Me, Myself & Them

Me, Myself & Them

Dan Mooney

PARK
ROW
BOOKS

PARK
ROW
BOOKS

Recycling programs
for this product may
not exist in your area.

ISBN-13: 978-0-7783-0777-8

Me, Myself and Them

For questions and comments about the quality of this book, please contact us at
CustomerService@Harlequin.com.

ParkRowBooks.com
BookClubbish.com

Printed in U.S.A.

For Nana, who is my past, and Ellen, Mikey, Emily, Gracey, Joe and Megan, who are our future.

Me,
Myself
& Them

MY BELOVED MONSTER

He watched the monsters watching him over his lunch of smoked salmon and brown bread. They didn't speak, or laugh or joke, they simply watched. Plasterer, the bulky clown, dressed in his usual workman's overalls, leaned against the door frame, his painted smile covering a gruesome frown. The Professor, his skin threatening to rot off his face and ruin his tweed jacket, rested his chin on his hands and sighed once without taking his eyes off Denis. Deano sat at Plasterer's feet, being hairy, which was his one exceptional talent. And then Penny... Penny also watched. Closer to him than he'd like. She was always closer to him than he liked. It was afternoon, but they weren't long out of bed, and as there wasn't a morning person among them, silence was not uncommon at this hour of the day.

They watched him clean his plate carefully, put on his coat and head for the door. He nodded to Plasterer as he passed him, and the clown clapped him encouragingly on the shoulder.

Nothing to be afraid of, he told himself. *It's just outside.*

The words were supposed to be a comfort to him, but a small voice in the back of his head quietly reminded him that they were a lie.

I remember when you weren't afraid of your own shadow. It's just outside, feel the fear, do it regardless.

He made his way out into the early afternoon, calling out his goodbye through the door as he pulled it firmly shut. He carefully placed the palm of his hand against the smooth grain of the door and gave it three precise pushes, taking care to apply the exact same amount of force each time. Satisfied with the door-closing procedure, he walked twelve steps to his gate and opened it, stepped out onto the street and shut it behind him, carefully counting each deliberate step as he moved. The low gray clouds closed in on the afternoon oppressively, a mild breeze tugging at his suit jacket, rustling the leaves on the trees, a whispered warning that he should have stayed indoors. The neighborhood kids watched and giggled. He smiled at them and nodded. They were used to his foibles, and he to their amusement. He set out for town, his perfectly polished black shoes striking a comforting staccato as he moved, a steady kind of rhythm that drowned out thoughts.

He was dressed well. Denis always considered maintaining his appearance to be something of a priority, and the act of maintaining his professional look was a chore in which he could lose himself happily. His suit trousers were expertly ironed and sat atop shiny shoes that covered perfectly pressed socks. Attention to detail is something that the normal person aspires to, but as far as Denis Murphy was concerned, if you don't iron your socks, you're living a lie, hiding your gruesome lack of concern from the world. His shirt, starched and crisp, was a pale pink with a darker pink tie to offset it. The whole ensemble was finished by his pristine gray coat, buttoned up, because that's how it's supposed to be worn. His gray satchel was carefully packed with a laptop, some paperwork and a pencil case containing all the required tools for the statistical analysis that paid his bills. As he passed a car, the glass threw his reflection back at him, forcing him to carefully correct a single aberrant hair that had strayed from his otherwise perfectly groomed head. Aberrant hairs were a significant problem for Denis Murphy, and the wind was most certainly not his friend. Sometimes he wondered if the breeze was trying to spite him. Most wouldn't have put his thirty years on him; he appeared to be a man in his twenties, but there was no mistaking his calm and confident manner, a learned behavior that betrayed no hint of his frighteningly complex daily routine. Tasks, tasks and more tasks. That was how Denis Murphy survived his day.

A careful, meticulous man, he awarded each job the relevant time he felt it deserved, depending on its place in his own personal hierarchy. Washing dishes was more important than cooking, maintaining the bathroom a higher priority than vacuuming the stairs. For some, household chores are that necessary evil that have to be tackled during commercial breaks on television, or on a Saturday morning when there's nothing on. For Denis, a daily schedule was written every night and completed on time every day. Each list presented a fresh order, a required routine that drove the hour forward. Denis was content to maintain the order of his day by the tasks that had to be completed. Not happy exactly, but content.

On this particular day, he had no work to do, and so his tasks were relatively simple. Walk into town—forty minutes. Purchase a newspaper and select a coffee shop—sixteen minutes. Spend some time with both of his friends—one hundred twenty minutes. Walk to the hospital—fifty minutes. Spend some time visiting Eddie—twenty minutes. Walk home—ninety minutes. Clean up the mess of four monsters—thirty minutes. (This one, upsettingly enough, could vary from day to day, depending on how boisterous they were feeling.) Prepare and eat dinner—sixty minutes. Watch television—

one hundred twenty minutes. Prepare the following day's task list—twenty minutes. Prepare for bed—fifteen minutes. Sleep—four hundred eighty minutes. Order and efficiency. There's nothing more important in the world.

He regarded the dark gray clouds above as he walked, considering the possibility of rain. Worryingly, they hung low in the sky, positively bulging with fat raindrops, ready, at probably the most inopportune moment, to shed their load. Denis was confident that if it did rain, the deluge would fall more or less directly on top of him alone, like some kind of sad cartoon character. He shook his head in exasperation, but immediately dismissed the idea of going back for his car. He had, after all, already closed the gate, and besides, the peculiarities of other road users were a concern. Driving infuriated him on a number of levels, not the least of which was that, despite the uniform rules that had to be applied to all drivers, there was a plethora of possible variations as each driver applied only the rules he or she believed to be most relevant to him or her at any given time. Signaling on roundabouts, for example. Slowing or, more important, not slowing when a traffic light turned amber. Changing lanes. To add to that, his new car had a digital speedometer, which meant there was no practical way to avoid looking at odd numbers. Odd numbers upset Denis. No, the car simply wouldn't do. His bicycle was out of the question for many of the same reasons. There was always the bus. He winced at the thought. What if someone sat next to him? They might even unwittingly touch him. What if they talked to him? Expressing their opinions as they leaned into his personal space, breathing their breath on his face. He grimaced. He would just have to chance the rain. He knew his friends would find his current predicament hilarious, and he smiled at the thought of how delighted they'd be if he told them that he had taken a bus into town.

He could picture both of them laughing heartily. No, there'd be no satisfaction for them today, not on this account anyway. He continued walking, the sharp click-clacking of his black shoes comforting him as the dark clouds overhead threatened to soak him to his skin.

The shopkeeper at his chosen convenience store eyed him with a smile. Another person used to his foibles. "How do you do today, Mr. Murphy?" he asked in his African accent, raising his hand and presenting it, as he did most days, for a high five. "What about that high five? Are you going to leave me hanging again?"

He had tremendous diction. Denis admired it to no end.

"I'm very well, Thomas. Thank you for asking. I'm afraid today, much like yesterday—"

"And the day before, and the day before that," Thomas said, cutting in.

"Yes. Just like those days too, I'm afraid I'm going to have to leave you hanging. I hope your day goes well though."

"I'm sure it will, Mr. Murphy. I'm sure it will. The usual?"

"Yes, please. The usual." Denis found himself smiling. Thomas was a nice chap. A regular fixture in his day who, like so many other regular fixtures in his day, gave him a sense of comfort. He still recalled with anxiety the day that a new staff member had served him and touched his hand as they exchanged money. He imagined that she must have told her friends about it in some bar or other that evening over drinks or cocktails. His meltdown that day had been up there with the best of them. He had spent an extortionate amount of money on baby wipes and tore through the packs, eyes wide with panic, frantically scrubbing while trying to maneuver himself so that she couldn't wrap around him the consoling arm that she was offering.

Oh yeah, that one would have made an excellent conversation piece. Her friends probably gaped at her as she told them how he had almost wept, and only left the shop when there were no baby wipes left.

Thomas placed his change on the counter and bade him farewell with a smile.

His shop was close to the Italian café. The inconsiderate clouds had threatened to make a good day bad, and so the Italian café with its unobtrusive staff had become the choice of venue. By such consideration did Denis Murphy make decisions. There were four potential options, and each one had its own particular charms on any given day. Set on a quiet side street, narrow from one end to the other, his coffee shop of choice was well protected from the elements by a canvas canopy and by the looming buildings that lined the street itself, acting as a kind of wind shield. Each shop front had been restored to a beautiful finish not seen in many decades, and though their colors were clashing, there was an almost beautiful uniformity to the two-tone color schemes, and their floral arrangements and hanging baskets. He took his favored seat, thankfully not occupied as it had been the previous Saturday, to text both his friends. He carefully unfolded the paper and, making sure to turn each page properly and refold on the crease, set about reading the day's events. The waiter brought his coffee, a latte, and placed it on its saucer directly in front of him. His teaspoon was wrapped in a serviette, and a fresh ashtray was produced on his arrival. All in order. He smiled at the waiter and nodded his approval.

"Enjoy," the man told him.

"Will do. Thank you."

Manners. Manners were so very important. Their application oiled the communication process in a way that was acceptable to everyone. As a result of his manners, Denis never offended anyone. No one ever begrudges a man who smiles and who shows courtesy to all and sundry. It was his own little defense mechanism in a world that finds people like him interesting until they become annoying. His foibles, for want of a better term, could be viewed as endearing to some, as long as they didn't overly impact on their lives. Denis made sure that he smiled and showed his manners as often as possible, to compensate for the irritation of having to individually wrap a teaspoon in a serviette, or pick up money from the counter-top and place the change back without simply handing it over.

His friends were late. No surprises there. Idly he wondered whose turn it was to try to get him that day. His friends had developed their own way of dealing with the day-to-day hassles of being friends with Denis Murphy. Each time they met, one of the two would try to do something to upset his sense of order. Something to test Denis's limits and force him to deal with their special brand of chaos. Some of their pranks were impressively elaborate. On one occasion, they had broken into the outdoor garden of a coffee shop in the small hours of the morning, removed a single cobblestone and dropped in a fish, three days dead, before replacing the cobble. The rotten fish raised a stink that drove customers out and wafted down the street for half a block. Sometimes a prank would back-fire drastically, as it had on the day of the smelly fish, which Ollie and Frank had expected would drive him away in a hurry. They had not anticipated that Denis would simply put up with the smell rather than deviate from a well-established schedule, and they were forced to keep their seats too, rather than lose face. The three of them had sat directly on top of a rotting fish carcass for one hundred twenty minutes. There was little in the way of conversation that day.

Other times their pranks were successful, and the resulting disorder would force Denis to beat a hasty retreat back to his house, where order reigned, more or less—his housemates were famously messy when they wanted to be. Ollie had scored one particular win with a bag of birdseed and a veritable army of pigeons had become willing accomplices. More often the attempts to sow some chaos into his life were simple things, like buttoning their coats incorrectly or dropping cutlery on the floor and threatening to use it afterward.

He didn't resent his friends for their hobby; quite perversely he was glad that what they called his "disorder" could bring them some amusement, even if it was at his expense. Personal tragedy or not, they had put up with him for a very long time—mostly with good grace, occasionally with more than a share of frustration. There is, however, a limit to how long one can go on being frustrated about something, so that eventually gave way to pity. Pity for Denis and his "condition," which was reflected in their tone and the concern in their eyes each time they saw their friend line up condiments on a table by order of size, or when they saw the panic on his face as he struggled to get the baby wipes from his satchel to clean a smudge from his perfectly polished shoes. Denis had very secretly hated that pity. They didn't know that he could see it, but he could, and it ate at him. Each look of sorrowful lenience made him want to cry or scream in equal measure. He felt the first stirrings of an angry bitterness that he repressed with logic. His expression, however, remained impassive. Finally, the pity had given way to amusement. It had taken nearly seven years to reach the point they were at now. They had arrived at a place where all three were comfortable enough with his foibles for both of his friends to mock them. Six or so years of consistent attempts to unbalance his sense of order had, somewhat paradoxically, become part of that order and owned its own place in his routine. Obviously he would never tell them that. They might stop. He shook his head at the absurdity of this particular line of thought.

Over his newspaper there was a flash of color. Bright pink. He looked up and saw her moving along the street, almost skipping. The bright pink had been the scarf that she wore half over her shoulders. Her hair was a dark brown that hung down past the scarf and was tied back with a knitted, many-hued hairband. A single lock of hair bounced here and there, plaited with tiny yellow beads. Her face was only partially visible, but he didn't need to see all of it to know that she was beautiful, with dark brown eyes and full, smiling lips. She was tanned and of average height for a girl, and exuded energy and cheerfulness.

Rebecca.

For one brief second of complete insanity he thought about calling out to her, but stopped himself as panic rose in his chest and gripped him aggressively by the throat.

Do it. Say hello. Do it now.

A surge of emotion, powerful feelings of something or other, tumbled in his head. His feet began tapping a rapid tattoo on the ground as he adjusted his tie, smoothed over his hair. His eyes darted all over the table; there must be something that needed fixing. He tried to restrain his foot. It continued tapping as his breathing quickened. *All is in order*, he reminded himself over and over. There was no need to panic. She hadn't seen him, and she was now almost at the end of the street. Soon she'd be around the corner and gone, and the world would be okay again. Nevertheless, he stared after her, and as she passed from view, there was another surge of emotion that felt bizarrely like regret or disappointment. He couldn't tell which. This of course made no sense. Denis Murphy had no time for the kind of chaos that Rebecca could bring into his life. He fought it down as hard as he could, adjusting the coffee cup on its saucer so that the handle pointed directly out on the right-hand side.

"Wow. I think you managed to get him without even doing anything. Good job." The voice seemed to float toward him through a haze. He was still looking at the spot where she had disappeared around the corner.

"You all right there, big guy?" came another voice. Frank's voice.

"What? Yes." Denis cleared his throat. "Yes. Fine. Thank you. And how are you?"

His two friends stood above him, looming slightly, as was their way. Frank Long, blocky and quite muscular despite his slight paunch, had a friendly if somewhat serious face, with a well-trimmed beard that stuck to his jawline, black, like his short spiky hair. Occasionally he wore glasses, although, when feeling vain, which was unusual for someone as pleasant and humble as he was, he would wear his contacts. Ollie Leahy was slightly taller than both of them, handsome with carefully maintained stubble, darker than his mousy blond hair, which he kept cut short and styled to look like it was permanently messy. Sometimes vain, but so genial that it could be forgiven, and almost always talking. He was a balance for Frank, who often contributed little, allowing Ollie to ramble instead, until the time came to shoot him down with a quip. They occupied the same space in Denis's head, a compartment specifically reserved for the last two friends he had who were still fully alive.

"Dude," Ollie interjected with his usual colloquialism. "You look spooked. Did someone start talking to you about fractions again? I know you have a thing for whole numbers. Seriously, just point him out and we'll kick his ass."

"Amusing," he replied, smiling at his friend.

"No, I don't think it was fractions this time," Frank said, keeping a straight face. "I know that expression. I've seen that one before. Did someone walk past here with a plate of rice and drop some of it?"

Dry was the only word to describe his sense of humor.

"Yes, Frank," he replied sarcastically. "A person walked up this street with a plate of rice. In fact, six people did. I hear it's some new kind of internet meme. Rice Walking. Huge in France."

They both chuckled.

"Honestly though. You okay? You looked a little rattled there."

"I'm fine, don't let it trouble you. Take a seat." Denis started his watch.

"We're on the clock again, Franky boy," Ollie said. "Better make this some quality conversation time. I'm going to cover topics relating to football, weather, housecleaning and gambling. You've got rugby, music and movies, Denis's extensive love life and romantic interests. Go."

Ollie's sense of humor was probably his most endearing and annoying trait. Denis found himself smiling nonetheless.

"Speaking of which…" Frank said. "I heard a rumor that Rebecca Lynch is back in town."

He delivered the sentence conversationally, but the look that he shot Denis was weighed and measured. He was waiting for a reaction. Suppressing the urge to panic again, Denis kept his face composed and tried not to look either of his friends in the eye. The swirl of emotions in his head was dizzying and frightening. Had they met her? Had they told her to walk by? Was this how they were trying to get him? If so, he feared it was working all too well. He clenched his thigh to stop it from rattling.

"Oh really?" he asked noncommittally. "That's nice." Nonchalance was an excellent shield.

"Damn. I tell you, man, I fucking hate it when my exes

are around," Ollie said, clearly preparing for another epic tale of a time when some ex-girlfriend said or did something that ended up with Ollie either having sex or being knocked out. There was a certain rhythm and formula to Ollie's stories. Denis loved them. He relaxed as his friend recounted the story. The details were no longer important; the words alone lulled him back into a state of comfort. Frank was still looking at him, possibly still hoping to see something, a spark perhaps of his old college friend, as opposed to this new tightly wound reality. There would be no hints of anything today. The momentary panic was almost gone now, and Denis found himself smiling again. The dark clouds also seemed to have passed. There would be no rain this afternoon after all.

On his way to the hospital, Denis found his thoughts straying, refusing to compose themselves as he liked them to. His friends had made no serious attempt to goad him today. They had either let it slide because of his obvious discomfort, or they had been in some sort of cahoots with Rebecca. He hoped it was the former; the latter didn't bear thinking about. The compartment in his head occupied by his two friends had no additional space for anyone else. Least of all her. And therein lay the problem. She was like the classic pink elephant; once she had been mentioned there was no way to stop thinking about her.

The darker clouds had been replaced with the lighter fluffy variety; white and endless, they robbed the day of any real shine, but they weren't threatening. His shoes pop-popped as he walked to the hospital, carefully reading the oncoming pedestrians from a considerable distance in order to minimize the chance of contact. He had an extraordinary gift for it. His mind, however, continued to flit and twirl, leaping from thoughts of panic attacks to deep brown eyes to practical jokes. It was his least pleasant walk, but such was the case every Saturday. The purple flowers he carried weighed a ton. As was also the case every Saturday.

The sliding door to the hospital swooshed as it opened, and Denis moved quickly to dodge the people walking in the opposite direction. The jaded receptionist dismissed him with a look. His particular brand of weird had stopped being charming about a year after he had started turning up every Saturday, and he had used up whatever credit his politeness earned him when he went through an entire industrial-sized bottle of hand sanitizer the day a patient had accidentally touched him. He made his way through the winding corridors to Eddie's ward. His only other friend from his college days shared his room with five other patients. None of them moved or opened their eyes. Machines kept them alive. Next to Eddie's bed sat Ann and Ned, his best friend's parents, and on the cabinet beside them was a photo of a beautiful young blond woman with a little nose stud and big blue eyes that stared at him every time he came to visit. Even her name seemed to follow him: *Jules.* It whispered at him quietly from time to time. He ignored them as best he could.

Poor Jules.

There were some wilting purple flowers in a vase behind the photograph. He stood at the window in the corridor and looked in, feeling the grief grab him by the throat and squeeze. His eyes stung a little. A voice inside his head told him to remain calm. It was a voice of confidence and solid assurance. He listened to it whenever he felt himself stray from his new path.

Ann shot him a sad little smile, and Ned simply nodded at him. There always seemed to be a question in that nod. Denis felt that if he really put his mind to it, he could figure out what Eddie's dad was trying to ask him, but the voice warned him that he wouldn't like it a whole lot if he knew, and he certainly wouldn't like to ponder the answer.

You're going to have to eventually.

For twenty minutes he stood at the window looking in at Eddie, ignoring Jules and trying to outthink the grief that felt like it might strangle him. Throughout it all his face remained impassive. When the allotted time was up, he put the flowers on the floor next to the door and nodded to Ann and Ned. He didn't enter the room. He never did. Turning into the traffic of walking germs and sickness, he began his long journey home.

It struck him en route to his house that it would be a day like this that the monsters were most likely to be throwing their own miniature party. At times it seemed like such impromptu recreational activities were attempts to cheer him up, shockingly misguided attempts that resulted in the type of chaotic merriment that caused him to follow along behind them cleaning as he went. Order abandoned in favor of unrelenting and seemingly pointless destruction. Perversely, he found contentment in reestablishing order in their wake and in that small way, they did actually help him to regain focus. He wondered sometimes if it was worth the hassle. There had been talk the night before of a popcorn fight. He made no effort to understand the kind of thinking that makes someone consider a popcorn fight as a worthy way to spend one's time. He focused instead on the time it would take to collect each individual popped kernel, and then tackle the salty mess that would cover the floor of his living room. It was usually the living room. They tended to prefer messing communal areas, and kept their bedrooms quite neat.

They'd moved in not long after he had bought the house. At the time he was struggling, mentally, to cope, and so he tolerated their antics as they tolerated his, and after a while they had reached a level of routine with one another. If he was honest with himself, he tolerated them because he imagined that life might be just a little lonely without them, and the house was big enough to accommodate five people comfortably.

As he approached, his sense of disquiet grew. The lights were all on, including the porch light, which was utterly point-less at seven o'clock on an August evening, even one as cloudy as this. The upstairs windows were all open. Denis was cer-tain he had closed each of them before leaving the house. Leaving them open was not the kind of oversight he permit-ted himself to have. He opened the gate all the way out and then closed it, starting his foot-count to the front door as the latch struck behind him. After his twelve paces he gave the door three carefully weighed pushes before inserting his key and letting himself in.

Inside the house it felt like the calm after a storm. Some-thing stirring in the air. Popcorn littered the hallway. Some-one had taken a crayon to the wall and drawn a picture of the outside of the house, crudely. The sun shining down on the house had sunglasses on and wore a cheerful grin. The piece of childlike art was signed *Penny O'Neill*. Other than the art-work, the walls were bare. No photographs, no artwork, no cutesy signs reading *Bless This Mess*. Beige. Beige and un-imaginative and magnificently uniform.

They were waiting for him in the living room. The coffee table had been turned upside down, and all four of them were balancing on one leg each, their hands outstretched to each other for balance. Penny O'Neill, her long feline tail flick-ing back and forth idly, regarded him with tawny eyes and a smile. Being the tallest of the four, she could easily see over Professor Scorpion's head. Her body, that of a perfectly pro-portioned woman covered entirely in soft shimmering blond fur, seemed to tremble with the effort to remain balanced. A woman, but also a cat.

"Hello," she said in her usual smoky voice.

"What are you doing?" Denis asked with a weary sigh.

"We're playing a game of balance," Plasterer told him. His confident, masculine voice, as always, sounded strange coming from his unusual features. His clothes, rough looking workman's overalls, complete with utility belt, and the paint-spattered white T-shirt that seemed a little too snug over his muscular torso, were also at odds with the thick layers of clown makeup he wore on his face, the multicolored wig he wore on his head and the bright red nose. Two white gloves adorned his hands, and his tanned arms were thick with muscle. His clown shoes seemed to provide no advantage in the game of balance.

"Is that you, Denis?" Professor Scorpion asked, as if it could possibly have been anyone else. The rotting flesh around his mouth sometimes seemed to rattle when he spoke, as though part of his lip would simply fall off if he shouted too loudly. It never did, and for all his apparent decorum in his tweed jacket with its leather elbow patches and his beige chinos and polished shoes, the zombie could be one of the most boisterous of all of the housemates when he wanted to be. Deano, as usual, said nothing. Humanoid hair balls never do. His expression gave away nothing either. Humanoid hair balls don't have expressions. He shook a little, causing the slightly shorter hair around his arms to wave a little.

"What's the object of the game?" Denis asked, as he began to collect popcorn from the floor of the living room.

"The last person to keep their balance wins," Plasterer told him.

"Surely the first person to move wins," Denis replied. "After all, the first to move is the only person guaranteed not to fall on their faces. Once one moves, the other three are going to fall."

In retrospect, Denis should not have said anything at all. The eruption of noise was catastrophic.

"If you move first, I'm going to choke that little kitten neck on you—"

"You better not even think of such a fiendish thing..."

"I know who's going to move first, he always moves first..."

"How dare you deign to speak to me in such a manner...?"

"I'll punch you in your back teeth..."

Even Deano shook with rage at the thought.

"Calmly now. Calmly," Denis shouted over the din, until there was silence. "I'll count to three, and all of you jump back at once. Then no one falls, and no one loses."

"Even better than that," Penny O'Neill said. "Everyone wins. I like winning."

"You do so wondrously at restoring such fallings-out to order," the Professor told him pompously.

"Before I count down," Denis interjected, "did you all wreck the kitchen?"

Silence.

"Right. I'm going to fix the kitchen as soon as I've put away the laptop. When the kitchen is in order, and I've prepared myself some dinner, I'll let you all down. Until then, you guys are going to have to figure this one out for yourselves."

He permitted himself a smile as he walked to the office. It wasn't very often that he managed to get one over on his housemates, and he intended on savoring it for a little while. Behind him, another fight erupted as Plasterer, the would-be leader of the group, attempted to encourage the others to follow his three-count, to no avail. The cacophony continued as Denis pottered about the kitchen, his rubber gloves on and sleeves rolled up. Fifty-four minutes exactly to complete the tasks at hand. The sugar had to be thrown out after it had been poured into several small piles and then designed into the shape of a smiley face. Someone had clearly licked part of it away. The crockery needed a wash after it had been made into a design not unlike the Eiffel Tower. Miraculously none of it was smashed. The offender in this case had clearly been so pleased with their work that the tower was to be preserved. Probably Plasterer. The others wouldn't dare touch it without his consent. Several more crayon drawings had been done; these on paper instead of the walls, thankfully. Denis set about cleaning up and wall washing as a competitive silence settled in the living room. After eating while listening to the radio, as was his way, Denis moved to the living room, freed his housemates with a backward count from three—a small resolution being required as to whether they would go on three or after three—righted the furniture, vacuumed the popcorn and settled in to watch some TV. Just as he was relaxing, she popped into his head again, for just a brief second, but before he could grab ahold of the thought, Plasterer interrupted him. The clown was staring from the kitchen doorway.

"How was your day? Anything unexpected?" he asked, his voice taking an edge that was not out of place on the burly clown. There was something in it, an implied threat, a note of menace.

"Nothing major. Normal day, really," Denis replied, as if he hadn't noticed the edge.

The room went silent as three pairs of eyes and a mass of brown-blond hair turned to regard him quietly. Their faces expressionless. He regarded each of them in turn, his face also expressionless.

"Nothing out of the ordinary at all?" Plasterer inquired again. "You went to town and the hospital?"

"Nothing to report," Denis lied.

For a few more seconds there was silence. Then Penny O'Neill yawned and stretched out beside Denis on the couch. Resting her head in his lap, her blond mane spilling across his thighs, she sighed contentedly. Plasterer tilted his head to the side for a second before he moved, taking his seat at Denis's left-hand side. Professor Scorpion settled into his normal arm-chair, his feet crossed on the footrest and just a hint of rotting flesh peeking through from between the end of his trousers and the start of his socks. Deano did as Deano always did and hunkered down on the floor.

"Let's watch *CSI*," the Professor said.

Plasterer nodded, though he kept one eye surreptitiously on Denis.

Denis smiled, only partly in relief. He surveyed the room and nodded in satisfaction.

You know, sometimes I think he wants to kill you.

GO AWAY, HEARTBREAKER

The following morning, Denis woke to the sound of his alarm clock. It sounded off loudly and evenly three times, as it did every morning before he killed it with an almost accusatory jab of his finger. Penny O'Neill was stretched out at the end of his bed. She slept above the quilt; her fur coat provided her with all the warmth she required. She usually slept almost perpendicular to him, but with a cat's propensity to stretch and roll at will. She was often found dangling half off the bed, her tail twitching in her sleep. She groaned loudly at the sound of the alarm clock and waved one irritated hand in its direction before drifting back to sleep. She didn't spend every night at the end of his bed, nor did she even start the night there, but seemed to come and go as she pleased. There was a kind of grace to her, even when she was half falling from the bed, a sort of languid perfection that often made him smile. She almost never frightened him. Almost.

Of the other three housemates there was no sign, but that was not unusual. They were not early risers.

"Good morning, Penny O'Neill," Denis said sleepily as he flipped back his covers and stretched his legs over the side of the bed.

A grunt was all the reply he got; standard response from her. Not much of an early riser either.

Sunday, as with every other day of Denis's week, was a day carefully planned in advance. Early-morning breakfast (high-fiber cereal, orange juice and black coffee)—ten minutes. This particular Sunday morning he was feeling just a little bloated. It happened from time to time, but Denis Murphy had no time for ailments; they interfered with his schedule. Next up was exercise (run followed by light core work)—one hundred twenty minutes. Shower and shave—twenty minutes. Then came the part of Denis's Sunday that had to be tolerated despite how much he disliked it. His mother's visit. He grimaced at the thought. It upset him that there could be no timetable for this whirlwind event. Her arrival time was at her discretion, her departure usually an uncomfortable mess of goodbyes or recriminations. There was no telling how long or how briefly she'd be there and equally no way of knowing how critical or how friendly she'd be feeling. Denis pushed the thought out of his mind in favor of embracing the tasks that lay before him.

Invariably he prepared no food for his housemates. They never ate it when he did, so he had stopped bothering. He did shop for them when the unfortunate need to grocery shop arose, and their list was a complicated mess of fats, oils, complex carbohydrates, E numbers, MSG and sugar. He didn't begrudge them. What would be the point? He prepared his own simple breakfast, cleaning the mess left over from a feast his housemates had clearly held in the small hours of the night before. Just as clearly, they were maintaining their protest against cleaning products in general and sponges in particular. Deano was by far the worst. He didn't so much eat as mash the part of his head where one assumed a face might be into a plate. Some of it disappeared into a mouth presumably, but by no means definitely. The rest of his pile of "food" gravitated toward the hardest to clean places in the kitchen, as though compelled by whatever magical powers a person who was entirely represented by hair might have.

His breakfast consumed and the dishes tidied and stored, Denis set about his exercises. It should be said that this was one of the few times that Denis didn't mind the rain. The exercise had to be completed and there was a shower waiting at the end; what was the harm if he got soaked? His housemates despised it when he came home wet and sweaty, his hair plastered to his head. They would berate the silly look he sported. Denis tolerated them, as most people do with their housemates. It was worth it to feel the exhilarating freedom he got from running. Each step seeming to carry him further away from his own thoughts and into a steady rhythmic trance in which there were no worries, no people, no blue eyes smiling in his rearview mirror from the back seat of his old car. Just a curious peace. There wasn't much rain on this particular Sunday, so there wasn't much ire to contend with when he finally arrived home. The crew was, however, awake.

"I'm back," he called after he'd performed the door-unlocking procedure and stepped through into the hallway.

"We know," came the reply in chorus.

Denis chuckled to himself. The chorus calls always amused him. After his shower, but before the arrival of his mother, there would be time to light the Sunday fire. Sundays mean a fire. It could be, though it rarely was, in the midtwenties temperature-wise, but this didn't change the fact that a fire was mandatory. There is, undeniably, something about a fire that makes a house a home. He rose from the edge of his bed, where he had carefully dried his feet and meticulously checked his toenails for cleanliness, and then did something so utterly surprising that he shocked himself. Without any justifiable reason, and apparently engaged by his own free will alone, he walked to his closet and pulled out a battered cardboard box. Misshapen by age and utterly out of place in the immaculately organized haven that was the bedroom of Denis Murphy, it was stuffed with photos. The box offended Denis on several levels: first, was the fact that it was so old and battered. It should have been replaced with a box that had retained its rectangularity. Second, there was no discernible filing system, not even an attempt at keeping the photos facing the same direction. They were simply packed in there any way at all, and for a brief second, his hand recoiled from touching such a disorganized mess.

Then he saw her again. With Jules. For the second time in two days, his eyes lingered on her, absorbing the beauty of her face. She was smiling at the camera, not a fake, posed affair, but a genuine smile that seemed to make her brown eyes sparkle even in the photo. Next to her on one side, with one arm draped lazily over her shoulder was Denis Murphy. Not the Denis Murphy he knew, but a different version. A stranger. His face was partially stubbled; his hair, longer than normal, was a disheveled mess. His eyes were squeezed shut and his mouth agape. He presumed the photo was taken in the throes of laughter. He was wearing a vest. It was the inside of a club. He looked ridiculous. On the other side of her, with her more serious, innocent face, was Jules. She had the hint of a tiny smile playing on her lips, but she was fighting to look serious, fighting to maintain decorum. She had always been the responsible one of the two of them. Just like their mom. Denis frowned at the picture as the memories flooded, all unwanted, into his head. The bass line of the music thumped and jumped up into his chest as people surged past them wearing garlands around their heads and shoulders. A beach party. A mess of drinking and dancing. He had been more than half cut, whipping back shots and practically inhaling beers. And kissing. So much kissing. In his mind's eye he snatched the camera from Eddie and forced him to cram in alongside them. Stretching the camera to arm's length, he took another photo of all four of them. Idly he wondered where that photo had gone.

I think she has it. I seem to remember it on the cabinet next to her bed.

His eyes were stinging, and he blinked to clear his vision. He considered placing the photo by his bedside, but thought better of it. Without a frame, it would simply lay there, and the common convention of tacking it with a pin would leave a small hole in the finish of his built-in headboard. Denis knew himself well enough to know that such a hole would keep him up at night. It had no place in a built-in headboard. He would eventually have to throw the whole thing out and buy a new one. And then what would happen to the photo? He reluctantly put it back in the box, which he replaced in his closet. It was only then that the shock of what he had just done hit him. His hands began to shake, and all of a sudden his mind was racing. The box suddenly seemed like the dirtiest, filthiest thing he'd ever touched. In fact, the whole room seemed to be unclean and out of place to his mind. He struggled to regain control of his thoughts; they flitted back to the hospital, and then to the club, and then to a roadside and shards of broken glass. He bolted to the closet and grabbed his cleaning products. To correct the anomaly in his behavior he spent thirty-eight minutes carefully dusting the bedroom, feverishly throwing himself into the task until his mind focused itself. Then he showered again, as though cleaning would simply wash away the absurdity of this random act of nostalgia. After a shower he could start again as if it had never happened.

He toweled himself dry and dressed in his well-pressed underwear and well-pressed socks, along with a pair of suit trousers, which were, predictably, well-pressed. He selected a shirt, this one a pastel green, and a darker green tie to offset it. His hair was combed carefully and styled with a respectable amount of gel. He washed his hands twenty-two times. Gel upset him, but not as much as messy hair. There was a trade-off in such incidents. He nodded at his own obvious pragmatism. As he made his way to the door, he heard the sounds of a conference being held in the hallway.

"It is most certainly a suitable gift for a Sunday afternoon visit," came the voice of Professor Scorpion.

"It is, but you all know he's never going to go for it. Think of the mess. Think of how he'll react. You know what a bitch he is about things like this." That one was Plasterer.

"But I think he likes her visits about as much as we do. He'll love this." The third voice was unmistakably Penny O'Neill's.

"Once again, the mess. All right, all right, calm down, Deano. I get your point," said Plasterer again. Clearly Deano was gesturing. Sighing, Denis opened the door and walked into the hallway.

"Oh hello, Mr. Bank Manager," Penny O'Neill said, mocking his crisp Sunday clothes with a curtsy.

"Good day, madam," Denis replied, affecting the tone he assumed was a bank manager's. He hadn't met many of them.

Penny O'Neill giggled girlishly.

"I believe you four were discussing something?" Denis inquired, looking straight at Deano. The hair ball shrank back from his gaze, as though there was something menacing about it. He was shy that way, from time to time.

"Your mother is coming to visit," Plasterer told him.

"And?" Denis began cautiously.

"We wish to give her a cake…" the Professor told him.

"Why?"

"…in her face," the zombie finished.

Denis laughed out loud in spite of himself.

"Told you he'd love it," crowed Penny O'Neill.

"Amazing," said Plasterer sarcastically. "Quick, Deano. Bake a cake."

"No," said Denis. "No hitting my mother with cake. Regardless of how hilarious it is. Remember how upset you all made her when you painted that teddy bear?"

They took on the manner of small children, staring down at their feet and scuffing at the carpet. It set his teeth on edge slightly.

"I'm sorry, guys, but no." They grumbled, Plasterer even going so far as to throw him a menacing look, but the big clown eventually ambled away, muttering under his breath.

Oh yes. He's definitely the one to fear.

Denis set about preparing for her arrival. He always felt like he should prepare properly, when in truth, there was very little to do. The house was immaculately kept, when he could control the four anarchists who lived with him. The cupboards seldom needed organizing, since he seldom disorganized them, and they got a thorough cleaning once a week. The floor was swept several times a day, and while it can never really be swept enough, it wasn't a job he felt that adequately prepared him for her arrival. The bathroom occupied him for a while. Since it was used only by his housemates, it had a tendency to get messier more quickly than the rest of the house, but Denis rarely allowed the situation to develop to serious proportions. There would be no repeat of the time that he got so lazy there was no toilet paper in there, and the toothpaste was being rolled up to squeeze out the last drops. That had been a complete disaster. Finally, there was only one job left to do. Light the Sunday fire.

He made his way to the living room, where four all-too-innocent faces beamed at him from their usual seats.

"What's going on?" he asked suspiciously.

"Nothing," replied Plasterer and Penny O'Neill at once.

"We lit a fire in the anticipation of our pending houseguest, but it seems to have gotten rather out of hand..." the Professor told him, to scowls from the couch.

Denis looked at the empty fireplace.

"Looks like you need to start again. This time try adding firing materials to the fireplace," he told them sarcastically.

"...in the kitchen," the Professor told him matter-of-factly, glancing toward the door.

It took a moment for this information to sink in, but when it did, Denis was amazed that he'd missed it. The smell of smoke was appalling. He bolted for the kitchen, where what was left of the toaster was sitting on the step by the back door, which had been left wide-open. Flames licked the wooden door where it charred and smoked. The light drizzle caused the melted plastic of the toaster to hiss occasionally. He stared at the lump of twisted metal and plastic. There were about a dozen melted candles leaking out of what was left of the slot for the toast. He dashed into the kitchen, grabbing the fire blanket and covering the flames, the acrid smoke stinging his eyes.

Dangerous, so dangerous. You need to be more careful. Really any one of them can kill you.

"Toasters aren't cakes," he screamed into the living room.

"Cool," Plasterer replied. "Wanna watch TV?"

Denis tried to contain his rage, fighting it down, smothering it.

"I'm going to compile a list," Professor Scorpion declared to anyone who would listen, "of other common things that are not, in fact, cakes."

Denis sighed and surrendered. The doorbell rang.

"Doorbells are not cakes."

"Get out of here," Denis barked in reply.

The curious thing about his housemates was that while

they were familiar with all the people in Denis's life, through endless stories, they had no interest whatsoever in meeting or engaging with any of them. This suited Denis fine, since he held tightly to the belief that neither his friends nor his mother would be overly fond of them either. And so, when the doorbell rang, there was a mass exodus from the living room, accompanied by a scampering noise, like the sound a child makes when he climbs stairs using all four limbs, at full speed.

"I'm coming," he called out, still trying to collect the destroyed toaster without burning himself. He headed for the door and pulled on it three times before unlocking it carefully.

"Hello, Mom," he said to her, nodding and smiling slightly.

"Hello, my dear," she replied, opening her arms and imploring him with her eyes. "Any chance of a hug this time?"

He stepped back from the offer and shook his head slightly. It broke her heart just a little more, he could tell. It was for precisely this reason that his mother's weekly visit was almost unbearable to him. Each week she'd call. Each week she'd ask for a hug. It's no great thing for most people, a simple gesture of greeting or of parting. A way of consoling or celebrating. And each week he would refuse her. She would wince ever so slightly and attempt to cover it up by adjusting her coat, or rearranging her handbag, but her eyes would show everything. Each week she came with the simple intent to love her son a little better, and each week he would refuse to love her a little better in return. For Denis, a hug was no small thing. The thought of just brushing up against another person was sometimes enough to send him into a panic attack. A hug? She may as well have asked him to take her to the moon. *How must she feel when she meets with her friends?* he wondered. *When their children, or in some cases, grandchildren, hug them, or kiss them on the cheek, or hold their hand.* She had only one child left, and he wouldn't even grant her a hug. Denis hated himself from time to time.

"Come in," he told her to cover the awkwardness of yet another rejection.

"Drizzly out there," she said conversationally.

"Yes," he replied. "Was out for a run this morning. Not great for August, is it?"

"No. Not great at all. I suppose we should be used to it."

"Yeah. You'd think we would be. Would you like tea?"

"Yes, please, that would be lovely. Have you a fire on? I can smell smoke."

"Er, not quite. I, er, was experimenting with something, and I kind of burned my toaster. Nothing major. I'll put a fire on though."

"Yes. Please do. It's nice to have a fire when it's bad weather out."

"It sure is."

This was the manner of most of their conversations. This was the manner of most of Denis's conversations with people. Sometimes she would arrive all guns blazing in an attempt to shock Denis out of his "disorder." Once, he even locked himself in the bathroom to wait her out. It worked; she had left the house that day in tears. A victory for order he recalled bitterly. Other times it would be just like this; polite chitchat with some subtle maneuvering until she could hit him with a question loaded with emotion. A salvo intended to rock him.

"Anything exciting going on at work?" she asked, as they moved into the living room.

"Nothing really," he replied, tactically placing himself on the armchair closest to the door.

An awkward silence settled around them.

"Did you get a new computer?" she asked finally. He had

not. They both knew that. It was something to say. She would say anything at all to help feel connected to him.

"A few months ago," he told her. "Still working fine. How's everything at home?"

"Good," she replied. "I was thinking of getting a new fridge."

"Good idea," Denis replied. "You've had that one for a while."

More silence. This round heavier than the last. She was building to something.

"I was thinking maybe I'd get one that has the ice dispenser on the front. Very fancy," she said with a half laugh.

"Yes, we've always been a fancy family," he replied. They had never been a fancy family. He was chasing conversation. It didn't work.

She was here because he wouldn't go home. He wouldn't go home because it smelled and looked like a shrine to another life. It smelled like Jules. His mother had to understand this. Perhaps she did, but more likely she did not, since it seemed more likely that no one did, or ever could, save for those precious four housemates of his.

Another silence settled in. She was smiling at him now, but it was fixed. She was building to what she wanted to say. He could tell.

"Eddie's parents tell me that you were out visiting yesterday," she said suddenly.

"Yes. I went to visit," he replied cautiously, feeling his chest and shoulders tensing.

"I think they'd like it if you'd talk to them, Denis," she said, choosing her words carefully. Doireann Murphy was all too aware of her son's tendency to retreat when she charged at him with such dangerous conversation.

"Perhaps I will," Denis lied. "Maybe next time." It was always maybe next time.

"They say that you're there every week. You bring him

flowers. Purple ones. Jules's favorite. That's very good of you."
Her face beamed sympathy at him.

"How do you take your tea again, Mom?" Denis asked. It
was a stupid question, and he knew it. He was well aware of
how his mother took her tea. How one takes one's tea is an
important matter, and such things never escaped his memory. He was beginning to get flustered as she dangerously
approached the topic that she always seemed to be steering
toward. A short retreat might suffice.

"Strong, please," she replied with a sigh. "Two sugars, just
a drop of milk." The battle for conversation was fought in
trenches of politeness and references to the weather.

"Will you come with me to visit your sister? You haven't
been in a while," she tried again, another probing attack.

Her face rose in his mind, with her nose piercing and her
sharp blue eyes, stabbing at the inside of his head. Her smile
and a memory of the sound of an ice-cream truck. It was an
old memory, not like the picture he had found earlier. She was
just a child in this memory. He pushed it from his thoughts.

*Don't push it, you prick. Don't you dare push it away. She de-
serves more than that, you selfish bastard.*

"How has work been?" he asked, completely ignoring her
question and calming himself. He could focus, bury the memories and go into full retreat. She could come at him all day.
She would find seven years of defensive work had more than
prepared his fortifications. Stalemate was the only winner of
the day.

They returned to polite conversation. Denis lit the fire and
they talked about this and that. Safe topics. Try though he
might, Denis remained permanently on edge when she was
around, as though she could at any minute attempt another
assault.

They discussed Denis's mortgage. His mother had been

financially very sound and had managed the family bud-
get for as long as Denis could remember. She offered advice
from the other side of the room, never hiding her desire to
sit next to her son and hold him. They talked about Uncle
Jack, his father's brother. Uncle Jack still kept in touch, calling and visiting. Denis guessed that he must feel guilty about
his little brother's abandonment of his family. His mother
had a lot of time for Uncle Jack. She had a lot of time for
everyone really. During this part of the conversation, Denis
carefully avoided any mention of his father. It was another
potential land mine. For a while they discussed driving, and
Denis joked about how much he hated other drivers. For a
moment, as he laughed at some quip or other about motor-
ists, his mother's face lit up, as if merely the sight of him smiling was enough to sustain her for another week. Her joy was
bitter to him. Bitter because it had to be dug up by so little
a thing as a laugh. By the time she got up to leave, Denis
felt like he'd been through a whirlwind. The required focus
to maintain polite conversation after one had broken their
mother's heart, yet again, was tiring. Something welled up
in his mind, something familiar and unpleasant. It was like
the tinge of regret he had felt the day before as Rebecca had
disappeared around the corner. Denis tried to push the feeling down, but it persisted as they made their way through the
house, desperately trying to find a way not to think about the
photograph of Rebecca with her too-beautiful smile. He was
still thinking about it as he showed his mother to the door.
She paused and offered him a hug, just as she had done arriving. Denis pretended to be checking on the clouds to make
sure it wasn't raining. She pretended that he really didn't see
the offered hug, and he could almost feel his soul shrivel up
inside him. When would she quit? At what point would she

just accept that he was broken and leave him be? Did Rebecca know? Had someone told her?

"Denis," cooed Penny's voice from back inside the kitchen. "I've hidden a dirty plate somewhere in the house. Somewhere it's likely to leave a stain, and I'm not going to tell you where."

"What kind of stain?" he asked, as his mind considered the grim possibilities.

"Why would I tell you that and ruin all my fun?" she replied.

He thought he could smell soy sauce, honey and flour mixed with water, and he had a strong feeling she probably shoved it under his cushion on the couch before replacing the throw on the back to keep him off the trail. He could practically see her doing it. She was right of course; it would stain. And badly. He might have to spend hours just scrubbing to get it out. He found the thought repugnant, and yet he let himself be dragged away by it and lost the rest of his Sunday evening to a sink and the effervescent action of his array of cleaners and cleansers. He went to bed a weary man.

"Wake up," Plasterer's voice barked, snapping Denis out of his dream.

He half woke but kept his eyes closed. His feet were cold; he couldn't feel his duvet.

"I said, wake up," the clown snarled at him.

And suddenly Denis was wide-awake and standing in the middle of his kitchen. He looked about in confusion. The last thing he could remember was falling asleep and dreaming.

"You were having a nightmare," Plasterer told him.

"Where's Professor?" Denis asked, the fog of sleep inertia still clouding his thoughts.

"Probably where you left him," Plasterer replied.

"In my dreams?"

"Something like that."

"You're not making any sense," Denis told the clown groggily.

"Rich, coming from you," Plasterer rejoined. "Don't step in the mess."

Denis looked about him, actually taking in what he saw for the first time since waking. The tiled kitchen floor was covered by a thin blanket of biscuit crumbs save for a tiny circle around the spot he was standing in. They must have torn the pantry apart to create such a fine-grained mess.

"Did you do this?" he asked Plasterer, trying and failing to keep the irritation out of his voice.

"Do you think I have nothing better to be doing?" the clown asked indignantly, but Denis thought he heard a note of amusement.

"If not you, then who?" Denis asked.

"Who indeed?" Plasterer asked back mysteriously.

"You going to help?"

The big clown just laughed as he walked about the room, his feet crunching as he moved.

"Wanna tell me about your dream?" he asked pleasantly.

"It was weird. You were in it."

"Naturally," the clown replied modestly. "I expect you dream about me often."

"Don't be stupid," Denis scoffed at him, refusing to admit that all of his housemates frequently occupied his dreams.

"What happened?"

Denis told him the story of the dream, struggling for details as the images, so sharp when he felt them, dulled second by second. In it, he had been standing in the hospital listening to Eddie screaming in pain while Ned and Ann smiled encouragingly at him. The Professor had stood beside him in the dream, holding wilted purple flowers, his attempted smile terrifying on his ruined, decaying face.

Then Denis had looked again, and it was himself in the hospital bed screaming, his mother sitting by his side patting his hand consolingly. Plasterer stood next to her, holding purple flowers and roaring at him to shut up.

He recounted the dream to his burly, heavily made-up friend in sleepy groggy tones. The terror had passed as soon as he woke up; all that was left was the memory of it.

"Typical you," Plasterer told him dismissively.

"Typical me? How so?"

"It's all you, you, you. And you're overdramatic."

Denis didn't consider himself a particularly dramatic person. Quite the opposite in fact.

"Anyway," the clown continued. "It's past my bedtime. Have fun cleaning. No more sleepwalking, okay?"

He disliked taking orders from the clown, particularly orders that were well past his ability to obey, but it did feel like sensible advice. His feet were too cold for more sleepwalking.

Denis thought about going to bed, but instead decided to tackle the mess. He wouldn't sleep if he didn't. As he cleaned, he thought about his mother, his poor mother, just as broken as he was, but she didn't have the support network he had. No one lived with her. He thought about her good nature and her quietly determined attitude. Jules had taken after her; he had not. In his youth he had been a rogue, fond of his drink, fond of his late nights, none too fond of hard work or responsibility.

You miss it. Don't pretend you don't.

He didn't miss it. The unpredictability of it, the flakiness. Turning up to class when he felt like it, returning calls if and when he felt like it, feeling things when he felt like it. And then justifying it all in the name of living his life. Explaining it all away with a simple "that's who I am" as if such words excused him from all blame. He was, he decided, as he cleaned crumbs from his heels, much better off without the old version of himself. He comforted himself with that thought as he gently eased himself into bed so as not to disturb Penny, purring in her sleep.

THERE YOU ARE

Mondays can be tough on people. For most people it's a result of returning to work after a weekend away from the grind, socializing with friends, sleeping in, spending quality time. For Denis, Mondays were tough because of his mother's routinely upsetting visits, and this particular Monday was harder again because of the sleepwalking and the nightmares of the night before. Not that he wasn't used to them; left to their own devices, Denis's thoughts would stray into nightmare territory often, and sleepwalking wasn't uncommon for him either. There was just something particularly jarring about his late-night escapades of the night before. To compound his misery, he had barely any cookies left. He busied himself, as only Denis could, in tasks and time-tabling. He worked, he printed things, wrote notes, scanned other things, pushed the buttons on the calculator. He had deliberately hunted for a calculator with larger, more raised buttons as he found the tactile sensation of pushing and releasing each button in rapid succession to be a wonderful, simple pleasure.

He ate a basic lunch, cold cuts on brown bread, soup made up from powder in a pouch with the easy-tear top. He performed the act of lunch making with solemnity under the supervision of his housemates who lounged here and there. Penny, Deano and the Professor moved about, sitting by the dining table, prim and proper, or perching on the counter, absently searching through the higher cupboards for something to play with, and then to smash. Only Plasterer didn't move around. He hovered by Denis's shoulder in the afternoon, flexing occasionally or pressing down on the counter as if testing it. His movement was a constant anxious movement, a sort of pent-up energy that had nowhere to go. They babbled at him as he moved. Why that soup? Why that bread? Why not something else? Why this house? Why not other people? He tolerated them as he moved about, smiling to himself from time to time. Their enthusiasm was palpable. After he had finished work, he set about preparing his dinner, only to realize he was going to have to get creative with his recipes, since almost everything edible had vanished.

Someone as organized as Denis Murphy never allowed his cupboards to go bare, but his housemates frequently found use for food items in their games and misadventures. Among the tremendous works of art they had bent their considerable creativity toward were the Leaning Tower of Pizzas, for which they had emptied the freezer and crisper, and the Milka Lisa, which took Denis over an hour to mop up and caused his house to stink, and which in turn caused him to have a panic attack. And then there was The Kitchen Chapel, for which the artists themselves had removed every single item from the cupboards in the kitchen and transferred them to the ceiling.

Because of their artistic endeavors, Denis frequently had to restock his home with new food and cleaning products. By the time he had cooked, eaten and ordered all the various provisions that a single man and four monsters required, Denis was all out of energy. He flopped onto the couch to unwind that evening feeling drained, pleasantly tired.

"You look tired," Plasterer told him from his spot on Denis's left.

"Bad night last night," he told the clown.

"Well, then, isn't it great to have us to tire you out?" Penny O'Neill asked from his right.

"Yeah. It's nice to have you guys around. Even if you are very annoying."

"Such eloquent and charming backhanded compliments," the Professor announced loftily.

Denis glanced at the zombie and found himself flashing back to the nightmare; Eddie screaming and the Professor smiling. He almost shuddered.

"Not to worry," Plasterer told him reassuringly. "You'll sleep like a log tonight."

But Denis didn't sleep like a log. Just as he settled into his bed he remembered the flash of a pink scarf, the brown hair, and for the first time in a very long time, Denis glanced to the other side of the bed and missed her presence.

On Tuesday, he received the grocery delivery from a wide-eyed delivery man who must have heard the racket Plasterer was making in the living room, since he appeared half-terrified. Denis tried to tip him only for the man to back away cautiously from him. He shrugged it off, carried out the door-locking procedure and went back to work.

On Wednesday, he had to take a phone call from work, while Plasterer pummeled the Professor all about the living room for reasons Denis thought he was better off not knowing. The call involved something to do with his handwriting being illegible, and someone called Marshall from Human Resources wanted an explanation. He tried to explain it all, while the bigger of his two monstrous housemates kicked the other in the ribs.

On Thursday, a man collecting for charity arrived at the

door, and Denis was forced into another awkward standoff when the man offered his hand for a shake and Denis had put his hands behind his back. He knew the man was offended, so he went to new levels of politeness and donated a substantial sum of money to compensate. Such were the trade-offs Denis made to secure a comfortable life of not touching other people.

His week progressed, as it always did, minute by minute, job by job, day by day, and at the end of each day, regardless of how well or poorly they behaved, Denis found himself sitting down with his housemates to watch television in good form. Tired, but content.

Rebecca intruded upon his thoughts from time to time, distracting him at a moment when his guard was down. A pop-up ad when he least expected it. An image of her, as she was when she had left many years before, and then what details he could remember from the previous Saturday. She was more tanned now; she looked more grown-up too. He wondered when she had plaited her hair. He was saved from these moments by his housemates, usually Penny O'Neill, who seemed extra-affectionate even by her own feline standards, and when the moment had passed, he found he could put Rebecca out of his head with a little effort.

It wasn't until Friday that Denis found his proverbial apple-cart well and truly upset.

His housemates were about to begin a game of Slide, where they soak the floor of the kitchen and then take turns trying to slide the farthest, when the doorbell rang.

As usual, they ran for safety, leaving Denis to deal with whoever was there. He always found that slightly unfair, that they knew how much he hated other people, but refused to even offer to answer the door when people came to visit. He limped to the door, his side aching. He had been sitting awkwardly all day, and now had the stoop to show for it.

He carefully carried out his door-unlocking procedure and opened it to the stranger. Outside stood a jocular-looking young man with dark skin and a short haircut. He was dressed in what Denis supposed might pass for "looking cool" these days. He smiled a tight smile of introduction. The kind of forced pleasantness most people display when in new company for the first time. The kind of forced pleasantness Denis could understand. He returned the smile with one of his own.

"Marshall," the man said by way of introduction, thrusting out one hand.

"Denis," Denis replied, whipping both hands behind his back.

The other man nodded knowingly. He knew. Somehow he knew about Denis. Which meant someone was talking about him. Denis seethed at the thought, but kept his tight outward smile showing.

"Can I help you, Marshall?" he asked, unclenching his teeth.

"Just wanted some clarification on something. I know we spoke on the phone the other day, but I wasn't entirely certain…"

He was from Denis's workplace, then. This was bad. Not quite his mother visiting levels of bad, but not much better. They must have been talking about him at work. About how weird he was, about how he was a recluse, how he had no one. He straightened as much as his aching side would allow—he definitely didn't want to add a deformity to the already outrageous stories about him. What else were they saying? For a moment he hated the young man, brandishing a sheet of paper at him and still babbling. Denis realized with alarm that he had not been listening.

"Would you like to come in?" he asked, more to cover for the fact that he didn't know what the man was talking about than out of any real interest in having a guest.

"Well," the man replied, clearly shocked. "If you don't mind?"

"Not at all," Denis lied.

It was only when the man was in the door that Denis remembered the game of Slide that had been about to begin.

"You'll have to mind the water all over the kitchen floor," he said as pleasantly as he could, thinking fast, "I've had a burst pipe under the sink. Been an awful nuisance."

"No problem," Marshall said, trying to look all about the house at once. No doubt he would report back to work on what kind of conditions the weirdo lived in. Denis was determined not to give him anything to work with. They could call him weird if they wanted, but Denis wouldn't give them any more ammo to fire at him.

He hoped Marshall bought the story about the burst pipe as he walked through the kitchen. He also hoped that a zombie, a clown, a cat woman and a fur ball wouldn't walk into the middle of the room and start trying to slide across it. He knew that would unquestionably raise some eyebrows. To his relief, they remained hidden wherever they were.

"Now let me take a look at that," he said, as he sat down in the office.

"Certainly," Marshall said, handing him the sheet. "You have a really nice house here."

He sounded surprised. As if he might have been expecting Denis to be living in tinfoil-coated walls covered in scraps of cut-up newspaper.

"Thank you," Denis replied, pleased to be bucking expectations. Maybe Marshall would go back to the office and tell everyone how normal he was.

When he saw the piece of paper that Marshall had handed him, he knew there was slim chance of anyone believing that. His heart sank. The page contained work he remembered distinctly doing—printed items and lists and bar charts onto which he had handwritten several notes before he scanned and emailed it back. What he hadn't seen before he sent the document was that one of his housemates had gotten their hands on it and scrawled all over it. *Mathematical ignorance*, said one note, with a line connecting Denis's notes. Along the side they had written *whose side are you on?* Farther down the page they had written *pointless* and across the bottom *everyone has a bottom, even you.* Somewhere sandwiched in between two lines of text were the words *can't you read between the lines?* The handwriting was crude, a rough approximation of Denis's. It looked like a child's forgery. He didn't know whether to laugh or cry, so he simply pretended it wasn't there.

"We were just wondering," Marshall asked delicately, "if you had made some kind of mistake and didn't mean to send this, and we tried to sort it out on the phone, but you seemed distracted."

It wasn't a work call. Or a social call. Someone had come to the house to see if Denis was nuts. He smiled as politely as he could.

"So sorry," he said, "I meant to write that on something else. A paper I've been working on. I must have gotten distracted. The stats all check out. You can go with this."

"Ahhhh," said Marshall, and Denis couldn't tell if he had bought the lie or not.

They sat there, looking at one another. Denis had no intention of saying another word, regardless of how weird that would make him look. He still thought the notes were funny, in their own way. The damage was done regardless.

"Well," Marshall said uncomfortably. "I guess that's it. If the stats check out?"

"They certainly do," Denis said pleasantly, trying to pretend like he couldn't see the problem. A poor end to his week, all things considered.

He showed his colleague, only the second one he'd ever had a conversation with, to the front door and then stomped back into the office to wait for them to show themselves.

When they did, it was just Plasterer and the Professor. The burlier of the two leading the corpse into the room.

"I know what you're thinking, Boss," Plasterer told him confidently.

"You do?"

"I do, but if you recall, I've already taken care of his punishment."

Denis remembered the kicking the Professor had received just a couple of days before.

"I must confess," the Professor told him in his pompous drawl, "that I am most honestly and grievously sorry for any inconvenience I've caused. I can assure you that I meant no harm. Just a gentle ribbing between friends, you see?"

Denis found it impossible to be mad at him. He was just so ridiculous.

He's not on the level though. He does what the clown tells him, and that should make you wary. If you were half smart you'd be wary.

"They're going to think I'm going nuts, you know," he told the two of them.

"Who cares what they think?" Plasterer asked. "Is it quitting time yet? Wanna play Slide?"

Denis laughed and shook his head. It wasn't a complete disaster. He didn't really care what they thought of him at work, it was just a minor irritation. He hoped the uncomfortable feeling in his gut would pass.

When Saturday rolled around, as it does, Denis found himself back in town, back at the Italian café with his newspaper and his coffee but alarmingly not back to himself. He had pressed his trousers as well as he knew how, and his entire apparel met and exceeded his own exacting standards of orderliness, and yet, as he walked toward the town center, he found his thoughts fleeting, hard to hold, and a vague sense of dissatisfaction settled on him that he couldn't shake. The bothersome nature of his young colleague's visit from the day before still nagged at him, but what was truly alarming, he thought to himself as he sipped his coffee, was that he found himself scanning the street for a scarf.

He had spent a whole week with her coming and going without any significant impact, but now he was quietly hoping she would show up again. He knew he didn't have it in him to actually talk to her, but it surely wouldn't do any harm to just see her again, flashing by as she went in her own toned-down style and that almost ever-present smile. His eyes scanned for her through all one hundred twenty minutes of his afternoon coffee with Ollie and Frank.

"Are we missing something?" Ollie asked at one point, trying to see what Denis was hoping to see.

"No. Sorry. Just a touch distracted."

"Want to talk about it?" Frank asked helpfully.

Ollie laughed at the idea. Denis never wanted to talk about it. No matter what *it* was.

"Heard anything from Rebecca?" he asked, trying to sound nonchalant.

"Yeah, actually," Frank replied, offering nothing further.

With dismay Denis realized that he desperately wanted to know what she had said, how she was, what she was doing home. There was no way he could ask without alerting the two of them about how he felt, and so he simply said, "Oh?"

"Australian visa expired. She wants to go traveling again, but there's a job offer on the table and she's thinking about taking it."

"Here?" Denis asked, still trying to sound cool.

"Yep," Ollie told him.

So Ollie had heard from her too. Was he the only one of their old gang that she hadn't contacted? He felt left out, isolated. He told himself that he didn't care, but it was hard to take. He wondered if she still played guitar and remembered the first time he ever saw her, performing at a house party.

"Very nice," he said, hoping he sounded sincere. They let it slide, Ollie moving onto a fresh story about how his girlfriend made him sleep on the couch. Frank watched him again, carefully weighing him up. Denis offered him a casual smile. He gave nothing away.

After the allotted time was up, Denis gathered his belongings and made for the hospital, stopping off to pick up the purple flowers. The sky overhead was a solid wall of white, overcast, but dry. His shoes pop-popped all the way to the corridor where he had stood for years now, and he took up his ritual position.

The room frightened him more than usual. It wasn't just the limp, unmoving form of his best friend, nor the sickly patients of the hospital moving here and there all around him; it was more. A tension, something coming from within himself.

The purple flowers from the week before were wilting a little, and Denis found himself back in his nightmare. The Professor smiling at him as he clutched the rotten bunch of petals. The memory of Plasterer telling him to shut up. He had to double-check that Eddie wasn't screaming. Ned and Ann smiled at him. They smiled the exact same way that they had in his nightmares. He fled the hospital after a measly twelve minutes.

He walked all the way home in shame and anger. As with the week before, he found that the party had raged in his absence and Denis spent his Saturday night unclogging the kitchen sink, which had been filled with something Penny O'Neill called Donkey's Breakfast Cereal. He didn't know what it was made of, only that it was lumpy, sticky and smelled of things that shouldn't be mixed together. He would have to order a host of new cleaning products. He lost himself in the cleaning again, and by the time he was done, the world had righted itself. As much as his world could.

The following day, Denis performed each of the appointed tasks at their appointed time and in the appointed manner. The soothing feeling he earned from running, each footfall propelling him away from his own thoughts, was complemented by the warm glow he got from organizing his life just so. He even felt that he could deal with his mother's visit, which would be happening, as appointed, at some time on Sunday afternoon.

Her arrival was the same as it had been the week before, and when he denied her the hug she wanted, a little part of him died all over again. She covered her broken heart with a tiny forgiving smile.

It wouldn't kill you, you know. At the very least pat her on the arm or something. Give her something to keep going on.

"How was your weekend?" he asked pleasantly.

"Excellent. I met Marge and the girls. We went to see a show. How was your week, love?"

"Just fine," he told her, deliberately neglecting to mention that a zombie had made him look like a madman and received a brutal beating from a clown for its troubles. He shifted on his seat, his muscles still hurt him from sitting awkwardly.

"Anything new at work?" she asked.

"No," he lied, as he wondered what her reaction might be to finding out that one of his work colleagues had been in the house. He decided against telling her.

They continued making idle chitchat—the weather, again, some new book or other, something about a new television show. He nodded and smiled his way through it, trying to pretend that the physical gap between them wasn't killing his mother slowly.

He waited for her moment, because he knew it was coming. Some weeks he could just sense that she was going to make him uncomfortable. She tried not to show it, fiddling with her purse. He ventured nothing, knowing that when it was right for her it would come.

She talked about the show she had seen, how wonderful it was, how brilliant the theater was and wouldn't he think about going to see the show? He nodded in what he hoped she would take as agreement while inwardly shuddering at the thought.

She talked about her plans for the new bathroom. Uncle Jack, in his guilt, was going to help her get it all done up. She didn't mention the guilt, but Denis heard it all the same. Trapped by his brother's absconding into being a permanent friend for his now ex-sister-in-law, because she had put up with so much. Because she continued to put up with so much.

She wondered if one Sunday Denis might like it if Uncle Jack came to visit. Denis tried to nod at that one, but he must have done it wrong, because his mother just looked alarmed at his expression and moved on. He liked Uncle Jack, but despised pity, so he wasn't overly keen on the idea of the man coming to see him. When she finally got around to asking him, it was so simple that it shocked him.

"Denis, love," she began tentatively.

This was it. Here was her moment for this week.

"Are you happy?" she asked.

Happy? Was he? He didn't know. He wondered if anyone knew.

"Of course I am. Why would you even ask?"

"It's just…"

She paused, trying to frame her thoughts. He watched her

struggle with it, various emotions playing across her lovely, kind, serious face.

"It's just that you live a different life now, and I know I barge into it, and it's because I want you to be happy. I just need to know that you're happy."

He looked her dead in the eye and lied.

"I'm happy. I promise."

After she had left, Denis pondered the question. Was he happy? Was anyone? And found himself back in the same peculiarly uncomfortable place he had been in the day before when he couldn't shake certain thoughts from his head.

Dealing with this unwelcome sensation was surely partly responsible for what happened next. Denis Murphy went off-book. He took his phone from his pocket and called Ollie. The phone had begun to ring when he realized what he was doing. He thought about hanging up, but it was too late to go back now; Ollie would call back, and if he didn't answer, Ollie would come to the house. Denis blinked in momentary confusion when he heard the voice on the other end.

"Hello?"

Silence.

"Denis? You there? Is the world ending? Have I slept a whole week and it's already next Saturday and we're supposed to meet for coffee again? Buddy?"

"Um." He coughed, embarrassed. "No. I'm here. I just wondered if you felt like a coffee today. Sunday. Would you like a coffee on a Sunday?"

"Sure I would, dude," Ollie said slowly. "You okay, big guy?"

"Yeah. Thanks," he lied. "I'm fine. Just wondering if you're not busy, that is."

"Never too busy for you, my friend. Italian place or Fish Place?"

The Quarter was the official name for what Ollie and Frank had dubbed Fish Place in reference to their misguided prank.

"The Quarter," Denis told him, smiling in spite of himself.

"Cool. See you in about half an hour."

Plasterer was standing in the doorway, watching.

"Just going to pop out for a bit," he told the poorly dressed clown.

"Yeah. So I see," came the reply. It was not friendly. Some people can invest a deep wealth of meaning into few words. Plasterer was one such.

Denis looked at his housemate closely. Through all the makeup his very slight frown was hard to see.

"All right there, Plasterer?" he asked nervously.

"It's just that Sundays are our days. No work. No friends. Just us and the fire once your mother leaves. What will I tell the others?"

"Tell them I'll be back in a while," Denis replied. "I won't be long."

Plasterer stood his ground. He seemed larger than normal somehow. Denis's mind could play tricks on him at the best of times.

Carefully now. Very carefully.

"It's just that Mom was a little difficult today," Denis told the clown. "I think I could do with some fresh air." He left it hanging. For a minute Denis felt like he was asking permission. This was new. He never asked permission from them.

Plasterer's frown deepened; under the thick makeup it gave his face more contours, more edges, but after a moment he nodded. Turning on his heel, he strode from the room, pulling the door closed behind him. Hard.

Denis sighed with relief.

The walk to town on this particular day came with a fundamental difference to the previous day: an umbrella. The modest umbrella was a source of unending contentment to Denis. It provided shelter from the elements. No spatter on his tie, no rain in his hair, no fear of sogginess that would cause the indescribable discomfort of trying to sit down in sodden trousers. Instead, it was protection of order from unpredictability. He laughed inwardly at his own disproportionate fondness for the common umbrella and conceded to himself, privately, that his friends may be right. He might just be a little odd.

The walk brightened his spirits a little. Strolling along, he could focus his thoughts on work, or avoiding that crack on the road instead of pointless nostalgia brought on by the picture incident. While walking with his shoes smartly rapping on the pavement, he could drown out the sound of his mother's voice asking him to love her, and he could forget the look in her eyes when his actions told her no. Forgetting things comes easily when you've spent several years working at it.

In town, Ollie, dressed in jeans with a ripped and dirty leg, a hoodie and a baseball cap, had deliberately chosen a table as far away as possible from Denis's regular spot. He had also added a fifth chair to the rectangular table, positioning it so that the chair was right at the corner, half facing away from him. Denis shuddered inwardly and made his way to his regular spot. The coffee shop was quiet, which was why Ollie had been able to get away with opening several sachets of sugar and emptying them all over the smooth steel surface. Denis was unsure which of them looked crazier: the guy who emptied sugar sachets all over a table and then walked away and sat somewhere else, or the guy who refused to sit at any other than one table, and then can't sit with the mess.

A waitress made her way outside and, seeing Denis, she busied herself cleaning his table, pausing to shoot Ollie a withering glance. She knew Denis by sight and knew he couldn't sit at any other table. Ollie beamed back at her, clearly pleased with himself. Denis shook his head and suppressed a smile. After the table had been cleared, he took his seat and waved Ollie over, ordered a coffee and watched his friend light up a cigarette.

"So what's up, D-Dog?" Ollie asked, affecting an accent.

"Nothing, just felt like a cup of coffee. What's up with you?"

"Don't think you're getting away with that one, buddy. It's a Sunday, which means, breakfast, exercise, cleaning, fire, your mom visiting and then television or movies all day. You think I'm not aware of your schedule by now? I'm pretty sure NASA uses you to program clocks at this point. So spill, what's up?"

Denis paused. Yet another departure from standard conversation. Twice in one day. Worse again, it seemed to Denis that ever since he had glimpsed a pink scarf over the top of his newspaper, he felt the comfort of his routine had been diminishing. It had served him so well for so long, and now this. Nothing was working out at all according to plan.

"A few deviations from the usual order. I'm just trying to reestablish my pattern," he told his friend.

"Interesting. By going for coffee you can just reset your weirdness?"

"Well, I could if you'd stick to the standard conversation."

"So what were the deviations?"

"That's not standard conversation," Denis replied irritably. Of his friends, Ollie was definitely the more irritating.

"Come on, just a little hint. One more tiny glance into the world of humanity's finest weirdo. What happened?"

"It's hard to talk about." That wasn't a lie. Most things were hard to talk about for Denis Murphy. "I just couldn't keep my own head today. Like it kept remembering things I didn't want it to remember. I'm just a little flustered that's all. You mind if we drop it?"

"Denis, you are definitely the strangest person I know," Ollie told him.

"Ever considered the idea that everyone else is strange and I'm the only normal one?"

"Briefly thought about that and then dismissed it on the grounds that I thought it was making me a weirdo too."

"Probably wise."

"Roisin wanted to come. I think she wants to be your friend too."

"I have a suitable number of friends."

"You have two friends, Denis. Two is not a suitable number. Give her a chance, will you?"

"Ollie, this is not helping. Now are we going to return to standard acceptable conversation or not?"

"Not until you promise to give my girlfriend a chance. You never know, someday you may find yourself standing in a perfectly straight and symmetrical line at an altar with me while I marry her."

Denis hesitated briefly. "If I promise to make more of an effort, you'll get back to normal-talk?"

"Absolutely."

"In controlled circumstances."

"Obviously."

"You promise?"

"Cross my heart in exactly even lines," Ollie quipped with a smile.

"Very well," Denis replied, resigning himself to having to navigate yet another awkward social event. "Now..."

"Okay, sorry dude, but heads up. Rebecca is coming..."

"What!" Denis exclaimed. His heart seemed to briefly stop in his chest, before kicking back into life at twice its normal rate. The panic must have been obvious in his face.

"Relax, she's... No, wait...she's seen me. Panic..."

"No way!" she exclaimed loudly, her voice floating to Denis from behind. It struck a note in his head. It sounded like wind chimes, but not the annoying ones. "Is that you, Ollie? It is you. Oh my God, it's so good to see you."

Stay calm. This is a good thing.

There was a warmth in her voice that Denis would have taken more time to appreciate if he wasn't in the grip of a full-blown war against an impending panic attack.

"Hey, lady," Ollie said, rising from his seat to hug her.

By some perverted logic, Denis figured she may not see him if he remained perfectly still.

Rebecca and Ollie continued hugging and exclaiming their disbelief at seeing each other, mere inches from the side of Denis's perfectly still head. In his periphery he could make out just enough of her features to bring sharply painful memories crashing back into his head. Her smile. How she tilted her head to one side when she was reading. Her singing voice and the way she looked at him while she strummed on her guitar. The way her lips pursed and her brow furrowed during debates—pub arguments really, but she was the undisputed champion. He could smell her perfume faintly. Still, the complete stupidity of believing that by not moving he could avoid a potentially painful reunion had not occurred to him, and so he was still sitting bolt upright, eyes forward and almost totally motionless when she spoke to him.

"Denis? Is that you…?"

"DENIS," Ollie shouted to snap him out of his reverie.

"Uh, yes. Hello." He tried to smile. He failed horribly, the result looking like a kind of half grimace that a lizard might make after eating something unpleasant.

"Give me a hug, you!" she told him, leaning forward, her arms extended.

"Please don't," he almost shouted.

And there it was again. For the second time in an increasingly worse day, Denis Murphy broke someone's heart. He would have cried if he could have figured out how. She looked beyond hurt. Before he had become what he had become, their entire lives together had been based on contact, often intimate, but always present. Holding hands, kissing, hugging, her arm falling lazily over him as they slept in their bed together. Her world of experience with Denis had been built on that constant contact. He rejected her cruelly with his revulsion, and he could expressively see the hurt it caused her.

"I'm sorry," he said, trying desperately to compose himself. "I'm not the hugging type."

"Okay," she replied slowly, looking at him, the hurt in her eyes pronounced.

"So...ah, you gonna have a seat?" Ollie asked, trying to break the awkwardness.

"That okay with you, Denis?" she asked, confused.

"Er, yes, er, of course," he replied, feeling himself break out in a sweat. "If you two will excuse me for just a couple of minutes, I'd like to use the bathroom."

With that, he practically jumped from his seat, and almost, but not quite, ran to the bathroom. At least now Ollie would have some time to explain things to her. Tell her all about him and his personality issues, and then maybe she'd just move on. Leave. Head somewhere else. Oddly enough, the thought of her leaving didn't make him feel any better. He splashed some water on his face and washed his hands repeatedly. It would be better if she wasn't here, he decided. With any luck, she'd be gone by the time he had finished drying his hands for the sixteenth time.

JUST EAT IT

She wasn't gone. She was sitting there when he returned to the table, directly opposite his seat, one hand idly playing with the single lock of hair with its many yellow beads. The rest of her long dark brown hair tumbled down her back and over her shoulders. Her loose-fitting, long-sleeved T-shirt had slid down one arm, leaving a beautiful tanned shoulder exposed. She was listening intently as Ollie talked in hushed tones. Undoubtedly he was catching her up on several years of compulsive behavior and trying to warn her of the pitfalls that come with conversing with Denis Murphy. He sighed bitterly as he walked back out to the covered smoking area. She would inevitably talk to their other old college friends and recount in half-horrified tones how Denis refused to hug her, and how his only remaining friends trod on eggshells lest his fear of odd numbers drive him from their company.

You know who's to blame for that, right?

Denis took his seat without a word. The conversation between Ollie and Rebecca cut off as he approached the table, confirming his suspicion that he had been the subject of their discussion.

"Sorry about that," he said, carefully positioning his seat

across from her, while briefly lamenting the lack of symmetry that Ollie had caused. Cursed odd numbers. Had it been Frank sitting there, the three of them wouldn't have felt so odd, but in her company, it needled Denis. He wondered about inviting the café's other regular customer to his table for balance, and then discarded the idea on the off chance that the man would attempt to engage him in conversation.

"That's okay," Rebecca replied, studying him carefully. "It's been a while, eh? How are you doing?"

"Very well, thank you," he said, shooting her one of his patented courtesy smiles. "And you?"

"Good. Just back from traveling. Six years living out of hostels and on beaches. I don't think I've done a day's worth of Event Management since college."

Denis suppressed a shudder at the thought of living in a hostel and sleeping in a bed that someone else had slept in the night before.

"Very nice," he lied.

"I'm not sure it would suit the new you," she said, laughing, not unkindly.

"I'm certain it wouldn't," he said, smiling genuinely for the first time since she walked in.

"Now there's the smile I remember," she said, her face lighting up in response to his.

"Yes, well, just because I'm orderly doesn't make me a robot," he replied, still smiling.

"Jury's out on that one, dude," Ollie chimed in.

"As it is on your questionable sense of fashion," Denis replied critically with a withering glance at Ollie's bright yellow hoodie.

"Score one for you," Ollie said, faking a look of hurt.

"What brings you home?" Denis asked Rebecca, more for the excuse to look at her again than out of interest.

"Visa ran out," she replied. "It's not so bad really. I was getting a little tired of it anyway. Was thinking of maybe trying China for a while, but a festival organizer has offered me a job here. Kinda too good to turn down. I left here because I was sure that there was no hope of a serious gig in this town, then I travel most of the world looking for one, and it turns out to be waiting for me back where I started. Typical."

Rebecca had earned a degree in Communications and Event Management. The university had given her tens of thousands to throw fund-raising parties and student events. She had a knack for it, a skill for organizing and a way with people the likes of which Denis had never seen in anyone else.

"So you're home for good?" Denis asked, his heart beginning to speed up again. He wasn't sure if he was frightened by the prospect or excited.

"Looks that way," she said. "Crashed with Mom and New Dad for a few weeks, and then came back here. Living in a hostel now till I get set up. Kinda suits me, really. I've been doing it for so long now, it's becoming second nature."

"To hell with that!" Ollie exclaimed. "Me and Ro have a spare bedroom in our place. It's not huge, but it beats the crap out of a hostel."

"No, I'm good, thanks," she replied. "It's only for another week or so while I find a place to stay full-time. It's a renter's market out there, so I get to pick and choose a place. Was thinking about sharing, but I don't want to end up living with weirdos."

"No. No, you don't," Denis agreed, thinking about the weirdos he lived with. He wondered what they were up to. In his head he imagined them playing hide-and-seek as they so often did. Badly. He had once found Deano hunkered down on the fireplace, holding a large vase in front of his face.

"So what brings you to town on a Sunday?" she asked.

"Denis is trying to reset his weirdness. I don't think it's working," Ollie told her.

"Oh?"

"Yeah, you see, there's three of us. Three being an odd number, Denis is unquestionably wondering if there's a polite way of making one of us leave. Three is only acceptable when it's me, him and Frank. Any other day of the week, three is intolerable."

Denis shot him a flat, unfriendly stare.

"I see," Rebecca said, taking Ollie's lead. "Any other odd numbers bothering you today?"

Denis cocked one eyebrow at her, but said nothing.

"Come on. This is my first time meeting the new version of somebody that I used to know. I want to know you again, Denis. So spill. What other odd numbers are annoying you?"

"There are three birds sitting on a gutter at the top of a building across the street. There are five small flowers on your T-shirt. Ollie has deliberately selected a bright yellow hoodie with the number seventeen inexplicably printed on the left shoulder. Don't look so offended, Ollie, it signifies nothing and you know it. Seventeen what, exactly? There are seven empty beer glasses on the table behind me, and there are thirteen condiments of various types in that ramekin—three mustards, five ketchups and five mayos."

The two of them stared at him, half impressed, half horrified.

"Also, you have thirteen beads in your hair."

She regarded him silently for just a few seconds before reaching into her bag. She produced a safety pin and carefully pinned back the T-shirt to cover one of the flower designs. Taking out a scarf, she draped it carefully over Ollie's shoulder to cover the unsightly number. She reached out and grabbed a small pack of mustard, one of ketchup and one of mayonnaise and stuffed them into her handbag, and then with delicate, beautiful hands, she carefully untied her plait, slipped off one of the beads and handed it to him.

"Unfortunately, I'm not the boss of pigeons, so you're going to have to deal with the birds. I don't work here, and I'm not feeling very energetic today, lots of fun last night, so I'm not collecting beer glasses, so unless you feel like doing that yourself, you're going to have to live with that too."

The smile he shot her was half wondrous.

"He can't collect the glasses," Ollie told her. "Someone else's mouth has been on them."

He nodded dumbly, still bowled over by her gesture.

For a second she just smiled, and then she burst into gales of laughter. Ollie couldn't help himself and joined in. For a few seconds, Denis tried to resist the urge, but there was something contagious in her melodic laugh. He chuckled in spite of himself.

"Thank you," he told her seriously after they'd collected their breath. "It's not easy, dealing with me. I know. So thank you."

"I have some bad news for you, Denny," she told him, using the nickname that only she used, once upon a time in a previous life. "I'm back home, and I'm not going anywhere, so I'll get used to you, if you'll get used to me."

Oh that's nice.

His heart started hammering again. She muddled his head, over and over. She had always done that to him, even when he was someone else. He wasn't sure if he was going to laugh or cry.

"So. I've got to get some shopping done. Then go back to the hostel. How do you guys feel about some dinner tonight?" she asked.

"Smashing plan," Ollie replied.

"Ah, not me. I've got something planned," Denis mumbled half-heartedly, trying not to look either in the eye.

"No, you don't," Ollie said firmly. "I'm bringing Ro, and Frank, and he's bringing Tash, and your date with your DVD player or your TV can wait. You promised to make more of an effort, and that starts now."

Denis could feel his face crumple. This was quickly turning into the worst Sunday ever.

"Wear something nice," Rebecca told him with yet another stunning smile. How could one person smile so beautifully? It didn't really seem right.

"I'm going to scoot. I promise I'll wear a perfectly even number of flowers this evening," she said, as she gathered her belongings. "Oh some phone numbers."

She reached into her bag and began pulling things out. Denis felt his muscles tighten up in discomfort as she produced an array of bits and pieces. Was there no end to this bag? Ollie spied his discomfort and tried to cover a smile.

"Quick," he told her, "get that phone and get moving, I think you're giving Denis a heart attack."

Denis breathed deeply.

She took the numbers as Denis tried to compose himself, and left with a laugh. If he didn't know any better, he'd swear she had done that on purpose.

Ollie was looking at him, an odd expression on his face.

"Time for you to start living life again Denis," he told his old friend. It sounded suspiciously like a threat.

He made his way home. It was more reeling than walking. He tried to compose himself.

Back at the house the four housemates were still in the middle of the worst game of hide-and-seek that anyone had ever played. For starters, none of them were actually seeking, which meant that all four had gone their separate ways about the house and were hiding. Unfortunately, their hiding places were every bit as atrocious as Denis imagined they would be. Penny O'Neill was stretched out, facedown, in front of the living-room fireplace. "I'm a rug, I'm a rug," she was whispering, over and over. Deano was headfirst into the cabinet under the sink, his hairy lower back, legs and his inexplicably hairy feet blatantly obvious to anyone who may have taken the time to look.

Plasterer was in the bath with a washcloth over his head, and the Professor stood at the top of the stairs, his face locked in an expression that could only be described as his "hiding face" while holding a book. "I'm a bookcase," he whispered at Denis as he walked by.

"Of course you are," Denis replied.

"PAUSE GAME," came a roar from the bathroom. "The Boss is home. Action Four News Team Assemble."

There was general panic as all four scrambled around and past each other en route to different rooms. On reaching one room, and realizing there was no one there, they would bolt, at top speed, to a different room, usually passing each other on the way. Denis sighed to himself.

"I'll be in the living room," he called out. "Join me when you're done."

It took fifteen minutes for the crowd to calm themselves before joining him, during which time he was able to assess the damage done during his absence. Surprisingly, the break from the standard Sunday routine hadn't affected them too badly. The milk would have to be thrown out, as it now had most of a bag of frozen peas floating in it. The butter too, which had peas mashed into the top of it in a kind of checkered pattern. Several of his ties had been nailed to the door that led to the utility room, and a wash had been put on. One of them had evidently decided that several of his books needed a good, thorough cleaning. He set about making things right again as the four slowly wound themselves down from all the running and stair-climbing. Deano, who had made his way to the living room first, was obviously not done yet, and was rolling back and forth across the carpet.

"Mind your hair," Denis shouted to him.

Deano froze in place. Then shook in what Denis assumed was a laugh.

By the time he had finished tidying the mess, all four were waiting in the living room.

"How did your day go?" Plasterer asked, his tone unpleasant. "It's a Sunday, and you went for coffee. Fucking coffee on a Sunday."

"It went fine," he replied. "I was trying to reestablish the order. I really don't like it when things unbalance the order."

"Neither do we," they replied in chorus.

"Liars. You find ways to break the order around here."

"Only for fun though. And only at the right time," Penny O'Neill replied. "Even we know that Sunday is for TV and movies. Today's no ordinary Sunday though, is it?"

"No. Sadly it's not. I have something to tell you all." Denis took a deep breath. The four facing him leaned forward in unison.

"I'm going to dinner."

Three of them applauded. Plasterer did not. He folded his arms in front of his chest unhappily.

"What? Applause? Why?" he asked, dumbfounded.

"Why not?" two replied in unison. Plasterer tsked irritably.

"Don't do that," Denis told them. This response was most unexpected.

"Don't do what?" they replied in unison.

"That," he snapped.

"Aaaaaaaah," they replied.

"You're all very annoying," he told them with a half smile.

"I think you'll find that is not the case," the Professor told him, raising one rotting finger in protest. "This one is Deano, the lady is Penny O'Neill and the undisputed champion at breaking all of my fingers when we arm wrestle is Plasterer. I am Professor Scorpion. So I think you'll find that not one of us is Very Annoying."

The others, even Plasterer, had begun pretending to sleep midway through his declaration, and Denis found himself playing along, allowing his head to drop onto one shoulder and making slight snoring noises. Penny O'Neill giggled now and again.

"Very well," the Professor announced sourly. "Your point is well received. I shall desist from my modest attempts at humor for the time being."

More applause.

"So is it Frank and Ollie for dinner? Or your mom?" Plasterer asked coldly.

"It's Frank and Ollie, but also—" Denis hesitated; this wouldn't be easy "—their girlfriends."

"Shock," Penny O'Neill cried in mock alarm, her tail standing straight out behind her.

"Horror," Plasterer added drily. He didn't look like he was joking, but it was hard to tell under the makeup.

Definitely not joking, you idiot. Not that one. No, no. That one is dangerous.

"I'm not permitted to partake of humor," the Professor told them grumpily.

Deano just shook alarmingly.

For some reason, Denis had decided not to tell them about Rebecca. If pressed, there could be no solid reason for not doing so, just a sense that perhaps it would upset them. If she had half the effect on them that she was having on him, he'd be cleaning the crayon off the walls for a week. His hand was in his pocket, idly rolling the bead she had given him in between his fingers.

"Why?" Plasterer asked.

"Well," Denis stalled, he had to give them a reason. One that didn't include her. They wouldn't like it. "Ollie sort of bullied me into it, and he's my friend, so I just thought, maybe it's not a terrible idea."

"It is," Plasterer told him gruffly.

"No," Penny O'Neill asserted firmly, "it's not. It was bound to happen at some point. You wouldn't want him falling out with them, now, would you?"

Plasterer looked at her. It was a good argument. Falling out with them would mean breaking the routine, and the clown simply loved the routine.

"It's about time that you engaged with your friends' better halves," Penny O'Neill told him. "And by better halves I mean their girlfriends. No one's actually able to split themselves in half. That's stupid. Plus, then you'd only be allowed to talk to the good half, because the bad half would think you're an asshole."

Denis looked at her, bemused. "Obviously," he said finally.

"What are you going to wear?" she asked him, plucking at his coat.

"I don't know," he replied. "I was told to dress nice, but I thought I always did dress nice."

"You dress well. Not nice," Plasterer told him, apparently warming to the idea. "There's a difference."

"There is?" Denis asked.

"Yeah. Anyone can dress well. All he has to do is buy some nice stuff and then spend exactly forty minutes ironing it. Then he can toddle off being well dressed. But if you take those well-looking garments and you wear them to look good, and I mean real good, then you're dressing nice. And that's different. Dressing nice gets you the ladies. I should know."

"You should know, should you?" Penny O'Neill asked, cackling with laughter. "Real lady-killer, eh?"

"At least I don't look like some slutty cat," Plasterer told her, his clown hair bobbing around as he shook his head at her.

"Meeeeow," she replied. "We can dress you nice, Denis. You just leave it to us."

Denis looked at them all suspiciously, as every one of them looked everywhere but at him.

"Why do I get the feeling I'm going to regret this?"

"Suspicious nature," Penny replied, taking him by the elbow. "You've always had it."

"I think you four may have earned such suspicion," Denis told them as they made their way upstairs. "I seem to recall needing new nightwear after you had convinced Deano to shred mine in a blender."

"A minor detail," Plasterer said, his face crinkling underneath his clown makeup. He was definitely coming around.

Don't be so sure.

"Then you spent six hundred euro on my credit card buying women's pajamas," Denis added.

"For the record, I think you looked rather fetching in those," the Professor told him.

"Can't believe I let you talk me into wearing them," Denis mumbled.

In his bedroom, the three began a mission to dress him "nicely." For some reason this involved tearing through the room. Plasterer took little part initially, just barking at them every now and then, but as the rumpus continued he seemed to warm up.

If Denis had reservations about this entire event before they had started ripping his room asunder, he certainly had them five minutes into the adventure. There was seemingly nothing that didn't need to be pulled out from every nook and cranny in the room. At first he tried to keep them in line, but it quickly became obvious that they were running on their own steam now, and in such situations, he had learned to simply sit back and let them work it out of their systems. They argued over clothes, such discussions frequently boiling over into shoving matches, until someone else suggested something that united two previous enemies back into allies. Denis sat there as they selected his attire. Finally, they came to a consensus on an outfit. He looked at it. It reminded him of college. It looked like something he might have worn on a night out back in his early twenties. The shirt was one of his better dress shirts, but the top two buttons were undone, and no tie was permitted. The suit jacket was a light gray. From somewhere they had produced a pair of jeans that Denis had forgotten he owned, as well as a pair of Converse running shoes. He was horrified at the ensemble.

"I'm not wearing that," he told them. "That is not dressing nice."

"You're wearing it," Plasterer told him, adjusting his white gloves menacingly.

"I am?" he asked with a slight catch in his voice.

"You are," they replied. In unison.

He dressed himself with an audience of one. Plasterer watched him as he disrobed and stepped in as he slipped on his jacket. The big clown reached out and adjusted the collar.

"We have a system, Denis," he told him in a low voice. He clearly didn't want the others hearing. "And you're messing with it. Dressing up and going out isn't part of the system. When we leave the system, bad things happen. Remember that."

With that he turned on his heel and walked from the room. Denis had thought the clown was warming up to the idea.

He stared after him for just a minute before he shook it off. "It's just dinner," he told himself. "Nothing to be afraid of." *Be afraid of that one.*

And so it was that he headed into town that night, having locked his door, checked it three times for safety and counted his way down the driveway, to meet five people for dinner. It was nearly seven years since Denis Murphy had gone for dinner with five other people. He couldn't remember the last time he'd gone outside his house without a tie on. He felt exposed. His running shoes made no satisfying pop as he walked. The unbuttoned shirt allowed the evening breeze to get down his top and ruffle the material against his skin. His muscles tensed involuntarily with each breeze, as though they could sense his discomfort. His hair was undisturbed by the wind, as Penny O'Neill had liberally applied the hair product to give a spiky effect. It was, Denis assumed, trendy. It was a dramatic change from his usual Sunday evening. No cop shows, no acronyms for investigators, no Penny O'Neill laying her head in his lap. It had been a long time since Denis Murphy had experienced significant changes in his life. None of them were comfortable. None of them were easy. Change, Denis concluded, was very much the enemy. And still, despite all that, he found himself oddly excited by the prospect of dinner. No doubt both Ollie and Frank would be agog at his choice of attire, and Rebecca, after demanding the dress code, would probably have something to say about his altered image too. He could hardly think straight every time she skipped into his head.

As was typical for any meeting with his friends, he was the first to arrive. Ollie had texted him the location, and his phone had told him how to get there. Not early, not late, but almost exactly on time. If the world was trying to impose change on Denis Murphy, it was in for a tough time of it; there were certain things that simply couldn't be wrested from him. Punctuality was one of them. The door to the restaurant presented certain problems, however. It had a stain on it. Right on the handle. It looked like ketchup, or perhaps jam; he was unsure. What was certain was that that tiny little glob could single-handedly deny him access to the restaurant all night. He looked through the glass at a waitress and shot her one of his courteous smiles. She waved back, but made no move to get the door. He stood there. Awkwardly. She beckoned him to come in. He smiled again and sort of nodded in the direction of the door, but made no further move. The waitress looked at him curiously. No doubt, she was beginning to think that this man was something of a weirdo, and, Denis thought to himself, she may be correct. Dressing up was fine and good, but weirdness had a way of outshining even the snappiest of casual wear. They stood there, regarding each other awkwardly through the glass panels of the door.

"Idiot," a voice muttered. Frank had arrived and reached past Denis to take the door handle. Clearly he didn't recognize his friend.

Denis jumped back, startled. They had almost touched. He tried to cover his shock, but it seemed that his clothes had done that for him. Frank and Tash were both looking at him with something approaching awe.

"Denis…" Frank almost whispered. "You look like you."

"Let's not make a thing out of it," Denis told him, almost snapping. "I was told to dress nice. This is the best I could manage."

"You did a good job," Tash told him, her brown eyes flashing at him. "I think I might just ditch this fella in favor of a better offer."

Tash didn't know any better and hadn't realized that talking to him like that was pretty much off-limits. He almost turned tail and ran. Only the thought of disappointing Rebecca kept him in place. Frank had dressed for the occasion too, as had Tash, who always looked glamorous. Her dark skin contrasting with the cream dress she was wearing, making her stand out for style as well as natural beauty.

"Thanks, Denis," Frank told him sarcastically. "The one night you actually behave like a normal human you have to go showing me up."

"The man has style, my love," she said, appraising Denis. "Think you might give this guy some tips, Denis?"

Denis didn't trust himself to speak, fearing that if he did it would end up being a quick apology before fleeing, so he nodded dumbly instead. The restaurant was an assault on his senses, and it took all of Denis's willpower just to step through the door. Inside, thick beams of stained dark wood supported the low ceiling, stretching from the front door all the way back to a private dining-room door. Platforms here and there gave the feel of split-levels, with banisters separating the dining area into little sections, rows of wine bottles stuffed with candles standing solemnly on each partition. It was positively claustrophobic. It was, to compound his sense of growing unease, a mess of odd numbers and haphazard seating arrangements. In between two tables, one rebel had turned his chair sideways so he could address diners at both. A fork, still smeared with the sauce of some meal or other, was on the floor next to a table. Here and there children moved about, as if attached to no one in particular. It was a busy restaurant. Sunday was most obviously a family night out. The subtleties of this level of social interaction were quite beyond his comprehension.

"Can I help you?" asked the waitress who had been smiling at him through the door. She leaned forward into his personal space.

He took a backward step, watching her warily in case she tried to touch him.

"Unless you're a qualified psychiatrist and a one-woman pharmacy rolled into one, I doubt very highly that you can help him," Frank told her smilingly.

"Witty," Denis replied, still watching the waitress.

"We have a reservation for about now," Frank told her. "Six people, under the name Lynch. If you could arrange to have the six seats spaced exactly evenly apart, that would probably help my terrified-looking friend here."

"Genius," Denis grumbled at him as Tash barked some good-humored laughter.

The waitress covered her disgust at his behavior and showed them to their seats, eyeing Denis like he was some form of visiting alien. The other waitresses would surely find her story about the weirdo in her section hilarious. And then he stopped thinking. Just like that, all thought vanished from his head as Rebecca walked in with Ollie and Roisin in tow. The other two may as well not have existed; in fact, the entirety of the restaurant may as well not have existed. His eyes feasted on her. A slim black skirt, with a slightly loose-fitting white blouse, its sleeves rolled almost all the way back up to expose the skin of her arms, bedecked with bangles. Her curly hair was tied back, with what looked like a leather strap. Her black pumps were worn over bare skin, no tights or stockings needed for her smooth, tanned legs. She was glorious.

"Close your mouth, Denis Murphy," she said with a smug smile as she took her seat.

Denis started. He had been staring. His mouth hanging open. Ollie was snickering as he held out a chair for Roisin. Denis had never met Roisin before, and was impressed that

Ollie had found someone to match him. She seemed outwardly
pleasant, and taller than most girls to equal Ollie's height advantage. She had a pleasant face, but she was clearly nervous
of him. He tried not to let it darken his thoughts as her eyes
darted away from him and then slowly back again.

"I take it you approve of the getup, Denis," Rebecca stated,
clearly enjoying the moment. "It was a real experience trying to get myself dressed up in the hostel. Privacy is a little
hard to come by."

"Six bangles on each arm," Denis replied. "Even and symmetrical. Thank you."

She winked at him.

Frank and Ollie exchanged glances. Denis was sure there
was meaning loaded in the look, but it would take a far more
intuitive mind than his to decode it, and so he simply ignored
it. He was introduced to Roisin who, clearly having been
briefed by Ollie, made no effort to shake his hand. His relief
was tempered by remorse. What great lengths his friends had
to go to to accommodate him, and even after all this time
they had not given up. It would have made a normal person
cry. Denis simply looked at them both and nodded. He hoped
they understood.

He didn't contribute much during dinner. Mostly because
he had to keep his head down to avoid seeing things that made
his skin crawl, but also because he feared that if he opened
his mouth he'd say something that Rebecca would take offense to. Oddly enough, he also found himself considering
both Tash's and Roisin's feelings. They chatted amiably, with
Roisin casting him occasional glances. He just kept his mouth
shut, smiling politely at the appropriate moments, laughing
when called for and nodding seriously when he felt he must.
What surprised him most about the entire event was not that
he had lasted this long, but that he hadn't had a panic attack

or collapsed out of pure revulsion. The smudges of dirt on the aprons of the staff were bad enough, but the tightly packed restaurant space meant that they had to squeeze by him, almost brushing him with their dirty clothes. He suppressed a shudder every time they did. He watched the clock from time to time. One hundred fifty minutes was the time allotted; he mentally counted down with every glance. And yet for all of that, Denis had to admit, he was enjoying himself a little. He appreciated the easy manner his dining companions had with each other; the way Rebecca slipped back into Frank's and Ollie's lives, like she had come back from a two-week holiday and not a six-year hiatus. The way they all laughed so easily, so frequently.

"Denis…"

He looked up. He had been daydreaming. They were talking to him. They were all looking at him.

"I'm sorry. World of my own. Can you repeat the question?"

"Frank was just saying he's never been to your house. You bought a place and everything. No housewarming?" Rebecca inquired.

Here they were. Right at a topic he had no interest in discussing. They had ventured from the safe waters of comfortable chitchat to the reefs of personal interest.

"It's something of a sacred space," he told her guardedly.

"Do you have housemates?" she asked.

"No," he lied. He'd been doing quite a bit of that over the last two days, he realized.

"I heard it's huge," she persisted.

"It's a big place all right," he agreed.

"And it's just you in there on your own?"

"Yep."

There was an awkward silence as everyone realized they

had hit a point in the conversation that was going to force Denis to retreat. His eyes involuntarily flickered toward the door. Rebecca had been watching him.

"Don't go…" she said.

It wasn't far to the door. A quick dash.

She looked at him again; there was something in that look. A question and a promise and a hint of something, something he wanted. It was enough to keep him in his seat.

"Not yet," he replied, sighing.

"Anyone following anyone cool on Twitter?" Roisin asked, changing the topic with a look in his direction. Ollie nodded at her. The easy rhythm of the chat that had been flowing for most of the dinner seemed to kick in, and in a moment, the table was back to comfortable and easy conversation. Rebecca looked at him with slightly narrowed eyes. He'd have paid to know what she was thinking.

After dinner, Denis made his goodbyes quickly. There was something ridiculous about dragging out a farewell that seemed to go hand in hand with awkward emotional responses. He preferred to avoid rather than engage such situations. Ollie and Frank had smiled approvingly at him as he bade everyone good-night. They were clearly proud of him. Privately he would have to admit that he was ever so slightly proud of himself. Just once, he had proven he could be sociable. Rebecca had not smiled at him as he left. She had looked him very seriously in the eye and simply asked him to stay in touch. He wondered about that as he made his way home. Obviously there was a type of layered meaning in it, but Rebecca hadn't been around him long enough to know that such things were not easy to grasp for the socially inept. One dinner didn't make him the man about town. He still very much counted himself among the ranks of the socially clueless. He pondered what she could have meant, and idly daydreamed about how soft her hands must be as his running shoes softly patted the ground.

The door was open, and he was in the hallway before he realized his mistake. The gate was open. He hadn't counted any of the steps to the door. The key had slid perfectly into the lock without one attempt to test its security. A well of panic surged up from his stomach. The gate was open.

Calm down, you big baby.

"Help," he shouted into the dark and silent house. "Help me." The gate was still open.

OPEN THE DOOR

The streetlight pouring into the house cast an eerie shadow across Plasterer's face as he appeared at the doorway. Penny O'Neill was just behind, and slinked past him to stand by the coats that hung in the porch. The Professor and Deano stood at the bottom of the stairs watching him. Out on the road, the next-door neighbor arriving home from the pub called out. "You okay? Is everything okay?"

"Shhhhhhh," Penny O'Neill whispered to Denis. "It's going to be okay. Listen to Plasterer. He'll fix this. Shh, now."

Denis looked at Plasterer. Panic had erased his ability to think. The gate was still open. The intrusion of others into his life was a burden that must be borne, but not this, not this kind of negligence. Not from himself. It was unacceptable. The clown returned his look with a frown, his arms folded across his broad chest.

He's getting bigger, you know.

"Is something wrong up there?" came the neighbor's voice again, tinged with alarm.

"It's okay," Plasterer told him, his voice low and steady. "It's going to be okay. Tell him that everything is fine. You just got a fright."

"I'm... I'm fine. Thank you. Sorry for the disturbance. Just got a bit of a fright," Denis called out to the street. His eyes locked on the gate for a moment. It was still open.

"You sure? Want me to come over?" came the reply from over the hedge that separated Denis from the outside world.

"Tell him that it's okay. There's no need. Apologize again. Make a joke. Laugh it off," Plasterer advised, his voice bubbling with something aggressive.

"No, no, really, that's fine. I'm embarrassed enough to have been jumping at shadows. I don't want my shadow scaring you too," Denis called back, forcing a laugh. He sounded surprisingly calm even to himself.

"Very good," came the reply. "Good night."

The sound of footsteps signified the neighbor's retreat into his home. The rattle of keys at the door. Click. Slam. Once again Denis was alone in the night air.

"Well done," Plasterer congratulated him admiringly. "The fat bastard should be minding his own business."

His voice came out in a growl before he returned to his soothing tones.

"Now, I need you to walk back to the gate. Count the steps all the way. Close it. Count them all the way back. Wipe your feet on the mat, twenty times each foot. Close the door. Lock and unlock it ten times. You'll be fine. We can get you through this."

"Listen to Plasterer, Denis," Penny O'Neill practically purred. "You'll be safe again before you know it."

Denis did as he was told, the chill night breeze cold against his freshly sweaty skin. He counted the steps to the gate, all the way open, all the way closed, counting all the way back. His breathing was ragged. The panic was subsiding with each carefully numbered step, but the memory of it lingered. Penny

O'Neill hugged him tightly when the door was closed behind him.

"Now," Plasterer continued, "label each door in the house. A single A4 sheet for each room, in block capitals. Then shred them and do it again. After that I want you to alphabetize the breakfast cereals. I'm going to overcook porridge in the microwave, and when I'm done, you can clean that. I also want you to clean the insides of the bottles of all the cleaning products and then put the cleaning products back in. Next, you must plan tomorrow. Include some time for a coffee in the afternoon. This time you go alone. No girlfriends or any such nonsense. You have no business hanging around with girlfriends."

There seemed to be something in his voice that suggested he knew about Rebecca, but that couldn't be. He must have been referring to Tash and Roisin.

"Time you remembered the plan," Plasterer said in a tone that brooked no argument.

Denis embraced his tasks with his usual efficiency. There was no room for thinking when there was work to be done. Eventually he returned to the living room to turn on the television. He knew it was the living room for certain because he had just labeled it so. On his way he had passed the kitchen, which was, unquestionably, the kitchen. The label said so. He sighed quietly as he sat. How did this happen to him? Things like this never happened to him.

"This happened because you broke the rules, Denis," Plasterer told him. "You deviated from the course. We know the course, and we're comfortable with it because we know it. When you change it, when you do these things, you're allowing in thoughts that don't help us. They make us weak and unsure. We need to be sure, Denis. All of us."

Denis nodded dumbly.

"Turn on the television," Penny O'Neill instructed him

as they each took their regular spots. "We'll watch a movie before bed, and then I'll curl up at your feet and the whole world will be right again."

"I'm not sure if this is the time to interject," the Professor interjected. "But what about left? If it's all right, then it's entirely unbalanced. Remember that time we all stood on the right-hand side of the room and it nearly toppled over?"

"It's okay, Professor." Denis smiled. "She meant that it would all be correct."

"I doubt it highly. People are idiots."

"Agreed. But we persevere."

"We do."

Denis could feel himself unwinding. This room was safety. This house was safety. Outside was not. Tomorrow's plan was ready, and it included two hours of coffee-socializing, but Denis vowed that those hours would not be spent in the company of Rebecca Lynch, or Natasha Kane, or Roisin Dermody. Maybe not even Frank and Ollie. No. It was time to put a stop to the nonsense of the last two days. Dinner dates and running shoes with jeans. Ridiculous. Why not just chop a mohawk into his hair and wear those leather jackets that no one ever bothered to wash? Safety would be restored. Order would be restored.

"You're not ready yet," Penny O'Neill told him cryptically. "Not yet. But I'm sure you will be eventually."

He hesitated for just a moment before telling them.

"It's a girl," he announced quietly. "Rebecca. She just showed up. It's thrown me a little. And by a little, I mean a lot."

"Women can have that effect all right," Plasterer replied somewhat bitterly.

"As if you'd know," Penny O'Neill shot back.

"What am I going to do?" Denis asked them.

"Nothing. You're just going to be you. You're mostly good

at that," Plasterer told him in a lukewarm declaration of confidence. "We know all about this Rebecca, and the only way you win in this situation is if you put your head down, do as you're told and stick to the plan."

Denis shook his head.

"You're going to be okay. Someday you'll laugh at this," Penny O'Neill insisted, her voice calm.

He didn't bother to ask what she meant. She was half asleep anyway, her blond mane spilling across his lap. She was warm. He was comfortable. This was safety. Everything was going to be all right.

Denis woke the following morning as the very personification of determination. It was a sight to behold. Never before had anyone so carefully and determinedly brushed their teeth. Never was a bowl of cereal the subject of such relentless eating. In the history of well-pressed trousers, there had never before been seen a pair as well-pressed as those that Denis put on that morning. The gel for his hair was calculated precisely to provide maximum hold with minimal wastage. His tie was retied no less than six times in the dogged pursuit of tie perfection. Denis Murphy took on Monday morning like a dog digging for a bone. There was no wasted movement, no reckless disregard for excessive use of the space on his spoon. If you could have measured his morning coffee, it would have been consumed in equal mouthfuls, such was his focus on the task at hand. The patented computer program that had been his brainchild—as well as the subject for his undergraduate thesis—crunched numbers and data like no program had ever done before, but even that was a poor shade of efficiency next to Denis Murphy.

Denis's home doubled as his workplace. Recession had made such a house, a proverbial palace, accessible to Denis. Recession and, of course, a more than healthy salary. His work suited him well. All that was required was a laptop, a printer, a scanner and a working internet connection. Data was emailed or faxed to him. He analyzed it, compared it, ran it through the program he had devised in college, which collated such information and utilized website analytics to project future coverage. Clients could come to the company he worked for looking for marketing solutions, and Denis provided all the necessary facts and figures for optimum growth and development. Strategies to achieve this were left to people who were more personal than he was. Frankly put, that meant just about anyone, but since his data and results were all impeccably researched and analyzed, he was invaluable to his employers. Thankfully for all concerned, he could be perfectly invaluable from home. Denis was under no illusions about his absolute uselessness in the modern working environment, and believed, probably correctly, that his colleagues would be just as frightened by the idea of him coming to work as he was by the notion of having to share a lunchroom or toilet with other staff. Some things were simply not acceptable to someone with his particular idiosyncrasies. His office was perfect for his requirements also: white walls untouched by photos or pointless artwork, a study in minimalism. His desk and chair functional to the point of severe. In fact, his whole house was a monument to simplicity. During the recession, armed with a generous paycheck every two weeks, Denis had applied for and received a mortgage. He had even shaken the bank manager's hand on conclusion of the deal. He had to wash it twenty-two times, each wash taking exactly two minutes before he felt comfortable handling cutlery again. The mortgage bought him a four-bedroom detached house in a quiet development just outside the city center. He had a large backyard, two living rooms—one of them converted to a bedroom—a wide, bright kitchen and an office. Ideal. He also had a separate garage that the real-estate agent assured him would make a lovely gym. Most of the bars required for lifting weights had rough edges for better grip alongside smoother edges toward the middle of the weight, a situation that was uncomfortable for Denis, and so it stood empty, save for when his housemates went in there to paint on the walls for apparently no reason.

Now they stood by the door to his office beaming at him and occasionally thumping each other about the head and shoulders, again for no apparent reason. Deano was covered in clothespins. He looked uncomfortable in the way only a human hair ball could look uncomfortable. Hairily.

Denis made phone calls to head office, wasting no extra words, save for some polite salutations, which weren't really wasted, considering he had decided it was in his interest to keep the work people onside. It wasn't manipulation as such, but more a pragmatic approach to office politics. At some point, his particular social needs may impact on their lives, and being nice now might help on the day that he required something in return.

You can't avoid it forever, you idiot.

For two hundred ten minutes Denis worked. He made coffee efficiently and drank it in fourteen minutes. He then worked for a further seventy-eight minutes before lunching for sixty minutes. Then he worked for a further one hundred twenty minutes. During this time, he ignored his cell phone. It was staring at him in a most accusatory fashion, but he blanked it out all the same. At four, having put in an efficient, productive and most of all orderly day's work, he sent his final email and clocked off. His phone was waiting. It had a habit of doing that. The text message waiting on it was short and simple: Nice to see you last night, Pudding. Coffee?

I'm bored. His mind, ever so briefly let off its leash, traveled back to a time when Rebecca called him Pudding. His nickname, Denny, which had a barely humorous link to an Irish meat company, had earned him an additional nickname: Pudding. He tried to recall a time when he had found someone naming him after a tasty, if disgustingly produced, breakfast meat to be a good thing. In his memory he heard her voice chant it in a bar while he slammed seven shots in a row, racing Ollie to the last one before leaping onto a table to soak in the adulation of a heartily impressed crowd of inebriates that had included Jules and Eddie. Ollie had vomited on the floor. The crowd was doubly impressed. Ollie had always been the lightweight of the group, with Eddie and Frank competing for the heavyweight championship of drinkers. He shook off the troublesome thought, but dithered over a reply. In no way was he prepared for another onslaught. She confused his brain, and his brain was not a fan of being confused. Equally he was unprepared to face the consequences of such; the abandonment of order. Today had been, to this point, highly productive, not just from a work point of view, but in terms of reestablishing the pattern and rhythm of his life.

"You don't have to reply," Plasterer told him, seeming to materialize at his shoulder, his thick face paint dangerously close to smudging Denis's work shirt. There were grains of sugar stuck to the paint around his lips. "Forty minutes into town. Newspaper. One hundred twenty minutes' coffee time and home to watch *Criminal Minds* with us." His smile would have been reassuring if not for the sugar crusting on his mouth. Denis could practically taste it.

"You're right. Again," Denis told him, snapping the leather cover of his phone shut. "Try not to make a mess while I'm gone."

"I'll be good, but there's no stopping the other three reprobates."

"Pffffft. Liar." Denis smiled. "See you in a while."

He made his way to town as he had done ever since he bought the house. Same route. Same cracks in the pavement to be avoided. Same noise of the world intruding on his ears. Thomas was waiting in his chosen convenience store.

"The usual, Mr. Murphy?" he asked in his foreign accent. He had, Denis concluded, a wonderful smile.

"Indeed, Thomas. And thank you. Hope you're having a lovely day." He flashed his courteous smile back, feeling a vague sense of disappointment that his smile would never compete with the man's behind the counter.

"Would be a better day if I could get a high five…" he replied, still grinning.

"A nice offer, but sadly, I must—".

"Must decline," Thomas finished for him. "I know. See you tomorrow, Mr. Murphy."

"Good day, Thomas. Thanks."

He made his way across the sheltered side street and under the canopy, taking his usual seat. The waiter, businesslike in his black uniform, brought his latte without ceremony, placing it with the handle pointed at a right angle away from Denis to the right.

"Enjoy," he said. He always said that.

"Thank you. I will," Denis replied. He always replied that.

On the same street as the little coffee shop were several other businesses. Women in smart suits strode down the street against old men who seemed to amble aimlessly with nothing but time on their hands. Some women, with strollers or tugging reluctant children behind, bustled with shopping bags and boxes. A beggar, dressed in old, filthy clothes, his face a mask of dirt, wandered here and there, thrusting out his hands to people. He was largely ignored. His eyes landed on Denis, who quickly began assessing his chances of getting out of the man's path before it was too late. If he did so, he'd have to leave without paying. If he went to pay, he'd have to confront the man outside the shop. A perfectly good and orderly day was preparing to descend into a mess of hand-scrubbing and awkwardness. And then it got worse.

Just as the man was making his final approach, he was caught by the wrist by a beautiful young woman, with deep brown eyes and a stunning smile. A woman who wore beads in her hair. A woman with a first-class honors degree in Communications and Event Management. A woman with a terrible knack for being in Denis Murphy's head. She took the man by the arm and, smiling, pressed some money into his hand. They spoke, just out of earshot, but loud enough for him to know that their conversation was amiable and friendly. He cursed his luck. Was there a chance that she was following him? He once again wondered if this was some elaborate prank by Ollie and Frank designed to shock him back to what they called normality. It seemed a little sophisticated for Ollie, but Frank could pull it off. The beggar was moving on, a smile on his face. Rebecca had that effect on people and try though he might, Denis was unable to avoid smiling at her as she made her way to his table.

"Avoiding me?" she asked.

"Trying to," he fired back before he had time to think.

She just laughed at him. "And why would you do such a thing? Aren't I wearing symmetrical enough jewelry today?" She did a little turn as she spoke. He couldn't help himself and found his eyes drinking in her form.

"Eyes off the ass, Pudding," she ordered with a half smile.

"Don't call me that," he replied, a little harsher than he'd intended. If it bothered her, she showed no signs of it.

"Why not?" she replied.

"It's not my name. It's a strange meat by-product that no one should eat," he told her, asserting himself. It was high time he stopped allowing her inside his head. He was making a stand this time.

"It is your name. I named you it. And you used to love it. You once snorted like a pig when I called you Pudding in bed."

"I once did a lot of things," he replied coolly, outwardly calm as the memory of a bright sunny morning in bed crashed into his head like a train. The rays were spilling through a gap in the curtains and bouncing off everything in her room. He lay naked underneath the covers, staring at the ceiling as the first stirrings of her awakening reached his ears. She had wished him a good morning and called him Pudding. He had snorted like a pig. She had laughed like a bell ringing.

"Now there's something we can talk about—" she ventured.

"No. That's not something we can talk about," he retorted, cutting her off. "You do not have a special pass, Rebecca. I don't talk about these things to anyone. You are no different from Ollie, Frank or anyone else."

"I think I am," she replied, her face stern with his rejection. "But we can let that slide. What are we allowed to talk about?"

"Events of the day, politics, sports, weather…such things." He realized that his tone and language had taken on a pompous quality that made him sound like he was auditioning for an Oscar Wilde play, but he couldn't help himself. Emotive language was not going to help. It's what she wanted.

She narrowed her eyes for a moment, clearly irritated, but the stern quality of her features eventually gave way to a smile. Damn her smile.

They sat in a slightly tense silence for a while. Denis was determined not to give ground.

"I'm sorry," she said finally, her face growing serious. "This can't be easy for you. But it's not all about you, you know. This isn't easy for me either. I came back here, moved into a crappy hostel and the one thing that was keeping me motivated was seeing you and the guys. Especially you. I came back expecting to find you, but what I found was some stranger wearing your face. Every now and again there's a flash of the guy I used to know, but then it vanishes behind that grim expression you always seem to wear. Like every moment of the day is a battle that you have to win. Not easy for me to swallow, you know."

She was right. All too often Denis was aware of the difficulty he presented for others, but in three days he had barely considered how she must feel about seeing him. She was also right about the stranger. She didn't know Denis Murphy. Not anymore.

"I'm sorry," he told her.

She sat looking like she expected more. Truth be told, he wanted to say more, but it seemed that his brain had passed on orders to his mouth and the apology was about as far as he was going to go. One would think that controlling one's brain is a relatively straightforward process. It is not.

But his mood softened considerably, and the two eased into more amiable conversation. They chatted about this and that, her new job, the fact that she'd have real money to live on, instead of whatever meager wages she scrimped by on during her travels. It was enticing to her, financial stability. He talked about how he had managed to climb up a few rungs on the managerial ladder without ever having to leave his home. Then they both marveled at how old they had become, how their priorities had shifted, leaving them in an adult landscape that their younger selves could never have foreseen, prioritizing finances, insurance and groceries over fripperies, luxuries and booze.

She laughed at his reclusiveness and made fun of him, but never probed too deeply; Denis never gave too much away, and despite his reservations, he found himself enjoying his time with her. Her easy, relaxed manner soothed him. Her conversation was, for want of an expression that didn't belong in a 1950s screenplay, sparkling. She was witty, bright, funny and insightful. In his daily routine, with its particularly ordered timeline, there was little room for reminiscing and so he had forgotten that she was so much more than simply graceful and beautiful. She had a way of lulling him into a sense of comfort. That led to mistakes though. He would have to be on his guard, he realized. Even now, sitting here, he was aware that she was slowly creeping into his head again. Vigilance was needed.

"Denis? You there?" She had asked him a question. He had been thinking about vigilance and missed it.

"Hmm?" he replied, aware that the noise and his facial expression were working together to make him look like an idiot.

"I asked you why no one has ever been in your house." The question was innocently asked, without a hint of confrontation or probing.

He blinked at her. She arched her eyebrows at him.

"Do you want to see it?" he replied.

Now it was her turn to blink at him.

"You're welcome to visit," he told her. It sounded wrong coming out of his mouth. What would his housemates make of this decision?

"I'd love to," she replied, clearly stunned. "It might be nice to get out of the hostel for a bit, visit a real house. There's something so transitional about living in a hostel. It's hard to unwind. Might be nice to chill at yours for an evening. If you're sure you don't mind? I could just hang with Ollie if it makes you uncomfortable though."

There was a surge of something in his chest. An emotion. Not a new one, but one so rarely felt that it was almost alien to him. A distant part of his brain remembered it. Jealousy. Irrational jealousy. As if there was any other kind.

"You can stay with me if you like. Plenty of rooms in my house."

The words were out of his mouth before he knew it. He hardly believed it was possible for him to say such things. It was as if someone else had taken over control of his mouth. The words sailed through the space between the two of them and straight into her beautiful brown eyes, which lit up as they struck home.

"Denis, that's a lovely thought, and I'm blown away by your offer, but are you sure you want a houseguest? What if I put one of your forks in with one of your spoons?" she asked with a half smile. "I can always just stay with Ollie. I'm sure he won't mind if I change my mind." The first comment was not said unkindly. It wasn't intended to hurt, but for some reason it did, all the more because he had involuntarily flinched at the thought of the fork mixed with the spoons. Some cutlery just shouldn't mix, and it was blatantly obvious that forks had no business with spoons. The second comment hurt even more, and another surge of jealousy battered him at the mention of Ollie's name. Distantly, he dissected the emotion; there was nothing about Ollie that upset him. Nothing about his friend's house upset him. There was no part of this feeling that he liked. It was a tumult inside his head, a feeling of intense panic at having invited her, that ping of jealousy that had slid up on him from nowhere and a sense of excitement hidden in the middle of it all. A sense of something that might be.

"Hey, it's my house, isn't it? I'm sure we'll get on fine. It has to be better than a hostel, right?" He tried to sound nonchalant, but that's not easy for a man who flinches at the thought of a fork and a spoon sharing a plastic cutlery tray.

"Pudding, I'd go back and pack my stuff right now if I thought that you really wanted me to live in your house, but I'm not sure you do. I don't know what you're trying to prove to yourself, but Ollie and Frank have been with you through all of your ups and downs, and they've never been past the porch. Are you really sure you want, or are ready for, a housemate?"

A part of him wanted to smile. He had dealt with all kinds of housemates for many years now. It was the thought of those housemates that shocked him back to reality. He was inviting her to live in his home, but it wasn't just his home. It was theirs too. What if she tried to sit in the Professor's seat or, even worse, Plasterer's?

But what if she stays with Ollie or Frank instead of you? You wouldn't like that.

He couldn't tell which was worse. Something of his torment must have shown on his face, as Rebecca sat up and looked at him in alarm.

"Something wrong, Denny? I didn't mean to offend, I just want to know if you really want me to stay with you?"

Two voices seemed to be screaming in his head now. One said no. The other said yes. Denis simply said, "I have to go. If you wouldn't mind…" He left some money on the table for her to pay for his latte. He was gone before she could object. The rhythm of his shoes pop-popping on the sidewalk was more rapid than normal, matching his accelerated heart rate. He could just take it back. Text her and tell her he changed his mind. He didn't want to. Through town, avoiding the cracks.

Over the bridge. Past the stadium. Gate open, closed, steps counted, lock tested, home safe. Denis heaved a sigh of relief.

The Professor met him in the hallway.

"Deano tried to set fire to himself a while ago. No conceivable reason. We had to tie him to a chair. He wasn't happy about it so we set fire to all the tea towels to cheer him up. He's sleeping now."

Denis looked at the Professor and sighed.

"Anything else?" he asked.

"Not precisely. Something happen to you? You look frightened."

"Two days in a row, Professor. Two days in a row I've seen her and three times I've done something that I regret."

"Any chance she's a witch?"

Denis gave him a flat, unfriendly look.

"All options must be explored," he announced loftily. "Anyway, what did you do this time?"

"I invited her to live with me."

The Professor broke into gales of laughter. Denis had been expecting a drastic reaction—the Professor was unpredictable at the best of times—but he certainly hadn't been expecting laughter. He doubled over, clutching at his sides, tears careering down the ruined mess of his face.

"Wait till Penny O'Neill hears of this. This is better than good. You? Her? Living with one another?" He was laughing so hard that some of the words were barely coherent. The others, drawn by his mirth, appeared at the door to the office, Penny O'Neill swaying more than walking, standard for her, really. Plasterer seemed to burst into every room; even when he was strolling there was something about him that hinted he was always on the edge of exploding.

"What's all the racket? Jokes? Can the zombie tell jokes?"

he asked as the Professor attempted to pick himself up off the floor.

Penny O'Neill cocked her head to one side questioningly.

"Nothing. Haven't you got anything better to do?" Denis snapped.

"Not really," she told him. "We've burned all the tea towels and painted all the crockery, so we were actually getting a little bored. It's not as much fun playing games with three people, but Deano tried to light himself on fire, which is odd because he never really does anything without being told by one of us, and nobody said anything about fire to him."

Denis sighed again.

"So what's he laughing at?" she persisted, pointing a finger at the Professor, who had regained his feet but was continuing to shake with glee.

"You'll never believe it," he told them, still trying to compose himself from his laughing fit. "Our lordship has asked that woman to move in here. With us."

The Professor began howling with laughter all over again, holding Penny O'Neill upright as he did. Sometimes in life, even your nearest and dearest are utterly without sympathy. Plasterer was most certainly not laughing. He was looming. Denis pushed past them disgustedly to free Deano in the kitchen, who was struggling against his bonds.

"Relax, fur ball," Denis told him. "I'm setting you free."

Deano quivered slightly at being let loose and then bounded out into the corridor to join the other three. If he had a tail, Denis was sure he would have wagged it.

The floor of the kitchen was still a mess of charred tea towel remains, and the crockery, which had been painted crudely with a collection of faces, some smiling, some frowning, stared at him from the kitchen side table, like a little army whose primary weapon was judgment. The smell of singed material was strong. Their constant, wanton destruction should have bothered him more, but for the first time in a very long time, he felt a serious need for it. Now he could lose himself in the task of cleaning and tidying, all of the thoughts and irritations of the day, all the conflict, the struggle for clarity that seemed to come with just thinking about Rebecca Lynch, the stupid opening he'd left her, all of it could be left behind so that tidiness and neatness could be imposed on the mess that his four housemates, some of them still howling with laughter, had made. The quiet voice in his head told him that at some point a decision was going to have to be made, a decision about what to do with Rebecca and whether or not she had a place in his life. That decision would not be made today though. Today was a day for cleaning and reasserting the correctness of a tiny universe belonging to him and four housemates. A universe that existed within the confines of a securely locked door. Guests not welcome. He would have hummed with satisfaction if humming was a thing that Denis Murphy permitted himself to do.

The fact that guests were not welcome in this little universe, and very infrequently tried to impose on it, was the main reason that Denis got such a shock when the doorbell rang. All mirth in the hallway ceased. He walked out of the kitchen to check it. His four housemates were lined up, single file, just inside the office door. They wouldn't be seen there. He knew before he opened the door that it was Rebecca. It couldn't be anyone else. No one else would simply turn up. She had a knack for invading his space. A singular talent that had no practical use in the real world, but was disastrously damaging in this universe.

"Invite her in," Penny O'Neill whispered as he passed the door. "You two can hold hands and kiss and stuff." Her tone was mocking. Denis didn't like it very much, but he ignored it and, after testing the lock, turned the key and opened the door, just slightly.

"You can't just take off like that, Denny. It's rude," Rebecca said, her tone stern. She was not pleased.

"I've had a long day," Denis told her. "And I'm tired. If that's all you've come here to tell me, then please leave."

The words seemed to strike her face like a slap. She looked as though she was about to well-up, but then, strangely, she just shook it off.

"If you think you can drive me away, you're wrong. If you think I'll give up and just avoid you, you're wrong. Like it or not, Denis Murphy, we're a big part of each other's lives. We were for three years. We all went through a terrible tragedy and clearly it's hit you harder than us, but that doesn't mean you can wallow in self-pity all your life. We all lost someone dear to us, and you don't have a monopoly on that. I don't care if you were the only one of us there. You don't own our grief. I'm not about to let you ruin your life feeling permanently sorry for yourself."

Denis tried not to hear her words. They stung him inside and out. Something was leaking out of one of his eyes. He drew a breath to say something, but nothing came out.

"You can have tonight off," she told him, her tone not softening a whit. "And you can have tomorrow to think things over and straighten yourself out, but on Wednesday, I'm coming over here to view one of the rooms, and if I like it, I'm moving in." With that, she turned sharply on one heel and left. She never closed the gate on the way out.

Rationally Denis knew that he could simply say no. She didn't have keys, there was no way for her to gain access to his home, but somehow he knew in his heart that if she decided to come in, she was going to be coming in. For a Monday that had started so well, this day was turning into a complete disaster.

"I don't like her, Boss," Plasterer announced coldly from the office. "Now lock the door twenty-two times and help us tie Deano to something else."

GOOD LUCK MOVIN'

Time, for something that seems quite objective, is remarkably flexible. Pots being watched still boil water, regardless of what the old saying tells us. For Denis, that Monday night and the Tuesday that followed were a lesson on the flexibility of time. Wednesday morning seemed to be rushing toward him like an asteroid, and he was utterly powerless to prevent what would certainly be a shocking impact. For all of this inevitability, he still managed to do a remarkable amount of worrying, which made minutes drag and made hours unbearable. All at once things were moving too fast and too slow. Time, it seemed, was not his friend.

He spent Monday evening in relative silence. He cleaned up the mess that only four fully adult children could make and prepared dinner. He cleaned up again. He watched some TV and, before he went to bed, he cleaned. For their part, his housemates let him be. They played their games and destroyed the house while Denis moped about. Even his usual formulaic cop dramas couldn't help. He loved cop dramas. Particularly the ones that followed the same pattern: bad guy commits crime, good guys are stumped, red herrings emerge, among them a sure suspect for the grisly crime. The enigmatic genius of the group makes some excellent off-the-cuff quips and is generally misunderstood by all of his peers, but then he saves the day and the bad guy is apprehended. Occasionally the show threw something of a curveball and the bad guy got away, or one of the good guys got injured, or worse, killed. These episodes made Denis sad and forced his housemates into an orgy of destructiveness, which inevitably kept him cleaning for hours. Worse still were the episodes, very infrequent as they were, when the characters in the show became emotionally attached to one another. These episodes caused an internal struggle within Denis that could, if the episode in question was particularly soppy, keep him up at night.

On this night, there were none of the booby-trap episodes, but he couldn't make his mind be still. He thought back to the grim determination that marked Rebecca's behavior at his front door, and found himself remembering the smell of her perfume. He tried to focus on potential solutions for keeping someone as dogged as she out of his life, and found himself idly rolling the single bead she'd given him around his palm while he thought about how her jawline looked so perfect when she tilted her head to the side. His to-do list for the following day was written in handwriting that was so appallingly bad, he had to cross through it and start all over. He briefly considered burning the book rather than permitting such an egregious scrawl-stained page. He decided against it. There would certainly be no coffee the following day. Going outside was becoming increasingly problematic. He went to bed unhappy.

It had been a long time since Denis Murphy had gone to bed with genuine happiness. Usually contentment was the best he could manage. At some point, early in his adulthood, going to bed happy had stopped being a goal for him. Surviving each day was in itself a victory, if a hollow one. It had not always been the case. The upheaval of the last few days had stirred something in him. He was recalling things. Sharing a house with Ollie, Frank and Eddie had been a happy time. A time when going to bed was a thing done in the small hours of the morning, after drinking or playing computer games or watching movies surrounded by friends and family. For the first three years of adulthood, going to bed meant Rebecca Lynch next to him and waking up meant listening to Ollie singing in the shower. These memories seemed to reach inside him and tug at emotions that Denis was unprepared and entirely unwilling to confront. Nearly seven years of changing his life, changing his behavior, changing everything he had been had almost erased those old days of sleeping late and sharing company, but they hid deep inside him, and now they were struggling to get out.

He could beat it though; he knew he could because he'd done it before. His housemates had always helped him with that. They asked no questions, they made him work, they didn't care that he used to cry himself to sleep. They were company during the very rare moments when he felt lonely, and with their help he had faced down challenges before. He would do it again.

Denis's Tuesday morning was an unusual start for him. The alarm rang, three times, as it usually did, but this time it came with a chorus of imitation voices. Three of them. They were lined up next to his bed, looking straight ahead and mimicking the alarm noise in perfect unison. All except Deano, who had taken his place but, as ever, said nothing.

"Good morning," he bade them groggily as he rolled out of his bed.

"Good morning," they replied together, each of the four heads tilting to exactly the same angle as they regarded him.

"What do you want now?" he asked, rubbing the sleep out of his eyes and scratching his head.

"We want to help," they said together, remaining entirely still.

"I'm not sure if you four have ever wanted to help me with anything," he told them as he made his bed.

"Not so," they replied.

"What do you want to help with?" he asked.

"She's coming tomorrow," they told him in one voice.

"I'm aware of that," he replied testily.

"Oooooooooooooooh," they chorused, mocking his tone.

"You call this helping?"

"We want to help," they repeated. They were behaving strangely, which for four people who made games out of trying to seal themselves into couch cushions was really saying something.

"Not now. I need to have breakfast, shower, dress…"

They echoed every word he said seconds after he said it. It was eerie.

"We can discuss it later. There are things to do now."

They laughed. "We can help you, you know. After work it shall be."

Denis shook his head and went about his routine. Breakfast—sixteen minutes. Shower—ten minutes. Ironing—twenty minutes. For a man with Denis's considerable intellect, such things shouldn't really occupy too much of his brainpower, and yet the way he approached them allowed him not to think. Thinking was the enemy. Three of them followed him here and there. Deano, Penny O'Neill and Professor Scorpion went wherever he did, supervising the meticulousness of each job, as if mentally preparing for the best way to undo that work later on. Plasterer did not join them. He sat at the breakfast table and waited. By the time Denis joined him, Plasterer had laid a place for himself; his bowl was full to the top of shredded newspaper. He'd poured some white paint from under the utility-room sink over the paper. The bowl was certainly destroyed, but miraculously not a drop of the paint touched the tabletop.

"I was never going to get the table," Plasterer told him confidently. "If I did, we couldn't talk, because you'd be having a meltdown."

Denis nodded in agreement as he attempted to measure exactly forty grams of Bran Flakes in the small scales in front of him.

"You know that I know the score," Plasterer continued.

"I do?" Denis asked, arching an eyebrow skeptically.

"I do," he said, nodding. "And I know that you know that I know the score."

"Is that a fact?" he asked.

Plasterer was nodding like a madman now.

"It is. You know that I know that you know that I know the score."

"What's the score then?" he asked.

"TEN NIL TO THE MONSTERS," came a pair of voices from the living room.

"Ignore them," Plasterer told him. "They don't need to have this little chat with us."

Denis was becoming confused. There was little doubt that Plasterer took the lead in most things that his housemates did, but his leadership was at best laissez-faire, and at worst a complete fiction. How much could the worst-looking clown you've ever seen really control anyone? There was something about his tone too. Something alarming. Something that seemed too familiar. They'd never shared this kind of familiarity before. His facial features, so difficult to read under the mountain of makeup, seemed to be smiling knowingly.

"Go on," he told the slightly grinning Plasterer.

"Your problem, Denis, is that you're approaching this the wrong way. She thinks you're broken. She wants to fix you.

That's how it is with some of them. The more you behave like someone who's broken, the more she's going to fixate on fixing things. If you'll pardon my alliteration. And I think there was some assonance in there too."

"YOU SAID ASS," the living room seemed to call out.

"Shut up, idiots," Plasterer barked in exasperation. "You too, Deano," he added as an afterthought. "You're not playing it right, Boss. That's what the score is. There's a way for you to play this and win. Reel her in and then close her out. Invite her in like it's no big deal. Quit panicking every thirty seconds because you think her eyes sparkle like the sea or some crap like that. Just chill."

His voice changed tone several times during the speech, and once or twice it sounded like he was doing impersonations of movie characters' voices.

"I don't understand, Plasterer. I know you're trying to give me advice, but I'm not sure if you're talking to me or picturing yourself in a movie."

"Little of both, Boss, little of both," he replied with a smile. "What I'm saying is that you're a mess. You were a mess the second you saw her and you're a mess now. What you need is a return to order. To you. If you want to get there, and I'm pretty sure you do, you'll need to get over this tiny little hurdle. It's only small, but you've convinced yourself that it's a big deal. It's just a girl. If you want your life back, you bring her in, show her your life. Convince her you're happy. Convince her that you like your life the way it is. Be nice, but not too nice. Be friendly but not over friendly. When she realizes that you're not broken, that you don't still secretly crave her touch, well, then she goes away, and we get our house back. You don't still crave her touch, do you?"

"Of course not," Denis replied sharply, remembering the softness of her hands and the way she liked to link arms.

"Then this plan will work. Trust me."

"I don't know, Plasterer. This is our house." Denis could hear a tone of pleading in his own voice.

"It's not our house, Boss, it's your house. She won't even know we're here."

"Of course she'll know you're here," Denis replied spluttering. "Half the neighborhood knows you're here. Last week you dismantled the old bicycle I had in the garage so you could make the world's crappiest marching band. The noise disturbed people for miles. I'm pretty sure she's going to know you're here."

The clown looked at him steadily, unblinking, unflinching. His look said, "don't be stupid," but it hinted at something else too, something Denis was missing, something important. For the life of him, he couldn't work out what it was that he was missing here.

"Tell her nothing, Boss. Say nothing about us. We'll behave. We'll stay out of the way. We'll all stay in my room, and you and her can stay in the rest of the house. We can play when she leaves, and we'll even clean up afterward."

Denis considered Plasterer. There was something wrong about this conversation, something deeply and truly wrong, but if his life depended on it, he couldn't put a finger on it.

Please, reach for it. You need to understand this now, before it's too late.

"I'll think about it," he told his housemate.

"She can't know we're here, Boss," Plasterer told him, his voice quiet.

Silence descended on the room like a dark and moody blanket.

Denis wanted to ask why not, but Plasterer's tone had taken him by surprise.

"She can't know. You know she can't know. And I know that you know that she can't—"

"Oh cut it out," Denis snapped.

"I'm right though," Plasterer said. "She should stay. She's worried, and she won't go away until you let her in, so just let her in for a while. Once she sees that you're okay, then everything will be fine. She'll let you be you, and you'll have another friend. She'll move into her own place when it's ready, and then you can add her to the list of people you meet for coffee. Everything will be fine. But you can't tell her we're here. Ever."

"I won't," Denis almost whispered. "I won't tell her you're here."

"Promise?"

"I promise I won't tell her you're here."

Plasterer nodded, satisfied.

You poor idiot. You poor, sick idiot.

"Time to eat, Boss," Plasterer told him. "Then you can work, and I can get back to eating paint."

Denis nodded. It was the tone that was so wrong, Denis thought. Something about it frightening him. Something too quiet. Something brooding. He shook his head. Another task had to be done.

After this, his day seemed to right itself. If he was honest with himself, and he frequently was, then he'd have to admit that he wasn't just worrying about Rebecca's reaction to him. He was worrying about how she'd react to his housemates. The thought of them hiding themselves for what little time she'd be staying seemed like one less worry to have playing on his mind. He tackled his day easier after this.

Tuesday was also bathroom day. This is not to say that on this day and only this day could Denis face the relevant duties one associates with a trip to the bathroom. He was organized, but not that organized. No, each day of the week had its own particular area of cleaning responsibility. It was actually something of a rare pleasure when cleaning his home. It was the one room of his house that he wished his housemates would consider off-limits for their wide array of destruction. Sadly, they never did, and too often they would ruin it with scribbles and notes written on the mirror after showering, or by plugging up the sink and leaving the taps on to very slowly and quietly fill the bowl. It never reached spill-over point, but he imagined on the day that it did, they'd throw a party all around the house to celebrate the destruction. He wondered what bizarre changes he might have to endure in a house that Rebecca Lynch shared. His bathroom was, as ever, immaculate. Surfaces gleamed and taps sparkled. Whole armies of massively self-impressed cleaning-product advertisers would gnaw on their own livers with envy at how spotless Denis Murphy's bathroom was. There was always a trade-off however, and Denis was fairly certain that if he could remember what envy felt like, he'd feel it about their social lives and ability to casually walk on the beach without worrying about whether or not it had an even or odd number of grains of sand.

During the afternoon, he worked. More numbers were crunched and more data was analyzed. At one point in the day he got an email that almost knocked him off his newly reacquired stride. It had an emoticon in it—a small little nodding yellow head that smiled at him from the end of the correspondence. He couldn't take his eyes off it. He wondered why it was so happy before realizing that, for just a moment, he had been genuinely curious about what was making it smile. That's a tough realization for anyone. The moment you realized you're questioning the motivation of a computer icon. He shook his head. The email also had a compliment for his last report. It read: That's gr8 work. He stared at the digit lost in the middle of that sentence for at least six minutes. It had no business being there. He shook it off eventually. The nature of his work from home was more than a benefit for him, but every now and then other people attempted to interact with him in a wholly unsatisfactory manner.

For all his preoccupation, his mind constantly returned to her. She'd be coming. A decision was going to have to be made, and so that night when the work was done, but before the television could be switched on, he sat them all down for a chat.

"Can you guys join me in the kitchen?" he called out as he sat himself at the table, his tea steaming before him, placed carefully on its coaster.

Three of them shuffled in and lined themselves up. He examined them critically for a few minutes. They were most certainly an unusual collection. Penny's tail was flicking back and forth again, which typically meant that she was amused or annoyed. Denis had never learned to tell the difference; with Penny, there frequently was none. Deano was hiding behind the Professor's shoulder. He'd become more and more diffident in the last few days. He made a mental note to speak to Deano about that. Not that he'd be able to understand the fur ball.

Plasterer was a different story. He sauntered in, folded his arms and leaned casually against the door frame, his bulk filling the space in a most intimidating manner. He watched the other three almost paternally before nodding at Denis to begin.

"So. I may have invited a woman to live with us," he announced. "Your thoughts?"

This was, of course, a mistake. He knew this. Asking for input from any of them at the same time was never wise. They roared their opinions, first at him, and then at each other. Oddly enough, they were all agreeing with one another, but none of them seemed to realize it.

"I THINK SHE'S LOVELY AND IT'D BE NICE TO HAVE ANOTHER GIRL AROUND HERE."

"I THINK IT'S A GREAT IDEA AND WHY NOT? IT'S ONLY FOR A WHILE AND THEN SHE'LL BE GONE."

"IT WAS MY IDEA IN THE FIRST PLACE."

"LITTLE CHANGE WILL DO US GOOD."

Deano was doing a wonderful job of articulating someone who might have been shouting if he knew how. His arms waved wildly and his hips seemed to gyrate. He hopped up and down a little. Denis couldn't help but smile at him. Plasterer simply watched his friends and shook his head gently at them, as if suffering the fools for their excitement. Denis sat back and watched them not argue with each other for a few minutes before they sort of drifted into quietness.

"Done?" he asked.

Four heads nodded at him.

"I'm a little worried that you guys will mess with her, like the way you mess with me."

"We don't mess with you," Penny O'Neill purred at him.

"Yes, you do," he assured her.

"I practically guarantee you that we'll be the very soul of good behavior," the Professor declared. "Why, I shall this very night prepare a list of the very best of people who ever were good, and then I'll swear on that list that we'll be even better. Then we can all eat the list."

Denis shook his head but was interrupted before he could answer.

"But I like playing games," Penny O'Neill said, pouting. "I don't see why—"

"You know very well why she can't know," Plasterer interjected. He was looming again, and Penny shrank back from him. They all did, moving a little farther away from the hulking clown. Denis noted the subtle change, but since Plasterer was helping him on this one, he wrote it off as good fortune. In hindsight, that may have been a mistake. Now the mood had shifted, and three of them were cowed, submissive while Plasterer stood tall. He nodded knowingly at Denis.

Oh shit. I think you've fed him too much. He'll kill you, Denis.

"Time for bed, Boss. You've got a long day ahead of you."

Penny O'Neill had crept into his room at some point in the night, and she slept curled up at the foot of his bed, one long, slim, furry leg dangled over the edge, and her foot twitched occasionally. Denis remembered when he used to sleep like that, back when he lived in another world, one that ran parallel to this one, so close that they were almost the same. Except that he knew better. The rules were different in this world. His alarm clock told him that it was four fifteen. It never told him anything else except the time, and it did so silently. He admired its dedication to chronology as much as anyone can admire the work of an alarm clock. He slid quietly from the bed and padded down the stairs. It wasn't unheard-of for him to wake in the middle of the night. Sometimes he got up, sometimes he didn't. Sometimes nightmares woke him. Vivid and shocking, they would echo in his head for hours after waking, and no amount of paperwork or relentless scrubbing of the back of the toilet or dogged polishing of the wires that poured from the back of the entertainment center in the living room could make that stop. These nights were his worst nights, and in his fear and panic he would call out to his housemates who would descend the stairs like a tornado, destroying all in their wake. He would clean as they went. Not so tonight. On this night he just made his way down the stairs and into his kitchen to make tea. There was a light on in the living room.

"Somebody awake in there?" he whispered loudly.

"No," a voice whispered back.

"Are you sure?" he asked.

"Positive," the voice told him. It was the Professor's voice, the rotting flesh near his lips betraying him.

"What are you doing up?" Denis asked.

"Painting all the crockery with the paints you bought us," the Professor told him matter-of-factly.

Denis was about to ask why but decided against it. With the Professor, such answers could take all night. Instead he filled himself a glass of milk and ambled in to see the zombie. The cups were stacked in the living room awaiting the careful strokes of the master artist inside.

The Professor sat in his usual chair with the stand lamp behind it casting an eerie glow around his rotting frame. His hands were poised delicately as though mastery of art could be acquired simply by posing in just the right manner. The paintings on the crockery were crude at best. Mostly smiling faces again. One or two sad faces. Standing proudly apart from the others, watching, were six cups. One had the face of a frowning clown. One a cat. One was purple and its eyes were dead. One was just eyes peering through a mass of thick yellow paint strokes. The other two were just slightly apart from those four.

"Why is Plasterer frowning like that?" Denis asked.

"That man is positively frownlicious, Denis," the Professor told him. "For such a well-muscled man, he seems remarkably unhappy at times. Don't let that painted smile fool you."

"Why has Deano got eyes?" Denis asked, ignoring the implied warning. The Professor could be remarkably dour at times. "I've never seen Deano's eyes. I guess I always knew he had them, but they're never visible."

"Don't let our little furry friend fool you either. He goes

along all right. He does as he's told. But only for now. He's watching it all. He's just waiting for new orders."

Denis shook his head at the cryptic response. The Professor was at his strangest now.

"Have you ever wondered, Denis," he inquired, "as to why we all fit ourselves into boxes? Metaphorical ones, I mean. Everyone knows that fitting yourself into a literal box is among the most fun things you can do to pass the time. It's the metaphorical boxes that seem to really contain us."

"I've never thought of it to be honest," Denis told him, sipping his milk. "Safety I guess."

"Not that safe in there, I think," came the reply. "Not when it suffocates. Plasterer loves boxes. He'd climb in them all day if he could. He'd put you in them too."

"What about you?" Denis replied.

"What about me?" the Professor asked, puzzled.

"Would he put you in there too?"

"Heavens no. We live in the same box you see."

Denis shook his head again. There was no making sense of the Professor when he was in such a mood, sitting in his lamp-lit chair, expounding on matters of philosophy as he painted smiley faces on cups and plates.

The last two cups were smiling also. One of them had yellow beads in its hair.

Denis went back to bed.

The following morning proceeded as usual, save for the marching of his housemates, who were running drills on the hallway landing and preparing to hunker down in their shared bedroom as soon as Rebecca arrived. Denis executed his morning on schedule, save for the minor irritation of having to scrub one of the bowls clean for his high-fiber cereal. One should not discuss such matters, but a healthy bowel is important in one's day. Perhaps the only difference today was an extra-special effort at grooming. Privately Denis would have to admit, only if pushed on the matter, that this was entirely for the benefit of Rebecca. Outwardly, this was because one should always maintain high standards of personal hygiene and appearance. He gave a thought to the possibility that she may take a look at the house and find it unsuitable to her needs. This would surely be a relief to him and the others, but for some reason it didn't feel like a good thought. It made his stomach tighten. He shook it off. He avoided thinking about the last thing she had said to him at the door before she had announced her decision to come and view a room. It had hit him harder than them, but why wouldn't it? They weren't there. They didn't have to see. They arrived at the hospital after it had all happened with their red eyes and their hugging. Not for them the sound of screaming and the distant wail of a siren, getting closer and closer.

Plasterer stood in the doorway. He was gritting his teeth noisily.

"You look like you could spit nails. And not fingernails either. Hard nails. Like the ones the Professor used to nail all those books of yours to the floor that time," Plasterer told him.

"Sorry. Distracted. You guys finished pretending you're an army?"

"We are an army. An army of five. Unstoppable too. No wily women with beads can dare prevail against us."

"Plasterer, she's not the enemy. She's just going through what Frank and Ollie went through at the start. She'll grow out of it." The words rang hollow even in his own ears.

"Maybe. Maybe not. One way or another, we're prepared and ready."

"They're the same thing."

"You're the same thing."

Denis gave him one of his patented flat unfriendly looks. Plasterer remained impassive.

"Anything else?" he asked the clown.

"We're ready for fallout. When she gets here, it'll be like we vanished into thin air."

Denis nodded and returned to his duties. Socks don't iron themselves, you know.

For someone as preoccupied with time as Denis, there are certain aspects of life that you simply have to learn to accept. For example, no one else ever operated on such a rigid time schedule as Denis. Inevitably, everyone else was late. This normally wouldn't trouble him if it meant that he could simply take out his paper and read while he waited, but this was not the time for such things. A veritable tsunami of rational-life destruction was bearing down on him, and it didn't even have the decency to tell him when it was going to ruin his week. He tried texting. Well, at least he tried to try texting. He took the phone out and sat staring at the screen. He played with a number of options for tone. Stern about punctuality? She'd laugh at it. Casual and offhand? She'd take that as license to turn up whenever she wanted. Mildly curious? She'd see right through it. He opted instead for an extended period of procrastination and text reflection. Basically, he just sat there, continuing to stare at the screen, even after it had gone into sleep mode and was entirely blank. The housemates were playing Slaps in the living room. This game involved slapping each other. The rules were not complex. They rarely were with his coterie. There was a stunned silence when the doorbell finally rang. The four tiptoed out of the room in a highly exaggerated manner and proceeded up the stairs. Penny O'Neill hovered slightly behind, perhaps wanting to catch a better glimpse of the woman who would be sharing their home.

Denis's heart was pounding as he headed for the door.

He absently fixed his hair, which, of course, did not require fixing. He cleared his throat and cleaned his teeth with his tongue. He tested the door three times, as was customary, and opened it. She was standing there, smiling as usual. That smile burst through the dark clouds in his life. He instantly felt better upon seeing it, and the smile he returned her was genuine. That is, until he realized that she'd come fully packed. Her belongings in a pile around her with Frank and Ollie unloading even more from Frank's flashy car.

"Hey hey, Chief," Ollie called. "There was no way I was missing a chance to see the inside of your house. Me and Frank have twenty between us on which of us finds your porn stash first!"

Denis swallowed hard. He should have realized that such things don't go off without a hitch.

"I thought you were just coming to view the room."

"Changed my mind," she told him presumptuously.

"Now either give me a hand with the bags or at least make some coffee for my manservants." She was smiling at him still, but something in her look told him that she was also measuring his reaction. There could be no sign of cracking now. He hoped the housemates were well hidden.

"Come on in," he told her.

For some reason he felt a remarkable relief as he spoke.

JUST DON'T ASK

They came as intruders to his house. No matter what kind of nice face he put on it, all the forced politeness and offhand charm in the world wouldn't change the simple facts of the situation. They were not welcome here, and yet, here they were. To add insult to injury it was barely one o'clock in the afternoon. Sure, his mom came and went on Sundays, but her visits were spectral; she floated in like a ghost and left like one too. She hardly counted as a visitor. These though. These were visitors. They unloaded the bags, with surprisingly little chitchat, and then the three invaders set about exploring.

Ollie pawed through Denis's things, hefting some as if to check their weight. He marveled at the wonderfully large television, his fingers leaving greasy prints on the smooth, glossy black screen. He idly tapped at some of the keys on the ultraslim keyboard that sat, glorious in its precision, directly in front of the computer's monitor. He dragged his hand along the office wall as he walked around the room and fidgeted with the cases that held the DVD collection Denis loved so much. Frank did less fidgeting, but walked from place to place, checking things. Inspecting his belongings as though he didn't quite believe that they were there. He looked in closets, noting how normal everything seemed. He checked and checked, searching for signs of some kind of rebellion against order. Had they looked in just one of the upstairs bedrooms they would have found at least four examples of rebellion. Thankfully, that disaster seemed, temporarily at least, to be avoided. Rebecca checked neither his things nor his cupboards nor even her room. She checked him. His face hurt from the effort of affecting a casual smile. Central to Plasterer's plan was that everything seem okay. It was the only way to make them leave. Smile through it now. Clean everything they touched later. She knew though. He was sure that his mask never slipped, but somehow, she knew.

"Get out, idiots," she told the other two, not unkindly. "You're making my landlord uncomfortable."

"I should think so," Frank replied. "He bought this house six years ago, and this is the first time I've managed to get in the door. I keep expecting to find chopped-up bodies in the closets or something."

Ollie laughed his agreement.

"I'm not uncomfortable," Denis lied.

The words were barely out of his mouth before Plasterer made him wish he'd never opened it. A shock of multicolored hair was poking out from behind the kitchen to utility-room door. All of their backs were to it. He tried not to stare. A face followed the hair, since hair seldom goes anywhere alone. Unless it was Deano, obviously. His smile was slipping a small bit; he could feel it. He tried to put it back on. Plasterer was staring at him from the door.

"Yeah, say what you like, buddy boy," Ollie told him, "but you look hugely unhappy. And frankly, kind of creepy."

Plasterer made frantic, aggressive shooing motions in the air behind their backs.

"No, really," Denis lied again. "It's totally fine. You guys want to sit down in the living room? I'll make some tea…"

Plasterer was now slowly waving his arms back and forth and mouthing the word *no*, over and over. He pointed at the living room and struck a pose so similar to Penny O'Neill that Denis thought he might laugh out loud at the absurdity of it. He started when he realized that she might be in the living room, but covered it by pretending to yawn. What if she was there, sprawled across the couch, her head hanging over the edge of the seat, her long mane spilling onto the floor? He killed the momentary panic and hoped it hadn't shown on his face. He forced himself to look polite and inquisitive.

"It's nice out, isn't it?" he asked no one in particular. "Maybe we should go out the back?"

The Professor might be hiding out there. Badly. He really was terrible at hiding.

"Nah, it's all good, Chief," Ollie told him. "We'll let you two lovebirds stop pretending that you're not going to share the same room and get out of here so you can get all nostalgic with one another." The emphasis he put on the word *nostalgic* allowed little room for wondering at his meaning.

Plasterer stopped moving instantly. His arms cut off mid-gyration. Instead, he stared balefully at the back of Ollie's head. He raised one hand and pointed a finger threateningly at Ollie's back. There was something chilling about it. Denis had often found his housemate imposing, even frightening, but this was something worse, and for a short second, Denis feared for his friend's safety, so furious was the clown.

"Right, then," Denis said suddenly. "I'll show you out. I still have work to get done today, and I'm sure Becks wants to settle into her new room."

Now Plasterer was staring straight at Denis. So was Rebecca. And Frank.

"Becks, is it?" Ollie chuckled. "See, you're right back where you left off. C'mon, Frank, let's leave them at it."

Becks. He had called her Becks. A cluster of memories exploded in his brain. In each one he was calling out her name, and it seemed to leave a sweet taste in his mouth. He'd never called her Rebecca. He had called her Becks. He had once twisted his ankle badly and had been laid up for a few days while Rebecca had played nurse for him. He had milked it to an extraordinary degree, moaning exaggeratedly and calling out her name, Becks, over and over whenever he wanted tea or a cookie or for her to hand him the remote. Eventually her nursing skills slipped and she threw the remote at him. He had laughed for half an hour straight that day as she fussed over him and apologized for the little bump she'd put on his head. He fought down the shining memory quickly and savagely. None of them should be held up to the light too closely. He forced another smile and showed the boys to the door. Plasterer had made himself scarce again. As he passed by the living-room door, he glanced in. Penny O'Neill was nowhere to be seen either. He sighed as he locked the door and triple-checked it for security. He thought the hard part was done.

But his day did not get much better. Not even a little.

The first problem was preparing a speech to explain why he lived with four housemates who he'd never mentioned before. He was certain that she'd run into them, or that in their usual exuberance, they'd play a game that would result in them setting fire to something. Then the cat would be out of the bag, and so it would be better to tell her now rather than risking a plan to hide them from her. Besides, why hide them at all?

Remembering Plasterer's grim words of warning, he decided against it. It seemed wrong to tell her, and he realized just how insane he would sound, if they had hidden. So he held his tongue and tried not to worry about it.

The second problem turned out to be photographic. Initially he had not considered Rebecca's love for all manner of photography to be any kind of problem, that was until she attempted to introduce it to the kitchen and living-room walls. Denis didn't hang photos. There was, he would have to admit some time later, a great deal of charm to them. They attracted dust and would therefore be a cause of some satisfaction during cleaning bouts. It was their content that offended the senses. The small one she tried to hang on the kitchen wall was a photo of the two of them sitting in the car of a Ferris wheel. As per usual, he was grinning like an idiot in the photo. It shocked him to think that of the admittedly few photos he'd engaged with in recent times, he seemed to smile like a moron in most of them. Rebecca sat next to him in the photo, one hand gently resting on his thigh. She had gotten cold that night, and he'd given her a zip-up hoodie to wear. They'd gone to a pub afterward. He drank dark stout and she had hot whiskey. Jules had come in, looking for all the world like a mirror of him with blond hair. She drank hot whiskey too. For a brief second when he first saw the photo, he could smell cloves.

Plasterer would have hysterics on seeing this photo, and the others would likely follow suit. He could almost hear them laughing now. He told her to take it down. She smiled sweetly, like only she could, and ignored him.

The second photo was of the two of them with two friends of hers from college. They were sitting on the lawn outside the library building, books arrayed before them, not studying. He had been in the middle of saying something, and even then he was grinning like a fool. No one should show off that many teeth that often. She was listening to him talk. Her face was serious, with just a hint of unimpressed. He had been explaining why he'd chosen to climb up the side of a construction site the night before. They ended up having a real argument about that, but as they always had, they made up soon after.

"I don't see what the problem is. The frames are classy. They'll class up the place."

"It's fine the way it is, Rebecca."

"Call me Becks."

"No."

"What's wrong with photos? Our old house was covered in them."

"This isn't our old house."

"No doubt about it. It's way cleaner."

"Right. And it belongs in this universe, not the other one."

"Other universe?"

"Nothing. I just meant that it doesn't fit on the wall." He swallowed hard, the word *universe* was a poor choice.

"I like it. Reminds me of the old days."

"I hate it. Reminds me of the old days."

She looked at him for a long moment, taking in the last sentence with a face so full of sympathy that he had to look away.

"Just one?" she asked.

"Just one," he said, sighing.

She chose the Ferris wheel picture. The argument had cut into work time, and Denis found himself somewhat alarmed. Rebecca's arrival had been hard to take, and it was still early in the day.

After he'd worked for the appropriate amount of time—with time added on for stoppages—Denis made them dinner. A simple stir-fry. It took twenty-two minutes to prepare and serve. It took twenty-six minutes to eat it. While they ate, they talked. Sometimes about college, a little about work. They were still talking when Rebecca made tea and brought it to him just before his cop shows started. She picked a spot on the armchair by the fireplace and curled up her bare feet to sit on them. Her dark brown curly hair spilled over her shoulders, and she rested her chin on one hand that was propped on the arm of the chair. She looked beautiful. He felt like telling her this but held his tongue. Just as he did so, he spotted movement in the doorway. Deano was on the Professor's shoulders. They teetered precariously and wobbled from side to side. He started to get up to help them.

"Everything okay?" Rebecca asked.

"Hmm. Yes. Of course," he replied, waiting for the crash. It didn't come. He sat back down again. The show started, and a ball of fur rose up behind Rebecca's head, so close he was sure that the hair would fall down over her eyes.

"Are you staring at me?" she asked.

"No. Yes." Deano dropped down behind the armchair. "What's the appropriate answer to that question?" he asked glibly.

She smiled at him mysteriously and turned her head back to the TV. The fur ball that was Deano slunk quietly out of the room. Denis heaved a sigh of relief.

The rest of the night passed without incident. It didn't pass without the *dread* of incident, which had taken up residence in his head, but it was quiet enough. When the time came for him to call it a night, Rebecca opted to stay awake and watch TV. Denis considered staying up too, but that would cut into the four hundred eighty minutes of required sleep. So he decided not to and simply headed for the door.

"Denis," she called after him softly.

"Yes."

"I liked it earlier when you called me Becks." She was smiling at him again.

He nodded.

It was never going to work. In one night she had already threatened to turn his entire life upside down. He wouldn't last a week. Two would be a disaster without a doubt. And what if she needed three? His house would be full of pictures and smells before he knew it. What if she decided to decorate it? There'd be colors and paint drips everywhere. A tight fist of panic made a small ball of worry out of his stomach. His housemates were waiting in his room. Penny O'Neill sprawled across the end of the bed; Deano curled up in a ball on the floor. The Professor stood, frozen in the corner, like a terrible statue of a respectable zombie. Plasterer reclined on the bed.

"It'll work, Boss," the clown told him. "Stick to your guns and it'll work. You can do this. We got your back."

He nodded again.

"And, Boss," he added, his tone unfriendly. "No more Ollie in the house."

He nodded once more.

And so he stuck to his guns. Through Thursday, when she put the small square pepper mill on top of the salt mill and he almost fainted, and into Friday when she insisted on watching a reality TV show about someone building a house and he thought he'd die of shock. Through all of it, he found a pattern slowly emerging. A pattern of seeing her chaotic ways as her own warped kind of order. Like the antiorder. It had a shape, if you looked hard enough for it. Throughout the invasion, the housemates' heads popped around corners and floated up from behind couches, always attached to bodies of course, but those bodies always in places that they never should be. She never saw them, and they made a game out of not being seen. Skulking, one would emerge from the bedroom they now shared, declaring themselves to be "On a mission," and they allocated points for how close they could get without being spotted. Denis remained remarkably calm on such occasions. He was beginning to get a grip on this ridiculous domestic espionage. For her part, when she wasn't attempting to destroy his entire world, Rebecca just smiled and talked and played her guitar. She chatted about the great big things in her life, and the plans and ambitions. She talked about the small little details concerning her job and her daily motivations. She washed her hair and even dried the bathroom floor after herself—after she'd spotted Denis on all fours drying it while trying to stave off the panic attack. She smelled like lemons sometimes and oranges other times, and often she smelled like a strange kind of woodsy incense that tantalized his nostrils. She had always smelled like that. He had always loved that smell. Every afternoon she'd go to her room to practice her music, and her voice would float down to Denis from upstairs. When she began singing, there was no way he could work. He sat, transfixed, moving only occasionally to scrub at his eyes.

Through the weekend they continued the dance, but now they could escape from the house since neither of them had to work. They drank coffee and chatted some more. There seemed to be an endless supply of things to say to each other. On Saturday afternoon he went for his paper, and she insisted on buying chocolate. Thomas, who worked behind the counter, took one long look at her, then him, and then smiled broadly and winked at him. Denis found himself smiling sheepishly as he felt his cheeks redden. It was the first time he'd properly blushed in recent memory and would be recorded as such in the Denis Murphy Book of Records. They met Frank and Ollie for coffee, and Denis was struck by a perplexing sense of déjà vu. They'd sat like this, the four of them, too many times for him to recall. Only the last time Jules and Eddie had been there too, their fingers intertwined. He and Eddie typically led the charge in all matters of joking and messing, with Frank often the butt of jokes and Ollie helpless with laughter while Rebecca punched his arm and scolded him to be nicer. Jules, the youngest of them, was always the quietest. Now, four of them sat here again. It was not an unpleasant feeling, and Denis leaned back in his seat and crossed his outstretched legs before him in comfort. It's a universally understood truth that a man sitting with his legs crossed and stretched out in front of himself is extremely comfortable.

That Sunday morning his mother arrived as she always did, rang the doorbell as she always did, but this time she was smiling broadly when he answered. As she always didn't. Clearly Frank and/or Ollie had told her about the return of Rebecca. He had forgotten, as he worked double time to keep his life intact after she had smashed into it, that Rebecca adored his mother and his mother adored Rebecca. The hug he once again refused her was instead returned by his ex-girlfriend. It was a bitter thing to watch that someone gone so long from this frail woman's life could give her more love than her own son was capable of. Denis swallowed his shame. He had grown a great skill at that. His mother was still beaming as he handed over her tea on its little saucer, which was both wonderful to see and galling a little too. Denis couldn't give her such satisfaction. So he sat in silence while the two women in his life—not counting women who were also cats—caught each other up in whirlpools of conversation that seemingly would never run out of energy.

This isn't a bad thing you know. This a good thing. A healthy thing.

And there it was again, that feeling stabbing at him. Jealousy. Like a bristle growing in his belly. He couldn't understand its source. Perhaps it was Rebecca, who could connect so easily with his mother. Perhaps it was his mother, who was stealing his time with Rebecca. He couldn't tell, but it was attacking his insides. He tried to remain calm. He put on his best smile and excused himself politely so that he could go to the kitchen and examine his illness more closely. There would always be a logical way to deal with such things, and rational thought was the cure for what he had. He was alarmed to find Plasterer standing by the table. Waiting for him. Something about the way he stood was wrong, shoulders hunched over slightly, as though he was ready to compress and then explode. He gestured toward the living room angrily. The Professor stood in the doorway, shaking his head sadly from side to side. Denis wrinkled his forehead at them; it seemed like the thing to do. Something was most certainly amiss. Plasterer pointed accusingly at Denis, who wrinkled his forehead a little more. Plasterer stooped his almost ungainly clown body over and took a stack of crockery from the lower cabinet. He walked with the armful of plates right into the center of the kitchen, his stride purposeful. He extended his arms fully and then tipped his head at Denis warningly. The Professor moved to put himself between the two, one hand reaching toward Plasterer, the other toward Denis.

"They're upsetting him. He doesn't like it when they do this," the Professor told him in a whisper so low that he seemed to be talking to himself.

Denis shook his head at Plasterer. "No," he whispered.

Plasterer nodded at him insistently.

"Please," Denis whispered intently. "Not now. They're having so much fun. Please. You promised."

"This isn't their house," Plasterer told him angrily. "It's ours. We don't want either of them getting too comfortable. That's not part of our plan."

"Why is he doing this?" Denis asked the Professor, close to tears.

"It's unnatural to him. He doesn't like feeling this way. They're hurting him, so he's hurting you."

"Make him stop," Denis implored.

"I cannot," the Professor whispered. "He's doing it for you, you know."

"Not like this, please," Denis begged Plasterer.

"Necessity is often a cruel and demanding mistress," the Professor whispered sadly.

Denis shook his head helplessly.

"Will you make them leave?" Plasterer whispered.

"I'll make them leave, very soon. I promise." Denis's voice was strained as he whispered.

"I don't believe you, Denis. This is for your own good. We stick to the plan. This is not their home."

Plasterer released the plates and they plunged into the ground with a sickening crash, spraying shards in all directions.

The room next door went quiet for a moment before Rebecca called out, "You okay in there?"

"Er, yes. Fine," Denis replied. "All is fine. I'm just a little clumsy. Ignore me."

"They better not," Plasterer whispered in his ear as he bent down to collect the larger shards. "No one ignores us."

"You want a hand?" his mother called.

"No. No, it's fine. You two carry on," Denis called back.

"They really better not," Plasterer whispered again. "It'll only get worse." He was leaning right into Denis's ear.

"Let me help you," Rebecca called. He heard her teacup being placed on the side table. Plasterer smirked at him and backed out of the room far too casually.

"No," Denis shouted, much harsher than he'd intended to. A stunned silence answered him.

"I'd better leave," his mother said eventually.

"I think she'd better too," Plasterer agreed, as he moved toward the utility-room door.

The two in the other living room said their goodbyes in low murmurs as they headed for the front. The plates had been smashed in the middle of the floor. There was no way of explaining why he'd taken them out of the press, or what he was doing with them. He simply kept his head down and cleaned. His mother had been so happy talking to Rebecca. Finally, some happiness for the woman whose life he'd ruined. It had been so long since he had seen her happy. If he could remember what crying was like, he'd have done that then and there. Instead, he cleaned. He cleaned often, and more and more it seemed like he cleaned in place of doing things he'd long since forgotten to do.

Rebecca walked back into the room, having seen his mother out, and gave him a look. He imagined it was equal parts pity, scorn and anger, but in reality it was utterly unreadable. He couldn't stand it for more than a few seconds, and so he turned his attention back to the broken plates. She stood in the doorway for a few minutes more, not saying anything, and then abruptly turned and walked up the stairs. Denis scrubbed the wetness off his cheeks and went to fetch a brush.

It was later that afternoon before they spoke again. Denis spent the intervening time polishing and carefully cleaning all eight pairs of shoes in his bedroom. Penny O'Neill lay on her stomach alongside his bed, her knees bent so that her feet could kick absently behind her. Her tail seemed to flick from heel to heel as she kicked. He couldn't see her from the far side of the room, the bed was in his way, and so her voice seemed to come from nowhere. From Rebecca's room, the sounds of some mellow singer-songwriter emerged into his hallway, a hallway that hadn't heard the sound of music until she had invaded with her army of memories and smells. He tried not to hear the lyrics, all lost loves and unrequited passion. For some reason it stung the inside of his brain.

"Why did he have to go and do that?" Denis asked Penny O'Neill bitterly.

"Oh you know him. Action man himself. He told you that it had to be done, and I don't like agreeing with him, but that kind of behavior can't be tolerated," she told him.

"I could have gotten them to leave," Denis replied.

"But would you have? There's the thing, Denis. You were enjoying their company. It's a terrible habit to form. Where's the control?" Her voice was patronizing.

"It wasn't a big deal. You guys are making a way bigger deal out of this than is necessary."

"It's because we love you, Denis," she purred at him. "We only want what's best for you."

"Yeah, well I—"

There was a knock at the door. The music was no longer playing.

"You talking to someone in there?" Rebecca's voice called out.

"I was just talking to myself," Denis replied. "I was thinking of an apology, actually. For my clumsiness earlier."

"Really?" she asked, sounding unconvinced.

"Honestly," Denis lied.

"You're sorry?"

"Absolutely."

"Good. You can make it up to me. Frank and Natasha are having dinner at their house and we're going."

Denis groaned inwardly. She had very neatly trapped him with that one. Saying no now would make his apology seem insincere. Saying yes would mean eating a dinner that could potentially be a disaster. There's no way to tell someone that you only want peas if none of the peas mix with the rest of the dinner and you can guarantee that there'll be an even number of them on the plate. This was why the outside world remained a constant mess to Denis. Peas. And other things of that nature.

"Of course. I'd love to go." He grimaced as he said it. Penny O'Neill was chuckling quietly to herself on the floor.

"Turncoat," he muttered at her.

"What was that?" Rebecca asked.

"I said where's my coat," Denis replied, as if he didn't know.

"It's in the exact same place your coat always is, Denis. It's never anywhere else. Now let's get moving. I don't want to be late."

For a man who wears politeness as a form of armor against judgment, Denis Murphy was particularly aware of the social graces that go with being a dinner guest. He brought a bottle of wine with him to the table, though he drank absolutely none of it. The effect it had on Rebecca, however, was much more positive. She hadn't been hostile on the way to Frank's place, not exactly anyway, but it was clear she was still annoyed. As dinner went on, and Natasha's charming ability to put people at ease kicked in, she mellowed, and once again, Denis found himself in a social setting that he didn't find repugnant on every level. In fact, he was beginning to enjoy himself a little, which on a Sunday, when he should be watching one of his movies with his housemates, was a serious break from the norm. He wondered if this was what normal people felt like every Sunday. He grimaced; it was one of his natural gifts as well as his default reaction to everything outside his home. "Normal" was that other world he used to live in, and thinking about it too much was dangerous. He tried it on sometimes, and he almost made it appear as though it fit, as long as no one looked too closely, but it was seldom comfortable. In just a week he had managed to lose a part of himself and couldn't tell if that was a good thing or a bad thing.

"That's a lovely tie, Denis," Natasha told him.

He had at least won that argument before they left the

house; his right not to dress like a man eight years younger than himself was something he held very dear to his heart. Those running shoes he'd worn to dinner a week before had probably had their last ever outing.

"Thank you," he replied while trying to catch Rebecca's eye.

"Can't get this guy into a tie for love nor money," Natasha said, gesturing at Frank.

"Seriously, Denis, stop showing me up. I think she's getting a crush on you," Frank said, feigning exasperation.

"What can I say, when you've got it, you've got it," Denis replied.

"Listen to this guy." Rebecca laughed. "Mr. Smooth here nearly had a meltdown when I hung my coat on the back of the kitchen chair."

"Standards," Denis announced loftily, "are to be maintained at all times."

"I hear you," Frank joined in. "You're not the only neat freak you know. If I wasn't here to keep the place in order, the house would fall down."

Natasha arched an eyebrow at him.

"Momma's busy bringing home the bacon," she told him. "Besides, you do it better than me."

"He learned from the best," Denis told her with a chuckle.

"Oh please, you were a pig in college," Rebecca said with a gentle punch on the shoulder.

She had touched him, and curiously, he didn't mind. He shot her a warm and very genuine smile. One week was all it had taken, and he really had lost a little bit of himself.

After dinner they sat out in the backyard, under the red-hot glow of a gas lamp. There was something very tranquil about Frank and Natasha's life. Frank's affable but slightly solemn demeanor was matched perfectly by Natasha's charm and conversation. Their home together was decorated well;

brightly lit and there was no spare wall that wasn't fitted out for storage. Each shelf was packed, from the floor to the low ceiling: books, ornaments, spices, cooking utensils. He marveled at the peculiar order of it, which was a strange kind of medley of organization and space-saving. The living-room furniture seemed lower to the ground than usual furniture, giving their house the sense of being cozier for some reason. The whole place seemed to be a perfect reflection of the life they shared. Denis envied it a little, but understood that there was no way he could live with such chaos. The tea jar was bright red, but its coffee counterpart was green. It was hardly bearable. He guessed it wouldn't be long before these two were married. For that matter, Ollie and Roisin were in a much similar boat. It made him feel somewhat lonely, so he made his mind refocus on something else. Domestic bliss was not making him feel wonderful.

In a quiet moment while Natasha and Rebecca talked shop, Frank motioned Denis to one side.

"I like seeing you like this, you know," he said with a little half smile. "It's not like the old days fully, I mean you've still got your shields up, but it's a nice change."

"I like who I am," Denis told him. "You all keep wanting me to be something I'm not. And I don't like that, but I have to admit, it's been a nice evening."

Frank marveled at him until he became uncomfortable.

"Now go away," Denis told him, rejoining the ladies.

At the end of an enjoyable evening, Rebecca insisted they walk most of the way home. Fearing a return to the bad books he'd been in earlier, Denis acquiesced. For a while they didn't speak, but walked in companionable silence. They were so close their shoulders were nearly touching. It was the first time in a very long time that Denis almost touched someone without panicking.

"Why did you break the plates?" she asked without warning.

He didn't know how to answer that. His first impulse was to blame Plasterer, the actual culprit, but the words stuck in his mouth. She didn't even know Plasterer was in the house. She'd think he was a lunatic. Then when they got home and saw him, she'd want to know why they were being kept a secret from her. That couldn't be allowed to happen. She might leave, and even though that was the eventual aim of the plan, for some reason the thought of it made him feel sick to his stomach.

"I told you, I'm clumsy," he eventually replied. His eyes were stinging with the effort of lying.

"It's okay," she whispered soothingly.

At home, Rebecca insisted that there was time for a movie before bed, and selected a horror film from the DVD collection. Denis found other people's fascination with horror films unusual. They barely phased him while they were apparently revered as a genre for their ability to terrify the viewer. Why would anyone choose to terrify themselves? People just might be the weird ones after all. Rebecca jumped several times during the movie and then laughed at her own fear. When the movie was done and the good-nights were shared, Denis made his way to bed. It had been a long week and he was bone tired. Tired of trying to hold on to his way of life. Tired of being confused. Yet still he couldn't sleep, so he lay staring at the ceiling. He was wondering if Rebecca was still awake when the answer tapped lightly on his door and crept in on silent feet.

"I can't sleep," she told him.

"Neither can I," he admitted.

"I'm not going to touch you," she assured him carefully, "but I am getting into your bed."

His breath quickened, whether in alarm or excitement, he

couldn't tell. She was the only person with whom he had ever shared a bed. He hoped that he looked relaxed, but his heart was hammering in his chest. He knew it would be bad for him, bad for his housemates. He knew that no one would like this and he should object, but he didn't want to. He wanted to feel what it would be like to have her fall asleep beside him again, just like old times. Even knowing that he wanted this felt like betraying his housemates, but he couldn't fight her again. He wouldn't fight her just for them.

He was so very, very tired of fighting her.

He nodded slightly at her. It was all the permission she needed.

She climbed in, the left-hand side as she always did before. Neither of them said anything, but Denis watched her curl up and her eyes droop slowly closed. Denis was watching her so carefully he didn't notice Penny O'Neill arrive in the room.

She stood alongside his bed, her face a mask of fury, tail lashing from side to side.

He was so very tired of fighting everyone.

He returned her stare with impassive eyes. This was his bed. His room. If she didn't like it, she could go back to hers, he thought to himself.

"Good night," Rebecca murmured sleepily, without opening her eyes.

"Good night," he whispered back, still staring at Penny O'Neill. She was trying to cow him, but he wouldn't be beaten so easily. He eventually half shrugged and went back to looking at Rebecca. Her hair spilled over his pillow. Even in her sleeveless top and pajama bottoms she looked beyond beautiful, and he could feel something stir deep inside himself as he stared at her. Penny O'Neill turned on one heel and left. He didn't even see her go.

CAN'T STAY HERE

Denis's alarm rang three times in a display of consistency that seemed to be otherwise sadly lacking in his life. He was, he found, at the farthest point away from Rebecca that he could possibly be. She was, he found, in possession of most of the quilt. It was her way, he remembered.

"Morning," she murmured sleepily.

"Good morning," he said.

She smiled at him through half-closed eyes and rolled over to go back to sleep. There was a time when he was the one who rolled over and tried to go back to sleep. She'd elbow him in the back and tickle him until he either got up or fell out of the bed. Either way he'd end up laughing. Now, however, he simply stepped from the bed and commenced the morning rituals. Tasks needed completing, and he'd have to be in top form when she went to work. There was a showdown with Penny O'Neill on the cards.

He embraced the new day with the vigor it now required, just as he had the previous Monday, with the determination that only Denis Murphy could muster. When one's trousers must be the most well-pressed in the universe on a daily basis, one learns how to approach a task with a relentless drive that would give a jumbo jet pause. His cereal was measured to perfection. His shower took exactly ten minutes. His attire was immaculate and his tie was pristine.

He tried not to watch Rebecca prepare for her day, first because she was a thorough distraction in her nightwear. For some reason her pajama bottoms and top ensemble was alluring to him, even as one hand scratched her messy hair. The main reason was that she prepared for her day the way she lived it: chaotically. She brushed her teeth and hummed at the same time. She allowed water to drip from her hair and towel onto the rug of the hallway as she prepared a load of laundry for the washing machine. She ate her breakfast *after* she had cleaned her teeth. A flake of cereal escaped her bowl, and she picked it up and popped it in her mouth. Denis did his best to ignore it. When she was ready and about to head out the door for work, they had a moment. For just a second as she passed him, she stopped and moved to kiss him on the cheek; in that same second Denis departed from his own head and watched in horror as he leaned in to accept the kiss. The moment of absolute insanity passed in the blink of an eye as both of them realized what they were doing. Denis jumped about two feet from Rebecca as though she was threatening to stab him. She made a face that seemed to indicate that she realized the horror she had almost inflicted on him. She said a hurried goodbye and shot out the door. Denis got the alcoholic disinfectant and applied it to a facial scrub and rubbed it four times on each cheek just to be sure.

He went to his office, took his seat and swiveled to face the door. They'd be coming through at any minute, he surmised. He was not wrong.

Like a whirlwind they burst into the room, brooding, menacing. Plasterer was the front of the storm, with Penny O'Neill behind him, her face contorted in anger. Deano and Professor Scorpion flanked them.

"Good morning, kids," he began.

"Whose side are you on exactly?" Plasterer hissed through clenched teeth. Denis knew that they had simply been waiting for her to leave before unloading on him, and that it would take a new type of tactic to contain them now.

"I'm on Denis's side," he replied. "Which should mean the same side as you, since you're on my side too."

Deano cocked his head and scratched it, confused. Professor Scorpion raised one hand as if to say something, then stopped. Penny O'Neill's tail stopped lashing angrily.

"Oh very clever," Plasterer told him contemptuously. "You can fool these idiots with that kind of talk, but not me. You let her sleep in your bed? You think this is going to get rid of her? I'm starting to think that I may have to take some drastic steps to bring you around here, Boss."

"Don't be so dramatic," Denis snapped. "She stayed in my bed. So what? She's not living in my house forever. I couldn't stand the disorder, and you all know that, so calm yourselves. I didn't have the energy to fight with her about it, and besides, the more I fight her, the more she fights back. That's her way. Let me handle this. We've got a good plan. Let me see it through."

Plasterer seemed to consider that.

"She took my spot," Penny O'Neill complained, pouting.

"She borrowed it, that's all. And I'll wash the sheets, hell, I'll even burn them if it makes you feel better, so you can have your spot back."

Penny O'Neill began to purr. Professor Scorpion walked around so that he was now standing next to Denis, facing the others.

"This kind of insubordination doesn't bear thinking about.

It doesn't bird thinking about. It doesn't even *fish* thinking about. You should all be ashamed of yourselves," he told them as if he hadn't been standing next to them ten seconds beforehand.

"Fish thinking?" Denis asked.

"Fish thinking," the Professor agreed, nodding his rotting head. "Would you have preferred panda thinking? That's a variety of bear."

"No, no. Fish thinking is fine." Denis didn't want to argue. He'd won an ally in the conversation and placated two others. Only Plasterer remained to be convinced.

"I'll go along with you on this one, Boss, but I'm a little concerned," he said finally. "I don't think that this is what allies do to each other. This is our house, and she shouldn't be able to move about so freely. It's nearly been a week since she got here, and she's getting more and more comfy. Next thing you know she'll be bringing girlfriends over here, and they'll be putting on makeup and leaving pink crap lying all over the place."

"This is temporary," Denis assured him. "She will not be here long so you needn't worry, but if we push her out, she'll push back, and we'll be in a longer war than we need to be. Humor me."

Plasterer grunted.

"Now, I've got to get some work done, so why don't the four of you go make a giant mess somewhere."

They duly obliged.

Clever. Very clever. If you're careful, he won't murder us. Or you won't. Or whatever. You get what I'm saying.

For all of his talk, he knew it for the stopgap it was. There was no way that this could continue indefinitely. They would oppose her, and though she didn't even know them, she would oppose them. Not openly, but in her way of living and her manner and her life. Her very existence opposed them; her selflessness versus their self-obsession, her openness and honesty versus their secretive seclusion. They wouldn't mix, couldn't mix. In Western parlance, this house wasn't big enough for all of them.

And so Denis's life pattern reestablished itself in a new form of order. Early in the day for work. An hour to clean up the mess his housemates made. Dinner and TV with Rebecca in the evening. Bedtime at night. Sometimes he would stare at his door for a little while after he'd turned out the light and wonder whether she was asleep, and whether she might come in and join him. She did not. Three sharp alarm calls later and he could repeat the new order all over again.

This comfortable period was not without its mishaps of course. When one lives with four housemates of the caliber that he lived with, there could be no such thing as an easy life. Plasterer had taken to leaving banana peels on the floor of the kitchen in a real life imitation of a computer game, hoping that she might trip on them. Rebecca had taken to laughing at the frequent banana peel appearances and thought it was a practical joke that Denis was playing. She periodically forgot that the Denis Murphy she once knew was not the same man as the Denis Murphy she had met on her return from her travels. Once upon a time, practical jokes were his bread and butter. Once upon a time.

Deano had taken a shine to the photograph of the two of them hanging in the kitchen and would often take it down and walk around the house holding it and staring at it. Distracted by the picture, he all too often missed the fact that the Professor was lying in his path and he'd trip over him. Things were getting broken about the house, and he was finding it hard to come up with excuses for why. He was sure she was beginning to think that while she was at work, he was walking around the house smashing things.

One afternoon she had come home for lunch, startling all of them. It was a break from the new established order, which was troubling enough, but it was also a very inopportune moment. Plasterer was standing in the middle of the office with a bucket of filthy water and the mop. The game they were playing seemed to have no more rules than "dodge the muddy water." Denis was soaked in it.

"Hey, Denny," she had called from the hallway. "I brought lunch."

Plasterer had frozen on the spot, the mop dripping water on the floor. Penny O'Neill had slunk into a hiding spot behind the door. Professor Scorpion put on his "hiding face" and picked up a book. Deano dived under the desk.

"I'm a bookcase," the Professor whispered as Denis made his way to the door to peek out.

Rebecca walked through the kitchen and into the utility room without looking in his direction. He dodged out of the room and locked the office door, then bolted for the stairs.

"You there?" she called.

"Yeah. I spilled ink on my shirt and trousers so I'm just changing. I'll be down in a minute," he called from the stairs as he removed his trousers.

"You spilled ink on yourself? What a disaster. I'll get the yellow pages and look up a counseling service."

"Smart-ass," he called back, chuckling.

Disaster had been averted, but only barely. Denis reminded himself that he'd have to have another word with her about upsetting the daily schedule. That day had been a particularly good day for Denis. With the door to the office locked, his housemates had no way of playing ridiculous pranks or poking their heads out from doors where they shouldn't be, and so he had sat in some comfort with her while they ate.

"It's just that you always do dinner, so I thought I'd take care of lunch for a change," she told him proudly. Rebecca Lynch had many strengths. She was intelligent, caring, funny. She had a sharp insightful mind. Notably, cooking was not one of those strengths. Denis had always been the chef in their relationship.

"It's lovely," Denis told her, around a mouthful of couscous and meatballs. "Who made it?"

"Ha ha. Now who's the smart-ass?" she asked, feigning offense. "I picked it up in town. There's a neat pop-up café not far from my office. New Dad recommended it."

"Does he know you call him New Dad?" he asked.

"I call him New Dad to his face. He lets me get away with it. It's a minor form of rebellion."

"How's Regular Dad?" he asked.

She pursed her lips, which in the unspoken language of Rebecca that very few people could speak meant "I disapprove." He decided not to push the matter.

"Do you think people can stay in love forever?" she asked eventually.

"I don't know," he told her. "It would be nice to think that most people have that capacity, but I just don't know."

"Do you remember when you stopped loving me?"

His eyes were stinging again. He tried to force a smile, but for some reason his mouth refused the order, and suddenly his lip felt like it was shaking.

"It's okay," she assured him. She looked worried. She looked upset. Perhaps she knew what the question had done to him.

Denis composed himself as best he could. He remembered her standing at the screen door by the side of his parents' house. It was like a scene from a remembered nightmare. She stood there, her hair soaked from the rain. Her eyes were puffy and red, and she called to him through the glass. He sat there and watched her. From four feet away he had sat and watched her. For an hour she had banged on the glass. She had been calling things through to him, but he couldn't hear, or didn't want to. He just sat there staring at her and through her all at the same time. The cast on his arm was wet with tears. That was when he remembered how to cry. He suppressed the memory. His greatest talent in his life, the suppression and destruction of thoughts and ideas that upset him. He scrubbed the wet from his cheeks.

"Is this lamb?" he asked her.

"Yes," she said, nodding sadly.

They ate and sat in a cold, lonely silence, and when he was finished, Denis smiled his weak smile at her again and went back to work. He tapped relentlessly at his keyboard and battered his calculator and tried not to hear the sounds of her pottering in the kitchen.

Eventually, she came back to him; she offered him a look. It was a "don't worry about it" look that suggested they move on from the afternoon's discomfort. He smiled a stronger smile.

That afternoon they went for coffee. Roisin and Tash joined them. In less than two weeks his two friends had become five friends. Thankfully this meant symmetry when having coffee, with even numbers occupying a table being infinitely more appealing to him than odd ones. Roisin had a way of scrunching up her face when she laughed that he found charming. Tash was as bubbly as ever. When he lived in the other universe, it was common for Denis to hang around with several girls at the same time, but it had been seven years since he lived in that place, so there was a tremendous novelty to sitting down in the company of three women. He affected his best offhand charm and was pleased to see he could make them laugh. He poked fun at his own idiosyncrasies with self-deprecation that was as humorous as it was endearing. The waiter in his favorite Italian café looked shocked to see him sitting there in the company of three ladies. Thomas in the convenience store newsagent had laughed openly when he had walked in to buy his paper. He had almost insisted on a high five that day.

What none of them could see was the effort he was expending in the name of this exercise in sociability. A man walked past them at one point with the most offensive ketchup stain on his T-shirt. A small child spilled Skittles from a plastic bag all over the street in front of them. A woman at a nearby table pushed around spilled sugar from a sachet as she talked loudly on her phone. Her lipstick was uneven. A man with flyers wiped his nose with the back of his hand before placing a flyer on the table. Rebecca could see his jaw clench at the sight of it, and took immediate action with a facial wipe and his germ-killing hand sanitizer. He was grateful for her help. There was no mention or acknowledgment of the lunchtime conversation. His one departure from his new venture into socializing was that when the appointed time was up, that was that. One hundred twenty minutes had been spent in the act of engaging socially, and that was enough. He made his goodbyes and headed for home.

He had lied to his housemates the morning after she had slept in his bed. Lied right to their faces. He had no idea what the plan was, and he found this concept both terrifying and thrilling. For a man who lives in a constant stream of tasks and achievable goals, the lack of control when it came to Rebecca was very much a love-hate feeling. He knew the time would come when she would leave the house; she had to. That did not make him feel good. At times he yearned for the consistent dependable life he shared with his housemates, but too often, lately, that had been getting away from him. That feeling of control was eluding him and, with the reckless abandon of a man who just might decide not to clean his teeth before bed, part of him was embracing this new order. He couldn't tell his housemates, obviously, but something told him that Plasterer already knew. The onetime unofficial leader of the foursome had become the führer of the group. While the other three played games of Bat the Light Bulb and What's in this Bin, he watched over them, saying little. More often than not he sat directly at Denis's side. He talked more than he played. He talked about their plan. He lamented their lack of order. As if the four of them had ever attempted to establish order in this house. He still had to cover for their ludicrous behavior, including running to a local shop to buy towels after all of them mysteriously vanished, only to turn up hanging from the branches of a small tree in the backyard the next day. How he had missed them when he was putting his clothes on the line the day before he'd never know.

The weekend came and went almost without incident. His mother had visited again, and he had been more or less ignored again. Plasterer threatened to cause another scene, but this time Denis had asserted himself and the pugnacious clown had backed down. He'd had dinner at Ollie's house that week, and in a move that stunned even him, he left the house wearing a tie, only to remove it when out of sight of his housemates before unbuttoning the top two buttons. Rebecca had said nothing as they walked, but he thought he saw a faint smile playing about the edges of her lips. He watched those lips a lot.

It was early the following week before Denis suffered his first major setback. He had always felt that there were changes that came during one's life, and such changes were often to be embraced, but from time to time, one had to step back and realize that too much change could be a terrible thing. Rebecca had, quite early in the week, expressed an interest in getting out in the evenings more. Denis could understand her desire; it had to be tough for anyone trying to live to his timetable. He'd perfected the art over years. For someone like Rebecca or Ollie, it could be tolerated only for so long.

"C'mon," she urged in a voice near a whine. "Let's do something. Anything."

"You're more than welcome to do anything you like, Becks, but I'm staying here. *SVU* is on in less than five minutes," he told her cheerfully, referring to one of the grittier cop shows.

She flounced from the room in a pout. All too often she reminded him of a darker version of Penny O'Neill.

"You want to go see a movie?" she called from the kitchen, opening and closing cupboard doors as if the answer to boredom lay within.

"Oh absolutely," he told her sarcastically. "Give me a seat that someone else has sat and sweated into any day of the week. And popcorn from a trough? It's my favorite. And all the popcorn on the floor? It makes wonderful decoration. What about the sound of other people eating? Is there anything more melodic than that?"

"Point taken," she shot back sourly. "Hey, where do you do your grocery shopping?"

"Online," he called back, not seeing the trap being laid out before him.

"You're running out of stuff. Let's go shopping."

"What stuff?" he asked, trying to divert her.

"Stuff," she answered in a tone that brooked no arguments.

"What if just you go and I mind the fort?" he tried.

"What if we both go and I don't have to kick you all the way there?" she countered playfully.

"Have you heard of the internet? It makes it so we don't have to leave the house."

She came to the door of the living room and looked at him sternly.

"And that's why it's destroying civilization, now put your shoes on and let's go."

She fixed him with a glare as she said it. She knew, even as he did, that he would simply be unable to refuse her. He felt his will dissolve.

"Fine." He sighed, setting the TV to record.

"I'm just going to run to the bathroom and then we can take off," she said cheerily. She just loved getting her own way.

He reached for his keys and wallet when a white-gloved hand grabbed him by the wrist.

"Where do you think you're going?" Plasterer asked. Penny O'Neill stood at his shoulder, keeping watch.

"We're just going grocery shopping," he said, alarmed.

"Oh are *we* now? Are *we* just going grocery shopping?" There was spit forming on his lips.

"It's not a big deal. We won't be long."

"This is a mistake, Denis. A huge mistake. When was the last time you were in a grocery store? Food and packages that have been handled by the thousand or so customers that come in every day. Floors dirty. Nothing symmetrical. There'll be pudding there, Pudding." His tone was mocking.

"You ready?" Rebecca shouted from the downstairs bathroom.

Plasterer released his hand. They looked at each other for what seemed like an age.

"You're going to regret this," Plasterer told him.

"I don't need to ask your permission to live my life. I thought we were friends."

"We were until you betrayed us," the clown hissed back.

"Let go," Denis commanded. They resumed their staring

contest. Finally the clown backed down, shaking his head as he crept back up the stairs with Penny O'Neill in his wake.

"I'm ready," Denis told Rebecca.

"Can I drive your car?" she asked.

For a moment he hesitated. As long as he wasn't driving there couldn't really be any harm done, and the car was just sitting in the driveway.

"Sure," he said finally, tossing her the keys. "I don't think I can remember the last time I drove it. I sometimes start it up and let it run, just so the battery doesn't die, but actually driving it..." He really couldn't remember.

Rebecca looked excited by the prospect. As he recalled, she drove like a lunatic, all rally corners and speeding. He tried not to be intimidated by the gleam in her eye.

And so off they went. To shop for groceries. In a grocery store. But only after he'd checked the lock three times and counted the steps to the gate.

The grocery store was a mistake. Plasterer had been right. It was huge and messy. Not messy to most people's eyes, but Denis sought out the mess. An odd number of shopping carts in the loading bay, one of them sitting casually on its own across the line between two parking spaces. Denis should have walked home immediately, but his newfound sense of recklessness urged him forward. He carefully adjusted his tie, which, of course, needed no adjusting.

Rebecca parked incorrectly with the tires still in the turned position, one of them sitting on the line that marked the end of one space and the start of another. To Denis, that line was the very essence of order. People came to parking lots in their hundreds, and the cars parked in a neat and orderly fashion defying, or so it seemed to him, the natural inclination of people to do as they feel whenever they felt it. In a lot of hundreds of empty spaces, this simple act of bad parking would inconvenience nobody, but it was the abandonment of what should have been the epitome of structure. He tried to ignore it.

Inside the store the escalator handrail had a thick streak of what looked like rubber but actually could have been anything. Denis refused to touch it. Rebecca either didn't spot his discomfort or was in no mood to pay attention to it. She talked and talked while Denis fought off the rising panic. Denis Murphy had no business being in a grocery store. They made their way along the aisles with a basket. Lines of boxes of tea seemed to stagger in no particular order. One brand was sitting among another brand, offensively and smugly refusing to be where it should have been.

"I don't like this…" Denis said uneasily.

"It's just a store, scaredy-cat."

"To you it's just a store, to me it's a giant mess that other people have put their hands on."

"Suck it up," she replied.

Denis always felt that "suck it up" was a particularly terrible expression. He grimaced at it. Onward they plunged through rows and rows of mess, scatterings of products and labels. The evening staff was clearly in the process of restocking the shelves, and the discarded cardboard crates and boxes littered the aisles. Denis navigated each one like a man picking his way through a field of quicksand. Rebecca continued to chatter. Something about picking guitar strings, or sliding strings or something of that nature. Denis wasn't really listening. Something in the back of his head told him that if he could make it through this minefield, he could stop thinking he was a weirdo, he could bask in his own congratulations at his ability to blend in with those around him who had no respect for control. Another voice, speaking in tones Plasterer would understand, told him that this was not his place. This was wrong.

Rebecca casually picked items at will, flinging them into the basket with no regard for what went where. Denis argued with none of her purchases, saving his energy for fighting off the anxiety that was threatening to drown him. At the checkout a runny-nosed woman served them in between sneezing. She used the same tissue every time. By now there was no hiding the feeling he was having.

"Almost there," Rebecca said comfortingly. "I'll get you a treat if you can survive this."

He didn't care that she was speaking to him as though he were a child. She bagged their items and all of a sudden it was done. He heaved a sigh of relief in spite of himself.

"We're leaving?" he asked.

"In two minutes," she replied in a tone that he knew was a lie. "We're just popping into the clothes section. I promised you a reward, and a reward you shall have." She was forcing joviality, an insincere friendliness that must have been masking her contempt for his ridiculous behavior. No one could really understand him.

They made their way into the clothes section, which was, blessedly, in better shape than the grocery department. Denis walked with her, trying to calm his ragged nerves. He had survived it, but the panic wouldn't go away. She picked up items of clothing at random, plucking at the fabric as she walked by. Some of them she held up before him, trying to imagine how it might look. Shirts, trousers, ties, even a hat that he immediately dismissed. Hats mess hair. Mess is bad. QED. She stopped at a low shelf unit and picked up a pastel yellow T-shirt by some designer or other. It had stripes here and there in red and blue. Denis imagined that this was what "cool" people wore. He had owned one just like it in another life. That's why she picked it up. It tugged a memory from her brain just the way it did from his. Whatever memory it stirred in her he couldn't say, but for him it was one that he had worked almost seven years to forget. They had cut him out of a T-shirt just like that in a hospital. It had been caked in blood and shredded in parts by broken glass. There were long blond hairs attached to it.

"I think you'd look amazing in this—"

"No," he said abruptly.

"C'mon, scaredy-cat, I know you're only dying to get out of those shirts and ties."

"No, Rebecca," he insisted.

"It'll look great with the jeans you wore to dinner the week before last," she persisted.

"NO." This time he shouted. A loud and forceful shout.

"Denis…don't shout at me." She seemed shocked and offended and scared all at once.

It was too much for Denis. He'd hurt her, he knew that, but she hurt him too, and she didn't know or didn't care.

"You can't just make people wear T-shirts," he told her. She had to understand. Except, no one ever understood, only his housemates. "You don't just get to come into someone's life and wreck it and make them wear T-shirts that are yellow. No one gets to do that." He wasn't quite shouting, but he wasn't far from it. His tone was cold and angry, and he could do nothing about it. He could see the hurt getting worse and worse in her eyes. She would hate him now. "You don't get to just change someone because you don't like the way they are. You don't know me. This is me now." He gestured at his clothes. "You think you can just walk down a street with your thirteen beads in your hair, and everyone has to be like you want them to be. Well, they're not. Some people are different. Some people can't have thirteen beads in their hair.

Some people like discipline. They like knowing what their day holds. They like being in charge of their lives. Some people need to know the time, and they need to know their day. They need to know that what's waiting around the corner won't come smashing into them and ruin their lives. I'm not who you think I am. This is me. This is me." The last line was almost a shout. Denis turned and walked out of the store, picking his spot so that he didn't step on any of the cracks in the plastic floor tiles. He walked home at a powerful stride, his heart hammering.

The doctors had thrown the T-shirt on the floor after they cut it off. He was screaming in agony and grief. An orderly pinned down his thrashing legs, and they injected him with something. He felt the stinging tears rolling down his cheeks. He counted the steps from the carefully closed gate all the way up to the door. Checked the lock. Turned the key. Plasterer was waiting for him at the end of the stairs.

"I warned you," he growled.

TRY TO FIX

For fuck sake. Get a grip on yourself, you maniac.

Denis made tea while Plasterer sat in the living room, clenching and unclenching his fists. The big clown looked as though he might spit nails. As the kettle boiled, Professor Scorpion stood behind Denis, a ketchup bottle in one hand, a BBQ sauce bottle in the other. His feet were planted against the ground as though he was bracing himself against the backfire of the two condiments, while spraying the walls with a look of rigid determination etched on his rotting face. The brown and red sauces made splatters on the wall that reminded Denis of scenes from gory slasher films he used to watch. The blood slipped and slicked its way down the wall in rivulets. The sound of the liquids escaping the plastic was rude. Penny O'Neill walked around as the Professor sprayed the walls, dipping shredded newspaper in water and glue, which she would then fling at the ceiling with venom. Some of them stuck, some of them hung down and some of them made blobs on the kitchen table. Deano followed Denis as he walked around the kitchen surveying the damage. "It'll be all right. Everything will be all right," Penny O'Neill repeated absently as she fired glue balls. There was a hard edge to her voice. Hard but brittle underneath. Denis made the tea with trembling hands and carefully placed the tea bag into the organic waste bin. Deano reached by him and lifted the bin over his head, emptying the contents all over his hairy body. Most of it splattered Denis as it headed for the floor. Denis ignored the filth for the time being. The Professor was on the move again, emptying flour into a bowl while he cast serious sidelong glances at Denis. He made a fist in the bowl and hurled it about, powdering the room. He grunted in satisfaction as Denis was forced to stand aside to dodge the worst of it. Penny O'Neill dumped what was left of the glue and water on the kitchen floor, where it began spreading with slow inexorability. There was no need to tackle it just yet. She'd be coming home for sure, but not anytime soon. Her text had said she was going to Frank's to let him cool off. Plasterer had nodded knowingly when he found out. He called for a meeting, and tea.

Denis followed the suggestion, grateful for the opportunity to let someone else take the lead, though ever so slightly concerned by the domineering attitude the clown was displaying. There was no controlling the situation, no way to fight the mass of thoughts that surged through his head. They were making him nauseous. The organic waste on his clothes wasn't helping. The walls still looked like they were spattered in blood. It ran in little tears to the floor.

"I know you feel guilty," Penny O'Neill told him, as if speaking to a simpleton, "but it's going to be all right. Everything will be all right, you'll see."

"Do I?" Denis asked, confused. It was nice to know that's what he was feeling. The tremble in his hands was probably an indicator of something. Penny O'Neill could be exceptionally helpful when she felt like it. Her tail was flicking from side to side, and her hips swayed gently as she moved about the kitchen.

He made his way into the living room, the tea perfectly balanced on the saucer. Tiny ripples ran across the liquid.

"Penny O'Neill says I'm feeling guilty," he said to Plasterer.

"Maybe you are," the clown replied, sitting back in his seat and regarding Denis coldly. "Sit down. You'll ruin the couch."

Denis sat down. No point in arguing. Plasterer had been right all along. Denis had been reckless while the clown had urged caution. He had done this to himself with his stupid behavior. A Monday night, and instead of *SVU* while Penny rested her head on his lap, he had a ruined kitchen and stains on the couch.

"We've got a failed experiment here, Boss," Plasterer told him in a calm and measured tone. He was still clenching and unclenching his fists.

"We do," Denis replied.

"It was a fine idea, don't get me wrong, but you've screwed the whole thing for us. It's time to bail. Hit that parachute cord and land safely away from that plane crash waiting to happen."

"It hasn't already happened?" Denis asked. That was odd. The grocery store definitely felt like the plane crash. She hated him now. There's no way she couldn't.

"Not yet. Not with that one. She's determined, you see. Remember what Frank and Ollie were like at the start? It'll be worse with her. This one doesn't know when to quit."

Plasterer shook his head slightly as he spoke.

"Do we move out?" Denis asked, still confused. He briefly forgot that he owned the house.

"No, no, no. You see what she's done to you? What *you've* done to you? You need to tell her to go. Tell her you're sorry, and that you want to keep being her friend if she'll have you, but she has to go. I think we can agree on that, right?"

"Will that fix everything?" Denis asked. "Will that make everything go back to the way it was?"

"I'm not so sure, Boss. It might, it really might, but she's got a lot of dog in her. She'll not take it easy, and she may redouble her efforts. That girl wants something you no longer have, something we don't want to give, and she's determined to get it. She may come back, but right now we're working on damage control. It's time to cut her loose."

"It's time to cut her loose," Denis echoed. "I'll tell her in the morning."

It felt good to have the decision made, sort of. Something else was blossoming at the same time as his sense of relief, a nagging feeling that this was all wrong. Once she was gone, she'd be gone, and he'd be back to normal. That should have filled him with contentment, but it didn't. Perhaps he was still feeling guilty. He decided he should ask Penny O'Neill about that. No, for some reason there was a sense that this wouldn't be the great wonderful restart that he wanted. It would be something different. He tried not to focus on it.

See what he's got you doing? How he's got you thinking? This isn't you, it's him. And it's you.

"Don't think about it too much, Boss," Plasterer warned him. "Try not to think at all. It works for Deano. Clean instead. You love that. The walls are a mess in there, and so is the ceiling and the floor. I'll order them to behave and you clean up."

He was right again; Denis did love cleaning. He could just let it all fall out of his head while he cleaned. Turn on the radio and listen to some classical music and clean. That way when she arrived home she'd see a completely spotless kitchen. She'd understand, a little anyway. She'd get that he liked things a certain way, and maybe she'd hate him just a little less. He steeled himself for his three big jobs. He'd wash the flour off his hands, get the kitchen clean, then he'd write his to-do list for tomorrow and first on the agenda would be telling her that she had to move out.

He never told her though.

He got out of bed at the appointed time and fixed things in the appointed way. The bed was made, the pajamas consigned to the laundry basket, the laundry basket consigned to the laundry room and the pajamas, as well as some other odds and ends, were consigned to the washing machine. Teeth were brushed the appropriate number of times and a tie tied the appropriate way. He wasn't just dressing and preparing for his day, he was getting ready for war the only way that he knew how, clad in armor of office shirt and trousers. The only way he knew how. Somehow though, she had fired the first shot before he even got up. She was already out of the house, and sitting on the kitchen side table was a tidy cardboard box in which three expensive-looking ties sat, carefully rolled and stored in top condition. Next to the box was a note that read:

Denis, I'm sorry. So very sorry. It is your life and your house, and I'm a guest here, I know that. There's no reason for you to change the way you are, you're just fine to me. I'm going to give you a little space for a few days and stay with Frank and Tash. I'm on the end of the phone if you need me and I'll be back on Wednesday.

Love,
Rebecca

He read the letter four times. *Love, Rebecca*. He read that part eight times. He folded the letter carefully and placed it in his wallet. The notepad paper, with the tiny little flowers on it, made a stark contrast with the Spartan wallet he carried.

"What's that?" Plasterer asked, walking into the room, adjusting his gloves.

"Just my wallet," Denis said hurriedly. There was no reason that Plasterer had to know what it was. He was altogether too pushy about his advice anyway. Denis opted to keep the note to himself. In fact, where Plasterer and his other housemates were concerned, he might just keep more than a few things to himself.

"How did you sleep?" he asked the clown, as he fixed his morning coffee and weighed his breakfast cereal.

"Fine," grunted Plasterer. "I've got Deano hair in my mouth though. That fur ball is great as a hot-water bottle, but he makes a shocking mess. Where did we ever get him?"

Denis smiled at the thought of Plasterer and Deano spooning each other.

"Did you tell her?" Plasterer asked.

"She's gone out already. Says she's going to give us a few days to settle down."

"She's smart, that one," Plasterer observed, clearly unhappy. "Knows you're likely to pull the trigger on this one. She's making her move first, and waiting for you to think your way into another decision."

"Probably," Denis agreed nervously. He couldn't tell the clown that she had written him a note, or that she had signed it *Love, Rebecca*. He definitely couldn't tell him that it made him happy and relieved. He said no more, and went about his perfectly normal day.

And so it was that Tuesday operated exactly as it should. There was routine, room cleanings, an inspection of his housemates' room, which looked as he expected it would—as though a bomb had hit it. He had to apply in writing for access to their room. He was an automated cleaning machine and no stain, mark, scuff or pile of dirty laundry was safe from him. He stopped at Rebecca's room and wondered how she had managed to get so under his skin that he was already calling this her room. Hers. Like it belonged to her, as if somehow she belonged in his life. Downstairs, Plasterer smashed a bowl into the wall. For fun.

In the evening there was *NCIS*, *SVU* and *CSI*. Wonderfully structured acronyms that made him relax into his evening. Deano curled up by his feet as they watched TV, and the effect was warming. The mood in the house was markedly different, even the Professor could feel it. He shuffled about the house with increased energy and urgency, and he even managed to say a few sentences with fewer than thirty words in them. Denis was proud of him. Work was done and things filed. It was lovely, and it should have been all Denis wanted, but something felt missing. Her spot on the couch was empty and her absence conspicuous.

His batteries were fully recharged by Tuesday night, but he looked to where she usually sat, and imagined her there laughing and discussing people and things about her work. Penny O'Neill sat with her head in his lap, purring contentedly. Her blond mane didn't seem as comforting anymore. He tried to think of something else and found himself idly wondering what it might be like if her hair was brown, dark brown and ever so slightly curly. And so by the time Wednesday rolled around, he found himself losing concentration during the afternoon. She would sit with him that night, he thought to himself. She would eat the dinner he cooked and tell him that it was lovely. There was something about this that enticed him. He tried to steer his mind in another direction, but it seemed always to float back to her. He would have to try harder. It's an easy enough task to perform if you know how, and Denis

Murphy was an expert in not thinking about things he didn't want to think about.

Her arrival was without incident. She said hello quietly, not looking in on him, pottered about the kitchen with some things and went to her room. She arrived back a few minutes later and put on a wash. Nothing was mentioned about Monday night. Nothing was mentioned at all. He sat during her arrival, bolt upright, breathing heavily through his nose. Next to him at his desk, Plasterer sat motionless. Something about his body language seemed to be giving him away though. He was hoping she'd walk in, hoping she'd see him. Denis cringed inside and silently begged for the moment to pass. He heard her move back upstairs, and he sighed with relief. Plasterer just blinked.

Denis made dinner as she went about her evening. The tension was palpable; it floated all about the room. He pushed his way through it with even, measured strokes for each chop of each vegetable. Every now and again he'd look at her as she walked by, doing this or that. She did the same, shooting glances his way as she passed. The radio did all the talking. Eventually, she sat down at the table and unfolded a newspaper. She left it right in front of where Denis would typically sit. He tried to suppress a smile. She pretended not to notice it. He set the table for dinner, laying two places. Now it was her turn to try not to smile while he pretended not to notice. She cracked eventually, when her dinner was served. He returned the smile. Penny O'Neill had been right. Everything was going to be okay.

They ate in silence for a while, both smiling occasionally at one another. The tension had evaporated, and they were back to the comfortable familiarity that he had begun to get so used to.

"How is it?" he asked her eventually.

"Delicious," she replied.

Denis had been a clever enough wordsmith in his day, but right there and then, he could think of no words to describe the elation he felt. Her simple blessing, one barely significant word, meant more to him than a month's worth of well-ironed socks.

In the doorway, behind Rebecca, Penny O'Neill and Professor watched. They hardly moved, just stood in the doorway watching. He ignored them. It's not easy ignoring a long-legged blond woman who also happens to be a cat, any more than it is to ignore a rotting corpse that also happens to be a professor, but Denis managed. There was no way that he was going to allow this moment of reconciliation to be ruined.

"How has your week been?" she asked.

"Fine," he replied. "I got a lot of work done, and lots of ti-dying and cleaning. I missed you though. It wasn't the same without you."

Suddenly, Plasterer was in the doorway. He gestured for Denis to come to the doorway. Rebecca smiled at him, her most brilliantly wide, utterly heartwarming smile. It made his heart race. It made him think of afternoons sitting on grass with his head in her lap while he read. Plasterer gestured again, impatiently. Denis smiled back at her and asked if she'd like some tea. Plasterer shook his head from side to side, seething, before slowly turning and making for the stairs. Penny O'Neill and the Professor both backed away in perfect unison and then turned and marched up the stairs. Deano stood in the hallway; he had been hiding behind them. He crept behind the hall-way door and continued watching them through the gap be-tween door and hinges. Considering how hard it was to read the emotional responses of a hair ball, it was something of a guess, but Denis felt that Deano was pleased. There was no way to know if that was true; he just had a feeling. Later that evening, as they sat by the TV, watching sitcoms that made Rebecca laugh in the most adorable way, Denis decided to make tea. In the kitchen, Plasterer stood by the kettle.

"You think I don't know what you're doing?" he leaned in and whispered, his voice calm, but loaded with the threat of reprisal.

"I don't know what you're talking about," Denis whispered back.

Careful now.

Rebecca was calling something from the living room. Something about an actor on the television. Denis couldn't hear her with Plasterer whispering so close.

"The others are confused. They expected her to be gone by now, but I'm not confused. I know what you're doing. And I think you're an idiot. A fool of a boy who doesn't know what he wants. You can't tell where the real danger is, and you can't even decide what you're feeling from one minute to the next. You're an emotional cripple, Denis, and on top of that, you're blindly stupid and massively ignorant. But that's okay. You run the ship—for now. So I'll just wait here until you come crawling back to me, like you always do. Something will go wrong, and Plasterer will be there to fix it again. Eventually you'll realize that I'm what's good for you, Murphy. When you do, you know where to find me."

Oh fuck.

Rebecca was calling out something else. Something about the same actor. Denis fixed a smile on his face.

"Stop watching me," Denis told Plasterer shortly. "I've got company."

Plasterer nodded at him slowly, but something told Denis that the clown wasn't agreeing with him, he was deciding something. Denis didn't want to think about what exactly was being decided here, so he chose not to.

"Sorry," he called in to the living room, never taking his eyes off Plasterer. "I was in a world of my own there for a little bit. Gimme a second. I'll be in and you can tell me about it."

The look the clown gave him was unsettling. Like it was sizing him up, weighing and measuring him for the kill. He'd seen Plasterer bully the others, he'd watched the clown grow in strength, and confidence, and now it seemed that might be coming around to haunt him.

The week rolled on, as weeks do. Wednesday became Thursday, which wasted twenty-four hours being itself before it became Friday. For Denis Murphy, those delineations weren't real, and so Wednesday's tasks became Thursday's tasks and so forth. More and more, time on his to-do list was being allotted to watching television, something Denis did a lot of during the week. It relaxed him to sit with her and just let the time pass. She relaxed too. And laughed. Sometimes she stretched when she was tired. She would lock her fingers together and then twist her hands over her head, and the natural curves of her body became so much more glaringly obvious. Denis found himself staring and hoping she'd get more tired, so she might stretch again. It reminded him of a cat. Penny O'Neill was in his head and at the door at the same time. She was watching him again, just like she had at dinner. It was impossible to tell what she was thinking.

For their part, his housemates seemed intent on ignoring both of them. During the afternoons, while he worked, one or two of them would casually ruin something in the kitchen. One day they took a pair of his trousers, tied off the legs, filled the whole lot with fruit and then proceeded to smash them off a wall. It seemed to Denis though that their hearts weren't really in it. He barely saw them anymore. Where they were, what they were doing were curiosities to him, but it seemed that pulling at that particular string would likely tangle him in something he wouldn't care to get out of. For so very long they had been his truest friends. He had relied on them, and they on him, and now they were ignoring him. Years of late-night chats with the Professor about books or movies they'd read or watched. Nights of waking from a nightmare full of the sound of his sister's screams only to find Penny O'Neill sprawled across the end of his bed. Now not one word passed between them, and they were hiding from him. Except for Plasterer. Not for him the cold isolation of the others. He would often sit with Denis all day long. They ignored each other, their cold war stretching onward, all day side by side. It was unnerving, but Denis vowed there would be no surrender. By Friday evening the standoff was so tense that Denis found himself massaging the back of his own neck to calm himself.

Rebecca arrived home in the early evening, calling out her hellos as she walked in the door. Plasterer made no move to hide, instead sitting back with his hands behind his head and giving Denis an appraising look.

"You in the office?" she asked from the hallway.

"Yes," Denis replied, his voice strained. "Don't come in!"

"Er...okay," she called back, sounding amused.

He realized what she thought he was doing and blushed. Better her thinking that than walking in to see him and Plasterer.

"Can't get away with it forever," the clown snorted. "You'll never hold it all in, you know. You're like a sick person trying to mask your symptoms. Eventually something will show."

"Shut up," Denis told him casually. They were the first words they'd spoken since Wednesday. He left the room, locking Plasterer in as he went. He was still blushing. No doubt she'd take that as confirmation. He was happy enough for her to think what she wanted to.

"How was work?" he asked casually.

"Great," she told him, shaking out her hair. She looked like she belonged on television in some ad for hair-care products, except she was real, and standing in his kitchen. He realized he wanted to brush one of the stray locks of hair behind her ear. He had done that absently for three years. He was sure that sometimes she'd shake out her hair just to turn that one curl loose. She'd do it just to give him the chance to push it back over her ear. For a second he thought about it, but re-covered in time to stop himself. He thought he could hear Plasterer laughing to himself in the office.

"What would you like to do tonight?" he asked loudly to cover the sound and tried not to look at the office door.

"Er..." She paused, thinking. "I don't know, how about some coffee in town and a movie when we get home?"

"Sure, sure," he replied. "We should go right now though. How about it?"

"Give me a few minutes, will you? I just got here. By the way, how come you never clean the guest room at the top of the stairs? I went in there this morning for a hair dryer. It's a disgrace."

She had been in his housemates' bedroom. He froze.

"It's cool. The mess doesn't bother me that much," she said, laughing.

What if she'd seen something? What if they found out? The standoff would escalate. He hoped Plasterer had not heard. There was no sound from the office.

"I'll take care of it tonight," he told her, trying to sound calm. He walked to the office door to double-check the lock.

"There's no problem. Your house, your rules."

THUMP. Plasterer pounded the door from the inside.

"What was that?" she asked, as she walked out the door to hang her coat.

"Nothing," he replied, rattling the key in the lock. "Just making sure this door is okay. I worry about burglars."

THUMP. The clown pounded heavily again. He must have heard that she had been in his room. Even Denis rarely went in there, and never without permission. He had once wandered into the room in search of something about a week before Rebecca had strolled down a street and back into his life. Plasterer had destroyed his clothes in retaliation. He didn't like people in his space.

"I think the door is okay," she told him, walking back in. "It sounds like you're trying to punch your way through it." She looked confused.

"I'm sure it is. Listen, I'm just going to do a few minutes' more work. You stay out here, and we can go for coffee when you're ready."

She was looking at him strangely. He left his fist on the door. If it sounded like anyone was punching it, she'd think it was him and not Plasterer.

"Okay," she said slowly. "I'll call you when I've had a bit of a nap."

He unlocked the door and went back inside. Plasterer was back in the seat by the computer, his hands folded on his lap.

"Told you that you won't be able to keep it together," Plasterer said smugly.

"And I told you to shut up," Denis snapped back at him. This was not going well. Denis was slowly beginning to hate when Plasterer was right.

"You're sick, little man," Plasterer told him. "And I'm the fucking cure."

"No, you're not," Denis replied, but his voice cracked; it lacked conviction.

"You think she wants you, sickie?"

"Why are you doing this?" Denis asked. His voice sounded whiny even to himself.

"I'm what fixes you when you panic. I'm what keeps you being able to function. You're nothing without me, little man."

Denis felt himself getting angry, but swallowed it. It would be tough, but he could find a way through. He had to. He tried to aim his most contemptuous look at the clown. It had no effect, and so he walked out.

The struggle went on. It was a fact of life for someone in his position; sometimes you just have to struggle through. Others can float like leaves on a breeze through their day, but for some, for Denis, there was a constant struggle to get by. He wished it otherwise, but that's life.

He sat by his computer next to a clown in workman's overalls, who said nothing to him, but watched his every movement.

There was some respite in evening coffee in town, a combination of time with Rebecca away from his housemates, and escape from a power struggle that Rebecca knew nothing about. But when they went home, it resumed exactly where it had left off. Penny O'Neill seemed to skulk around every corner, watching Rebecca resentfully. There was no doubt that Plasterer was leading them in a mini revolution against him. He had made it perfectly clear that there was a path to returning to the life Denis knew and understood. The simple quiet life he had earned for himself through years of patient determination. That path started by removing Rebecca from the house. The trouble was, he didn't want to anymore. At some point last week he had, but now that panic seemed to be a distant memory, replaced by a feeling in his stomach that he thought he might remember if he focused, but that he enjoyed nonetheless.

Rebecca left the house to go shopping on Saturday and to meet with Natasha and Roisin, which was a relief only in that she wouldn't be there to witness the escalation from standoff to running battle. Escalation is exactly what the monsters wanted. A week or so of silence and half-hearted attempts at ruination were replaced by a new offensive. For his part, Denis stayed home and struggled to keep up with the whirlwind of destruction that was being wrought on his abode. Deano and the Professor ignored his every attempt to speak to them, which left Plasterer smirking from Denis's seat in the office. Penny O'Neill spoke to him only once, to ask him why he didn't love them anymore. Denis had no answer for her. His housemates had been almost his entire life for years now. If he could have had them and Rebecca and live in harmony he would have, but he knew that would never work.

Something told him that it would be a disaster. Something told him it was one way or another and never shall the two meet. This new behavior and new territory was deeply unsettling for Denis. He found his eyes following the Professor and Deano in particular. They had been his closest friends, but now they took orders only from the clown.

"Why are you doing this?" Denis asked Plasterer again while cleaning coffee beans from inside his printer.

"It's for your own good," Plasterer told him. "We want the old you, the old us, but you're on a path of self-destruction that we have no control over. We need to get you back to what you know. We want you back at the helm, Captain." His tone was soothing a little, charming even. "You're the boss, the leader, the brains behind the operation. This isn't a mutiny, it's an intervention. The sooner you realize that I'm right, that we're right, the sooner we can all get back to being happy."

"Why can't we be happy with Rebecca?" The question was asked before the thought was fully formed.

"Because you're you, we're us and she's her," was the cryptic reply.

Denis sighed.

★ ★ ★

Now, for a man in Denis Murphy's metaphorical boat, alcohol is simply out of the question. When he lived in the other universe, he had been something of a proficient drinker. In a culture where being able to hold your alcohol is considered a valuable attribute, Denis was highly regarded. He drank, and played a guitar, and sang. He could indulge in high jinks with the best of them, and delve deep into philosophy with old-timers propping up the bar in quiet pubs. He was a drinker in a drinkers' world. In this universe, however, where coffee stains on a tie are the cause of horrendous panic attacks, and anything spilled inspires a terror that "normal" people can only imagine, alcohol had no place. For seven years, Denis had been a teetotaler, but on this particular Saturday, with his housemates throwing various temper tantrums, Denis decided that he would love a drink. In a quiet bar. Preferably with Rebecca, Ollie and Frank. Natasha and Roisin would be welcome too, he grudgingly admitted. So when Rebecca arrived back from town and tentatively broached the topic, Denis nearly hugged her. Nearly. He wasn't so full of relief that he would deliberately touch another human being, but even contemplating it was a sure sign of just how much stress he was under. Rebecca smiled the same mysterious smile that she had worn when he had removed his tie one night not too long ago. It was a victorious little grin, and a paltry effort made at concealing it. So that evening, after dinner, they went to a pub. His housemates stood on the landing at the top of the stairs watching him as he put on his long black coat. He looked straight back at them. Plasterer shook his head slowly and turned away in disgust.

Decisiveness, the quality of being able to make timely decisions, was not a strong suit of Denis's. When life is ordered, and a list made out for tasks, a timetable for existing on a day-

to-day basis, there is little room for indecision. When one de-
viates however, there is a gnawing sense of worry. What if one
makes the wrong decision? What if that decision has horrible
consequences? What if it has great and amazing consequences
that lead him to further disregard discipline, which in turn,
leads him to make another reckless decision that has horrible
consequences? What if he killed someone by making terrible
decisions? The variables were simply too many to count, and
so Denis walked quietly alongside Rebecca, trying with all of
his mental powers, which were not inconsiderable, to push it
from his head. Not wishing to push her luck too far, Rebecca
walked alongside him saying nothing.

He imagined a world where he would sit in a bar, and drink
a beer, and laugh loudly. Maybe even a little too loudly. He
would tell a story and a small entourage of friends and rela-
tives, impressed with his confidence, would laugh with him.
Ollie would pat Frank on the back, and they'd both exclaim
what a charmer he was. Rebecca would look at him admiringly. His mother would hug him and boast to her friends that
her son was a great storyteller. Seconds later he contemplated
a world where he returned home and Plasterer had led a full
coup d'état, and his house would be burning to the ground.
Then his thoughts got darker; he thought of a world where
Ollie and Frank were dead. Killed by some terrible calam-
ity, and once again, doctors were cutting a T-shirt away from
his scarred and cut skin. He could hear Jules screaming. She
screamed so loud.

"Denis…"

Rebecca had been speaking to him.

"Are you okay?" she asked tentatively. Clearly she had not
forgotten the last time his head had wandered into that world.

"Yes," he lied.

"Wanna go in?"

They were outside a bar. A small, tidy-looking bar that had not been open during his college days. This was a good sign. There would be no monsters waiting for him in here.

"Of course," he told her, forcing a smile.

She smiled back at him, and they entered. Inside, the low ceiling trapped some of the smoke from a small fire by the door. The bar, which ran along the back wall, was manned by a friendly looking woman. The wall behind her was equal parts spirit bottles and bric-a-brac; old horns hung next to pictures of Elvis and Marilyn Monroe. The whole place seemed a curious crossover of old world and new, where customers of various ages sat in comfort with one another. Frank and Ollie, Natasha and Roisin were waiting. Ollie was wearing his "lucky shirt." Denis laughed when he saw it. No one commented, but it was obvious to Denis that they were shocked he was there. Shocked he was laughing. It was a sad indictment of his life that he had become such a recluse that his mere presence in a bar was the cause for such surprise.

"Guinness?" Frank asked.

Denis took a deep breath, gathered what was left of the old version of himself and squared his shoulders.

"The usual," Denis said, nodding as he prepared to take his first sip from a pint glass in seven years.

They were all smiling at him. He smiled back.

VERY OLD CIRCLES

The first sip was bitter on his tongue, and he forced himself to drink it out of a pure stubbornness that was ingrained deeply in him. The second was the taste of every drink he'd had in nearly five years of college life. He was in another universe again, the old one. It smelled of bars and cigarette smoke. It smelled of Rebecca's perfume too. It sounded like laughing and joking. It looked like smiling. Denis found himself lost in it. He was drunk from the second sip, not on the alcohol, but on the freedom.

By the time the first drink was finished, he had stopped looking at the stains on the floor, at the overspill from the taps and at the unkempt regulars who had been drinking all day with a determination that matched his own. He spent the time as he sipped that first beer simply listening and smiling, rarely contributing to the conversation. In turn, Frank, Ollie and Rebecca cast him sideways glances to check that he was okay. He couldn't blame them for worrying. For quite a while his modus operandi was to bail when things became difficult, but that was when he lived in the universe that his housemates lived in. They didn't live here, not in this bar, not with this Denis. Here, he was Denny. On his second drink he joked a little, he made fun of Ollie's shirt and reduced Roisin to helpless fits of laughter with the story about Ollie's attempts at talking to older women during college. Ollie and Frank both returned fire with jokes about his tie and shirt combinations. They mocked his regularity, and he lapped up the laughter they inspired in him.

"Serious question," Frank announced, his face straight. "Exactly how many minutes did you agonize over the shirt and tie?"

Twelve was the answer. Denis said nothing, just smiled.

"C'mon," Ollie interjected. "You don't think he picked it tonight, do you? He had this combination picked on Monday morning. It was item number twenty-four on the list. There is no item twenty-three because everyone knows you can't divide twenty-three evenly."

The laughter kicked in again. So often, Denis wondered if people were laughing at him. At his ways, his oddness. Were they sharing a joke about how he lived his life? Now, they were laughing with him. It felt good. He couldn't remember the last time he had laughed so much in such a short space of time. Frank tended to laugh quietly, and it suited his demeanor, while Ollie's laugh was half a cackle and caused heads to turn. Somewhere, way in the back of his head, he could hear Plasterer growling at their laughter. *How dare they?* the clown would ask. Denis ignored the growling and bought a round of drinks.

Good. Good. I'm proud of you. So proud. You're doing great.

They moved onto another pub, where Denis entertained the woman who worked behind the bar with a new answer to the question; "How are you?" every time he passed her or bought a drink. At one stage, on his seventh or so beer, he told her in confidential tones that he lived with four monsters who were trying to take over his home in a war of attrition where cleaning products were his only weapons. She laughed and shook her head. He winked at a young man who was nearby who shot him a broad and friendly grin.

He went back to join the others, but as he did so, his foot caught on a floorboard and he stumbled a little, his hand reached out to steady himself and found the small of Rebecca's back. She half caught him. There was a momentary silence from the group before Ollie let a guffaw of laughter escape. Denis had to admit, people falling over was invariably funny when you are on your seventh drink. His hand felt good resting against the small of Rebecca's back, and she hadn't shied away, so he left it there. For some reason this made him feel immensely proud of himself, and she smiled her mysterious victory smile. Denis may have been fighting a war for control of his home with his four housemates, but Rebecca was fighting a war with them too. A war for ownership of Denis's attention, and each little victorious smile marked a moment where she took ground from them and made it her own. Denis didn't mind too much. She didn't know she was fighting a war with them, but she knew she was winning. Before, they had once whispered "elephant shoe" at each other instead of saying "I love you," in a competition to see who would crack and tell the other they were in love first. He wanted to whisper it to her right then and there. He smiled at her until he caught her eye and then blew her a cheeky kiss.

It was all so familiar to him. The easy banter, the camaraderie, the winking and the blowing of kisses. He'd walked this way for a long time. He began to wonder why he had ever left. At some point, he couldn't be sure when, Rebecca decided it was time to take him home. It may have been when he climbed onto one of the bar stools or it may have been when he tried to convince Natasha to swap clothes with him, but she had decided and so she took him by the hand and led him out into the night. They left the others in gales of laughter. Clearly he could not quite hold his drink like he used to.

"Do you think crazy people know that they're crazy?" He slurred his words slightly as they walked home, hand in hand.

"I don't know. I guess it depends on what kind of crazy they have. Why?"

"I don't know. I just wonder, if you met a crazy person and you knew they were crazy, would they be aware of it too? Or what if you met someone who was crazy but you had no idea, but they did because they can hide it really good." His tongue was now independent of the rest of his body.

"You think I'm crazy?" she asked playfully.

"I think you're loop-the-bloody-loop," he shot back.

"Look, it's nothing you need to worry about. No one thinks you're crazy, just a little eccentric, that's all. Some people might even find it charming," she told him with a sidelong glance.

"Some people, eh?" he replied, smiling slightly. "You fancy the pants off me," he told her boldly.

"Someone's very sure of himself this evening." Now she was smirking.

"I'm fighting a war, you know," he told her in a conspiratorial whisper. He hadn't meant to say that; it just kind of came out.

"I know you are, Pudding. You'll win it too. Eventually," she told him comfortingly.

"Will I though? The clown is wily. You wanna know something? I'm a tiny bit afraid of him."

"You've been watching too many scary movies," she told him.

He decided to attempt to exercise some control of his mouth and shut up for a while. Her skin was so smooth, and her hand fit his perfectly. She smelled amazing, and as they walked, the light night breeze caught her long hair and made it bounce just slightly. She was the most beautiful thing he'd ever seen. The exercise in keeping his mouth shut continued, and so he never told her this.

When they got back to the house, Rebecca made tea, while Denis wandered into the living room. His housemates weren't there. In this universe they didn't bother him when he was with company. He picked his Eels album from the CD rack. There was something about owning an actual CD that Denis loved. He had the downloads too, of course, but the act of taking a CD from a case and placing it in the machine held a charm for him that couldn't be replaced. He put on "Last Stop: This Town" and turned it up. He didn't care if he woke them. Let them come downstairs if they wanted to. He was in no mood to be told what to do this evening.

"Awesome," Rebecca said as she made the tea. "I love this one."

"I think I love it too, but I think I mostly just love the backing vocals." He sang with the track while Rebecca watched him in amusement. He danced around a little. Laughing, Rebecca joined him. If ever there was a song that was unsuitable for two people to dance to, it was this one. They danced anyway. Her hands ran across his back and over his shoulders, down his chest. He held her by the waist. Over their shoulders, standing in the darkened hallway, Penny O'Neill and Plasterer watched silently. Denis spotted them, but was past the point of caring what they thought or what they did. He danced on. When the track finished and the other songs began to play, they sat on the couch.

"Are you sure you're okay?" she asked. "I don't want you to rush yourself. This is a lot of change for a man who times his bowel movements, and I don't want you rushing if it means that you'll hurt yourself. I want you to be okay with everything."

"I'm okay," he assured her. "I just feel a little bit freer than I've felt in a while," he said, slurring his words. A tiny voice that sounded suspiciously like Penny O'Neill told him that he'd regret this all in the morning.

"My Beloved Monster" came out through the speakers.

"Dance again?" she asked.

"If you would do me the honor?" he asked her pompously.

They danced around the living room, in a slow, small circle. His arms were all the way around her back, her hands locked behind his head. He smiled, stumbled a little and then kissed her. It was as though she'd been waiting for it all night. Her lips met his eagerly, her tongue and his finding each other with easy familiarity. With his eyes closed he could only smell and feel her. She smelled amazing and felt wonderful. They stood kissing for a while, and then Denis found himself feeling a little dizzy. He sat back down on the couch with a smile that he knew must be stretching across his face, another stupid grin. He stretched out and she joined him, easing her back against his chest. He swung one arm over her, and she clasped his hand.

"Elephant shoe," she whispered, but he was already asleep.

What woke Denis the following morning was a feeling that can hardly be understood except by those who have already felt it. His stomach roiled and rebelled. His mouth tasted dry and dead. His head pained and pounded. His hands were shaking. There was a jumble of feelings. He was on his couch, wearing the clothes he had worn the night before. The mess of it started a panic attack, which caused a headache, which made him lie back down and forget the panic attack. He had held her hand. They had danced. He had kissed her. The horror of it was mixed with a tinge of excitement and another wave of nausea, and he forgot both the horror and the excitement as he tried to keep the contents of his stomach inside him. There was no sign of his housemates, and for an hour or two he dozed on and off while his TV played the gentle reassuring sounds of *NCIS* in the background. When he finally made a solid attempt at getting off the couch, he found a note from Rebecca.

Gone to have lunch with your mum. You can take a whole day to yourself to recover. Enjoy the hangover, Romeo.

Love, Rebecca

He smiled as he read it, a sickly smile cut short by another wave of nausea. He looked about the room. Two teacups sat on the coffee table. He'd spilled some on the smooth surface of the table. It sat there, a little puddle of tea, mocking him. He tried not to stare at it. He noticed a stain on his shirt. He'd spilled some drink on it. The stain judged him from the front of his shirt, and just like that, the enormity of what he had done hit him like a kick to his already sick stomach. He bolted for the bathroom and emptied his stomach. Flecks of vomit made their way onto his shirt, and he fought to peel it off while he retched. His shaking hands couldn't control the buttons of the shirt, and he found himself nearly ripping it. He tried to compose himself. Instead, he vomited again. Water leaked from his eyes, and his nose ran. It was Sunday afternoon, and he had done nothing. He had slept all day. He was losing it badly now. His hands were shaking; he needed to regain control.

"You're pathetic," Plasterer told him from the doorway as he leaned his bulky shoulders against the frame of the door.

"Please, Plasterer, please," Denis begged. He didn't know what he was begging for.

"Did you think it would be so easy? Just walk into a bar

and suddenly you're the old you again? Did you forget why you left that universe? *Did you?* You're so pathetic."

"Please," Denis begged again. He still didn't know what he was asking for. How had this happened?

"It happened because you've been drunk since she got here. And drunk means no control. We can't have 'no control.' We need control. When we don't have it, bad things happen. When you're drunk, bad things happen. Very bad things."

Denis looked at him for a few moments. He had stopped vomiting. "Help," he begged.

"Fine," Plasterer said, wearing his very own victory smile. "Action News Team…get to work."

The others bounded by the bathroom door, freed from whatever restraints Plasterer held over them. There was no doubt now but that he was their leader. Dictator even. They whooped and bellowed as they burst throughout the corridors in a flurry of destruction that threatened to engulf the entire house.

"My gift to you," Plasterer told him. "Order."

Denis picked himself up from the floor of the bathroom, his shirt now all the way off, exposing his torso completely, with the stripes of his horrendous scars that crisscrossed his skin in shiny welts.

"I'm going to shower," Denis told the clown. "When I get out, you call them off and I'll fix it all."

"Good." Plasterer nodded. "Maybe you and I need to share command of this ship, eh? Maybe that's what we need. Shared responsibility."

Denis turned away and set about cleaning up his mess. His head was a tornado of pain and competing panic attacks. He had touched her, kissed her. He scrubbed himself in the shower until he felt like his skin would peel off. He had let her touch him. His mind kept flashing back to them dancing, her hands roving across his chest. He got sick again. Mixed with the fresh memories were old ones. Jules had put her hands on Eddie's chest too, reaching around him from the back seat. His sister always had such dainty little hands. His eyes began to leak again. *This is all her fault*, he thought to himself. *She wants what she can't have; she wants a person who doesn't exist. I don't exist.*

He toweled himself dry and fixed the bathroom to a standard that he found acceptable, then stepped out into the battle zone. The attack had ended quite quickly, a small string of attacks, coming and going like a summer storm. It seemed that they lacked the energy for sustained assault. He dressed and cleaned at a forced march. His hangover made for an interesting war wound, and he fought through the pain to reestablish his badly needed order. By the time he was done, and the melted candle wax had been painstakingly cleaned from the kitchen floor, he felt much better. Plasterer had watched the whole ordeal, quietly offering encouragement. His troops stood behind him, ignoring Denis.

The doorbell rang.

Five heads swung around to look at the door.

Through the glass he could see the cut of an average-sized man.

"It's a trap," Plasterer told him. "Don't answer it. We've been ambushed."

Denis walked by him and headed for the door. He checked the lock three times before opening it. It was Eddie's dad. He looked like his son. He also looked nervous.

"Denis," he said by way of greeting. It was clear that he was trying to smile. He was failing.

Oh fuck. This isn't good.

"Mr. Reilly," Denis answered. Inside, his head voices screamed a warning at him. *Run. Hide in the bathroom. Close the door. Run.* "Would you like to come in?" he asked instead.

"I would. Thank you."

Nervously, he stepped through the door. Denis's housemates were nowhere to be seen, and so he stood there. A middle-aged man, his hair receding slightly, a small mustache on his lip. When Denis had lived in the other universe, Ned Reilly had been a regular fixture. Softly spoken and generally kind, he had tried to ingratiate himself with the young people his son called friends. He was often seen in a bar or on a road trip with the gang, almost part of it, but just outside. Eddie had never been embarrassed by his dad. They were close.

"Can I make you some tea?" Denis asked, while every muscle in his body twitched with the urge to run.

"That would be lovely. Just a drop of milk, please," Ned replied.

Denis made his way to the kitchen to boil the kettle. The Professor loomed up beside him from nowhere.

"He must leave. He must leave immediately. Or you must. It is imperative that one of you leave this conversation now. No good can come of this."

"I can't just make him leave, Professor," Denis whispered.

"The enormity of the situation that you are about to enter is lost on you, Denis. You are not capable of this. Extract yourself from it immediately."

"Are you talking to me?" Ned called from the living room.

"Er...no..." Denis replied. "Just thinking out loud."

He gave the Professor a helpless look and made his way back into the living room.

"How have you been?" Ned asked, when Denis had served tea and sat down.

"Fine," Denis replied, lying. "Nothing strange."

"You haven't been to see us in a while," Ned told him.

Denis looked at him for a moment and then realized. It had been three weeks since he had been to see Eddie at the hospital. Three weeks to lose complete control of his life. For seven years or so he had dedicated twenty minutes each Saturday to visiting a friend who was, for all intents and purposes, dead. In three weeks he had thrown that out the window. His friend still clung to what some called life. For nearly seven years he'd held on, and Denis had forgotten him in three weeks.

"I'm so, so sorry," was all he could say.

"No, please…" Ned protested. "I think it's a good thing. You've been holding on for too long, Denis. Your family, they're worried about you. I know the boys are too. I still see them."

"No. It's not acceptable. It's not." Denis's eyes were leaking all over again. They stung so badly. His cheeks were wet. "I'm so fucking sorry—"

"No, Denis, please," Ned protested again. "Don't cry, honestly. I… I've been meaning to talk to you for years now, but it just never seemed right. There's something I have to tell you. I should have told you years ago."

"How could I do this to you?" Denis asked him. His vision was blurring; he blinked away the water.

"No, Denis, I don't want you to think it's like that." Ned was reaching out to him. Denis jumped back from him on the couch.

"Please, please don't touch me."

"It's okay, Denis. Listen to me. Nobody blames you. Nobody. Not me, not Ann, not your mother. You need to stop torturing yourself."

Torturing himself? If his eyes weren't stinging so badly, he'd have laughed at that. He hadn't started torturing himself until Rebecca arrived.

"Please listen to me," Ned said once more. "I wanted to tell you for so long. I just couldn't. It was nice to see someone other than me and Ann coming to see him. I wanted you to move on, but a selfish part of me wanted you there. We only go once a week now too. We had to move on too. We were just going when you were. Saturday, our only day, and only because we couldn't hide from it if you weren't."

Denis had slapped his sister's hand playfully as it reached around to embrace Eddie's chest. They had all laughed. Seconds later she was screaming and Eddie was silent.

"I'll come back," Denis told him, blinking again. "I'll come back right now."

"No, Denis, you're not listening. No one blames you. You have to stop doing this."

Denis jumped up and bolted for the bathroom again. He was sure there was nothing left to throw up, but he was going to try anyway.

"Denis… Don't leave…"

Denis left him standing in the living room.

"I warned you," the Professor said as he sat on the edge of the bath. Plasterer made his way into the room; his makeup was smudged where tears had traced tracks through it. It was hard to imagine the big clown crying, but clearly he had been.

"I warned you too," Plasterer told him, his voice thick with emotion. "It was a trap. She tricked us. Took your mother out of the game. Cleared a way for him. She had this planned. The sneaky bitch planned this from the start. Get that fat moron out of our house."

Denis shook his head numbly. "Look what I did to him. To Eddie. To Ann. To Jules. I did it. To my mom. To Frank. To Ollie. Look what I did to everyone. I can't make him go." The words escaped him in shuddering sobs.

"Why do you offer such protests? We're trying to help you." The Professor wrung his hands as he spoke, his rotting flesh knitting together.

"You have to make him go. We need him gone. He's ruining everything. And it's all her fault," Plasterer added. He didn't cut quite the authority figure with the marks of tears cutting through his clown makeup, but for some reason it made him appear horrendously sinister.

"I can't. Stay out of sight. All of you." Denis wiped his eyes and made his way back down the stairs.

"Don't you fucking dare tell me what to do," Plasterer replied, blinking away a fresh tear.

"Just...just please, stay here."

Denis couldn't wait for an answer; he brushed past the two of them and headed for the living room.

Ned was still sitting there. His eyes red and puffy from crying. He tried a reassuring smile, but his lower lip quivered and another tear leaked out.

"You were his friend, Denis. His best friend. He loved you. He loved Jules too. Please understand that we know you didn't mean it. It was an accident."

"I must do better," Denis told him, ignoring the pardon. "For you and Ann. I promise I'll be there next Saturday. I'll bring flowers."

"Denis," Ned said, his tone grave as he tried another avenue of attack. "Have you ever spoken to anyone about it? I mean, have you had any counseling? Grief counseling helped me to no end. I needed it. I was full of rage and bitterness, but it helped me to become okay."

"I'll bring the purple flowers that he used to buy for Jules. She loved them. Mom loved them too. They used to argue over them when he'd drop them at the house. I think Dad was a little jealous about that. Jules was his little girl, you know. That's why I always pick those purple ones. He just loved buying them for her—"

"Perhaps if I set up a meeting with my counselor you'd

think about going around to see him?" Ned interjected. Denis ignored him.

"No one brings her flowers now. Well, maybe Mom."

Something clicked in his head; the part of him that lived and relived that moment shut itself down, and a new compartment opened. His mind shuffled into that compartment, where it was quieter, where he couldn't hear the screams and sirens.

Don't turn away from it now. Don't. Lean into it. Face it. Face it, you cowardly fuck.

He was detaching now and he knew it; there would be no more stinging eyes. If he detached far enough, no one would be able to reach him. He was remembering Jules leaning over Eddie's shoulder; her long blond hair, which shed all over everything, had spilled a little bit across Eddie's shirt.

"Denis. Are you listening? I really think you could do with talking to someone. I meet your mom from time to time, and she tells me that you haven't spoken with anyone since it happened. Is that true?"

"Would you like more tea?" Denis asked. He could fight this to a stalemate if need be.

Ned nodded.

Denis made his way to the kitchen. The Professor stood by the fridge, shaking his head mournfully.

Plasterer blocked his access to the sink.

"Listen up and listen carefully," Plasterer told him. He had fixed his makeup. "He leaves and he leaves now. No arguments. You make him leave."

"I can fight this one myself, Plasterer," Denis assured him. He could feel himself receding. Growing colder, more distant. "It's like Mom. I just withdraw and withdraw. They get the message eventually. Trust me."

His words sounded cold even to himself.

"No. You're not listening," Plasterer said, echoing Ned

Reilly. "If you don't get him out now, I'm going to hurt him, I mean really hurt him. I'm going to go in there and beat him. I'll use the damn lamp, the one with the marble on the bottom. I'll beat the man bloody. I'll bash his fucking head in."

Plasterer's face was contorted, giving him a bizarre look underneath the smiling makeup. "I'll beat him until there's nothing left of him. No one gets to come in here and make me cry. No one. Get him out, or I swear, I'll ruin him for the rest of his life. Do you want that on your conscience? Him and his son? Is that what you want? Get him out. Now."

The last words were snarled at him through clenched teeth.

Get him out. For his own safety. If you don't, the clown will kill him. Maybe us too.

Denis nodded. His hands were still shaking terribly. He realized he was afraid. He had known anxiety and panic, sadness and bitterness for years, but it had been a long time since he'd felt fear like this. It gripped him. This threat was not idle. It was terribly real.

He made his way back into the living room.

"I think it's time you left," he told Ned coldly. He could see the hurt and the disappointment in his best friend's father's eyes. He could only break the hearts of those who loved him most.

"I really think we should talk for a while," Ned replied.

"I think you should get out now. In fact, I'm wondering what you're still doing here since I just told you I would like you out of my house." The words came out of Denis's mouth, but they felt like Plasterer had just said them. A sharp dagger of bitterness and regret stabbed him in his chest. Ned Reilly would never know that Denis was doing this for his own good. He was helping the man. Ned would never know.

"I know it's hard, son," Ned told him, gathering his coat and brushing down the front of his trousers. "But you'll have to deal with it eventually. I'll be here for you if you ever need me."

It was such a beautiful thing to say, all things considered. Denis felt his eyes stinging again at the man's generosity. Ned Reilly was such a good man.

"Get out," he said anyway, despite the kindness. "Now," he added, with a grim finality.

And Ned left.

After he was gone, Plasterer walked into the room. "I didn't want to do that, but it's time you realized that there are certain ways to deal with situations. Let's not have a repeat of this." The clown was practically shaking with the rage.

"I want Rebecca," was all Denis could reply.

"Not for long you don't," Plasterer told him.

TEAR THAT TRICKLES

They sat on the couch. All five of them in a room that seemed to be closing in on him by the moment, the walls shrinking, the roof drooping low over his head. If he stood up, he could have scraped at it with his crown. No one spoke. Penny O'Neill sat to his left, staring straight ahead, eyes fixed on a spot on the wall. She was coiled tight. Plasterer was on his right, lounging in the chair, with his hands folded on his stomach, casting sideways glances at Denis. Beside the clown sat Professor Scorpion, as rigid as Penny O'Neill, eyes staring into the distance. Deano had taken his seat nervously next to Penny, twitching every now and again. If his eyes could be seen, they'd have been seen darting this way and that, looking at nothing in particular, except every now and again throwing a furtive glance at the ceiling. Denis never knew how long they sat there in silence, but it must have been hours. The sun was going down on another disastrous Sunday, and Denis sat waiting for the woman who had made this wreck possible. After Ned had left, they had argued with him.

"It was a trap, don't you see that?" Plasterer had asked him acidly. "You think it's a coincidence that she happened to visit your mom on the day that he calls on you? Don't be so naive."

Denis simply looked at him.

"You shouldn't have let him in," the Professor told him sadly. "From the moment he gained access you validated him. Do you truly believe he'll stop now? He's much akin to her. She won't relent either. They must be excised." His dead, sunken eyes served to make his face seem ever more sad. It was a bitter admission from the corpse.

Denis sat there.

"This is ridiculous. Look what you've done to our lives," Penny O'Neill chimed in. "Look what you've made of us. We were a team. We rowed as one, and we lived comfortably, and then you brought her in here and now look where we're at. Are you proud of yourself? Are you happy with this decision, Denis? Because you're ruining everything that this house represents."

Denis stared at the wall.

Deano shook nervously before doing a little tumble. He banged his head on the coffee table.

Denis just sat there. Every now and again he'd look Plasterer's way to gauge the great clown's reaction. The makeup hid so much; there was no telling what he was thinking. He simply sat there returning each look straight back.

The memory of Ned's face wouldn't leave him alone. It haunted him. The man had reached out, broken as he must surely be from seven years of watching his son live and not live at the same time. He had acted with compassion, and the best that Denis could manage in return was a stinging rebuke and an order to get out of his house. Like the many times that he had refused his own mother a hug, Denis knew that this was breaking the heart of someone who was already heartbroken. He heaped misery on top of misery. He was a walking, talking symbol of everything broken in their lives. A living, breathing representation of everything that they'd lost. They needed him to be better, needed him to lean on, but he didn't need them. He needed order and things to be arranged a certain way and well-pressed trousers. He needed umbrellas in case it rained and teaspoons that were wrapped in serviettes and Plasterer and Deano, the Professor and Penny O'Neill. He did not need Rebecca. He knew in his head that he did not. No one told the rest of him though, because she was all he could think of. He wanted her here. He wanted her to make everything okay. He wanted to swap his housemates for her, but there was no way he could, because he needed them, not her. He needed them to balance him out. He would always need them, as long as he lived in the same universe they did, and as far as Denis Murphy was concerned, he was going to die in that universe. He would live there all his life, and then die there, not in some other universe surrounded by alcohol and T-shirts and pictures of his sister on the wall.

Rebecca did not live in that universe, so why was she here? And why did the thought of her leaving make his stomach knot up? He grimaced at nothing. He started as the rest of them grimaced at the same time. Had he said that out loud? Perhaps they were grimacing just because he was.

Denis counted the tiles that marked the edge of his fireplace. There were sixteen tiles in total. He counted them again. Still sixteen tiles. His housemates sat with him, silently, two on each side. They did not count the tiles, but simply permitted him to do so in peace and quiet. They could have objected; they chose not to.

Sixteen tiles, who fucking cares? Get a grip on yourself, you child.

He counted once more, this time aloud. There were sixteen tiles on the edge of the fireplace. He was still counting out loud about half an hour later when Rebecca arrived home.

"You home?" she called cautiously. Something in her tone gave her away.

"I knew it," whispered Plasterer sharply. "She knew all the time. She knew he was coming. She did this to us, Denis. She did it."

"Shut up," Denis told him. "I'll deal with her."

"Oh yes," Penny O'Neill added sarcastically. "You've done such a wonderful job so far. This can only go well for all of us."

The Professor grunted, but didn't leap to Denis's defense. He stood up, and the others all stood up with him.

"You stay here," he told them.

"Who are you talking to?" Rebecca called.

"No one," Denis replied, closing and locking the door to the office just as she walked into the adjoining kitchen.

"Ned said that you had someone over earlier."

"So you did send him?"

"No. I didn't send him. He wanted to come over, and he asked me if it would be okay. I just got out of his way, that's all. He needed to tell you some things, and you threw him out of the house. Are you happy about that?"

"Ecstatic," he told her flatly. "And since when do you decide who comes and goes from this house? I make those decisions, and it's always no one."

"Do you know how long he's waited to say these things to you? Do you know how many times he's waited for you to speak to him?" she asked, angered by his dismissal.

"Do you know how many years I've lived in peace and quiet until you came along and started manipulating my life?" he shot back.

She scoffed, "Peace and quiet. You live in misery, and don't forget, you're the one who asked me to move in here."

"You practically forced your way in the door," Denis told her incredulously.

"Be that as it may, I'm not prepared to watch you come back to life just to die on me again."

"Don't say things like that," Denis pleaded.

He realized she had very carefully worked the situation around. Now he was pleading with her. He should have been furious. Idly he recalled the Professor asking if she might be a witch.

"Don't tell me what to do," she returned.

She was on the offensive now. This was not going according to plan at all. In his imagination this was a much more decisive victory for him, but he definitely felt like she might have the upper hand in this case.

"I... I have... I have a life." That was better. "And it suits me. I like it that way. We all do."

"We?" she asked. "You think the rest of us like you living your life like this too?"

Denis nearly heaved a sigh of relief. She thought he meant "we" as in him and her and Frank and Ollie. What he had actually meant was "we" as in Plasterer and Penny O'Neill, Deano and the Professor. It was admittedly an easy mistake to make.

"No. It's not that. It's just..." He paused. She gave him a long and steady look. Penny O'Neill had been right to be sarcastic. Rebecca trounced him every time.

"Time out?" he suggested embarrassingly.

"Fine," she told him, turning on her heel, her hair flicking out behind her like the angry lashing of a cat's tail.

He waited until she'd made her way up the stairs and closed her bedroom door before opening the door to the office again.

"Oh bravo." Plasterer applauded sarcastically. "That was marvelously handled. You're truly a genius at the subtle manipulation of the female kind. Please, teach me your ways."

Denis gave him a very unfriendly look.

"Told you that you can't handle it," Penny O'Neill an-

nounced loftily, her tail swinging from side to side. "It's time
you let someone else handle this for you."

"I can do it," the Professor announced, placing one hand
dramatically on his chest. "I know all about the female psyche.
And I know all about how to handle witches. And that one
is most certainly a witch."

"Burn her at the stake?" Plasterer asked bitterly.

"No, no, no," the Professor told him. "I shall woo her."

Denis would have laughed out loud at the idea of a pompous, slowly rotting Professor putting on Ollie's "pulling shirt"
and trying his hand at some pickup lines in a bar. Would have
if he wasn't cornered in his own home. It was then he realized that they were considerably more relaxed than they had
been since Ned Reilly left the house. They were joking, their
fury diminished.

"What's going on?" he asked them suspiciously.

"We have an idea for how you're going to do this," Plasterer
told him with a determined edge to his voice. "And it's always
calming to have a plan. As well you know, Boss."

"What's the plan?" Denis asked.

"We're giving you a timetable. It's how you work. But we
need a little motivation in it too. So it's like this—you have
twenty-four hours to make her leave. If she's not gone by this
time tomorrow, we're going to make her go. Make her like we
made Ned go. And make no mistake about it, Boss, you'll be
the enemy at that point too." Plasterer leaned in threateningly.
His voice was low and even, not the furious hissing, snarling
animal he had been earlier, but he was looming now, a new
kind of threat. "We'll start an attack like you've never seen
before, against her and against you. We'll set fire to things.
We'll go in her room and we'll destroy her personal belongings. We'll go in your room and destroy your stuff. We'll cut
up your ties and piss into your socks. We may even go outside

and take this shit to the neighbors' houses. We will not stop until we've driven her away from you so completely that she'll never want to look at you again." Plasterer smiled smugly. "It's getting to decision time, Boss. It's her or us, and I think you know that you need us an awful lot more than you need her. I'm not sure you'd be alive without us, would you?"

Denis shook his head.

Is that a threat? Is he threatening to kill you?

"Even your pet fur ball and this turncoat—" he gestured at the Professor "—agree with me. We know what's best. And we're watching you, Boss. We're always watching you."

His words rang inside Denis's head like a hammer hitting a bell. Here was what it all came down to. There was no way that the two universes could coexist. He had been stupid, borderline insane, to ever think they could. He was going to have to ask her to leave, ask her to let him have his life back, so he could have his housemates back. The truce wouldn't last forever, and there was no way he could win a war against them. Therein, of course, lay the rub. He couldn't beat them, and he knew this. No one would ever understand him like they did. No one would ever accept him like they did. They didn't just endure his idiosyncrasies, they encouraged him. They let him be himself in a way that no other person in the world ever would. His mother wanted him to do things he couldn't, his ex-girlfriend only saw the Denis from the other universe, his friends routinely played pranks to expose the hilarity of what he was to them: a joke. A shade of someone they once knew. A clown to be laughed at. Their own pet weirdo. Only his housemates would ever truly love him for who he was. Yet they also knew his every weakness. They knew when he was isolated, when he was vulnerable. Six years of living with one another gave them all the tactical advantage, and in the pit of his stomach he knew that he couldn't match them for ferocity.

The flip side of this was what Rebecca saw in him; she saw the alternate universe Denis Murphy, she saw his potential to be great again. To be loved by people and admired by strangers, to have that easy way that helped him to succeed at almost everything he put his hand to. She saw his ability to be whatever he chose, not what the world had made him. She saw something great inside him and she, with gentle hands, was coaxing it slowly from its hole.

And so he would have to decide.

They had stayed true to Plasterer's word. They were always watching. As Denis struggled to think of a way to end his awkwardness with Rebecca, they watched. As he pottered about the kitchen hunting for grime and scrubbing at nonexistent stains, they stood at his shoulder. When he went to the bathroom, they stood outside, and as he opened the door, they were waiting. He made tea and they watched. They never said a thing as he fixed a cup for Rebecca. She was in her bedroom, playing her guitar as he stood outside her door with a teacup; they were standing on the landing, the four of them. Watching him. They ducked against the wall when she opened the door, out of her line of sight, but still in his.

"What do you want?" she asked brusquely. She was more than able to drive home her irritation. He felt hugely aggrieved that he was offering her apologies, but he had to get her back onside. He didn't want to ask her to leave while they were fighting. He wasn't sure if he wanted to ask her to leave at all.

"Truce?" he asked plaintively.

"Are you sorry?"

"Absolutely," he lied. How had she managed to make this his fault again?

"Okay," she said, smiling. "Truce it is. I'm sorry too. I know how you feel about visitors, it's just that you've been different lately, and we kissed last night and then I come home and you're all extra-Denis."

He smiled. Extra-Denis. He had been a little extra-Denis today. He was beginning to hate Sundays.

"Tea?" he asked, thrusting the cup at her to cover the awkward moment. He'd actually forgotten about the kiss. No wonder she was mad. It had been a long time since he'd kissed those lips, and now his memory of their latest kiss was blurred by alcohol. Thankfully, the worst of his hangover had passed. The sick feeling in his stomach had a new cause now. He swallowed as he led her downstairs to kick her out of his home.

Don't do this. Don't you dare… Not now, not when you're so close. And then he didn't tell her.

Good. Please see that this is a good thing. Now is your moment. Now is the time to grow. To be better. Please get better.

Instead, they sat at the kitchen table and talked as if nothing had happened; there was no mention of Ned Reilly, no talk of the kiss, nothing said of the dancing or any of the nonsense he'd spoken when he was drunk. They just chatted about various things. Several times during the conversation he imagined he saw an opening to tell her, but each time he lost his nerve or got distracted by something. He realized he was famished. He hadn't eaten all day; he'd been too sick, and now, with evening on them, it was far too late for a dinner. Far too late unless Rebecca Lynch was in your life, in which case, dinner could be at whatever hour she chose.

"Let me make us something to eat. You go watch cop shows, and I'll work on dinner."

"It's nearly nine o'clock. You want to eat dinner at nine in the evening?"

She smiled at him and nodded. The Professor was right. She was unrelentingly stubborn. He decided to let it pass and watch some television. As he got up to walk to the living room, he saw them standing in a shadow in the hallway. All four of them. If you weren't looking for them, you'd miss them, slightly obscured as they were, but definitely there, and they were watching her. Not him. He closed the door on them and moved to the living room.

The wonderful thing about owning a television is its capacity for absolute brainlessness. When one is in possession of a brain that works as hard as Denis Murphy's does, then one needs to find the ways and means of cutting off its circulation from time to time, numbing it. One could forget that one's house has been invaded when television is doing the thinking for you. Menacing clowns and depressed zombies are all well and good, but they're no match for Emily Deschanel playing a socially awkward genius.

Denis watched *Law and Order* and *Bones*, and marveled at how crafty the bad guys could be, but how the good guy, through hard work and taking the road that isn't always the easiest, could win out in the end. His brain went into standby mode, and he ignored the fact that four faces were pressed against the rear window of the house, looking in at him. He'd never seen them go outside the front door before. He'd always accepted that they liked being inside, and tolerated them for who they were. He would normally have paid it more attention, but the shining sedative in the corner was relaxing him. He didn't even mind the ads, which normally he objected to on the grounds that they offended his principles. They offered perfect lives in exchange for money. Denis blamed advertising for a lot of his worries. In an advertising-free universe, people wouldn't know what happiness looked like, and then they wouldn't think him unhappy just because he didn't behave like they did. It never occurred to Denis that he was stalling. It never occurred to Denis when he was avoiding something difficult. It hadn't for nearly seven years now.

Seven years of avoiding… You're an expert.

The smells from the kitchen snapped him from his reverie. He had never known Rebecca to cook anything, but the smell was wonderful. His stomach rumbled loudly. He had to take a look. While waiting for the meal to cook, Rebecca had also used his downtime as an opportunity to put on a dress and fix her hair up. She looked stunning. Denis stood with his mouth open. She had lit candles and poured wine. His kitchen had been transformed from a simple utility area where he performed basic domestic functions to a romantic scene lifted straight from some kind of Hollywood feel-good rom-com.

"Close your mouth, you'll catch flies," she told him with another victory smile.

"Sorry, it's just… You look stunning. Again." He was blushing, and he knew it.

"Sit down," she said, gesturing to his chair. "Chicken-and-leek Stroganoff, with rice, and some naan bread. I used to make it in Australia. A friend of mine was a chef."

Denis could only smile, although he felt somewhat disconcerted. He had always been proud of the fact that he did all the cooking, thinking that it was a skill he had to offer her. She had obviously enjoyed the fact that he liked cooking for her, and left him to it. And now this.

The romance was marred only by the fact that Rebecca had at some point opened the door, and sitting down, she placed herself with her back to the hallway. Four figures shuffled in and stood watching. Plasterer had his arms folded and regarded Denis with only the slightest nod. Penny O'Neill and the Professor stood behind either of his burly shoulders, both shaking their heads slightly. One in bitter disappointment, the other in a resigned sadness. Deano stood apart from them. Denis had a nagging feeling that this meant something, but he was distracted by a curl of hair that fell across one of Rebecca's exposed shoulders. He leaned over and brushed it back behind her ear. She smiled beautifully. Plasterer bunched his fists angrily in the hallway.

"So…" she asked him coyly as they prepared to tuck in. "How much about last night do you remember?"

"Enough," he told her, smiling.

"The dancing?"

"Obviously," he replied, blushing a little more.

"You realize you used to be able to dance, but now you move like a robot."

"Come on," he said, feigning offense. "I've still got some moves."

"Ha. I'm not so sure, Denny," she replied.

"Don't call me that," he told her absently. She was goading him. Later on she'd try again, and talk him into a dance. He figured that's where this line of conversation was going.

"You know, if you want another dance, all you have to do is ask. I have the entire Eels back catalog."

She laughed, and the sound of it made his heart beat quicker.

"You used to listen to them all day," she recalled with a smile. "And gangster rap, which you absolutely cannot pull off."

"Yeah, right," he replied mockingly. "I'll have you know I'd make an excellent gangster."

Plasterer raised an eyebrow from the hallway. He held his silence.

They ate quietly for a while, but it was clear to Denis that there was something she was waiting for, something she was holding back.

"Ask it," he told her after a while of watching her struggle.

"You know me too well." She smiled ruefully.

He nodded and waited while she hesitated again, pushing some of the food around her plate with her fork.

"Why do you want to be lonely so badly?" she finally said.

The question took him by surprise. He wasn't lonely, but she didn't know that he had four housemates before her, and would have when she was gone.

"I don't," he almost whispered.

"You block everyone out," she pressed.

"I know," he said, and started at his own voice. Had those words really come out of his mouth? Now Plasterer was shaking his head. His fists still bunched in frustration.

"Sometimes I think you're letting me in, and then just when I think I'm understanding you, I'm outside again, looking in at you, and you seem so unbearably lonely."

"I'm fine," he said, trying to assert himself. A strange voice in his head seemed to whisper, *No, you're not,* but he ignored it.

"See, right now, you're doing it again. Sometimes you're so honest, and sometimes you just lie for the sake of it. I can stand the obsessive behavior, I can put up with the fear of shops and yellow T-shirts, but I can't bear to hear you lie to me, and to yourself. It's like you've been doing it for so long you don't even know it, except sometimes I think you do."

"What do you want me to do?" he asked.

"Let me in," she replied, leaning forward intently.

"Do you remember the last day you saw me before you left?" he asked her suddenly.

"Yes," she replied, waiting.

"I wanted to let you in. Really, I did. I couldn't though. I couldn't do anything. It's like a weight inside your head. It keeps you stuck to the same place, and sometimes you can move around with it but you feel slow and sluggish. Some days you can't move at all, or you can't get out of bed, because this weight in your head, it just takes everything you have to keep breathing, to keep wanting to breathe." He told her all this in a quiet, dispassionate voice.

She nodded and her eyes glistened.

"It was all I could do just to sit there crying," he continued. "Every day, it took everything I had to get up, and some days I failed and just slept all day. I'd wake for an hour or two at a time, but I couldn't get up, so I'd stare at the walls. I cleaned my room from time to time, just so I could feel like I had succeeded at something. Then you were there, banging on the glass door. You wanted to come in, but if I let you, I would have had to talk to you, and tell you things and comfort you, and I just couldn't. I know it's selfish—that's who I am now. There are some things that I just can't do, and it usually involves people. I can't handle people anymore. I hate them. They hate me back. I have so few people left, and sometimes I wonder if I'd miss any of them if they all left. I think I'd be okay with it. I worry every day that if everyone left me, I'd be totally okay with that."

There were tears now, but she held them back bravely. So many tears in such a short few weeks. Denis had none left, but it seemed everyone else had oceans of them.

That's good though. Better than ever before. Well done. I'm… I'm proud of you.

"Do you still want me to let you in?" he asked.

"Yes," she said, nodding, wiping her button nose on a handkerchief.

He sighed, suddenly exhausted. She didn't know he was going to ask her to move out tomorrow. He was going to make her leave. The thought caused a lump in his stomach.

"Tell me about the people you have left. Tell me why they're still here."

He smiled in spite of himself. "They're still here because they don't give up. Mom, Ollie, Frank, even Thomas. And now you. Sooner or later, you're all going to have to give up."

"Who's Thomas?" she asked curiously, wiping away the remaining tears.

And so he told her about Thomas, and his constant high-five attempts. His relentless need to put his hand against Denis's hand seemed to represent everything about Denis Murphy and all the people in the other universe. They pushed and intruded; he politely declined. The back-and-forth of constant battle that made up his day. He talked about the coffee shops and the newspapers and his fear that every person he encountered must think him the strangest creature they ever saw, and he despised that about them. Despised the curious looks and the pity, despised the knowing glances and the fake half smiles. He told her about his life now. His universe. Everything except his housemates, who he left out. They stood behind her, watching him, watching her.

He talked to her while mostly looking at them, only glancing back into her eyes every now and then until eventually he just ran out of words. Then there was silence, the words gone.

"Can we have that dance now?" she asked after he went quiet.

"Yes," he told her. This time he wasn't even drunk, but he didn't care. Tomorrow he'd be kicking her out of his house, and possibly out of his life, so tonight, he would take what she would give. He didn't play the Eels this time; he played Bell X1 and they danced around and around in a very small circle, his hand resting on the small of her back, his other hand holding hers. He couldn't stop staring at it, her fingers entwined in his. Her breasts were pressing against his chest as he held her, and her head was tilted to the side to rest against his. His housemates had left the hallway in disgust, but back in a dark corner by the door he could make out the furry shape of Deano, hunkered down watching it all. He thought the fur ball approved, though he couldn't tell why.

"I was lying earlier," she told him quietly. "You dance beautifully. I've missed it."

"I missed you too," he said.

"I'd like a kiss now," she said, tilting her head up at him.

He looked into her brown eyes and smiled at her. For a minute or two he held back; he wanted to kiss her, but he didn't want the moment to end, both of them dancing by candlelight in his kitchen while the music played from the living room. It was a moment to savor, and he rolled it around inside his head and let it wash over him. But he knew she would only wait for so long. Rebecca Lynch most frequently got what she wanted. She leaned in, and he answered her invite.

When their tongues met, it was a journey back to a thousand kisses before, in the other universe. In bed, on dance floors, in the car, in the park, on the grass, standing at the stove, standing at the sink, on the couch, by the sea, so many kisses shared. They ran through his head in a flicker of memory like subliminal messages, and his hands answered the call, one of them cupping her chin, the other sliding up her back to the clasp of her dress. She pushed back gently and looked him in the eye. There was none of the usual twinkle of humor there; instead there was a question. Silently she asked him if he was sure. He returned her look, silently telling her that he was. She eventually turned and led him from the room, holding his hand, up the stairs and into his bedroom.

They kissed again, this time it was not a gentle kiss, but a kiss filled with need. It was almost forgotten; the kiss stirred something that had been dormant in him for so long, and he found himself remembering desire. Her dress couldn't be taken off fast enough; he fumbled with the clasp a little, and she giggled, almost nervously as she calmly opened his belt. The kiss became more passionate; his hands were practically clawing at her now, and she wasn't laughing but gasping at each opening, her hands pulling at his tie and shirt. They fell onto the bed, naked, and what little capacity for thought was obliterated. In this moment there was no Denis, there were no housemates, there was no dead sister, no dying friend, no Ned, no Mom, no Frank or Ollie. They were two, and they were becoming one.

It was hours before Denis woke. She was sitting at the end of his bed, still naked but with a small blanket pulled around her. She had opened the curtains on one of the two windows in his room, and moonlight spilled in.

"You okay?" he asked softly.

"Yeah," she told him, turning and smiling. Her smile lit up her face like he'd never seen before. He drank her in, the desire to hold her again growing.

"You still snore like a champion," she told him, laughing. "And you still have some of those moves you were talking about earlier too," she added archly.

"Get back over here," he ordered jokingly. And she did.

They made love again, this time more slowly, each movement between them gentle and considered. Afterward, she rested her head on his chest, kissing him every now and again.

"Did they hurt?" she asked sleepily, tracing the scars that ran across his chest and down over his stomach.

"They hurt me every day," he replied, stroking her hair. He lay there, holding her and staring at the ceiling.

"Elephant shoe," he told her, but she was already asleep.

CAN'T GET ENOUGH

*S**tay calm now, this is not the end of the world.*
For the second day in a row, Denis Murphy didn't wake to the steady tones of his own alarm. He was slightly distressed, but he drew in a steady breath and let the panic roll over him until it began to pass, as he knew it eventually would. When you are a connoisseur of panic, you learn to know such things. It was Rebecca's alarm that woke him, blaring out some ridiculous hip-hop anthem from her phone. Rebecca groaned in the bed, rolled over, tapped without looking on the screen until it went quiet and rolled back into him. She rested her head on his chest and sighed. He drew a deep breath and calmed himself again. Her head felt nice resting on him; it was worth the momentary flinch and the sensation that he was unclean. This feeling also passed.

"Morning," she murmured sleepily.

"Good morning," he whispered back, tentatively reaching out a hand to stroke her bare shoulder. He ignored the silent scream inside his head to stop and instead drew her closer to him.

"Your snoring sounds like someone ripping bedsheets,"

she told him, her fingers once again caressing the scars across his chest.

"You hog the quilt," he retorted playfully. "And you grip it like a vise. I had to practically drag it off you."

"I get cold," she said defensively.

"Me too," he told her. "Thankfully you're half a hot-water bottle."

She laughed softly.

"Do you have to go to work?" he asked.

"Yes. I'd love to stay here, but I'm not about to call in sick to a job I only started a few weeks ago. You stay in bed, wait for me. When I get back we'll order Chinese and download some old '90s cartoons and just relax for the night."

He smiled at her. There were times in his life when his mouth seemed to act independently of his brain, shooting out suggestions and declarations that led to anxiety and panic attacks. Before the previous night, his asking her to stay in bed with him all day may have provoked just such an attack, but today it caused a mere moment of trepidation. He felt the pang of regret when she said no, not the relief he expected to feel.

"There's that smile," she told him, reaching one hand up to brush his cheek. He was powerless against her, he knew that now, but he didn't mind.

She showered and dressed, planted a lingering kiss on his lips and left for work. Denis sighed contentedly and basked in the moment. A moment of freedom that was barely tinged with his usual fears and worries. He soaked it in for as long as he could, but such moments are glorious, and if milked for too long, can end up turning quite sour. He decided not to let that happen and bounced from his bed to shower.

He dripped on the tiles of the bathroom as he stepped out of the shower, the water making pools that ran together and collided into new shapes and islands in reverse. He looked at them for such a long time, waiting for the moment when they upset him to the point that he would have to mop them. The moment never came. He hummed a Barenaked Ladies song to himself as he brushed his teeth. He was careful not to let any spittle hit the mirror, or miss the sink, but he didn't count the brushstrokes like he normally would. This seemed to liberate him further, and he whistled while he dressed. He briefly worried about whether or not his whistling would wake his housemates, but that concern passed too, and he went about his morning at a pace that would have frightened him at any other time in the last six years. A leisurely pace. He practically sauntered into his kitchen. Denis fantasized that if there had been anyone else present in his house to see him, they would have thought how relaxed and casual he looked. As though he hadn't a care in the world. He made breakfast, carefully avoiding making any mess, but he didn't measure the cereal before he poured it into the bowl. Instead, like a rebel who refused to bend to authority, he just emptied in the amount of cereal that he felt like eating. It tinkled merrily as it hit the bowl, a little melody of congratulations for him.

He considered waking his housemates but decided against it. There would be time enough for that showdown later on. They were expecting him to kick her out today; what a surprise they were in for. Their war was over. He owned the house. They would be told, in no uncertain terms, that Rebecca Lynch wasn't going anywhere. He imagined the look on Plasterer's face when he told him. In his mind's eye, he played out the conversation.

"Plasterer," he would tell the clown. "It's time you learned to live with her or move on, because I'm the boss. I'm the captain of our ship. You're my troops and, dammit, you will obey orders."

Plasterer would cower at his confidence and authority.

He set about his work for the day. He played music as he worked—the band Fred. It was half-past ten when the phone rang. He looked at it, a sense of unease grabbing him by the belly and the throat all at once. Not enough to panic, just enough to make him tense. It rang and rang. He refused to answer it. Frank was calling him. Why would Frank be calling him?

The call went unanswered.

Then it started to ring again.

"Answer it," Plasterer told him from the door of the office.

"What?" Denis asked, his confidence emptying from him like water from a bucket.

"Answer the phone, Denis," Plasterer ordered implacably.

"I don't feel like it," he replied, trying to reassert his sense of authority.

"Answer the phone now, Denis," he was told.

It was still ringing. The sound of it seemed to scream into his brain.

"Hello…?" he finally said, punching the button to take the call.

"Denis?" Frank asked. His voice sounded thick. Something was wrong.

"What is it?" he asked, frightened.

"I'm sorry, Denis, I'm so, so sorry." A sob escaped his friend.

"Frank… What? What is it? You have to tell me what it is? What did I do? Who did I hurt?"

"You didn't do this, buddy, this isn't your fault. I'm sorry. They pulled the plug this morning. They've been preparing for so long. I'm sorry, Denny."

"Pulled what plug?" he demanded, but he already knew.

"Denny, you have to listen, this isn't your fault. I'm so sorry. Eddie died this morning."

Denis began shaking. His stomach convulsed. The phone

dropped to the soft carpet and bounced. His knees were hopping up and down. He grabbed at them with his hands to stop
them and found himself rocking back and forth on the seat.

"Denis? Talk to me, Denis…" The voice coming from the
phone on the floor seemed so very far away.

Eddie had been laughing. He'd held Jules's hand tenderly as
she reached around the passenger seat to hug him. He used to
bring purple flowers to their house. Denis mocked him every
time. Kiss ass he used to call him. He brought those purple
flowers to the hospital.

"Denis, please," the voice on the phone said. "It's not your
fault. You have to talk to me, Denny."

This was why Ned had stopped by the previous day. He
had come to tell him. Denis had kicked him out of the house
before he could.

Plasterer sauntered across the room just like Denis had earlier that morning. If anyone else had been present, they would
have thought that the clown didn't have a care in the world.
He reached down to the floor and picked up the phone.

"Denis doesn't feel like talking," he said into the handset.

"What? Denis, look you have to talk," he could hear Frank
reply.

"Go away. Leave us alone," was all the clown said, and he
cut off the call.

Denis's whole body was still shaking. Something was building inside him, something huge and monstrous. Something
unstoppable.

"Did you think it was going to be so easy?" It was Penny
O'Neill's voice. "Did you think you could kill two people
and it would just go away because you talked some woman
into your bed? Is that what you thought?"

"Eddie…" Denis tried to say.

"You're a breaker of families. A ruiner of lives. You think

there's comfort for you?" This time Penny and Plasterer were speaking in unison, their voices mixing into one, slamming into his head, each word a battering ram that tore at his ability to think.

"What are you going to do now, Denny?" Plasterer asked him, his voice like acid.

"I don't know. I don't know. I don't know," he replied. He was still shaking. The room was spinning.

"Clean the kitchen," Plasterer ordered him.

"It's not dirty," he heard himself replying.

"Dirty it then."

Denis found his feet; they seemed to reel underneath him. Eddie used to nudge the back of Denis's pool cue when he walked by during games to give himself an edge. Denis used to poke him with the cue when he tried it. Both of them would laugh. He walked into the kitchen and took the cereal boxes. He opened them and emptied the contents on the floor; the sound they made this time was a rushing sound, like a waterfall. He got lost in it for just a moment. It seemed to roar in his ears.

Eddie used to go to soccer matches with him. He had no idea about the game itself; he went purely as company. He'd shout, "Go team," and "Yay sports," to mock Denis's love of the game. It was playful ribbing among friends. Ollie and Frank would go too. Afterward they would head to a bar and drink pints of Guinness and play pool. No girls allowed on these nights; it was just for the four boys. Jules and Rebecca would object to being excluded. Denis would hug them both and go anyway. Denis tore out the contents of one of the cupboards and then sat on the floor, opening sachets individually to empty them. Tearing at the lids of salt-and-pepper canisters with fingers like claws. The Professor sat with him. For just a minute his face was Eddie's face, but then the moment was gone. The Professor was not his usual pompous self. There was a sinister quality to him in that moment, a brooding menace that seemed to make him seem larger than normal.

"Where did you go, Denis? Why did you have to stop visiting him?" The Professor almost sobbed for him. His words cut into Denis's brain.

"I don't know," Denis replied, his eyes leaking bitterly. "I promise I'll visit now. Every day. I'll visit every day."

"Sure you will," Penny O'Neill interjected sarcastically. "Just like you visit Jules every day. Your own sister, Denis. Your mother goes once a week. She brings purple flowers, doesn't she? You sit here instead."

Denis climbed to his feet and began emptying out the cleaning products. He poured them into the sink, making a cocktail of sharp-smelling foulness. He took the dishcloths and dipped them into it. He flung the cloths against the walls of the kitchen. He had seen his housemates at their most destructive; he knew exactly how to make a mess, a mess that would take him hours to clean. He had learned from the best.

The house he had shared with Eddie and Frank and Ollie had frequently been a mess, and so, more often than not, they would hang out in Rebecca and Jules's house. When they did clean, it was to loud music and it would be a pretty slapdash job. Eddie would choose the music, and more than anyone else, he hated cleaning.

He stopped and looked around to survey the damage.

"Keep going," Plasterer told him. In the doorway, Penny O'Neill and Deano watched. The Professor was still sitting in the mess on the floor.

He pushed on. He took the bag from the vacuum cleaner and emptied it on the already ruined floor. He began to boil water in all the pots, allowing them to overflow and burn the top of the stove, bubbling and hissing at him as he walked tracks through the filth. His eyes stung all the way through his tasks. Plasterer watched from the door into the hallway, Penny O'Neill and Deano from the door into the living room. The Professor helped him with his work. The floors, the walls, the ceiling, each was destroyed. His cupboards emptied of everything. His feet still felt shaky. His shoes were beginning to crush him, so he took them off and stood barefoot, with water leaking from his eyes, down his cheeks and onto the floor while the others just watched him. Soon it would be time to clean up, but just like that, all the energy went from him, and he sat down in the mess and filth he had just created and buried his head in his hands.

With his eyes closed, his imagination went into overdrive and a thousand memories burst from the depths of his mind like an avalanche that would sweep him under entirely. Eddie playing pool, holding hands with Jules, smoking a cigarette out the passenger window of the car. Eddie studying in the library, throwing a Frisbee, pulling out a seat to let Jules sit down. Eddie's mangled and crumpled body with the oxygen mask being fitted to it. Blood all over his T-shirt. His cigarette had burned a scar into his hand. It was distinguishable, somehow, from the mess that was the rest of him. Eddie lying in his hospital bed with the machines beep, beep, beeping throughout the room. Eddie's hand, being held by his mother, Ann, as he lay in the bed. For almost seven years.

His thoughts snowballed and started a second avalanche on a nearby mountain of memories. Suddenly it was Jules in his head. Jules as a little girl when he had to walk her to school. Jules in her school graduation dress. Jules and Eddie curled up on the couch watching movies. Jules's seat at the table for Sunday dinner, opposite his. Jules and Rebecca whispering and throwing looks at him and Eddie with half smiles. Jules's determined face when she insisted on sibling bonding time even though Denis wanted to watch soccer.

Now he imagined Eddie, with skin that looked like plastic. Like some life-size doll, lying in a coffin. No smile. No smirk. No clever retort or witty banter. Denis had killed his friend, just like he had killed his sister. It took him seven years to die, but time was irrelevant. The sense of utter helplessness overwhelmed Denis, and he screamed like an animal, his fists beating on the floor and splattering the walls with the mess that was all around him. He screamed until there were no screams left. He sat there in silence. His housemates had left. He was all alone.

It could have been minutes or hours from the time he sat down alone to the time that they returned. Without a to-do list, without a frame of reference for the execution of daily duties, there was little that Denis could use to tell the passage of time. The Professor had a watch, but he had made it himself out of cardboard, so it was hard to know how accurate it was at any time of the day.

"Would you have me assist you in the cleaning?" the Professor asked sympathetically as he surveyed the damage.

"Do you know how?" Denis replied glumly.

"I am an encyclopedia of knowledge, Denis. Let us dump it all in the bin."

"Sure," Denis told him. "Dump everything. Dump everyone. It's easier than sorting it all out."

"She'll return as soon as she finds out. You are aware of this, aren't you?" the Professor asked.

"Finds out what?" he asked, confused.

"When they tell her about Eddie. She knows this will have a tremendous impact on you, and she'll come home posthaste to address your issues and fix you all over again. You know how much she enjoys such things."

"I need to be fixed," he replied.

"No, you don't. You're not broken. Everyone else is broken. The sooner you remember that, the better. Do you remember what it was like before she came back? We were happy, Denis, all of us together. No one made us feel like we were broken. I fear that her presence has upset this. I am loath to agree with our aggressive friend out there, but she has changed you, and you must repair the past."

"But I'm so lonely…" The words came out of his mouth, and he knew that he meant them, but he couldn't recall ever thinking that before.

"You have us for that. That's why we're all friends."

"Plasterer isn't my friend anymore. I don't think Penny is either."

"They're just angry because you're turning your back on everything you believe in. Look at what she's made you do. Look at the mess you're sitting in. This is her fault, you know. With her hot yoga and her book clubs. She believes this is all going her way, that somehow she's in control of you, but she's really stripping you down and cracking you open, I regret to tell you. She's taking away a part of who you are. What will be left when she's taken it all?"

"She's my friend. I don't want her to leave."

A key turned in the door. The Professor's head whipped around at the sound. He gave Denis one quick severe look before he dodged out the door into the utility room, suddenly nimble where he had shambled before. Denis didn't move. He sat in the filth he had made and waited for her to see him. This was what he wanted her to see, not the covered-up version of his life that he'd been living with her, but the reality of who he was. The cleanliness, the order, the need for control. Now she'd truly understand. Now she'd see him for who he really was.

She walked into the kitchen and took in the entire scene in a single glance. She barely paused before walking to him and sitting down at his side.

"I'm so, so sorry, Denis. I'm so very terribly sorry."

Her eyes were puffy and red, her mascara a mess from the tears.

"I killed them both," was all Denis could manage to say.

"You didn't kill him, Denis, you didn't. Don't you understand? Ned was here yesterday to tell you that you didn't. To let you know that no one blames you for what happened. It's nobody's fault. Accidents happen."

"When you kill your sister and your best friend, that's something different. That's not an accident."

"What is it, then? What do you think it is?"

"Murder."

"Denis you can't go on like this. Look around you. Look what you did…"

Her words so closely mirrored the Professor's that it forced a bitter laugh from him. *Look what "you" did*, she said. *Look what "she" made you do*, was what the Professor had said. Who's to blame? In all things in life there must be responsibility. Was it hers or his?

"What's so funny?" she asked him angrily.

"Nothing. Everything. This is me, Rebecca. This is the reality of life for me. A mess, then order. Why won't you understand me?"

A silent voice in his head disagreed. *She's the only one who understands you*, it seemed to say. Denis was a mess because of all the voices, all the different opinions, all the perspectives that weren't his own. He didn't know what his own perspective was. Do this, do that, be this, not that, it was a cacophony he couldn't escape.

"It's not you," Rebecca disagreed, a hard edge to her voice.

"This is something else. It's the you that you've made up. You made it up to hide from the world, but you can't hide forever. Eventually you'll have to face it, Denis. Face your problems like a man. Stop hiding like a child."

Her words had the effect of a hammer, smashing his attempts to rationalize.

"I slapped her hand, you see…" he started. Then stopped.

"Tell me," she said. Her tone brooked no argument.

"I can't," he replied.

"Tell me," she said again. Harder this time.

"You don't understand. I can't. I can't tell anyone."

She didn't say anything, but her hand gripped his arm, vise-like. The message was clear.

"Jules reached out from the passenger seat. She used to sit forward in the middle of the back seat so her head would be popping in between ours. She had one hand over his shoulder, and I slapped it. I didn't do it hard. I just did it as a joke. And they laughed. And then they were screaming. I didn't look, Rebecca. I was somewhere else when I should have been there." The words came out in a rush. The police investigation into the crash had apportioned no blame, and Denis had been allowed to leave the station with only commiserations from the officers. He hadn't been able to tell them what happened. He told them he didn't remember, but he did. It was a terrible lie. The lie of his life, and the lie of their deaths.

"Were you drunk?" Rebecca whispered.

"No. Yes. Sort of," he replied. "I had two drinks, but it was hours before I got into the car. I just stopped paying attention. They were laughing. So was I. We were listening to something on the stereo. I don't remember what it was." His throat was sore. Tight.

"I slapped her hand, and then we hit it, and when we did everything slowed down. The car seemed to just crumple, and

Eddie was looking at me. He was looking right at me. Jules went by us both and into the windshield. The side of the car hugged Eddie, it just seemed to form up all around him, bits of metal and glass and Eddie. They all merged into one. Then I was asleep. I just slept, and in the background, the screams. They screamed and screamed, and I couldn't. I woke up, and all I could feel was warm. Jules was broken, she was just lying on the ground, broken. And the other driver was trying to help her. He was screaming too. Eddie wasn't screaming any-more. He was silent. His last words were a scream, and then he never made a noise ever again."

He drew a breath. She was still holding his arm, but not so tightly now, and her face was just like his mother's, a picture of pity and sorrow. He hated other people's pity.

"Go on," she whispered.

"They told me it would get better. Time would make it okay. You were there when they told me that. In the hospi-tal, while they checked on all my cuts. Nurses would rub my head with all their pity, and Mom would try to hold my hand. They were wrong though. I stopped being hungry. I forgot about eating. Then he killed himself. Like it was his fault. I was the one who wasn't paying attention, but still he killed him-self. And I was still alive. I killed my sister, and I killed him for driving his own truck. Didn't even go to their funerals. I was in the hospital. I sat in a hospital bed on my own while my parents and all my friends buried my sister. When they let me go home, everything was Jules. Everything was hers. My whole house was Jules and Eddie. My mother cried every day, and I couldn't. I had no tears. I don't know why I didn't. I just couldn't cry. Dad got angry at first. He used to make me get out of bed even though I didn't want to. He would force me and shout at me. When I wouldn't eat, he'd grab me by the jaw and try to make me. His hands hurt me, crushed me.

He had all these tears in his eyes. He'd scream and roar and shout and kick things in my room, but all I could see was his nose. It was the same as Jules's nose. She was his favorite, she always had been. Ned and Ann brought those purple flowers. Ned looks so much like Eddie. He would hug Mom and they'd cry. So many tears. All the time. And as good as none from me. It got so bad I couldn't look at anyone. You were always crying too." He looked at her as he said it. She was crying again. Fat, glistening tears rolled down her cheeks, just like they had rolled down Plasterer's the day before. He made the whole world cry. It was his great gift. Pain. For everyone.

"Go on," she said again, sniffling.

He had come this far. Further than he'd ever gone before. He wasn't about to stop now.

"Then Dad left. He took his things and went. I think he still talks to Mom, but I've never heard from him since. I try not to think about it, but you can't really blame him, can you? His murderer son kills the daughter he loves best, and then his home feels like a tomb, so he leaves. He really did always prefer her. I feel like I killed him too. It's like he's not with us anymore. Then Mom started needing me, and I couldn't be what she wanted. She wanted me back, but I was gone. I was in between places. I was slipping through the cracks. I didn't really exist. Then you were gone. You stood for hours at my door, just knocking on it and looking so sad. I couldn't look at how sad you were. I couldn't stand looking at how sad everyone was. I brought everyone pain. I killed everything. Jules, Eddie, Mom, Dad, Ned, Ann, him and his truck. He had a family too. So I broke them, as well. And you. How could I have broken you? How could I have done it?"

She swung her arms around his shoulders. That's when he realized he was crying. His body shook with the tears. Floods from his eyes. He wept like he had never wept before. He thought there were no tears left, but he was wrong. There were so many more tears.

"I'm sorry," he wailed. "I'm sorry. Eddie... Jules. Rick. Poor Rick, I killed him too. I killed him by slapping her hand. He didn't do anything, and then I killed him. Just a man driving a truck one day, and then he's gone. His family. His poor family. See what I do?"

She was talking to him, but he couldn't make out her words. They seemed to be coming at him through the fog of tears and anger and bitterness; the sound couldn't make it through, so he just kept crying. So many lives ruined. Ruined by him. Penny O'Neill had called him a breaker of families. She was not wrong.

"They promised me it would get better with time, but it never did. I just learned to live with it. I just bring it with me everywhere. I have to. I keep it here at home, and I try not to take it out of the house, but sometimes it just goes with me." The words came through clenched teeth and in between sobs.

"I've found a way to live with it. I just have to make sure I own it. I have to make sure I own everything around me. I can't get rid of it. I got out of the cracks in between life. When I realized it, I was here, in this universe, where I can control things. It's the only way I can live. I have to have it. As long as I have to bring it with me, I need to find a way to control it. So I do."

His face hurt from crying.

"You can't do it alone, Denis. Why won't you see that? It's too much for one person. That's what friends are for." Her words came through shuddering breaths.

"I have friends," he told her, looking at her through blurry eyes. "They help me. They understand me. They live in this universe too. They realize what I need, and they give it to me."

"Frank and Ollie?" she asked, the surprise cutting through her crying.

"No. Different friends. You've never met them."

"Denis, I've been here for weeks. I know that you have no one. I've seen you. You're like a ghost, Denis, sometimes you barely exist. I can't explain it, but I can help. I swear. I want to help."

She was doing exactly what they warned him she'd do. She was trying to fix him. She wanted him changed. It floated there between them for a few minutes while he calmed his erratic breathing. So much had just poured out of him, things that he had kept to himself for years and years. The knowledge of what he had done. He wore it like a cloak. He slept in it. He ate in it. He worked in it, and now he was giving it all away. He had given so much of it to her, he felt lighter, like he could float outside his own head and watch himself sitting in the filth of his kitchen floor, with her arms around him. Years and years of wearing his new life like a second skin, and now he was shrugging it off. All because she wouldn't let him hurt anymore. She was refusing to let him hurt. The dam burst all over again and he cried anew, but this time it was a quiet, regretful stream of tears, not the angry river from before. Tears for Eddie now, not for himself. Tears for the life his friend has missed. Her voice reached him again through his fog of regret.

"It's okay," she was saying. "It's going to be okay. I'm here. It's going to be okay."

He believed her.

He was wrong.

IN THE PANTOMIME

The days when Denis Murphy woke without some sense of trepidation about the day ahead were few and far between. The morning after he had cried all night and fell asleep sobbing while his ex-girlfriend whispered to him like he was a small child turned out to be no different. It was a sad fact of Denis Murphy's life that trepidation about the day ahead was a normal occurrence. It was also a fact of life for the thirty-year-old that no sense of anything came without a war, from a sense of something else. Every thought and feeling immediately fought for a place in Denis's consciousness with a variety of other emotions and ideas. Sometimes just thinking was a struggle. For example, on the morning after he cried like a small child, there was nervousness, uncertainty, a low-key alarm about what the ramifications of his actions would be; there was also a sense of wonder and freedom. He pictured Eddie in his old hospital bed, and found he could think of the man without the bitter sense of recrimination and self-loathing that had come with every other thought of Eddie since the accident. He felt sad. Calmly, he isolated that feeling and examined it as dispassionately as he could. Sadness was a surprisingly sweet feeling. On reflection, Denis realized, he probably just thought that because it was one of the very few emotions he could identify. He felt tears well up for his dead friend, but he didn't fight them, he allowed himself the moment of sweet sadness.

His alarm had not woken him that morning. He could remember Rebecca waking and detaching herself from him gently; he had half woken and fallen back asleep almost immediately. She had kissed his forehead and whispered to him, and he had smiled and tried to say something to her; he couldn't remember what. When he did wake, he didn't immediately get up. He decided to get up at his leisure and instead scrolled through the various news apps on his phone, reading about the world outside. He wondered idly if this was what normal people were like. Were there a million other men in the world waking up in bed with their girlfriends and feeling good, but somehow bad?

For a little while he imagined a world where Rebecca was his wife. On Sundays he'd fetch the papers from the shop, and they'd eat breakfast in bed. They'd have a dog that would always jump up on the bed and make him groan at the ruined sports pages, but he'd really love the dog deep down. Rebecca would laugh at him, and they'd kiss and eat Sunday dinner in his mother's house. It was a fantasy, but a fun one. He pictured himself being that guy for a while, and tried not to remember that he was, instead, a ball of neuroses whom people laughed at because he hated it when people used dessert spoons for eating soup, and in fact, couldn't eat soup himself without brown bread, buttered and cut into strips. Remembering things like that had a way of ruining perfectly good fantasies. Guilt concerning work eventually drove him from his place of comfort, and he finally managed to get out of bed.

He showered, carefully scrubbing as his mind drifted aimlessly. He found himself thinking of Eddie and Jules, and with thoughts of them came another great well of sadness; it didn't engulf him though, as it had once threatened to do, and he showered in peace. He also cleaned up the puddles in peace.

It wasn't until after he was dry that he got his first inkling of something being wrong. On the surface, he seemed confident, but he could feel the worm of uncertainty turning inside him. Something, as usual, was amiss. He couldn't identify that something. It would probably turn out to be not-usual at all. Still he gave himself a high five in the mirror for moral support. His reflection winked at him seriously. After dressing he made his way down the stairs to begin the cleaning of the kitchen, only to find the job done already. Rebecca may have done it before going to work, but that seemed unlikely. She knew what stock Denis put into cleaning, and its therapeutic effects. He looked in wonder at the spotless job. It was a job even he would have been proud of. He briefly wondered if the kitchen had become so accustomed to being clean that it had cleaned itself.

"We cleaned it, you moron," Plasterer told him, walking through the door carrying a large cardboard box.

"You did? I didn't think you knew how. I just assumed you were only good for destruction," he replied.

"We destroy so you can clean. Our relationship is like that. Yesterday, you destroyed, so we cleaned. There are certain things that are unacceptable. A filthy kitchen is top of the list," he said, placing the cardboard box on the table.

"You sound like me."

"Of course I do, moron. Six years we've been dancing this dance, but you're too stupid to see it."

"What's in the box?" Denis asked.

"None of your business," Plasterer replied, his tone unfriendly. Penny O'Neill and the Professor trooped in behind him, loyal dogs on the heel of their master. Denis couldn't believe he was thinking of them in such terms, but the atmosphere had turned sour. He could feel their resentment.

"Where's Deano?" he asked.

"Tied up in your bedroom. He's become insubordinate. He will be taught. So will you," the Professor replied, sitting himself at the table.

"What's going on here?" Denis asked, confused. Plasterer was leaning against the stove. He had replaced the white glove on his right hand with a red one. It frightened Denis for its sharp and unaccountable contrast.

"I'm afraid the nature of our relationship has changed. I asked you nicely, Denis. I truly did, but a direct course of action is necessary now."

"You were warned. You were told there was a deadline, but even if the deadline was next week, there's still no excusing yesterday," Penny O'Neill replied, digging her hand into the box. It was his box of photographs. Memories from the other universe.

"What are you talking about? Leave those alone." Denis looked at them one after another. The Professor and Penny O'Neill regarded him coldly.

"Ignore him," Plasterer instructed them. "He has to learn, and learn he shall. You don't just betray us after all these years. You don't get to just replace us with someone else. You don't get to tell anyone about our secrets."

"What secrets?" Denis asked. "Get away from the photos. They're mine."

"You're a moron, Denis," Plasterer told him. "A clueless moron who understands nothing. There will be punishment for yesterday. She will leave the house, and if you won't do it, we'll make it happen all on our own."

The Professor and Penny O'Neill began rifling through the photos, scissors in hands, and with slow, deliberate movements, they cut her head from the photos. Denis moved to stop them, but Plasterer moved faster, his red right hand reaching out to grip Denis by the throat.

"You don't get to be in charge anymore, Denis," he whispered sharply. A small speck of spit flew from his lips. "You're no longer the boss. I am. You're nothing now. A guest in my home. No more. You'll be tolerated, at best, but you don't get to make the decisions."

His grip was tight, and painful. Denis clawed at it with his left hand, trying to pry the fingers loose, but they weren't budging.

"Your reign of indecision and constant panic is over. There's to be a new order. I can do what you can't. Can face what you can't. I'm the strong one, the one with the power. You're sniveling and weak, and your lack of clear leadership is what makes you so unfit. Did you think I was bluffing?"

Denis was still desperately trying to suck in air.

"You were a peace-time general, at best. But this is war. A war of senses. A war of thoughts and feelings. And what are you to thoughts and feelings? Nothing. A ghost. You think you can logic this out? You cannot. You think there's a way to rationalize all of this? There is not. You're a killer of people, who loves a woman who left you and shuns his own mother. Yesterday you sat paralyzed until I told you how to fix it. You can deal with nothing, and so you shall be replaced."

With that he let go of Denis's throat, and Denis sucked in air in great gulps, his chest heaving. Plasterer seemed to be out of breath too, his chest rising and falling with the effort of maintaining his iron grip.

Denis looked at the Professor and Penny O'Neill for some support. It was not forthcoming. In fact, Penny O'Neill looked vaguely disgusted with him, as if looking at something repugnant. The Professor looked grimly satisfied, nodding slightly to himself before returning to his work. He even began humming "The Imperial March" from *Star Wars*.

Denis realized he was angry. A feeling. Strong in his stomach, a fire in his brain, and it was growing. It seemed to energize him.

"This is my house," he told them. "Not yours. Get out."

Plasterer laughed in his face, a long, hard laugh. It sounded like a cartoon bad guy. A really bad cartoon bad guy.

"I just told you to get out. I meant it. I'm fine without any of you. I don't need you. I have Rebecca, and Frank and Ollie. I have my mother. I don't need any of you." He shouted it at them, but the words still seemed to lack conviction.

"You have nothing. You think you don't need us? You're wrong. We wouldn't be here if you didn't need us. You're on the edge, Denis, and clinging on for dear life, but eventually you'll fall off. When you do, well, there's no telling what will happen, but I can assure you, it won't be good."

Professor was still humming "The Imperial March."

"I said get out. I'm not on the edge of anything. Get out of my house."

Professor was still cutting, his snips clumsy and brutal. Rebecca's head was all over the kitchen table.

He wore a small, angry grin. Denis couldn't tell if he was smiling at the slowly falling heads of his kind-of-ex-kind-of-current girlfriend, or at the futile shouting Denis was doing. He just kept cutting and humming.

"You don't get to tell us what to do anymore," Plasterer told him, this time coldly. "We're making a little present for your new friend. When she arrives back to the house, we'll have little presents for her all over the place. It'll cover the walls, her room, your room. We have many, many plans for how we're going to deal with this situation."

"Why?" Denis asked. Defeated. "Why like this? Why not just confront her, like you're trying to do to me?"

"You're a moron, Denis," Penny O'Neill told him.

It's happening. It's finally happening.

Realizing there would be no stopping Phase One of the plan to drive Rebecca from the house, Denis decided to rethink his strategy. He was confused and a little stunned by the brutal side Plasterer was showing, and the willing complicity of the others, but protecting Rebecca now became his priority. Plasterer had been right. Feelings and emotions were not his strong suit. Rational thought was where Denis Murphy stood out from the crowd. Logic would win this fight. He moved up the stairs and into his bedroom to find Deano bound and, somewhat pointlessly, since the creature had no way to talk, gagged. He was struggling with his bonds, squirming from side to side, wriggling to free himself. Denis crouched down to undo the belts and ties that had been used to restrain Deano. When free, he expected the small creature to leap away, but instead, Deano sat up, resting on his elbows as he regarded Denis quietly.

"Hardly a point in freeing you. You can't tell me anything, can you?" Denis asked him.

Deano nodded.

An idea, a thought was occurring to Denis. It seemed to him that he'd never truly considered his housemates. They were just part of his life, like coffee and hospital visits, something that intruded on his conscious hours. Something he had simply adapted to as par for the course. In a life that had been broken down into segments according to the time they took, there was little room for analysis. Denis realized that he knew almost nothing about them, nothing about their past. Nothing about where they had come from, and that was what tickled his brain. There was something wrong about that. Where had they come from?

Deano was nodding at him fervently now.

Almost there. Reach for it.

"What?" Denis asked him. "Show me, show me what you're nodding at."

Deano froze in place.

Dammit, go back… Don't let it get away from you.

Lights seemed to dance in front of Denis, and there was a pain in his head. It took a moment to realize that he had banged his head against the wall, or more specifically, Plasterer had shoved his head into it. The shock canceled out the pain.

"Looking for a little ally?" he asked. "He's utterly useless, you know. He refuses to accept anything. These last few weeks he's been unbearable, and I blame you."

Plasterer aimed a kick at Deano, his ridiculous clown shoes taking the fur ball right in the ribs.

"Leave him alone," Denis shouted at him, one hand still rubbing at his forehead where he had connected with the wall.

"Make me," Plasterer said, sneering, drawing back for another kick. Deano tried to squirm out of the way, but couldn't avoid the shoe.

"Fuck off, Plasterer. You fucking bully. You fucking monster."

"Only because you made me this way," Plasterer told him.

The thought in his head nudged again.

Don't let it slip away.

"What are you expecting here?" Plasterer asked. "Do you expect him to know? He knows nothing, just the calm moments and the struggle, that's all he's ever known. You don't understand it because you're a moron. Have you ever even paid attention to us? When I warned you this was coming, did you take me seriously? Did you think I was joking? I wasn't. You made a mess of everything by being you, so now I'm what's needed, as always, to fix your mess."

"But I always fix the messes," Denis told him. His head was throbbing.

"No, you don't. You clean. You're the housecleaner. I make the messes to give you something to do. To occupy you. I know what you're feeling before you do, and I can anticipate. For this, I am necessary. We don't need a cleaner anymore. You're only necessary because your name is on the deed for the house. Outside of that, you're nothing. Your old universe has no place in here."

Denis looked about the room for something he could use, a way out, a weapon, anything. He spotted a heavy, ring-bound book sitting up against the side of his open closet. It had been a gift from his friends for his birthday, a scrapbook. An idea hit him then, harder than the wall had. It caused considerably less of a headache. Keeping his body between Deano and Plasterer, he edged from the room, the fur ball limping behind him. He had to be careful here. Too quick, and Plasterer would know he was up to something. Too slow, and he'd give the clown another chance at kicking Deano. He made his way down the stairs at a half trot.

"The Imperial March" floated up toward him as he made his way down. The Professor was still humming to himself in the kitchen. Denis moved to the cabinet in the utility room and took his arts-and-crafts supplies, stowed so neatly. His shirt had come loose slightly as he had helped Deano. His hands involuntarily moved to tuck it in again, but he stopped himself, and instead tugged the shirt out. It was a small act of defiance, and one he felt wouldn't go a long way, but it was all he had at the moment. He took two cans of red paint from under the sink and brought them to the kitchen, placing them carefully in sight of the Professor. Penny O'Neill laughed spitefully at the sight of him as he walked through the kitchen with the satchel under his arm. He went to the living room and began cutting cards himself. Chopping slowly and methodically until his idea began taking shape.

In the kitchen, the Professor had stopped humming, and through the doorway, Denis could see him staring at the paint cans.

He reached out for the scissors again, but it wasn't where he'd left them. There was a sharp pain as the blade scored his hand. Plasterer was holding the scissors, his red glove shone brightly, and a small trail of blood was now trickling down one of the blades. Denis clutched at the hand.

"You've got some kind of plan, moron?" Plasterer asked him, waving the scissors in front of himself.

"How is it you're not sticking to yours?" Denis shot back, wiping the blood from his hand.

"All in good time," came the reply. "What is it you're up to?" Plasterer asked, his irritation tinged with curiosity.

Denis looked at him and frowned. It was an attempt at a dirty look. When he lived in the other universe, he had been involved in a fracas or two. Usually caused by Eddie. Back then he had been a master at throwing aggressive expressions, but now the simple act of frowning made him look more confused than threatening. Plasterer was not nearly so uncomfortable. He loomed, his broad frame casting a grim shadow that seemed to warn of violence. He wasn't always like that, but now Denis couldn't remember a time when he hadn't been. It was as if the new Plasterer had entirely replaced the old, and now he could only remember the intimidating version. He tried not to act frightened.

"You're nervous," Plasterer told him, relishing the words.

Back away from him while he has the scissors. No sudden moves. Carefully now.

The Professor saved the day, entirely by accident, striding as he did into the room, with one of the cans of red paint open.

"For all the people you've taken from this world with your reckless disregard for human life and your utter thoughtlessness. For all the crimes you've committed." The zombie shambled across the room and threw the contents of the paint on the wall. Denis tried to look horrified, but inside he exulted. Professor Scorpion had taken the bait. Penny O'Neill had followed behind, clapping her hands at the mess. It was all the distraction Denis needed, and he bolted from the room, carrying the tools for his personal art project with him. He locked the door to the sound of angry howls. He knew that it wouldn't last; they'd howl themselves out eventually.

He set about fixing it. They had cut nearly one hundred photos, removing the heads. Denis had been obsessed with the idea of printing photos and making a feature wall out of the memories of his four years of college. That had been before he killed Jules and Eddie. Before he had killed Rick by default. He still didn't know why he had kept the large box of photos, but he had. He quickly began cutting other heads from the photos, and began to apply them to the card. With luck, he would be able to turn their wanton destruction into something positive. He was going to make a collage for Rebecca. He allowed himself a quiet smirk as he set about his work.

There was a bang on the window outside. Plasterer stood knocking, slowly. Behind him, the Professor stood, fuming. Penny O'Neill's tail could be seen lashing. He had forgotten about the windows. Of course they'd climb out the window. He snatched up the contents of the photo box, as well as all his other bits and pieces and bolted from the room, up to his bedroom. The sound of feet thumping up the stairs behind him rang in his ears. Plasterer was chasing him. He made it to his room and locked the door. Deano looked at him, his head cocked to the side. Denis sat himself on the floor and crossed his legs. Plasterer began hammering on the door. Denis sat calmly and set about his work, ignoring him. The hammering continued.

"You can't stay in there forever," a voice snarled. It sounded like it was coming from inside the room, but Denis knew they were safely outside. He went back to work.

It was hours later that he finished. He had turned the terrible work his housemates had done into something that might pass as a romantic gesture, but it would be in vain if he couldn't figure out a way to keep Rebecca from coming home to their new order. The banging on the door, he realized, had stopped. He didn't know when it had stopped. He stashed the collage in the closet and then carefully picked his way across the mess he'd made on his floor.

He unlocked the door and poked his head out. Deano followed, urging him onward. He crept down the stairs in silence. They were in the living room; he could hear them. The second can of red paint was gone from the kitchen floor, but the room was otherwise untouched. He stopped to think for a minute before heading for the utility room again. For the first time that he could remember, his obsessive-compulsive behavior was serving him well. He threw almost nothing out, and so he had a large collection of various things that one accrues over six years of living in the same house. He removed the painting materials, including the plastic covering sheet, and made his way back to the living room. He could cover this one up too, a domestic paint job that he made a mess of, nothing more. Not an uprising of militant and angry housemates that Rebecca didn't even know she lived with.

There was a surge of pain in his hip as he connected with the table. Plasterer was sitting at its head. He had given the table a shove with the sole of his foot and driven it into De-nis's hip.

"Clever move, Denny. I didn't expect it," the clown said.

"Stay away from my things," Denis told him angrily.

"They're my things too," Plasterer replied. "Ownership is a fluid concept at the moment. Going to try to repaint the damage the Professor did? He won't like that. He's enjoy-ing himself in there, you know. When he runs out of paint, it might turn into a dirty protest. Now isn't that a thought?"

Denis walked into the living room with Plasterer's mock-ing laugh chasing him. Penny O'Neill was spotted in red paint. The Professor was covered in it too. It made him look as though he was bleeding heavily, adding to his already ter-rifying appearance. Denis had always been afraid of zombies. He wondered how he had ever put up with the man.

"You cannot prevail in your attempts to paint over this," the Professor told him loftily.

"No intention, old chum," Denis replied glibly. He set the painting supplies about the room in a haphazard manner. It made quite a mess. He made several journeys to the utility room to find more and more stock for his plan.

"Right," Plasterer told him, examining his new glove non-chalantly as Denis passed through the kitchen. "You're mak-ing it look like you did it. She'll think it was you and not the zombie. It seems you're only a moron when it comes to her. You can't win, you know."

A key turned in the door. She was home. This was the mo-ment that Denis had dreaded, but curiously, they all moved to conceal themselves. The Professor ducked behind the cur-tains. Penny O'Neill behind an armchair. Deano, who had been following him around the house, vanished up the stairs. For a moment, a dangerously long moment, Plasterer stood his ground, then with a snarl he ducked behind a couch.

"I'm home…" she called out.

"Hey," Denis called back.

"How you feeling today?" she asked, hanging her coat on a hook inside the door. There was a note in her voice. She was worried about him. It did not make him feel good.

"I'm okay. Was feeling creative, so I made you something. I tried to repaint the living room too, but I just ended up making a mess. I'll take care of it later."

She laughed, right until she stepped into the kitchen.

"Denis," she gasped. "What happened to you? You're bleeding from your hand… Your neck, it's black and blue… What happened?"

"I'm clumsy," he lied. "Just haven't done any decorating in a while, must be rusty or something. There was a bit of an incident in the living room, I got it all over the place. Disaster. I hurt myself too."

He tried to smile as he told her. To mask the lie. He was not great at lying. There was very little need to in his life; he typically just avoided the need to lie by running away from things that frightened him. There was no running away from her though. He wouldn't run from her again.

"Jesus, Denis." She was shocked now. "You're a mess. I mean…look at you. How did it happen?"

He smiled at her again. There was no way to explain.

"I told you, I fell over when I was trying to paint the living room."

"Denis, don't lie to me, for God's sake, what is wrong with you? You look like you've been fighting. What happened here?"

"Wait here," he told her, dashing up the stairs to fetch the collage. She was waiting in the kitchen when he came back, a look of confusion and anger mixed with something he recognized all too well. Pity.

She took the gift from him suspiciously. She inspected it closely. She was not pleased.

"Er… It's lovely," she lied. "Look, you haven't answered my question. This is a little frightening, Denny, and you're not helping the situation."

"You hate it," he replied.

"Denis, it's nice that you made something for me, but it's mostly cutouts of my head. You spent the day cutting out my head and painting the living room, all the while you look like you've been boxing. Is that a lump on your head?"

Denis nodded. There was no way he could tell her why he had made it, who had actually cut the heads out. What would she say to him? He'd sound like an insane person. He decided not to. Instead he said nothing. The Deano strategy seemed like the way to handle the situation.

"Sit down," she told him, her face hardening. "Denis, I want you to tell me what happened to you."

He did as he was told, taking his seat where the Professor had sat to destroy the photos.

"I think I know what's happening here," she announced after a long silence.

"You do?" Denis replied, confused. It seemed unlikely to him. A tall, aggressive clown with a red right hand trying to seize control of everything Denis owned seemed like a stretch.

"I think so. Are you trying to get rid of me? I don't know if you're doing it deliberately or subconsciously, but this card and the state of you? You're a mess. I know you well enough to know that you could have cleaned yourself up at any time today—in fact, you'd make a point of it. You want me to see you like this. You think it'll frighten me away."

"No," he told her. "I don't want to frighten you away."

"Good," she told him, her voice hard. "Denny, you know this isn't normal, right? Cutting heads from photos?" She was talking now as if talking to a fool. It was patronizing and annoying. He wanted to clarify what had happened, but something stayed his tongue. He let the irritation drain out of him.

"I know..." he replied glumly.

She took that as a sign that he had admitted defeat, and shook her head slowly at him. He smiled back, though he must have looked confused, since he didn't know what he was smiling at, or why she was shaking her head.

"Denis, I don't want to give up. You've had a lot on your plate and you're trying to deal with it, which I get, but don't forget we're trying to deal with it too. Eddie was my friend, as well. Don't forget that. If there's something that you need to say to me, now's the time."

Out of the corner of his eye, he could see Plasterer standing up from behind the couch. There was no way she could see him from the angle she was sitting.

Now was the time. Now was his chance. He could come clean, tell her about the clown in their house. He felt his throat tighten.

For fuck sake, do it.

"I know. I guess it's just everything that's happened," he told her, trying not to look straight at the clown. "I'm not dealing with it well. And I'm trying not to be such a weirdo, you know, with all my weirdo behavior. I'm just not good at it. It's not like I've spent the last few years being romantic. I'll be okay. I think I just need to get out of the house or something."

"Don't call yourself a weirdo," she said, not unkindly. "You're just different. And there's nothing wrong with it."

Plasterer was edging closer to the door. It was hard to tell underneath all the makeup, but he seemed to be grinning.

"I'll do better though, that's what I'm saying," he told Rebecca, trying to sound earnest and not panicked.

She could see through him. She could always see through him when he wasn't telling her the truth.

"What's going on?" she asked him suspiciously.

"Nothing. Just… I've been meaning to talk to you about something. Something that's been bothering me." Plasterer froze where he was, his eyes widening. He looked worried for some reason.

"Okay," she replied slowly.

"It's just that you've been so good to me, since you came back. Patient with me. And understanding. I just want you to know that I appreciate it."

Her face softened and she smiled at him for the first time. Plasterer's eyes narrowed, and he took a step back, considering.

"You know why, don't you?" she asked him, her face so beautiful and serious.

"No," he told her. He was staring at her a little now, he knew it, but it was hard not to.

"It's because I love you, you moron," she grumbled.

Oh.

Plasterer took a threatening step forward and then froze, as if held in place. Penny O'Neill emerged from her hiding place to stand beside him. She watched Denis with unblinking eyes.

Behind Rebecca, at the bottom of the stairs, Deano peeked around the corner. He waved his arms over his head in celebration. Denis could feel the sense of happiness rolling off the hair ball in waves. He could feel it in his head too. He knew she loved him, it was obvious, but it felt more than incredible to hear it from her anyway. He had heard it from her before, a thousand times and more, but never before had it felt like this. Like she knew what he was, and loved him in spite of it. He could hardly believe it. Even Denis didn't love Denis. He stared at her for just a minute, smiling broadly before he enveloped her in a hug.

"Elephant shoe too," he whispered in her ear, with a smile. "Can we go out for dinner? I really don't fancy staying here for much longer."

"I just got here, Denny. Let me get changed. Then we can make a move." She was definitely softening now. He felt he was past the worst. She hadn't seen through him. He'd fooled her, somehow.

"Please," he said, surreptitiously watching Plasterer.

She took another long serious look at him.

"Tuck in your shirt," she told him, turning back for the door. "And dinner's on you too."

He smiled to himself as they walked out the door. Behind him he could hear the noise of Plasterer punching his red-gloved hand into his white one. A minor victory for Denis, he knew, but the war was far from over.

ARE LONELY GUNS

Escalation is part and parcel of war. His housemates had at-tacked, Denis had defended and beaten back the assault, which means, typically, that escalation must follow. They had gone to dinner, and Denis had insisted on a long walk after-ward. As they strolled they talked. Rebecca's new favorite book, Denis's desire to start following soccer again; he'd been ignoring it for a few years now. They did not discuss the gift Denis had given her. Or the bruises on his neck. He could see it was troubling her and that she wanted to, but she was giving him room. It was a welcome respite.

When they finally got home, the house was in darkness and all was quiet. Suspiciously quiet. Denis barely slept for worry about what the next day would bring, and when the morn-ing rolled around, he delayed getting out of bed again, this time until he heard her close and lock the front door behind her. For their part, his housemates made no move against him until he got out of the bed. He had crept from his room to shower, and did so in peace and quiet, but when he emerged from the bathroom, Penny O'Neill and the Professor were standing in the hallway, looking at Rebecca's bedroom door. Denis moved to block them, stepping between them and the door while trying to look menacing. The Professor went to reach by him, while Penny O'Neill ducked under his outstretched arm. He grabbed at both of them, just as Penny O'Neill's hand took the doorknob. She managed to open it just a fraction, before Denis tugged her away from it and it slammed behind him again.

"Leave it alone," he barked, trying desperately to add a note of authority to his words. It's hard to tough-talk a zombie and a cat woman when you're only wearing a towel and still dripping wet.

"Stand aside," the Professor replied, still twisting and turning in the crook of Denis's arm. They were after her clothes. What they planned to do with them if they got them, Denis could only guess.

"We don't go in there," Denis grunted, as he struggled to contain the writhing cat woman.

"We do whatever we want in this house," Penny O'Neill replied, squirming.

A sound bubbled from the stairs, bubbled louder and louder until it burst from the landing.

Plasterer stood there, watching and laughing uproariously. It was unsettling for Denis in many ways. Once upon a time he had stood aside and watched the wrestling matches of his housemates while laughing to himself. It seemed that his house had come full circle.

I fucking hate that animal.

He wondered, as he pushed the heel of his hand against the Professor's forehead, if he had become the oddity, or if the oddity had become him. It made his head ache to think about it. During the scuffle, Deano stood in the doorway to Denis's bedroom, hopping up and down. Denis felt he may have been cheering on one side or the other, but it was impossible to tell which.

When he'd fought them off, he locked her door and stuffed the key in his laundry basket. Penny O'Neill glared at him balefully, and the Professor drew himself up as though he was preparing for another round, but on the landing, Plasterer just shrugged and made his way downstairs.

Denis dried himself, trembling slightly, and dressed slowly. How had this happened to him? At what point did he lose all form of control? For all their complaints and destruction, Denis himself had always been sacrosanct, but that just wasn't the case anymore. Now he was a target in his own home. It frightened him. When had they started dictating his life? He knew in his heart that he would have to tell Rebecca about them eventually, but the thought of it unsettled him greatly, though he didn't know why.

"If you tell her, she'll call you crazy," Plasterer told him from the doorway. He seemed to materialize at Denis's most uncomfortable moments.

"If I don't tell her, she'll think I'm crazy anyway. What have I got to lose?" he replied.

"A lose-lose scenario for you, which makes it win-win for me," Plasterer replied. "Don't you see that you're hanging on by a thread? Haven't you noticed yet? Are you that stupid?"

"You've not beaten me yet," Denis replied defiantly.

"You've beaten yourself, you moron," Plasterer told him.

For a moment, Denis's head spun. He tried to imagine why Plasterer would say such a thing. He put himself in Plasterer's head, and it caused his knees to wobble.

"There it is," Plasterer growled. "You're getting it. Go deeper."

Denis shook his head to clear himself.

"Go on, go back there again. Have a little think. Put yourself in my head. What do you see? Do you see yourself, Denis?

Do you see you with all my makeup on? Do you understand me now? My motivation? Do you?"

Denis shook his head again. His eyes welled up.

"I don't know what you're talking about," he replied hoarsely.

"Sure you do," Plasterer told him, unrelenting. "You're starting to understand, and in your understanding comes your defeat. By the time you fully get it, you'll have entirely defeated yourself."

And then he laughed a harsh, bitter, angry laugh. From out in the corridor the laugh was taken up by Penny O'Neill and the Professor. It echoed around the house.

He bolted from the room, pushing past them all. He almost stumbled down the stairs, and then he shot out the front door. He wasn't wearing any shoes, but it was too late to go back for them. He needed air. He sucked in great gulps of it and tried to calm himself. The children next door used to giggle at him. They knew he was weird. It had caused him to resent them just a little, but now he wanted them to laugh, he needed to hear it for some reason. It would remind him, he was sure. He walked to the green, across the sharp gravel, which cut at the soft soles of his feet, and stood at the edge of the grass watching them play. When they noticed him, he pointed to his feet and smiled. They didn't laugh. The one time he wanted them to laugh they didn't.

This wasn't going the way he planned. He made his way back to the driveway of his house and through the gate. He counted his steps to the door and back to the gate again. Then back to the door and then back to the gate again. He repeated this process several times before he realized that his neighbor, the friendly woman to his right, was watching him from an upstairs bedroom window. The realization knocked him off his stride, embarrassing him. Plasterer was right. He was losing it, badly. Trying desperately to compose himself, he went back into the house.

Plasterer stood in the hallway, smirking.

"Fuck off," Denis growled at him. "I fucking hate you, you animal."

He tried to make breakfast while they sat around the table watching him. They knew it too. He was losing it. Their mere presence now was driving him closer and closer to the edge. They didn't have to do anything, just sit nearby and stare. Deano didn't sit. He rolled back and forth on the living-room floor, like a child throwing a temper tantrum. Denis wanted to join him, his frustration building. He dumped the cereal into the bowl straight from the box, another pathetic act of defiance, as if by ignoring his usual customs he would some-how hurt them. The Professor sneered at the attempt.

He sat at his desk and opened internet browsers and checked his emails; he opened programs and began typing numbers. They followed him in and watched. Waiting for that inevi-table moment when he would crack. What would follow the cracking he didn't know. He figured they didn't either, but what they did know, one and all, was that pressure was build-ing and Denis would eventually blow.

He went through the motions of his job, making the odd attempt at upsetting them by refusing standard operating be-haviour, hoping somehow he could cow them with the un-expected. It was less than useless, they didn't care.

His phone beeped. He had left it on the kitchen table. Four heads whipped around to look at it. It would be her. Deano stopped rolling and sat, stock-still.

"Ooooh what's she going to say now?" Penny asked mock-ingly. "Something profound about flowers or something. And you can text her back and pretend you're not completely fuck-ing insane and she'll love you for being witty and normal."

Denis tried to mask his anger.

"Go check it out, Denis," Plasterer chimed in. "I give you my permission." He was smirking again.

They followed single file as he made his way into the kitchen.

It wasn't her. It was Ollie. Thinking about popping over for lunch, dude. You want me to bring anything? They were clearly checking up on him.

Little busy today. Rain check? Denis sent back. The last thing he needed was another person to try to hide them from.

He waited for the reply. The others stood all around him, leaning in close so they could read it when it came back. He could feel their breath on him, making him feel unclean. There was no space, no room to think.

The phone beeped again.

Cool, the text read. Denis heaved a sigh of relief. Their alarm was palpable. They wanted the chance to hurt him in front of Ollie, to do something outrageous and reckless. They wanted to ruin him.

He returned to his work, typing and sending emails. Deano returned to having a temper tantrum, this time on the couch, his arms slapping the pillows and cushions repeatedly. He seemed less enthusiastic about it this time. The other three returned to exchanging dark looks and skulking around him. Every now and again one of them would pace by the back of his desk and shove him. Every time they did he'd pound his fist on the desk. The bottom of his hand had begun to hurt. In the to and fro he'd forgotten he was barefoot. His feet slapped on the legs of his office chair. It made a satisfying sound. For some reason he knew it would irritate Plasterer, and so he kept doing it. After an hour or so the phone beeped again. The four of them materialized at his shoulder to get a closer look.

It was her this time.

Coming home for lunch, babe. Bringing salad and juice and coffee cake. Nom nom.

Denis's stomach tightened. Plasterer began to chuckle again.

"This is it, Boss," the clown told him, rubbing his red-and-white hands together. "What's your next move to hide us? What do you think you'll do this time?"

Denis could feel the panic rising once more. He tried to think.

Plasterer stood and walked to him. He put his red hand on Denis's throat and tightened it ever so slightly. Denis was slowly choking.

"Professor," the clown said, never taking his eyes off Denis. "Would you be so good as to go to Denis's room and collect the key to *her* bedroom door from his laundry basket please."

"I'm begging you," Denis started. "You don't have to—"

"Shut up," snapped Penny O'Neill. "This wouldn't be necessary if you had done as you were told."

The Professor walked upstairs, returning with a load of Rebecca's clothes.

"She's got photos in there, you know," the zombie told the others. "Lots of them. Photos of the two of them. And of Eddie. And Jules. The lot." He seemed offended by the photos.

"Next level," Plasterer told him with a consoling pat on the shoulder. He released Denis's throat. "You can go now."

Denis rubbed at his throat with his left hand, guiding Plasterer's hand away with his right. Like the previous day, he'd had a thought on how to dodge this, but he knew that if he let it show, they'd be onto him. They always seemed to be one step ahead. He made his way from the room as though he was reluctant. They ignored him leaving, except for Deano, who watched him all the way. Denis nodded at the fur ball, who nodded in return.

He made his way to the laundry room and found the old tartan throw he had used for the living-room couch. He pulled it out and threw it on his bed. From the kitchen he grabbed plates, glasses, cutlery and seasoning. He did all of this as silently as possible. If they heard him and came to investigate, they'd know what he was up to. It was painstaking, sliding the drawers open so slowly that the rollers on which they rested didn't betray his cunning plan. He collected the cushions with the least amount of red paint on them from the living room and bundled his entire stash together. His lawn, which was considerably larger than the other lawns in the neighborhood, was kept immaculately. Not by him of course. He couldn't abide cutting the grass since it would never be a uniform height. He paid someone else to deal with the horror of knowing that their work was for nothing and some of the blades of grass would forever remain uncut. He spread out the makings of his picnic on the lawn and marveled at how much time had passed since she had crashed into his life. Summer had turned into autumn almost without him noticing.

It was a nice enough day for early September and he was sure, though he didn't know why, that his housemates wouldn't come outside. He was still barefoot. She would love that; she loved being barefoot. He sat and waited for her to arrive, and tried to compose himself. It was a good plan, and he was safe here, though he didn't know why, but still he couldn't stop feeling Plasterer's fingers on his throat.

Easy now, just relax it a little.

He massaged his right hand and tried to relax until his breathing came easier. He dared not think about what they were doing with her clothes. One fight at a time, he told himself. It was all he was able to handle.

When she pulled up in the driveway and saw him sitting, cross-legged in his shirt and tie, shoeless, she broke out in a broad grin. He was aware that her coming home and Ollie's earlier text were related. In fact, it was possible that every move they made—her, Ollie, Frank, Ned, even his mother—was coordinated with him in mind. It was the pathetic kind of help he felt he needed and just the kind of decent thing they would do. They were clearly worried about him, and their plan was to keep him under close watch in the days after Eddie's death. Truth be told, he was worried about himself. Wandering around the streets barefoot, frightening small children. Not much of Denis's life had passed without feeling like something was wrong, but the last few days had felt more wrong than ever before. A fear building, a tension so tight that he knew it must be showing.

To boot, there was something gnawing at him about the conversation he'd had with Plasterer. Something about putting himself inside the clown's head. He tried not to think about it, but he couldn't. The feeling of control slipping away was permanently with him now. He had no way around it. He lied to Rebecca with a smile, a broad toothy smile that he remembered from days gone by. Each shiny, well-brushed tooth lied just a little more.

"Everything's better when you're barefoot, eh?" he said as she climbed from her ancient car. It was something she used to say over and over.

"Well, isn't this just a lovely surprise?" she asked. Still smiling.

She kicked off her shoes and sat next to him. Denis had positioned a place setting for her so that her back would be to the window. He didn't want to take the chance that she might catch one of them looking out from inside. In his mind's eye he saw Penny O'Neill peeking out from behind the curtains. Watching them. Judging him. Hating her. He put the thought down savagely, crushing it by staring at Rebecca.

"Did you tell Ollie to check in on me earlier?" he asked.

"Of course not," she told him. He could see that she was lying. She blushed when she lied.

"Of course not," he agreed, smiling.

"Are you ready for tonight?" she asked, changing the subject.

"Tonight?" he replied, puzzled.

"The funeral, Denny. Eddie's funeral is tonight."

A wave of nausea swept over him. He thought he might be sick, but he repressed the urge.

"It'll be okay. I'll be with you," she told him reassuringly, placing a gentle hand on his arm.

"Of course." It was not going to be okay. There were things that Denis Murphy believed he would never be ready for. Eddie's funeral was one of them. Ned would be there. And Ann. He would have to pretend to be sick. Better still, actually be sick. He was sure he could talk his body into it if needed. Hell, Plasterer would enjoy poisoning him.

"You have to go," Rebecca told him, as if reading his thoughts.

"Sure," he replied. "I know that. Of course I'm going."

She looked at him suspiciously and began unpacking their lunch from the two plastic bags she had brought. Salad mostly, with some fruit, yogurt and coffee cake. Her favorite.

"Do you still love me?" he asked. It was a random thought that just seemed to be floating about in his head, and then it was coming out of his mouth. It was his lack of control showing all over again.

"Of course I do, you moron," she told him, not unkindly. "I never stopped, Denny. Even when I was half a world away and getting all of my information about you from emails home, I was in love with you. I loved you when I watched you through the glass door at the side of your kitchen. From the moment I saw you singing while Eddie pushed you down the street in a shopping cart at three in the morning, I loved you." She was looking into his eyes. He was looking right back. There was something about her eyes, dark brown and lovely, that seemed to calm him. Every time she looked at him felt like a hug.

"You don't have to keep asking either," she continued. "It's not going to change anytime soon."

He smiled. Her words seemed to sink into his brain and stomach, untying the knots and loosening the panic that was beginning to take hold.

"Want me to pick out something for you to wear tonight?" she asked.

They were at the window. All four of them, standing in a straight line, Plasterer at the end, watching him.

"No. No, that's fine," he replied. There was no way she was going to be let into the house. "How's work today?" he asked as a diversion.

"Fine. Busy all morning. Festival planning for Christmas. Can you believe that? Already. Got some big plans, might need a marketing genius to help me with them actually. One of the girls at work is married to a marketing guy. They kind of do everything together. They kill each other though. Think we could work together?"

Penny O'Neill's tail lashed.

"Sure we could," he replied. "I'll point my giant brain at anything you ask, and you just stand around with a pen and paper and wait for the genius to come out."

She kicked him gently with one bare foot. She always liked putting him in his place when he talked big. He leaned back on his elbows. As long as she didn't go inside the house, this would be okay. If he could live outside with her on the lawn, it might just turn out to be a lovely life together, as long as they never went back inside. With her beside him, Denis felt he might even be able to take on the funeral home.

Sadly, for Denis, such moments of relaxation and clarity don't last long. She did have to go back to work after all, and when she did, after a long lunch of friendly flirting, his problems began all over again. Just before she left, she kissed him softly on his lips. Denis briefly wished that Thomas in the shop and the various waiting staff who knew him around the city could see that moment. That'd show them he wasn't a weirdo. He laughed at the ludicrousness of the thought. Inviting people to watch you kiss is not the done thing in polite society.

"What's so funny?" she asked.

"You," he told her, planting another kiss on her. From out of the corner of his eye he could see Penny O'Neill and Plasterer on one side of the window. The Professor was holding Deano by the scruff of his neck on the other side. When she had pulled out of the driveway, he turned to face them. Penny O'Neill narrowed her eyes at him, and Plasterer gestured with one finger for him to come inside. The clown would never allow him to go to the funeral. Nor would the Professor. They would resist it, just like he should. He wasn't ready for this yet. He wondered if he ever would be. Denis shivered and gathered his things to make his way back inside.

Plasterer loomed in the doorway, blocking Denis's way back in.

"You're not going," Plasterer told him.

"Who's going to stop me?" Denis replied, as if he didn't know the answer.

"I am. I'm going to beat the living shit out of you. I'm going to make pulp of your face." The threat was casually made, in a tone loaded with boredom, but the big clown was obviously agitated.

"Get out of my way," Denis demanded. Once again, he

was trying to give orders, but there was no command in his voice. He knew it even as he spoke.

Plasterer stood aside anyway. In the kitchen Deano paced back and forward, shooting glances at Plasterer and Denis in turn. Penny O'Neill and the Professor sat at the table, Rebecca's clothes in a pile in front of them.

"He's not lying," Penny O'Neill told him, sounding concerned. "You've gone too far."

"You thought you were so clever with your little picnic stunt, didn't you?" Plasterer practically spat the words. His mood was swinging from bored to raging. "Outsmarted me again? Think that was bright? I'm the one in charge here, not you. You don't get to go over my head. Not anymore."

"Over your head? Fuck you. I own this house. Me. I decide what's what, not you." The anger in his own voice was building; he could hear it. For the first time, he felt strong, maybe even a little frightening.

"You?" Plasterer shot back. "You're nothing, you little worm. Nothing without me. That little buzz you've got going on right now, where do you think you get it from? You get it from me, you little shit."

"I get nothing from you, and I'm giving nothing to you. I'm leaving now. I'm going to town, and I'm going to have a drink and wait for my friends and you can wait on me. Like you're supposed to."

The clown's eyes were wide; he seemed to twitch. His fury was rising, and with it a fear grew in Denis. A terrible fear. He had the marks on his neck to show just how violent his housemate could be. What if he wasn't going to back down?

The fist caught him on the chin, sending him backward and stumbling into the wall of the kitchen. He hadn't seen it coming. His eyes stung.

"What..."

A second blow landed, in his gut this time, winding him.

"Please…" he gasped. "Please don't."

Another fist, this one taking him on the lip, splitting it. He tasted blood, felt it wriggle its way down his chin to spatter his well-pressed shirt.

A sob tore loose from his chest.

"Please don't, Plasterer."

"You're not going to the damn funeral," Plasterer told him again. He touched his hand to his face, leaving blood on the white makeup around his mouth. "Why? Why do you keep resisting? Why do you keep thinking it's okay for you to carry on with her? Why do you keep thinking I'll allow you to change?"

Denis shied away from the clown. There was another blow coming. He could feel it.

"You mustn't persist in this, Denis," the Professor chimed in. He looked worried. He watched Plasterer warily. They were all frightened now. All of them except Plasterer, whose chest heaved as he struggled to contain the growing fury.

"The consequences of opposition here are dire. Tell him you won't go," the Professor insisted. Bits of his rotting flesh looked like they were going to fall away at any minute. "I implore you, Denis, I implode you, I imply you, please."

"I have to…" Denis whimpered.

Another fist, this one taking him in the eye, followed up by a sharp shove to his forehead, causing his skull to bounce off the wall.

"YOU HAVE TO DO WHAT I FUCKING TELL YOU," Plasterer screamed at him.

Another sob jumped from his throat. He was crying again too. How had it come to this? The lack of control, the chaos that was the inside of his head. He was spiraling now.

He's going to kill you. Oh Christ, you're going to die.

"She loves me," he told Plasterer, seeking to bargain. Clowns are not famous for bargaining. Plasterer even less so.

"We all love you," Plasterer spat. "I'm doing this for your own good." He was shaking from head to toe. "This is for all the things you can't do. You want all the eyes on you? They'll all know. Every one of them. Eddie's killer walking among those who mourn his passing. You think you'll be welcome there, murderer? And when Ned tries to hug you, the crazy old bastard, what then? When he wants to touch you? Will you shy away and show them all that you won't even hug the father of the man you killed?"

Denis's shoulders shook as his sobbing intensified.

"I have to go—" he started to say.

Another fist, on his cheek, below the eye. The pain stung, and spots danced in his vision.

"You're not going anywhere," Plasterer shouted. "And that bitch leaves this house today, or so help me God..."

"But I love her," Denis implored.

"If you love her, then prove it. Get her out of here. For her own safety. If she's in this house tonight, I'm going to do to her what I did to you, and then some. For her there will be no holding back. You've made me do this. You've pushed me too far, Denis."

"No," Denis whispered. He couldn't let this happen. Not to her. The blood dripping onto his tie was proof that Plasterer made no idle threats. "You can't hurt her."

Plasterer barked a short, bitter laugh at him.

"I can do whatever I want. I'll beat that woman bloody, from head to toe... Unless you do what you're told."

Do something, you fucking coward. Do it now, or you're as good as dead.

In this moment, Denis's future hung in the balance, suspended by the power of a clown. A decision had to be made.

She'd come into his life, and against his will had forced a place for herself. He did love her. He knew that now. He loved her hands and her eyes. He loved her laugh and her often quicksilver temper. He loved her sometimes deliberate dishonesty. He loved the endless well that was her caring and the iron will that was her resolve. He knew that she loved him too. She loved the bit of him that was buried deep down under the guilt and the self-loathing. She loved the bit of him that was about to drive her out of his home. For that last bit of him that was good and decent and nice, he would have to drive her out.

"What do you want me to do?" he finally asked the clown.

You poor bastard.

"Go to her room. Gather the photos she keeps. Of you. And her. And Eddie. And Jules. Bring them all back down here to me."

"What are you going to do with them?" Denis asked.

"Nothing. You're going to do it."

"What? What am I going to do?"

"Go and get them, Denis." Plasterer was cold now, his mood swinging back again. Denis wiped at the blood on his face and walked up the stairs. Deano sat on the top step, his head buried in his hands. He was crying. Denis ignored him and went into Rebecca's room. It was a mess. Her bed unmade as it must have been for days. There were photographs everywhere in a wide array of frames of every color and type. Paintings she had done herself hung alongside them. And a life-size cast-iron cat. Her clothes were thrown about the room. Carefully, with the tenderest of hands, he removed each photo from the numerous frames. There was one of the two of them by the beach, standing near a cliff edge, the sea stretching out in front of them. There was another of Jules and Rebecca at a restaurant of some kind. In a frame on the wall there was a scrap of paper. They had been at a lecture. Sitting near each other.

They weren't boyfriend and girlfriend then, but they had been on a few dates. They had slept together. Denis had scribbled the note on a piece of paper torn from his notepad. *You're so cool,* it read. Like Christian Slater. She had kept it, framed it.

When he had collected the photos, he made his way back downstairs. Plasterer was waiting by the table. Penny O'Neill looked on, sympathy etched in her feline features. That puzzled Denis. She had not been on his side recently. The Professor sat at the end of the table. His face unreadable. The knives were out, literally. Every manner of knife Denis owned sat before him. Bread knives, butter knives, carving knives, the lot.

"Sit," Plasterer said.

Denis sat.

"I want you to kill them all," the clown commanded.

"Kill who?" Denis asked, frightened now.

"The photos. I want you to kill every photo she has. We want no part of these memories. Kill them."

Denis looked at him in horror. This would break her heart. It would do everything Plasterer wanted and more. She'd never speak to him again. She'd never curl up next to him in bed, nudging at him in an effort to prompt him to wrap his arms around her.

"I can't," he whispered.

"You can, and you will. Or else…"

The threat hung in the air. There was no way to avoid it. It was this or watch him hurt her when she came home. He reached into that last part of himself that was decent, the part that cared enough about other people to do something that would make them hate you forever, to cut them loose for all time, for their own good.

He picked up the carving knife and slowly pushed it through the photo of them by the cliffs.

"Good," Plasterer murmured.

The Professor hung his head.

A tear, mixed with the blood on his chin, dropped onto the photo as he pierced it. He was crying again. Once freed, the tears came easily, and Denis cried as he cut up the memories of them she had held on to for seven years. He cried as he sliced each photo. He had to do it, to protect her. Plasterer nodded his grim approval as Denis tried to kill what was left of his connection to the old universe.

IF I SAW

When she arrived home he was sitting in the living room. "Denny," she called out, her voice cheerful.

He heard the sound of her dropping shopping bags on the floor of the kitchen. In a faraway part of his head, a little bit of Denis wondered what she had bought.

Her footsteps clacked on the kitchen floor tiles as she walked to the table. Her breathing could be heard; it was becoming erratic. She had started to cry. Denis could see her in his head, standing there as she picked up each ruined photograph, some with knives still in them. Each memory they shared skewered. Her clothes, untouched, were still piled on the table. A message to her that told her to get out.

"It's for her own good," Plasterer's voice seemed to whisper in his ear. "It's for everyone's good." The clown had long since left him, rounding up the others and heading upstairs, to leave Denis in his own silent hell. The red paint was still spattered across the walls, the DIY supplies still strewn about the place. He could see that for what it was now too: a desperate last-ditch effort to keep it all together.

She was sobbing now, crying loudly and sniffling. Denis suppressed the urge to get up and go to her. To tell her that he was sorry and he'd fix it. To beg her to stay. Instead, he sat there.

"What is wrong with you?" she asked him, her voice bitter as she walked into the room. She held the stack of ruined photographs, tenderly. She'd removed the knives.

He looked at her. In his head the answers screamed and rebounded through his skull: *I'm sick. I'm broken. I hate myself. I hate anyone who doesn't hate me. I hate people who think I'm weird. I think I'm weird. I need help.* He didn't voice any of these suggestions; instead, he continued to just sit there. He once again stared at her and through her, from his universe into hers. She was standing in the room and had no idea that he was millions of miles away from her. His facial expression was, he knew, entirely flat. He wasn't even in his own head. He could just see everything happen. His body was on autopilot, and failing to receive any orders from him, it responded only minimally.

She stared at him for the longest time, her eyes darting over the broken skin on his lips, the deep bruising on his face, the blood that had dripped onto his shirt. She looked horrified.

"Answer me, Denis. God damn you, don't do this to me again!" There was anger now, cutting through the shock and the grief. Her eyes were brimming with tears. A big fat one slid down her cheek.

He looked at her. His head cocked to one side.

"You don't get to do this again. Not again. You answer me, and you tell me what's going on. You tell me why your face is swollen, Denis. Tell me."

She wore summer dresses all the time, or so it seemed to Denis. No one else could wear one quite like her.

"Why have you splashed the walls with paint? Why did you do this to me?" She brandished the photos at him, thrusting them toward him accusingly.

She was even beautiful when she cried.

The fight seemed to drain out of her. Her shoulders slumped, and she looked at him with the most profound pity.

"I've tried everything. Everything. I can't try anymore. You need help, Denis. You need to see a professional. You can't go on like this."

The tiny voice in his head whispered, *Help me.* His mouth didn't move.

"I want to help you, Denis," she said, scrubbing tears from her face as she sniffled, anger tinging her expression through the shuddering breaths. "I'll help you if you go see a doctor, but I can't make you do that. If you won't, then you can have what you wanted at the start. You can sit here and rot, alone. When you're ready to help yourself, we'll be waiting, until then, you just sit there."

Alone. Plasterer's voice was in his head again, telling him that he was not alone.

"When you do things like this, when you behave like this, you're not even a person, Denis, you're a monster. You're Jekyll and Hyde, and about ten other things I can't even understand. Somewhere inside you there's a good person, but you have to want to find that person. Do you hear me?" She was still sobbing.

He could hear her. It was really a ridiculous question. He was only sitting a few feet away, and had clearly demonstrated time and again that he was not deaf. Of course he heard her. He blinked to let her know he could hear her.

She shook her head and turned from the room, defeated.

He sat there while she moved about the house. At one point he could hear her sobbing into the phone. Then there was quiet. Then more sobbing into the phone. He presumed she was talking to Frank, Ollie and his mother. The thought didn't faze him. They wouldn't be able to tolerate this treatment long. They'd been through it before. So he sat there. He was still sitting there when Frank and Ollie turned up.

Frank walked into the room and took his time looking around before staring at Denis. Denis stared back. There was no way to explain what he'd done or why he'd done it. They'd never accept that it was for her own good, and since there was no point, Denis opted for silence. Explanations here were quite pointless. Frank's facial expression turned from one of mild disgust to anger to pure and unrelenting judgment. Denis could read that expression. He knew it too well. Everywhere he went people judged him for his behavior. Those who couldn't understand and didn't attempt to engage with him or excuse him, ran straight for the cover of judgment or pity. He turned his face away from that just as he turned his face away from Frank. His friend shook his head sadly and walked out without saying a word.

More sounds of moving around echoed about the house; suitcases and bags being dragged, snippets of muttered conversations. He couldn't make out the words, just muted tones that seemed to sneak into his ears. Still he sat there.

Eventually, Ollie walked into the room and sat down next to Denis with a sigh.

"You've gone too far this time, Denis," he said. "I know you're not going to talk, and that suits me fine. I just want you to listen. Me and Frank, we're used to your shit. You hide in the bathroom to escape your mother, so she never has to see this nonsense, but Rebecca…"

Denis tried not to hear. This was not going to be fun for him, he knew that.

"She cares more about you than anyone I know. We tried to warn her that you're not the same, but she insisted that you are. 'Same old Denny underneath it all. He's just been hurting for too long.' That's what she was thinking of when she moved home, how much you hurt and how much she could help. You think she couldn't have gotten a job somewhere else? You think there wasn't work for her on any continent anywhere on the planet? Girl like her? You kidding? You're why she came home. After six years of no contact, she came home on faith alone. Faith that you and her are right for each other. She crossed half a planet for that idea. That woman loves you so much she'll travel across half a planet and then willingly volunteer to put up with all your bullshit. You love her so much you'll slice up her photos of the two of you and start clearing out her room?"

Ollie paused; he was waiting for some kind of response. Denis blinked.

"You're on your own, Denis. From now until you start coming back to the real world, you're on your own. Anything to say for yourself?"

Voices in his head began screaming answers again: *I'm a hostage in my own home. A murderous clown wants to kill everyone who's not me, and maybe me too. I love her, please don't take her away...* He didn't say anything. Somewhere in the middle of that jumble of voices, Plasterer's cut through it all. *You shut your mouth, moron.* Denis kept his mouth shut.

"I assume we won't see you at the funeral?" Ollie asked.

Silence.

"Thought so," he said.

With a shake of his head that was almost exactly like both Frank's and Rebecca's, he stood and made for the door. He stopped briefly and faced Denis for the last time.

"Sometime you're going to want people back in your life. You'll need them. I hope for your sake that it's not too late by then."

With that he left, the others in tow.

The front door closed behind them. The house was quiet.

Denis sat there.

"None of them would understand really," he told no one.

Silence. No one tends to answer like that.

"I'm not broken. I don't need help. Everyone else has a problem with me being the way I am, but you don't see me having a problem with them, do you? No. I don't go judging everyone else for being germ ridden and disgusting. I don't judge everyone else for their constant need to hug and kiss each other. You'd think they'd extend me the same courtesy, wouldn't you?"

No one answered with no one's usual answer.

"You know, talking to yourself is one of the first signs of insanity," Plasterer told him from the doorway.

"Are you happy now?" Denis asked, ignoring the quip.

"Not quite, but I will be. It's better this way, Denis. We have control of the situation when it's just us. I can control you, and you can be controlled, and trust me, that's just how you like it."

"I don't want you controlling me," Denis told him.

"Sure you do," Plasterer replied. "You want it because it helps you not to feel. Not to grieve. You let me control you, and you're free not to deal with things like funerals and sex and pushy girlfriends who want to spoon at half-past two in the morning."

"Can things go back to the way they were now?" Denis asked, seeking some form of silver lining.

"No, Denis," Plasterer told him coldly. "They cannot. You see, you breached the trust. You and that last little sliver of the old life that you represent are bad for us, so you're no longer allowed to call any of the shots. I'm moving into your room."

The words seemed to slap Denis in the face.

"You're what?" Denis asked.

"Moving into your room. It's the master bedroom and I'm

the master. You're not. You get the couch. You'll prefer it that way. You can let the TV play you to sleep, all those cop shows carefully turning off your ability to think. Perfect for you."

Denis felt the urge to cry again, but held it back. Plasterer seemed disappointed.

"Good night, Denis," he said by way of farewell. "Tomorrow's a new day. Try to look at it that way."

Denis sat on the couch. He was back in this universe again, but it was different now. He walked to the closet by the end of the stairs and pulled out a spare duvet. He walked back to the living room. He lay down on the couch and covered himself. He stared at the paint, now dry, which spattered the far wall. He did not cry.

The alarm on his phone woke him the next morning, but it wasn't the usual tone. It had been changed to some kind of pop-music monstrosity. The kind of noise that should have upset him, but it just made him think of Rebecca. Maybe she had changed it? Maybe he changed it himself; he couldn't remember. He was still fully dressed. He had slept in his clothes. They were now wrinkled beyond what anyone would consider acceptable, which itself was so far beyond what Denis Murphy considered acceptable that it was too extraordinary to be believed. Oddly, it didn't provoke a reaction from him. He swung his legs over the edge of the couch and stretched. There was chatter in the kitchen. The Professor, Penny O'Neill and Plasterer sat eating breakfast. It was cereal, actual cereal of the kind he himself would eat every morning rather than their usual fare of shredded newspaper and dish soap. Deano huddled in the corner, head down; he barely seemed to be alive. As Denis walked into the room, he saw a place had been set for him. His bowl was filled to the brim with the contents of the vacuum cleaner with water dripping down the side. All eyes were on him as he strode past the table and up the stairs.

His "breakfast" was still waiting for him when he arrived after showering and dressing.

"Eat up," Plasterer ordered.

"No," Denis replied.

"A healthy breakfast is the cornerstone of a productive day, Denis. I would have assumed that you were aware of the dietary importance of early-morning sustenance," the Professor chimed in.

"I want coffee. And a cigarette," Denis replied. That was surprising. He hadn't realized he wanted a cigarette.

"Stop behaving like a child and eat your dust," Penny O'Neill insisted.

Denis ignored her and made toast instead. He didn't bother buttering it, but choked it down without embellishment. For just a moment he worried they'd take it from him, but Plasterer merely looked amused as he watched Denis wolf down his dry breakfast.

"And what will you do for the day, then?" Plasterer asked.

"I'm going to work," Denis replied.

"Where?" Plasterer asked.

"Where do you think? In my office."

"No, I don't think so, Denis. Not today. We're having a party in your office for most of the morning, and you're not welcome to attend. On top of that, it's not going to be an environment for getting any kind of work done. Best go somewhere else to work."

"I'm going to work in my office," Denis replied stubbornly and realized, to his horror, he sounded whiny.

"Tut-tut," Penny O'Neill chided.

"Stop treating me like a child," Denis said, asserting himself, and stomped out of the kitchen. He wondered how long this could last. He had done as they asked and driven Rebecca out of the house. Why would they not leave him be now? Why were they being so vindictive?

He turned on his computer and opened the various files that required his attention. He click-clicked on the icons as needed and set about doing a day's work. Something he had been neglecting recently. For a precious half hour it seemed as though he was going to be left in peace, but soon his mind began to wander and thoughts of Rebecca and Frank and Ollie crept in. He got distracted for a moment and sat, staring into space.

"We were going to let you work," Plasterer announced from the door. "But since you're not doing anything anyway..."

The clown strolled into the room and started humming as he scanned the CDs on the wall rack. Penny O'Neill followed after, swaying, as was her manner. The Professor came in too, pushing Deano before him. The fur ball shambled in like a broken dog; he made his way to another corner and curled up yet again. Denis wondered how they had finally managed to break him, and regretted that he hadn't noticed his only ally sooner. They could have worked together.

"I just got distracted, that's all. I'll work, I promise, just please leave me alone."

"No," Plasterer told him cheerfully as he selected a Dean Martin CD and put it into the retro-looking sound system.

"Why are you doing this? Why won't you leave me alone?"

"Why are you doing this? Why won't you leave me alone?" Plasterer echoed, his tone mocking.

Denis spun in his chair and fixed his eyes on his computer screen, determined that he would get some work done, but it was pointless. The party kicked off around him as the three danced to Rat Pack music. Denis tried to focus as they jeered and mocked him. Every now and then, Plasterer would deliberately bump himself into the back of Denis's chair, or let a stray elbow glance off Denis's head. Each time it was a not-so-subtle reminder of the power that the clown held over him. He could beat Denis senseless if he wanted to; he had proven that already. For all that he despised this new version of his housemates, he was still very much afraid of what they could do to hurt him if they wanted to.

After three hours of struggling to work, Denis felt his resolve dwindling, before vanishing entirely. He had emailed none of his assigned tasks to his head office. His phone rang. The number that flashed up on the screen was his mother's. He ignored it. It rang again. This time it was his office. He ignored that too. Around him his housemates sang and danced. He tried hard to ignore them as well, and he had all but given up when the last straw arrived in the form of an email. It was his boss. A boss who barely knew him.

Denis, I'd like to have a chat with you tomorrow. Please be in my office at ten. Regards, Ger.

And that was all he could take. Denis was going to be fired. They had now officially cost him everything. Everything he owned, everything he cared about, everything he wanted was now out of reach to him, because his housemates owned it, didn't care about it or didn't want it. He sat on the couch in the living room and rested his chin on his hands. The party continued as they danced all around him singing "You're Nobody till Somebody Loves You." Tears stung at his eyes, and he tried to hold them back. He missed Rebecca so very much. A cheer went up from his housemates as the first teardrop fell.

The rest of the day was a blur for Denis, a nonstop series of torment and torture. He got no peace from them, not for a minute. They followed him everywhere. When he tried to go to bed, Plasterer shouted at him that it was his room now. Denis ended up on the couch again. Fully dressed again.

ME, MYSELF AND THEM

When they finally retired for the night, pushing Deano up the stairs before them, Penny O'Neill held back for a minute and watched him. For a long time she had been his only connection to femininity, and he could sense her feeling of betrayal that she'd been replaced by Rebecca. He thought of all the nights that he woke, terrified from some dream or other, to see her sprawled languidly across his bed, or the Sunday evenings after his mother had left when she rested her head in his lap while they watched television. He didn't miss it. He missed Rebecca. Penny O'Neill's long look at him was an invitation of sorts. She was asking him to be her pet, a new dynamic to be sure, but at least some connection with his life before Rebecca. He looked away, and that was all the answer she needed.

"You're pathetic," she told him, shaking her head.

"I know," he replied, turning on the couch and curling up.

He didn't hear her leave the room; he just knew that she was gone. He also knew that what was going on was not sustainable. There was no way he could live like this for long. Something would have to be done, something drastic, but there was no way of knowing what it was. His existence was quickly becoming a source of pain to him. He could try to sell his house, but he knew they'd never let him. He could move out, find a place to rent, but then he'd have to share with others, or face paying a huge rent alone, on top of a mortgage, an idea that was equally unsustainable. He thought about it for a few hours, seeking a way out. There had to be an answer. Eventually his thoughts drifted back to Rebecca. How sad she had looked when she had decided to leave was like a knife cutting at him. He had checked his phone several times during the course of the day to see if she would text him, or call. She didn't.

He tried to think of happier thoughts, and settled on the memory of her on the first night they had slept together in his house. The curves of her body, and the way she fitted against him perfectly, her soft smooth skin against his as he drifted to sleep. The memory was sweet and painful in equal measures. He held on to it tightly, even as it cut at him.

He felt that there was a solution to this somewhere, but it remained elusive. Some way to make them fall into line, some way to get around them, or through them. Nothing came to him. He spent the entire night struggling to think of how to fix everything. When his alarm went off the following morning, he was wide-awake.

The Professor shambled into the room, looking more dead than usual.

"If I were in your shoes, metaphorically speaking, I'd find this situation unbearable and intolerable. Not many other real people live in a manner such as this. Now, if I were in your shoes literally, I would be proud of how shiny my shoes are. For the former, I'm glad I'm not in your shoes, and in the case of the latter, I'm certainly regretful that I haven't given shoe care more consideration."

"It's as much your fault as it is his," Denis replied bitterly, refusing to stir from his prone position.

"It's as much your fault as it is ours," the Professor countered. "You'd realize that if you gave it some thought. You are responsible for all of this."

"Why can't we go back to the way it was?" Denis asked.

"I think if you examine yourself very carefully, you'll know why, but then, you've never been overly fond of introspection, have you? It hurts, so you don't do it. Eventually you're going to have to. It shows you what you're worth to yourself."

"I don't know what you're talking about," Denis replied.

"Not at the moment you don't, but since you're more like the walking dead than I am, you'll eventually have to look at what your life is worth. In that moment, you'll turn inward and you'll see what you've failed to see for six, maybe even seven years now. Will it be everything you secretly fear it will be? Or will it be hope? Will you see something that gives you reason to fight? If I were the kind to lay a wager, and I am, I'd guess that you'll look at what's left of your rotting mind and find nothing of value. Maybe that's just because I am who I am."

Denis looked at him for a moment or two. Noting the ruined face and exceptionally well-tailored suit, which was just a little bit too wrinkly. He had been wrong about his shoes too. They were shining.

"Why do you hate me?" Denis asked him after a long pause.

"What's not to hate?" the Professor shot back.

From the kitchen the sound of loud guffawing could be heard. Plasterer's loud guffawing to be precise.

"What's not to hate indeed?" he chimed in.

Denis found the spark of anger inside himself. He stood up suddenly.

"Going somewhere?" the Professor asked.

"I'm going for a walk," Denis replied.

"You do that," Plasterer interjected, now standing in the doorway. "Go out among your people. They just love you. You can hug them all and pick flowers out of the dirt and pretend that you're one of them. They'll know you're not, but you can pretend all the same."

It was the tone that hurt, not the thought of the people. Plasterer had chosen his words carefully for maximum impact; he wanted to remind Denis that he disliked being among people. He wanted his words to stir a fear in Denis that he may have to come in contact with other people. What the clown had not realized was that Denis hated being in his own home so much now, that the thought of being among people was oddly enticing, in a way that it hadn't been for some time now. He shrugged off the words and went upstairs to change.

He locked the bathroom door and changed his clothes as he listened to the echoes of mocking laughter drifting up to him from the kitchen.

"I know what you're doing in there," Plasterer called suggestively through the door.

"Fuck off," Denis said without much enthusiasm.

He didn't want to leave the bathroom, so he didn't for a while. He stood staring without looking at the mirror in front of him. He would go to town and drink. In the company of strangers he would erase his own ability to think in a place he knew they would never go. There, with dark beer and whiskey, he would find a way to make them quiet and a comfort all of his own making.

Penny O'Neill was waiting for him as he made his way out of the bathroom and down the stairs.

"Don't you look dashing?" she asked with a mocking smile. "Maybe you'll find the love of your life out there," she called after him as he trudged for the door. "I know women are just dying to meet a man who's terrified of odd numbers and can't bear to be touched. You'll be beating them off you."

She was trying to be clever like Plasterer had been. Women meant intimacy, and intimacy meant contact with others, and once again the words had been chosen to inspire fear in him, to make him pause, to fill him with doubt. He loathed Penny O'Neill and her ridiculous swaying walk, loathed her for her hatred toward Rebecca. He couldn't wait to get away from her. He let her words bounce off his back.

Their mockery followed him to the door of the house. Deano barred his path and began tugging at his coat as he threw it about his shoulders. There was something urgent about the way he was pulling at Denis. He was pointing at

Denis's face, jabbing his hairy finger at it, but the mockery of the others propelled Denis past the fur ball and out the door of the house. He deliberately neglected the door-locking procedure. He pointedly refused to count his steps. He had no idea where he was going, or why he was going there, but there was no question about it. He could spend not one more minute in that house with them. He strolled out the gate and deeply breathed in the fresh morning air, trying desperately to find something to enjoy in it. He used to do that a lot, when he wasn't broken. He picked up the pace, putting as much distance between him and them as he possibly could. Home was where the hell was.

ISN'T IT RICH?

A cloud of despair settled around his head as he walked from the house. His vision seemed darker, tinted with a kind of blackness that he knew instinctively was from within. There was something else too, a weight in his stomach that caused it to roil and heave, provoked as it was by the anxiety and overwhelming sense of isolation.

The local children were playing on the green again, kicking a ball with no apparent goal in mind. Denis hated their carefree running, their easy way of colliding with one another and their peals of laughter. Their game stopped as they saw him coming through his gate and out onto the road. There was no titter of laughter now; in fact, they looked alarmed at the sight of him. Perhaps it was his scowl, or his shoeless stunt of the day before, but they recoiled from him as he moved.

Their judgment was another sting, another arrow to the thousand that had gone before it. Why, he thought to himself, did everyone want to judge him everywhere he went? Why was his life something that other people felt they had the right to look down on? He felt the first stirrings of anger as he moved. Plasterer didn't tolerate other people's judgment. A thug and a bully he might be, but nobody looked down on the clown. In his mind's eye he could see the big man sitting in the armchair, his gloves, one white and one red, gripping the armrests.

Tell them to go fuck themselves, Plasterer seemed to whisper.

Denis ignored him, but scowled harder at the children anyway. Down the street one of their parents watched with a look bordering on alarm. She had always been a kindly woman, but now she was appraising him as if he might hurt one of her children. The anger rose in him. Never, not even once, had he been anything but polite to her and her lousy, messy children, and now she was judging him as if he was some kind of bad guy.

Tell her to go fuck herself too, Plasterer whispered from the couch. *What's her problem? Nosy bitch.*

Denis ignored the voice again, but it was harder this time. He wanted to know why she was being so judgmental. He swallowed the rising anger; it dropped into the ball of unease that was his stomach. Barely looking at her as he passed, he picked up the pace of his walk and headed for town. He toyed with the idea of taking the bus, but people are people and Denis was Denis and, in being Denis, was absolutely not in the mood for people, so he plowed on on foot.

His walk typically took forty minutes, but he was making good time, spurred on by the judgment of the people all around him and the cloud of despair that followed him. He considered the idea of trying to outpace it, but clouds of despair just don't work that way. It seemed to him that everyone was staring at him, as if they all knew what he had done. There was, of course, no way that was possible, but something about the way passersby looked at him caused his ire to rise further.

If this keeps up, you're going to have to punch one of them in their damn nosy heads.

Through his rising anger and Plasterer's running commentary, the cloud of despair still clung to him, and the feeling in the pit of his stomach continued to gnaw away at him. Something was terribly wrong. He chose not to examine it too closely.

He arrived in town in a record-breaking thirty-three minutes. He considered doing a lap of one of the blocks until his arrival time at the bar coincided with a much more satisfying number, but in the grand scheme of problems he was having, it seemed like an unnecessary flamboyance.

Outside a small hidden bar where he had gone to play pool and drink pre-match beers with Eddie and Frank and Ollie, an elderly man stood smoking a cigarette. His eyes widened when he saw Denis coming, and for a moment he stood blocking the door.

Get out of the way, old man.

"Move," Denis barked at him. His sharp tone surprised even himself.

The elderly man jumped to one side hurriedly.

Denis grunted at him as he stepped into the dark interior of the bar.

"Guinness and a whiskey," he snapped at the young bartender. His voice was independent of him now.

"You okay, buddy?" the youngster asked, as he dried a glass.

None of your fucking business.

"I'm fine," Denis snapped. "Guinness and a whiskey."

"Bit early for that sort of thing?" he asked, nodding in Denis's direction.

Oh this little shit is just begging for a punch.

"You gonna get me my drinks or not?" Denis shot back, raising his voice slightly.

The young man swallowed hard and began filling the pint glass.

He surveyed the bar as he took his seat. The pool table had

a long wooden particleboard covering it, stained with the rings of countless pints of Guinness and beer. The windows, tinted to keep the small cramped interior in permanent darkness, were dirty. Besides the bartender and the elderly smoker who had crept back inside warily, there were only two other customers, both men, apparently in their sixties.

"Is this some kind of a joke?" one of them asked as he lifted his pint.

You're a joke.

"No. This is a person having a couple of drinks. Got a problem?" Denis asked. He had had enough of being polite to people who judged him, enough of trying to please other people. The clown had it right all along. Take respect. Earn it. He had allowed Rebecca to demand a place in his life. He had tolerated Ollie and Frank joking at his expense. He permitted his mother to visit once a week even though it was hellish each and every time. For what reason had he done all this? To impress them? To pretend to himself and everyone else that he was okay? His rage grew a little greater, and his hand tightened around the pint glass as his drinks were placed before him.

The bartender shrank from him. That was good; they weren't judging him anymore, they were showing him the respect he deserved. He drank the Guinness in one swift motion and shook the empty glass at the young man behind the counter.

"More," he demanded, as he picked up the whiskey glass.

The bartender nodded at him, his eyes down.

And so Denis sat in silence with only his despair and his anger and the deep weighty feeling in his stomach that something was terribly wrong.

He didn't know how long he had been sitting at the bar when Eddie first crept into his head. He had drunk more than two for sure. He had been staring at the pool table when his friend's image reared up, unannounced and unwelcome, standing with the pool cue drawn across his shoulders, his arms across it. The bar was close to the stadium where the local soccer team played, and this had become a warm-up spot for the two of them, sometimes all four of them, on game nights.

Get out now.

He took the clown's advice and walked out, leaving a sense of relief behind as the customers inside released their collective breaths.

Outside, the sunshine stabbed at his eyes, and he winced. A teenager standing nearby saw him and laughed.

Punch him.

"What are you laughing at?" he growled at the youngster. His anger had a life of its own now. It seemed to be growing almost too big for his body. The tiny voice that told him this was all wrong was barely audible over the rushing sound of the fury inside that had burst its banks. Everyone decided everything for him, forced him into corners, made him play by their rules.

"Er...nothing," the youth replied, looking startled.

"Fuck off, then," Denis told him. The drinks had gone to his head, and he felt fuzzy as he made his way through the town. Still they judged him wherever he went. Each person passing him in the street looked at him with the knowledge of what he had done in their eyes.

Killer. Breaker of hearts. Who cares if they know?

He strode on, trying not to sway as he moved.

The next bar was a much more popular spot, but so early in the day only two customers and a lady behind the bar were waiting for him when he arrived. He strolled in, almost daring them to judge him. Daring them to pass a remark or laugh or do anything except keep their eyes to themselves.

"Can I help you?" the woman asked. She looked worried, almost disbelieving.

Watch your damn tone, Plasterer seemed to say.

"Beer and a whiskey," Denis replied, leaning toward her. He was trying to loom a little, like Plasterer did. Looming is an acquired skill, however, and it was not one Denis had picked up. So instead he just leaned, drunkenly.

"Are you sure you're okay to drink?" she asked.

What are you? Our mother?

"I'm fine. A beer and a whiskey," he repeated.

She hovered for just a moment before picking up the pint glass and filling it for him.

Denis turned to face the other two customers. They were staring at him. He stared back until they realized what he was doing and dropped their eyes.

After his third drink in the new bar, Denis began to feel that the plan was not working. He was definitely drunk now, and most of his thoughts seemed to float away before he had a chance to form them properly, but pouring alcohol into the mess of anxiety in his stomach had done nothing to quell it, and the cloud still hung about his head, coloring everything he saw in a shroud of darkness and misery.

He could no longer picture Plasterer sitting on the arm-chair, which seemed like a good thing to him. It occurred to him, through his haze, that drinking was a paradox much like so many other of his favorite activities. Here, he was trying to control his own lack of control. He had avoided drinking for so long. Feared it for the slightest hint in his mind that it had played a part in the death of his sister and his best friend. Now it was helping him, feeding his anger, which was feed-ing his sense of authority. It was also feeding the terrible anx-iety. It was putting Denis in charge of himself, a position he disliked, so he talked like the clown and drank like his old self and hoped people would not judge him to his face. His mind wandered to the last time he was drunk and the new bar he had been in with the gang. He had touched her there, had left his hand to linger on her back, and it was as if this little gesture had spurred her on. In this gesture he had ceded ground, and from there she had not stopped conquering him, piece by piece, until she had ruined his life. He had tripped. It was the ground's fault.

He hauled himself out of his stool as he decided to make his way back to that bar, back to the moment when he had silently given her permission to touch him. He reeled just a little as he moved, his shoulder colliding with a passing pedestrian.

"Oh I'm sorry," the man said without looking. Then he made eye contact and swallowed hard.

"Watch where you're going," Denis told him, turning on his heel.

It was still bright out, still early he guessed, but didn't bother to check. He weaved through a sea of judgmental faces, each one staring at him as though everything was his fault. He looked back with contempt. They could all rot as far as he was concerned. The tiny voice in his head urged him to think about the implications of what he was doing, to think about the people, not just his family and friends, but all the people who were looking at him. He refused and continued walking, secretly hoping that someone might bang against him again, but they didn't. They melted out of his path.

Inside the bar a handful of people sat around beers and coffee cups and soft drinks, talking cheerfully. It was brighter here than the previous two bars had been, and there was an air of joviality that he instantly found disagreeable. Conversations broke off on his arrival, a dark cloud into their otherwise bright days. He loathed every one of them with their healthy relationships and their clean hands. No blood on them. They were staring at him as he strolled up to the bar.

"Beer and a whiskey," he ordered.

"Absolutely not," the bartender replied. He was Denis's height, but burlier, with a large, expertly groomed red beard and short red hair that had been shaved at the sides.

"What?" Denis asked, feeling the anger swell and surge again.

"I'm not serving you," the bartender replied matter-of-factly.

"And why the fuck not?"

"I think you're crazy, and drunk, but mostly I just don't want to," he said casually.

Denis seethed at the judgment. He railed against it.

Punch him. Punch him in the face. Then they'll respect you. All of them.

"Get me the damn drink!" Denis shouted.

"No," was the reply as the bartender narrowed his eyes and leaned forward. "You're not getting a drink. I'll get you water and a face towel if you want, but that's about the size of it."

It was there for everyone to see. The pure undiluted judgment that was being thrown at him. This time he wouldn't let it slide. This time he would make someone pay. Denis stood his ground, his jaw clenched.

The bartender met his challenging look for a moment.

"Let me get you some water," he said, shaking his head as he moved away.

He had been blocking a large mirror that hung behind the bar.

As he moved away from it, Denis saw his own face.

It was a terrifying face.

Covered in makeup, thick white makeup, red around the lips, blue under the eyes. It was rough, a crudely drawn approximation of a clown's face. A clown he knew. Not the sharp, clear edges and expert style of Plasterer, but a jagged, terrifying mess under greasy hair that stuck to the white in places. The lip makeup wasn't smooth, but splotched on haphazardly. His eyes looked black and menacing and tiny in the hollow of his head.

He looked in horror at his own reflection. How had it happened? When? Were they playing a prank on him? Had they done it in his sleep? His memory stirred as he recalled being locked into the bathroom before he left. The implications stung him. He had done this to himself. Torn by the coup in his home and the smell of Rebecca's perfume lingering in the air, he had done this to himself and couldn't even remember it.

They had been judging him, all the way to town, everyone he met had been judging him, but not for who he was, for what he showed them.

"I'm sorry," he said to the bartender in confused dismay. "I'll leave."

The man was looking at him in a new way now, concern painted on his face.

"You okay, buddy?"

"No."

"You want me to call someone?" There was a newfound sympathy in the man's eyes. A touching gesture of humanity to a lost soul.

"I don't have anyone," Denis told him as the grim reality of that fact rammed into the inside of his skull.

He made his way out of the bar, on unsteady feet, trying not to make eye contact with the people he had frightened. They were all looking at him with concern now. Through the shock he found a small worm of hatred for their pity.

He had to go. Somewhere where there was no piteous looks

or fear or malice. No such place existed as far as Denis knew, and so he just walked.

His feet powered him through streets and past shops. His head was down, his eyes dodged people and focused on his shoes. Shiny and well-polished. His lips trembled as he passed groups of people. Anger now forgotten, he could feel the ball of uneasiness in his stomach growling at him until he could ignore it no longer. And so, as he walked he tried to feel it, really feel it in his body and in his mind, and to analyze it. He tried to unpack the feeling and see what it was. It had grown in him over days, but he felt like it might have always been there, hiding. Had he truly always felt this way? Why had he never noticed before? He pondered as he moved. He had no idea where he was going until he found himself standing outside Riverside Cemetery. Its cast-iron gates stood open in between marble pillars. The driveway leading in split an immaculately trimmed lawn, which was home to beautifully maintained shrubs and trees.

His grandparents were buried here. And possibly Eddie. Most important, Jules was buried here. He had never visited her. He listened for Plasterer's condemnation, but the clown remained silent. He walked through the gate tentatively and appraised the many hundreds of rows of the dead. Here, death was everywhere, old death and new, but for some reason it lacked the bitter sting of fresh mourning. In its place was a feeling of sadness mixed with something else he couldn't quite identify. He didn't know where her grave was, but knowing his mother and father, it would be by his grandparents. They had loved Jules. Him too. Both of them as a pair, really. His feet guided him as he took in the coldly beautiful headstones. Some were decorated with fresh flowers that seemed quietly dignified; others had the carcasses of long-dead petals sitting nearby, and Denis thought they painted an almost unbearably sad picture. He took it in as he walked, his head turning, hoping that no one else would see him in all his ridiculousness.

He found her grave before he knew what it was. Standing where he thought he might find it, with several bunches of beautiful, fresh, purple flowers nearby.

"Julianne…" he whispered at her gravestone as he sat down. "I'm so sorry."

The first sob broke through his crude clown mouth, spraying spittle on the headstone. He reached out with his hands to clean the spit.

"I'm sorry. I didn't mean to…"

The gravestone said nothing. That's the way of gravestones. It didn't judge him either though.

"They wouldn't let me go to the funeral. I was still in the hospital. After that I couldn't. I just couldn't. I'm so sorry."

If she was replying to him, her voice couldn't reach. The gravestone was certainly not giving anything away.

"Please forgive me."

He knew she couldn't answer. He figured she wouldn't have been mad at him anyway. She forgave him most things. Once she had been angry with him for a week after he and Eddie had fought. A full week. He had ignored her anger, and eventually she had come into his bedroom and thrown a shoe at him. When he laughed at her, she had laughed back. Just like that her anger vanished, and they talked that night, almost all night. He had apologized to Eddie the next day.

That had been the way with her. Often as reckless and stupid as he was, but with a bigger heart. She had guided him and in turn leaned on him for guidance. They had been a team. It had never been the standard older brother, little sister relationship. They were twins as far as he was concerned. Then he killed her.

Something about that thought stirred the ball of uneasiness

and made him queasy again. He sat on her grave and thought about it. The tears were still coming, but slowly, not in the great rush he expected.

"I should have come here sooner," he whispered at her grave. "I'll do better."

The knot in his stomach loosened. Something was giving way. He paused to think about it again. He was responding to the first thought, and focusing on fixing it. It loosened some more.

"I want to tell you that I've been busy, but we both know that's not true. I haven't. I've been…sort of hiding. You'd hardly believe it. I used to hate staying home, you know. I always wanted to be around people, now I just… I…"

His words failed him for a moment.

The grave waited patiently. Her name was all he could look at; it filled up his eyes.

"I don't really do anything, do I?" he asked the silent gravestone. "I mean, I just sort of exist. It's not really living."

He had stopped crying now.

"Fuck me!" he exclaimed with half a chuckle. "You'd hate it."

He sighed.

"You'd hate what I've become. God knows I do… Funny that. I didn't know I hated it until just now. Until I came to see you. But there it is. Still guiding me, I see…" He smiled at her and thought about her lovely smile. This time he didn't think about the blood and the shattered glass. He just thought about her lovely smile and her grumpiness in the mornings and how serious she could be sometimes.

"It's just such work all the time. And all the fear. I hate it. I hate that I gave in to it. I hate that I let them push me around. I hate myself for what I've done to you and Eddie and Mom and everyone. Most of all, I hate what I've done to Rebecca. And to myself. Sometimes I'm such an asshole."

If Jules had been there, she would have laughed at him.

He looked across the graveyard and admired the orderliness of it all. The rows and rows of graves, the uniformity of it. The grass between the graves was neatly trimmed, meticulously maintained. The walkways were swept.

A cool breeze brushed his face through his makeup and stirred his hair. There was a peace and quiet about the place that he admired. A reverential silence as if breathing too loud might offend the dead. He looked back at her headstone; funny how a piece of granite could appear friendly and familiar. He reached out to it and traced her name, and then he sighed.

"I guess I know what I have to do," he told her, climbing to his feet. "I'll see you again real soon. Thanks for the advice."

The cloud of despair was gone. Just like that. Perhaps it was hovering over someone else's head. The Professor's maybe, but Denis didn't care. Gone is gone. The uneasiness in his stomach had left with the cloud. He knew what must be done. He would do it. It would not be an easy thing, though he suspected that he was not special in this regard. It seemed like the kind of thing that anyone who did it found hard, but it was something that needed doing. For the first time in a long time, drunk but unconcerned by this, Denis Murphy had a purpose that fit him.

LIFE IS HARD

He walked home with the single-minded drive of a man on a mission. There was a blessed absence of thought, no confusion in his head, no part of him that told him he was going the wrong way or doing the wrong thing. He didn't think of what Plasterer would say, or how the Professor might react. His will was iron. Nothing was going to knock him from the path he had set himself. His housemates never even popped into his head; they didn't factor in this decision. The only thing distracting from his determination was a slight sense of euphoria. It might have been all the drinks. To be able to walk from here to there without a cacophony of contradictory thoughts was something of a novelty for Denis Murphy. The day seemed a little brighter now, the noise of the traffic less of an intrusion and more of a kind of energy, as though the world going about its business was a good thing for once. He tried to absorb as much as he could; it would help him do what needed to be done.

He walked through his gate, leaving it open, hoping the neighbors didn't see his horrible painted face. He unlocked the door and stepped inside. Plasterer was smirking at him from the hallway. Ignoring the clown, he made his way to the bathroom. His reflection looked perplexed and, for some reason, slightly bored. Then he went to the living room, where he took the DIY materials still strewn about from the days before and began to tidy up. He changed into some old jeans and a T-shirt in his room, the greasepaint smudging his clothes as he changed. He didn't care. Plasterer followed silently, with Penny O'Neill and the Professor in tow. He brushed by them as he headed back to the living room. A thought occurred to him as he walked: they were being too quiet.

He glanced at them to see Plasterer's jaw working furiously. His face was contorted in its now all-too-familiar mockery, but there was no sound coming out of his mouth, as though his rage was too great for words.

No sound at all. Just silence.

Denis decided not to think on it too much. There were things to do, if he could keep his will. He opened the paint cans and stirred them with a wooden spoon collected from the kitchen en route. Penny O'Neill stood there, concern painted on her face as she watched his every move. Still, no sound emerged. The Professor was gesticulating wildly, and he opened and closed his mouth as though he couldn't find the words. He looked more alarmed than the reanimated dead had the right to look. Curious, Denis paused his stirring to regard them casually. He waited for one of them to say something, but they just stood there, gesturing and scowling and jawing. No one spoke. He shrugged and returned to the task at hand. After carefully removing the decorations and fixtures from the wall, he set about painting. All the while they moved, stalking and circling him silently. Penny O'Neill even began weeping, without making a single sound.

He painted until the damage done by the Professor's outburst had been undone. With the wall slick and clean again, he began to tidy up. He wasn't going to leave a mess behind for anyone else. Plasterer stepped in front of him, his face a mask of pure rage.

"You fucking listen to me, you worm. You don't get to ignore me. I tell you what's what and you listen." His words came out, but they seemed to be coming from far away.

"No," Denis replied.

Plasterer brought his hands up. The red-gloved one looked like blood, and he pushed Denis in the chest. It seemed ineffectual for such a big man. Denis carefully put the cans and brushes down and shoved back.

Plasterer reeled back and tumbled to the ground with a yelp and a curse, his big frame hitting the living-room floor harder than it had a right to. He decided not to force the issue, but simply picked up his belongings and stepped past the shocked clown. Penny O'Neill was staring at him, dumbfounded. The Professor trembled a little.

"Don't you fucking walk away from me," Plasterer called out. "You need me. You need all of us. You try this crap, and you just wait and see if we don't fuck off and leave you to deal with this on your own. Picture that world, Denis—nobody to help you make sense of it all, just you, all alone. Terribly, terrifyingly alone."

Denis paused. He had been alone for such a long time. Even when he was completely surrounded. Not for much longer though. He walked upstairs, with the big clown struggling to his feet behind him.

"Don't you fucking walk away from me. Do you hear me?"

"Please, Denis, don't make him angry..." Penny O'Neill chimed in.

"This is a poor course of action." The Professor almost whispered.

Denis walked to the bathroom and ran a facecloth under the warm tap.

"What are you doing, you little shit?" Plasterer asked from the doorway.

"Please be quiet. I'm so utterly sick of listening to you."

He hadn't really expected the clown to stop talking, but when he did, Denis didn't think about it, he just enjoyed the momentary silence.

He was fed up of listening to the clown. Fed up of hearing what he was supposed to do and think. Plasterer had become irrelevant.

He looked at them, all three of them standing there. They were trying to talk to him, their mouths working furiously, but no sound was coming out. He watched them impassively as they stood there. Plasterer was the most frantic, his face contorted, wrinkling his makeup. Denis took a step toward them, and they shrank back. They seemed smaller now. Plasterer made a final futile attempt to block the door, his mouth still moving dumbly. Without thinking, Denis pushed him. The effect of the shove seemed disproportionate to the effort he had put in, as the big clown was lifted from his feet. Plasterer sailed through the air and slammed with force into the corridor wall. The Professor and Penny O'Neill stopped trying to talk and looked at Denis in fear. He brushed past them and made his way back downstairs, his face still wet and slightly red from his scrubbing. They followed him silently, almost sheepishly to the kitchen.

He turned on them once more, testing to see if they would flinch from him again. They stood, almost shoulder to shoulder, staring at him. Plasterer was no longer frantic; he looked docile. Denis shook his head at them and turned away.

He went to the utility room with the painting supplies, and when he came back, they were gone. He hadn't stepped out of the room for that long; it seemed impossible for them to have just vanished. Deano was waiting instead. The fur ball stepped to one side to allow Denis in.

"Where did they go?" Denis asked.

The fur ball shrugged at him. He didn't seem concerned and, consequently, neither was Denis, who sat down to write out his farewells. There were people who had to be addressed and loose ends to be tied up. He was going to have to tell the people he worked for, so they could start looking for a replacement. It was only fair, really. Denis was nothing if not considerate. The calm that had settled on him had all the sedative force of a drug. He was composed. He was ready. At least, he thought he was.

His first email, his most important, was the hardest to write. How to put right several years of wrong. He wrote and rewrote several times. He tried not to cry as he typed the words. Short and to the point. That's how she would prefer it. When finished it read:

Mother,

I'm sorry, more than you can know, for what I've put you through. I went to see Jules. It's funny, she's been gone for so long and yet I still feel like she's here with me, showing me the way. I needed her.

You probably already know, but I've become terribly lost, and something has to be done about that.

I wanted to keep myself apart. I wanted to be on my own. Where I can't hurt anyone. Somehow I've ended up here, and everyone I love is hurt by me. I'm sorry your marriage ended. I'm sorry I did that to Dad. I'm sorry Uncle Jack has to deal with guilt even though he never did anything wrong to anyone. I'm sorry I took Jules from you, sorry that I took Eddie from Ned and Ann. I'm sorry for poor Rick and his family. I guess I can't say enough how sorry I am.

I see now where I've gone wrong. It's taken me too long to see it, and you all had to suffer for that. I'll be grateful to you, to Rebecca, to Ollie and Frank, to Ned and Ann, to all the people who have tolerated what I am, until the end of my days.

If I could trouble you for another favor, please take care of the house when I'm gone. I think it'll be very empty without me, and I wouldn't like to see it fall into disrepair.

I know what I have to do. Too late I see it. I hope you can forgive me.

Your ever-loving son,

Denis

It seemed to Denis that the words were perhaps overly pompous, but at the best of times there's a little of the Professor in everyone. He sent the email and switched off the computer lest she reply.

You're doing the right thing, Deano told him as he sat on the couch in the office.

"You can talk?" Denis replied, though for some reason he wasn't surprised.

Sort of. This might be the first time you've listened.

"But you can now?"

You've given me a voice. It should be familiar to you. It's your voice.

He wasn't wrong. Deano's voice was coming to him as if he had recorded it himself.

"How did I give it to you? I never heard you speak before, ever. I wouldn't even know where to start with a voice for you," Denis replied, confused.

First time you've ever not ignored me actually, Deano shot back.

Denis was puzzled. Reading the body language of a ball of fur is no easy task.

"I didn't realize I'd been ignoring you before."

I tried to tell you many things in many ways. Unfortunately for us both, you're remarkably stupid for such a smart man.

"Tell me what? In what ways?" Denis asked.

It was always me being restrained, Denis. I was always being tied up. If anyone was cowed down or being bullied, it was me. I'm sure you noticed that, but I don't think you ever wondered why. I'm the one that was on your side, and for that, I rebelled when you rebelled. I fought when you fought, and when you were happy, I was happy.

Denis shook his head. Deano wasn't wrong; there was no question that he might be, but one must always find it difficult to trust a hair ball that talks to you in your own voice.

"I'm insane, aren't I?" he asked.

You're not well is how I'd put it. And by the way, I wouldn't trust me either. You're going to fix it now though, because this isn't sustainable. You can't keep going like this, and while you're fine for the moment, you know as well as I do that another day will come when something else happens, and suddenly you'll be listening to them again, and then when they want to they'll break you just like they did before.

"Where did they go?"

They're taking a break. Well-deserved if you ask me. You've been working them pretty hard recently.

"How do you mean?"

You'll get it eventually.

"Did you read my email?"

I did.

"Your thoughts?"

You write like the Professor talks.

"But it was good?"

I never said he didn't talk well.

"I'm doing the right thing?"

Well, first, you can't trust what I say, because I'm part of your problem. Second, you can't trust yourself because you're part of your problem too, and that's the problem. For what it's worth though, yes. I do think you're doing the right thing.

"Do you think they'll ever forgive me?" Denis asked. He could feel his anxiety rising up against his sense of determination.

Who?

"Rebecca. Mom. Ollie and Frank. Ned and Ann."

I don't think it's in any of them not to. They're good people. Did you know that you were surrounded by good people all of the time?

"Of course I didn't. I was too busy feeling sorry for myself."

Liar. Now I shouldn't be trusting you. Introspection is not one of your strong suits, Denis. If it was, then you'd hardly be in this mess.

"I don't want them to hate me forever."

I don't think they're capable of that. You see how they've always cared. All of them. How they never gave up on you?

"Except at the end."

They haven't given up on you yet, Denis. This is tough love. They're more worried that you've given up on yourself. Looks like it's working. She's a piece of work, that one.

"I've been lucky."

Not lucky, it's a sign of the kind of good person you are underneath it all that they stuck by you. If you were an asshole, they'd have left long ago.

"I meant lucky with her."

Oh good heavens yes. With her? Absolutely. Luckier than you'll ever know. I guess most people will go through their entire lives not knowing the kind of unreserved love she had for you. Most people will weigh up love and decide when it's become too inconvenient to continue. Not her.

"I did."

I know.

"I wish I hadn't."

I wouldn't worry too much about it now. Done is done.

"She deserves better."

Indeed.

"I should have been better."

Like I say, there's no point in griping about it now. You've done what you've done and been the way you've been. Now you're taking steps.

"I want the guilt to be gone, and the grief. I'm so tired of holding on to it."

Holding on to it is what made you sick in the first place, but you should always keep just a little bit, to remind you of what you've lost, only just a tiny little bit. These things, tragic though they may be, are part of life. They happen.

"That doesn't make me feel any better." Denis grimaced.

It's not supposed to, and it's only barely relevant. You've got a solution here. You've got to make it work.

"What will happen when I'm gone?"

Nothing. We'll leave too. We won't follow you though.

"I can hardly remember a time without you."

Be strong, Denis. Don't lose your way here. A decision's been made. You felt better the second you made it, even though you hardly knew you had. Stick to your guns.

"It's not easy, Deano. I'm lost again. In between the cracks again. And my major support for the last six years has been all of you. It's not easy to just throw that away."

Your major support has been yourself. You're doing the right thing by me anyway. There's got to be an endgame, Denis. You're on the right track.

"I guess I better get to it before I lose my courage."

Then this is goodbye. You won't be seeing us again.

Denis blinked and Deano was gone. Had he imagined it? The terrible thing about being insane, Denis realized, is that there's almost no way to tell the difference between real and imaginary.

He changed his mind and wrote two more emails, quickly this time, as he felt his iron will dissolving. The last thing he needed was for Plasterer to walk back in and change his mind for him. It was time. The house was clean, loose ends tied up. There was only one thing left to do.

I COULD TRY

Denis woke up in a hospital bed and immediately began scanning the room. He had been dreaming, well, night-maring, actually, if such a phrase exists.

Plasterer had been there, and Penny, and the Professor, drinking with him in a bar that seemed to get smaller and dirtier every time he took a sip from the pint of blood in front of him. Blessedly, the details began to evaporate from his mind almost as soon as he woke, wisps of smoke that were almost tangible, but not quite. He remembered he had been woken by a voice; it had drifted into the dream.

"I bet he's crazy. I always get the crazy ones."

Seeing no one, Denis began to feel panic rising in his chest. Were they here? What if they had followed him to the hospital when he had checked himself in the day before? What if they had heard all the things he had told his doctor about them?

He couldn't see them, but that didn't mean they weren't there. He began to hyperventilate.

"You okay over there?" the voice asked.

It was coming from behind a curtain. In his drowsy and drug-addled state, he had failed to remember that he was in a two-person room, and the voice belonged to his fellow patient.

He sucked in great big calming breaths.

"I'm fine," he told the voice.

"Besides the crazy, you mean?"

"Obviously," Denis countered and smiled.

He was going to ask the man what his name was when Dr. Davis strolled in, smiling warmly. It suited his face. Warm, open.

"How you feeling this morning, Denis?"

"Fine, Doctor, thanks."

"Just fine?"

"Better than I was yesterday."

"A good start, then. You can call me Dean, by the way."

Dean. His name made Denis laugh out loud.

"Mind if I don't?" he asked, composing himself.

"Up to you," he told Denis, joining in the laugh. "How would you feel about a visitor? I believe your mother got your email, and she's very keen on seeing you, but I don't want to put you under any stress for your first full day here."

"No, please. Send her in."

Dr. Davis nodded and withdrew, leaving Denis with his roommate.

"Is your mom crazy?" the voice behind the curtain asked.

"No crazier than me."

"Not much of an answer."

"Wasn't overly fond of the question, to be honest."

"Oooooh tetchy."

"Do you mind?"

There was something soothing about the idea of having a roommate for his stay in the psychiatric ward. However long it may be. A feeling of journeying together. Denis just worried that if he had to keep putting up with the not-so-clever quips, it might become a little trying. He was about to introduce himself formally when his mother walked in.

She didn't stop, or hesitate; she smiled a little sad smile and hugged him. It may have been the drugs in his system, or the realization of a first day back on a long road, but Denis didn't recoil, he let her hug him, and then, after a moment or two to calm himself, he hugged her back. He felt her arms tighten as she sobbed very gently for her poor, sick child. He gritted his teeth and endured it. Grateful that, for once, he could give her back something she had offered for seven years. A small gesture. Tiny, really, but a start.

"How are you feeling?" she asked, her concern stamped all over her face.

"Fine," he told her.

She nodded at him, but her eyes tightened. Something about her expression spoke of disappointment. He looked away so he wouldn't have to see it. The absurdity of his reply struck him.

"I'm not fine," he told her, in a rush, still looking away. "I'm not fine, Mom. I'm tired, and I'm sick, and I feel broken."

The medication kept the tears from his eyes.

She reached out a hand and clasped his.

"It's okay to feel that way, love. It's okay."

"I feel like I've gone insane."

He waited for a smart comment from behind the curtain, but there was only silence.

"I want to be better," he told her.

"And you will be," she replied.

"You might be," the voice said.

Denis looked at the curtain, then at his mother. If she had heard anything, she gave no sign. A worm of doubt crept into Denis's stomach. The doctor, his mother, two out of two people who couldn't hear what he could. Or could they? He had to know. He reached for the curtain.

"Can I get you something?" she asked.

Denis ignored her, stretching out his fingers, brushing the plastic material.

"Are you okay, love? Do you need something?"

Denis shuffled himself around on the bed to give himself more room and grasped at the curtain, pulling it back.

In the bed next to him sat a large, burly man, with thick dark circles under his eyes; his hair was messy and poked out here and there.

"Denis!" his mother admonished. "Leave that man alone."

"Do you mind?" asked his roommate.

Denis sighed in relief.

"I'm allowed to check," Denis told the burly man. "I'm crazy, remember."

During his first week in the hospital, Denis had four panic attacks and had nightmares of Plasterer every night. Hiding in the darkest corners of his mind, his onetime friend stalked Denis's dreams, spittle flying from his lips as he raged. Denis felt the memory of his gloved fist, recalled the feeling of his fingers closing around his throat and woke in a sweat. The clown followed him into his sleep, but apparently nowhere else. Dr. Davis adjusted Denis's medication accordingly. It numbed him at first, and he sat through his group therapy sessions in half a daze, but day by day the fog seemed to clear.

During his second week, Denis had only two panic attacks, and four of his nights were dreamless. He woke on the days after dreamless sleep feeling fresh, and almost powerful. He told his story in group therapy and found that for the first time in his life, he could talk his way through the crash, through the devastation without breaking down. He could still feel his grief, but it no longer consumed him entirely. Where once it had felt all encompassing, he now felt like he could look at it, as if from a great distance, and see it for what it was. He talked constantly: to other patients, to different doctors, to nurses, in groups and one-on-one. Denis found himself emptying himself of all the words he had, and filled up the space inside that they had occupied with a sense of well-being that had been lacking for so long that he had forgotten what it felt like. It was nice. He hoped to never lose it again.

His roommate, Stephen, as it turned out, was both a source of amusement and irritation in equal measures. He talked in his sleep, he talked to, with and at the television. He laughed at inappropriate times and scorned the other patients for being crazy. But he was nice. He often had a kind word, and for all his not-so-clever quips, Denis was glad of the man's company.

By the end of the third week, Denis's greatest source of anxiety was his impending release. His sleep had become regular, his dreams pedestrian, and his only problem at night was the sound of snoring from the bed next to his.

The thought of the outside world was both exhilarating and terrifying. What if they were waiting for him back in his house? What if they weren't? He tried not to think of them. Tried to force them not to be part of his reality. During the times that he was pretending they had never existed, his face took on a calm, composed look, his eyes faraway. To those watching from the nurses' station he was meditating.

On the day of his release he had his second, third and fourth visitors. They had come to move him home.

Ollie and Frank were tentative. In all their years of joking and messing and trying to shock Denis back into being human, neither had imagined that it might happen like this. They patted his shoulder as he sat with them in the communal area, still wearing his nightclothes. They made no jokes, but forced themselves into jovial conversation. He sat there and tried to put them at their ease, despite his rumpled hair and wrinkled pajamas. This was a brand-new Denis, one they had never known, one who wanted to be better, but knew that this goal might take a lifetime to achieve.

Rebecca didn't attempt to force joviality, she measured him with her eyes, seeing immediately what the others were still trying to figure out. A new person, built out of parts of the old one. Denis decided that she approved of what she was seeing, but even so, her wondrous, brilliant, wide smile that warmed her face remained absent. He had earned that. He had wounded her badly.

"Do you want me to stay with you?" she asked, cutting through the banal chitchat.

"I'll understand if you don't want to."

"That's not an answer."

He smiled at her, and for the first time since she walked in, she smiled back. A small, tentative smile, but a smile.

"Yes. I would like you to."

"Are you sure?"

"I think so."

He did think so.

They left that afternoon with the blessings of Dr. Davis and a long list of appointments he had to keep. Doctors, therapists, dietitians, counselors. His medicine bag he carried himself, while Frank and Ollie carried his luggage. He shook Stephen's hand and then passed the older man a box of antibacterial wipes so he could scrub his hands clean.

He stood at the gate of his house for a while before entering. He could feel the anxiety churning up his stomach, but it was smothered by a blanket of medication and a resolve to be better, to feel better, that he hoped would see him through the tough moments that were undoubtedly ahead. The front door stared back at him without saying a word. He opened it without ceremony and let them all in.

"I'm sure there's food that needs to be thrown out," he told them as they made their way into the kitchen.

"Don't be silly. Your mother and I took care of that two weeks ago," Rebecca replied.

Two weeks ago. He smiled at the thought. She never stopped caring for him, even when he couldn't see it.

He checked the living room for signs of life. Nothing. He strained his ears in his office, looking for any noise, a whisper of words being said. Only silence.

On soft feet, he climbed the stairs and checked each of the bedrooms one by one. Ollie, Frank and Rebecca followed in his wake, saying nothing. When he reached the last bedroom on the corridor, he paused with his hand hovering over the doorknob. This was where he had met them. This was where they had first come to him, and from this room they had taken over the house. He clenched his teeth, unlocked the door and stepped into the mess.

Inside the room was a mountain of memories. Jules's belongings, old textbooks, posters from the walls of the house he had shared with Eddie, with all of them. Eddie's Pennywise doll, Jules's first stuffed animal, now a shapeless ball covered in fur, photographs of him and his father, old clothes, scarves, hats, a comic book collection of *The Walking Dead* jointly owned by him and Eddie, a collection of He-Man, She-Ra and Battle Cat toys. A disorganized shrine to another life, to two other lives, really. Two lives he was leaving behind. No-where, among the flotsam, was there any sign of Plasterer, Penny O'Neill, Deano or the Professor. Denis let loose a long, shuddering breath.

The rest of the day was spent cleaning the room out. Some things Ollie and Frank kept, some Denis chose to hold on to. He remembered Deano's advice just before he had left, and kept just a little bit in memory of what had gone before. The rest was for the garbage. Not for the first time Denis felt the therapeutic benefit of cleaning, and supposed to himself that some things he didn't have to change.

Rebecca slept in her own bedroom. Part of him wanted to ask her to stay with him, but his better judgment told him that time would heal the wounds, or not, and one way or another he would have to live with whatever happened. It was a strangely comforting thought.

On a fine, sunny afternoon, two weeks after leaving the hospital, Denis made his way into town. He tried not to think about the cracks on the road and focused on more important things. When he reached the convenience store, he found himself smiling at Thomas, who initially didn't recognize him.

"Aaaaaah, Mr. Murphy," he said eventually. "Look at you. A new man. Your hair is very long, no?"

"Been busy. No time for haircuts."

"The usual today?"

"Please."

Thomas scanned the newspaper.

"And will you be leaving me hanging today, Mr. Murphy?" he asked, presenting his hand for the high five.

"Not today, Thomas." Denis high-fived the shopkeeper clumsily, and laughed at the astonishment on Thomas's face.

"See you tomorrow maybe."

In the afternoon sun, Denis sat in his usual café with his laptop and his coffee and wrote:

Dear Ned,
I hardly know where to start. First and foremost, I'm sorry I wasn't there for Eddie's funeral. He was the best friend I ever had, and I owe him, and your family, more than I can say. I don't

know where I went wrong. I don't know what started me down the road I went, but once I was on it, I found I couldn't get off. That's not an excuse for how I treated you, or Ann, just a way of explaining myself.

I've been seeking help, as per your advice. It's started me back on the road to recovery. I have no idea how this will all end up, only that I'm not willing to keep going the way I was. I have you and your kind words to thank for that. I want you to know that I may not have been alive to send this message to you if not for your love and generosity.

For the little this is worth, my door is open to you always. I hope that we can be friends, that we can grieve and share together the way I should have done a long time ago.

I hope you can forgive me.

Either way, I'll keep Eddie in my heart for the rest of my days, and you and Ann with him.

Thank you again,

Denis

He looked over it. Less pompous than his last email, but with a little leftover hint of the Professor. He decided he liked it all the more for it.

He watched the people walk by, studying their faces. As they poured by on the busy street, he saw the whole gamut of human emotion. It was visible on faces of every age and race and was specific to no gender. A river of people, carrying a river of emotion, driven by a great intangible force. It scared him a little. Rebecca stopped in front of him. She was beaming her typical warm smile. He smiled back. He had been sitting in the very same seat when she had walked past him so many months beforehand.

"You thinking heavy thoughts?" she asked.

"As usual."

She looked as though she might say something, but frowned instead.

"Something wrong?" he asked.

"No… Just thought I saw a really weird–looking clown. Thought he was staring at us. Must have been my imagination."

★ ★ ★ ★ ★

ACKNOWLEDGMENTS

If I was to thank everyone who had a role to play in making me, and this book, you'd have to read 498,113 pages of acknowledgments. We don't have the time, people... So just a couple of crucial ones: Mam and Dad, thanks for the endless support and encouragement even when I seemed like a weird kid. Ci, Jean and Paul, thanks for always being there for me, and for tolerating the vanishing acts. Mike, John and Tara, I'm glad you're all my family.

To Alex Dunne, at any moment of your choosing you may demand any limb or internal organ you fancy and it's yours. Thank you for the work.

For endless support and occasional bullying, my thanks to Grainne O'Brien, who remains the most like-me person I know. Let's never change.

To the other Amigos: Will and John, please change. Pete Moles's name is being deliberately omitted from this acknowledgment.

For all the others from the various gangs: theater, work, writing, school both primary and secondary, college, all my various jobs and the Banter Brigade—cheers for all the pints.

To test readers Enda Sheehy, Ciara (again) and Barney,

cheers for always thinking it was good, when it was really awful. To the Test-Readers-in-Chief, Eadaoin O'Neill and Paul Shinnors—thanks for telling me where it wasn't good when it was really awful. And of course Mr. Phil Shanahan, who gave this book its title when I was too lazy and tired to know better.

To Paul in Moviedrome. Thanks for the endless use of your computers and the stacks upon stacks of paper.

It's cliché for writers to thank their most beloved for their patience, but there's a damn fine reason for that. Thanks, Christine, for putting up with me. Despite the snoring.

Whatever success this book accrues will be fundamentally down to two people and two companies. My eternal thanks to Lauren Parson at Legend Press and Liz Stein at Park Row Books and all the others in both of those companies who have worked hard to help make this what it is. The fact that I have almost no idea what I'm doing has made all your jobs harder, and so I'm extra grateful for the help. You've made this a better book and taught me a lot in a frighteningly short space of time.

To Elaine Hanson, who has given everything to highlight issues surrounding men's mental health, thank you from the bottom of my heart.

Finally, and most important, thank you to Luke Bitmead. I wish I knew you. I think me and you might have been friends.

Stand up and fight.

QUESTIONS FOR DISCUSSION

1. If the Monsters are figments of his imagination, what part of Denis's personality do each of them represent?

2. Are Ollie and Frank enabling Denis by tolerating his regimented behavior and occasional rudeness? Is their mocking of him acceptable joking between friends or something cruel?

3. Is Denis fundamentally selfish in his relationship with Rebecca? Does he expect too much from her without giving enough, or is it the other way around?

4. At a certain point in the story, Plasterer begins his gradual rise to dominance. What fundamental changes in Denis empower this? Why has it happened? Is there a single triggering event?

5. Why is Deano without a voice? What does his powerlessness in the house represent? Why, ultimately, does it change?

6. Are the other housemates trying to warn Denis about Plasterer, or are they complicit in the clown's rise to power? Whose side are they on, or is that dynamic always shifting?

7. Eddie and Jules are not active characters in the book, but they influence Denis a great deal. What is their effect, if any, on the other characters—Ollie, Frank, Rebecca and the Monsters?

8. Denis's politeness to others is used as a shield to hide his true self from those around him. In a society that stigmatizes mental health, do you think this shield helps him or hinders him in the long run? Is he right to hide who he is? Do you think he would do more damage mentally if he revealed himself to others?

9. Is Rebecca's determination to help Denis ultimately damaging to him, or is she the catalyst that motivates him to seek help? Do you think she pushes him too hard?

10. If you could identify a single pivotal moment in Denis's journey during *Me, Myself and Them*, what would it be and why?

Read on for an excerpt from Dan Mooney's second novel,
The Great Unexpected, an emotional, humorous tale of two
nursing-home roommates and their unlikely friendship.

CHAPTER ONE

"Miller," Joel whispered across the space between their two beds. "Why aren't you dead yet?"

Miller, in a coma for over two years, said nothing. Instead his knobbly, decrepit old chest just rose and dropped, barely perceptible under the thin cotton sheets.

"Fine. Be that way," Joel told him.

Miller ignored him.

Joel Monroe had objected to Mr. Miller's presence when they'd first brought him in. Not that anyone paid his protests even the slightest bit of attention. A year before they wheeled in the corpse-that-was-not, Lucey had lived in that bed. He had gone to sleep every night knowing she was there and woken up every morning to see her already up and about, dressing herself, cleaning, pottering here and there and chatting quietly with the nurses as they came in and out with breakfast.

She had made living in a nursing home seem bearable, fun even, instead of the parade of indignities and insults it had turned out to be in the aftermath of her death. She decorated the place. Flowers in old vases she had collected from yard sales, photographs of their little family, the three of them at the beach, a tiny little Eva in his arms. She placed brightly colored throws on the beds which cheerfully canceled out the sterility of the place, made it nice. It was what she had been doing all their lives together: making things nice for him. She brought light where she went, and her laugh warmed any room she was in. To Joel's eyes she had never shown any evidence of her advancing years, for she was as bright and energetic as always, a force of nature showing no signs of abating. He, on the other hand had wasted away slowly while they were there, then rapidly after she had died. It was a cold place without her. Now the photos still hung on the walls, but Joel had paid them less and less mind as time rolled by. Occasionally he might glance at baby Eva in his arms and wonder what he had done to deserve being trapped in this place, trapped without his Lucey.

The ignominy of having her replaced by Miller was an insult that had stuck in Joel's craw. He had told them that he didn't want Miller. He didn't want anyone.

But after a while, he was, in fact, easy to get used to. He didn't chew too loudly, didn't care what programs Joel played on the television, didn't engage in pointless small talk, or interrupt the football when it was turned on. Outside of the times when the nurses came in to check on him, move him around and clean him, he was perfectly charming. Shocking conversationalist, but a fine roommate. That didn't stop Joel from resenting the staff for foisting Miller on him in the first place, but at least life was easy between them.

"If you're not going to eat your breakfast this morning, do you mind if I have your eggs?"

Miller, of course, said nothing.

"You talking to Mr. Miller again. Mr. Monroe?" Nurse Liam asked, as he bustled in with Joel's breakfast on a small foldable table. The orange juice hardly rippled in the young man's steady hands. Youthful, unblemished, not at all gnarled up like his seemed to be.

"Rudest man ever," Joel grunted. "Hasn't opened his mouth since he got here."

Nurse Liam smiled slightly at the joke. It wasn't new. Nothing in the nursing home was. Everything was old and over-used and on the point of breaking. Everything, down to the furniture, showed its age and its weakness. Joel tried not to think about it, but it seemed that wherever his eyes went there was infirmity and uselessness.

"Time for your breakfast, Joel," Liam told him, as if he didn't know.

"I'm well aware of what time it is, Nurse Liam," Joel replied testily. "I've been living here for five years. Eight in the morning has never been anything else other than breakfast time. For over eighteen hundred days and counting, it's been breakfast time at eight o'clock."

"All right, all right. No need to get cranky. Just making conversation."

"Well if that's your idea of making conversation, boy, then you have a great many things to learn."

Liam sighed and tried to force a tight smile as he nestled the mini-table across Joel's lap. He was used to Joel; he might have even liked him. Sometimes. A little bit.

Liam hated to be called boy, which naturally enough, meant that Joel found frequent opportunities to deploy the word. It wasn't that he didn't like the young nurse, quite the opposite; he had always enjoyed the young man's company. It was just something about the way that he, and all the rest of the staff at the home, spoke to him during mealtimes, or when the medicine was being dished out, or at bedtime. A sort of false tonality, a singsong quality that Joel was sure was supposed to be upbeat and cheerful but somehow felt like the voice a teacher might use when checking a ten-year-old's homework. He opened his mouth to have another pop, but thought better of it. Nurse Liam was one of the increasingly small number of things about this nursing home that Joel actually liked.

It was sometimes difficult for others to tell when Joel liked something, since his behavior changed not a jot.

Liam was in his mid to late thirties, a full forty years younger than Joel, but had about his face a certain quality of elderliness. It was something about his eyes, a sort of wariness that suggested he'd walked a harder road than perhaps he should have. Everything else about him was ordinary enough. He was a handsome type, with a long narrow face and a ready smile. He was tall but not looming and quite slim without appearing too skinny. There was nothing particularly special about him, except those blue eyes with their aged quality.

His hands moved deftly, with the steady calm and assurance of a man who had worked in his field for years. There was a touch of gentleness about them too, a familiarity with delicacy and breakable things. Joel wondered if he was the breakable thing. He supposed that he was.

Liam seemed to notice Joel biting his tongue, bottling up the urge to needle him further. His tense, forced smile relaxed into a more genuine one, and he cheekily tucked a napkin into the top of Joel's pajamas and then darted out of range before the older man could rip it clear and throw it at him.

"Insolent little…" Joel started furiously.

"I'll bring you some tea," Liam told him, laughing as he backed out of the room.

Joel sulked. To think that he had decided against ribbing the man out of some sense of loyalty, and then the little shit had gone and stuck a bib on him like he was some kind of child. Worse again, he had almost forced Joel into uttering a swear word. Joel despised profane language.

"You believe that, Miller? Can you believe the arrogance of children these days? The disrespect of them?"

Miller breathed. In and out.

"Miller, do absolutely nothing if you completely agree with me."

Miller did absolutely nothing.

He was an agreeable chap in that regard. He frequently agreed with anything Joel had to say on a variety of subjects.

"Nice to have you on my side again, old boy. When he comes back in I want you to give him the cold shoulder like only you can. Don't say a word to him."

"Some tea, Mr. Monroe?" Liam asked as he made his way back in.

"We're not speaking to you," Joel told the nurse matter-of-factly.

After breakfast Joel cleaned and dressed himself. He had been neglecting his appearance lately, which came as something of a surprise to him by the time he realized it. All his life he had been somewhat fussy about his appearance. His clothes were a symbol of his position in society. A small-business owner. A working man. He wore his clothing as a uniform, that passersby might know his rank and station. Up in the mornings to prepare for work, he'd wash, shave and fix his hair, before donning his shirt and tie and making his way to the garage. A shirt and tie, despite knowing that he was going to be pulling on his overalls and getting dirty for his living. The overalls were a symbol of his rank too, his usefulness. A man in dirty overalls is almost never an idle man.

The early stages of retirement had been no different; he had dressed smartly, shaved every day. His rituals had continued unabated. Right up until when Lucey died. Something had happened to him then, a little bit of his life force had left with her, and suddenly Joel found himself in the visitors' room, at five in the evening, in his pajamas and his housecoat, watching soap operas that he loathed, because it was someone else's turn to decide what channel they'd all watch on the common room television. For Joel the only thing worse than the outrageous stupidity of the story lines was the number of people who seemed to buy into them. Hilltop Nursing Home had accrued a small hard-core group of soap opera addicts.

Worse still were the days when he lay abed, not getting up, endlessly cycling through the channels on the small television in his bedroom, never happy with anything that was on, never happy with anything at all. Too unhappy and too unmotivated to just turn off the television and find something else to do.

When he had chanced across his reflection in the sneeze guard on the dining-room salad counter at lunch the day before, he had been shocked to notice the fuzz on his cheeks and the stains on his pajamas. His cheeks had appeared extra hollow, skeletal even, despite the fact that he still had some meat on his bones. He hated that reflection. In reaction, he had decided to arrest his decline, and so, after he had eaten, Joel hauled himself from the bed and set about cleaning and dressing with determination.

He plucked his nose hair. He shaved his cheeks. He swept his hair back with the wax his grandson Chris had given him for Christmas nearly six months before. After he was clean, he dressed himself. A white shirt, a simple brown tie and a wool jacket. Brown slacks and brown shoes. He straightened himself up and gave himself a look over. Not bad, he decided. Not tremendous, by any means, but not terrible either.

Joel had never developed a significant stoop. His father, an occasionally vicious man, had been adamant about three things: good manners, no swearing, and fine posture. He rewarded any display of these three handsomely. And punished any failures furiously. As a result, Joel stood quite tall, still approaching six feet. His years of manual work and playing football had toughened him, and so his frame was still substantial, with only the traces of a paunch showing around the buttons of his shirt. He still had a lot of hair. For now, at least. His father had died bald. Joel tried to pretend that there was no satisfaction in that for him, but that was a lie. He had been a little bit delighted about it.

"Stay here and guard the fort, Miller. I'm going for a walk."

Around nine in the morning in Hilltop Nursing Home, the corridors started to come alive as much as they could in a place where death is potentially around every corner. Having had breakfast, the residents began their days, and visited each other's rooms. The nursing staff, having only just started their shift with the delivery of breakfast, would be full of energy and enthusiasm. That would wane, of course, it always did. Sometime, after they had to convince Rose that the house across the street didn't belong to her brother, or when they'd had their first row with one of the residents' family members over what medication their residents should be taking, or when they had to change their first adult diaper of the day. The positivity with which they began every day would fizzle out. Nurse Liam usually kept his good spirits, and the little Filipino lady, Angelica, whose laugh could be heard from one end of the building to the other, was hard to wear down too, but Joel had seen it a time or two. Given long enough, Hilltop wore everyone down. Life. Life wore everyone down, didn't it?

And of everyone, this was most terribly true of The Rhino. Life had made her into something else. Something hard and unrelenting and, though Joel would never admit it to anyone else, something a little bit scary.

Florence Ryan, or The Rhino when her back was turned, was both the head nurse and the owner of Hilltop. It seemed something of a misnomer to call such a little woman The Rhino; her size indicated something altogether daintier. Her size was a lie. She was named for her relentlessness and her purposeful charge through the halls that scattered residents and staff alike.

Hilltop had belonged to her parents, and she'd grown up here. Worked here all her life, studied to be a nurse, inherited the family business, and now she ruled over the establishment with an authority Pol Pot would have been proud of. Like a blizzard she moved through the nursing home, with a kind of relentless, cold energy. Always threatening to destroy whatever she came in contact with. Even Liam and Angelica stood to attention when The Rhino was on the move, their good-natured smiles replaced with sterner expressions, almost severe, as though old Rhino herself was somehow contagious. The families of residents, vocal in their complaints when dealing with other nursing staff, stepped lightly when dealing with The Rhino, moderating their tones, fawning a little, and when she had finished wringing them out like a wet rag, The Rhino would plunder onwards, furiously.

He remembered with a chill the day she had found a family member smuggling in a bottle of whiskey for Old Tim Badger. Joel had watched as she seemed to grow in size, swelling outwards, Old Tim's son shrinking before her, contracting into himself until it looked like he might just shrink out of his own clothes. She had brandished the bottle of whiskey like a club. Joel could have sworn she'd grown a full two feet taller by the time she'd finished with him, while Old Tim's son looked like he might actually cry. Literal tears. Joel shuddered at the thought.

He tried to look nonchalant as he scanned the hallways for sign of The Rhino, but all he saw or heard were the sounds of the residents and staff happily going about their day.

"I don't think she's in yet," Una told him from her doorway.

"Excuse me?" Joel replied.

"You're looking for Mrs. Ryan, and I don't think she's here yet."

Una Clarke had been a resident at Hilltop longer even than Joel had. She had been friends with Lucey. They'd played bridge as a team. A handsome woman, she hadn't yet surrendered to the malaise that seemed to grip everyone in Hilltop at some point, and dressed herself well. She had never been a wealthy woman, and some of the clothes she still wore had once been Lucey's. It set Joel's teeth on edge, but there was nothing he could do about it.

"I was absolutely not looking for Mrs. Ryan. I have no interest whatsoever in the comings and goings of that woman," Joel lied, while trying to surreptitiously check for her out of the corners of his eyes.

Una chuckled at him lightly.

"You're looking very well today, Joel. You scrub up quite well when you bother to get out of your pajamas. What's the big occasion?"

Joel bit back a retort.

Una was wearing a neat navy cardigan with large golden buttons that Lucey used to wear on Saturdays when they would go to the market. Saturday morning was always the market. Lucey dragged him along once, and he had been surprised to find the vibrancy of the place charming. After that he had looked forward to it. A little early-morning date with his wife. She in her cardigan and he in his. She'd usually pick up some strange fruit or vegetable and work it into their dinner. He didn't always love that, but complaining to Lucey had been pointless. She'd listened to enough of it over the years that she let it wash off her, smiling at his grumbling and cooking whatever she pleased anyway. That little smile was a beautiful thing.

The cardigan looked well on Una. He hated that it looked well on her. He wanted to tell her that it looked nice on her. He also wanted to tell her to stop wearing his wife's clothes.

"Felt like it," he mumbled instead. Una wasn't the enemy. Come to think of it, Joel was struggling to identify who the enemy was.

"Makes a lovely change. It's nice to see you motivated."

Motivated. He didn't feel motivated. He felt something else.

It was something darker, malevolent but intangible. Something he couldn't explain that seemed to be resting just beyond the edges of his senses, waiting. It wasn't the first time he'd felt it, but there was something more immediate about it now, something more imminent. A bleakness that spread like a cloud around him, thickly, invading his space, his mind. He hoped it would pass.

"Yes. Well. Thought I could do with a shave and all that," he said, trying to come up with a way to end the conversation.

"I remember that jacket. Wasn't that a special occasion jacket?" she asked.

She was clearly thinking back to a time when Lucey had selected his clothing for him. He couldn't remember which of his clothes qualified as special-wear. He didn't want to think about it, or about her adjusting the collars of his shirts as she buttoned them up with her soft hands. She had dressed him for Eva's baptism. He had squirmed under her ministrations, mostly for show, because he loved when she fussed over him, and the more he squirmed the more she fussed. Eva had cooed and gurgled at them from her bassinet.

What a glorious day that had been. Sun shining. Lucey looking as beautiful as ever. Their families and all the neighbors out for the big occasion. It felt so long ago, and the memory of it somehow felt like it belonged to someone else. Someone happier.

"Just a jacket," Joel mumbled as he felt his breath quickening.

"What's on the agenda today then?" Una asked, noting his sullen demeanor.

"What's on the agenda in this place on any day of the week?" he shot back bitterly. "TV in the common room until they shove us into the dining room like spent cattle? Read a book and listen to Mighty Jim babble incoherently?" He couldn't quite understand why his voice was getting so loud. "Find a corner of a room to doze off in and hope that when you wake up you've killed enough of the day so you don't have to be bored living through it?" The last was almost a shout.

His words took him by surprise. They took Una by surprise. Both surprised, they stood awkwardly staring at each other for a minute. He heard them coming from his mouth, so he knew that he had said them, but he didn't know that he had been thinking them.

"Eh... Sorry. Don't know where that came from," he tried to explain quietly.

"Anything you want to talk about?" she asked.

"No. Really, I must apologize. That came out unexpectedly."

She looked at him with genuine concern.

"Maybe there'll be something good on TV today, eh?" he suggested, trying to force some joviality into his tone, trying to sound normal. "And that show we were watching last week was all right, wasn't it?"

She continued to look at him with concern.

"Maybe we should get Nurse Liam...." she started.

"No, no, no," he cut across her. "I'm fine. Perhaps I'll chance a game of chess with Mighty Jim."

He moved off before she could answer, his long strides taking him out of harm's way before she could insist on getting Nurse Liam. He tried to think about where his words had come from. It might have been seeing Una in Lucey's old cardigan. Or perhaps his quiet fear of Rhino. It could have been his frustration with being treated like a child. But Joel suspected it was that bleak something else that had settled on him. A part of him wanted to analyze it, understand it, but he feared it, feared looking at it too closely. He shook it off and went in search of Mighty Jim.

That afternoon, poring over the chessboard in the common room, Joel tried to ignore the nagging feeling that had been pestering him since his outburst that morning. His mind kept floating back to it as soon as he loosened his grip on his thoughts.

"What I say is relative. It should not become a dead end…" Mighty Jim whispered to himself as he waited for Joel's turn. Joel had long since given up trying to understand what the older man was saying. He'd been a resident here for nearly a decade, and his ancient face was lined, his back was bent, and his gnarled hands were crippled with arthritis. His mind had left his broken body many years before, and now he mumbled nonsense wherever he went, all the while wearing a great big grin plastered across his beaten face.

Joel remembered when Mighty Jim had been Mayor Jim Lincoln. A politician, sharp and savvy, in stylish suits with a serious demeanor and a handshake for everyone he encountered. He was a symbol of strength, authority, and command, a totem of manliness. He was unrecognizable now, which Joel suspected was just as well for Jim. The memory of the old mayor would live on as a powerful man, and not this bent old thing with dementia and a warped, semi-permanent smile.

The moment he had allowed his mind to wander, the cloud of doom returned, coalescing around his head, bringing its negativity and despair. He felt it almost as a physical sensation. He had felt isolated before; in fact, he had felt isolated since Lucey had left him here, on his own, but this cloud was new, new and terrifying.

Part of it, he concluded, was to do with the look of shocked concern on Una's face. She had been kind to him ever since Lucey's passing. Checking in on him, trying to include him in her Gardening Club, asking his opinion on soap operas and bringing him her unfinished crosswords to ask for his help. Joel had left school at fifteen, to start his mechanic's apprenticeship, so book learning was not his strong suit. He read often, but nothing highbrow. That had been Lucey's area of expertise. He had no answers for Una's crossword questions, but felt a small burst of gratitude that she would think of him anyway, despite his continuing and obvious limitations in the field. He didn't like the idea of upsetting her, after all her kindness. But it wasn't just that. There was more to his unexplained anger than he had managed to put his finger on. Mostly it was the terrible sense of despair that seemed to have crept up on him, a sense he couldn't seem to shake. Looking at it a little closer, a few moments of introspection might have helped, but that sort of thing was well outside Joel's wheelhouse, so he opted instead to try to ignore it again.

Joel moved his knight into position carefully. In hundreds of games with Mighty Jim, he'd never won a single encounter. Whatever terrible affliction had taken hold of his opponent's brain, it hadn't yet managed to get the part of him that remembered how to play chess. Frustratingly for Joel, he had never lost either. Games with Mighty Jim had the predictable charm of repeating the same pattern; Jim would go on the attack, wipe out half of Joel's forces, and then settle back for a stalemate that had no ending. Every time, Joel would tell himself he was done with this stupidity and vow to leave the old man to his pointless shenanigans, and days later he would inevitably find himself back at the table, determined to win this time. Just this one time.

"We simply must reach a greater understanding," Jim told him seriously as he moved his bishop into a killing position.

"Absolutely," Joel replied, as he tried to ponder a way out of the inevitable slaughter.

Behind them a burst of laughter from a gaggle of women, with Una sitting at its center. The laughter set his teeth on edge.

"The hell do they think is so funny?" he asked Mighty Jim testily. Joel did a lot of things testily.

"The romantic lie in the brain," Jim replied sagely.

Joel nodded. He wondered idly how much Jim understood, and how much Jim expected him to understand.

"The laughing doesn't bother you then?" he inquired.

"Ninety percent of people in the world that have a religion are all wrong," Jim replied, his broad grin breaking through. He laughed a little to himself, delighted, and returned his gaze to the chessboard.

His happiness set Joel's teeth on edge too. What exactly, Joel wondered, did the old devil have to be happy about? He studied the old wrinkled face across from him for a moment. He seemed happy. Genuinely happy. His smile, crooked sometimes, was not a false effect; he just didn't see or didn't care about the conditions he lived in. He didn't care about his own slow decline or the decline of the residents around him, He didn't care about the mediocre desserts or the constant stream of pills being shoved at him. He was fully senile and fully delighted about it. Ignorance truly is bliss, Joel thought to himself.

Across the room, rapt in front of the television, some of the residents had gathered to watch the soaps again. Joel shook his head at them and looked for his next move. There had to be a way to beat Mighty Jim.

Later in the afternoon, he sat in the common room by a window with a view all the way down the hill. It was a beautiful view, in its own little way, with tall trees that enclosed the gardens and would have been majestic, if they didn't feel like walls too tall to climb over. He flipped through the pages of the crime novel he was reading, enjoying the sensation of being transported away from Hilltop. It was a welcome distraction from the nagging feeling that something was terribly wrong, which seemed to be seeping into his mind, distracting him, infringing on his consciousness. Joel's reading intensified. Somewhere in his head Joel reasoned that if he read the words quicker, then he'd be less likely to be distracted by whatever it was that was imposing itself on him.

He read until he was bored of reading. Then he went for a walk, down the long drive toward the gate of Hilltop and around the path that ran outside the line of tall trees that circled the extensive garden. He walked until he was bored of walking.

In the evening time, at the appointed hour, which was always the same hour, Joel took his supper in his bedroom to watch football on the television. The food was good, though he would have liked to complain about it. He had no doubt that The Rhino had invested her money well when she had hired Cook. The woman obviously loved her work; she had stayed in the nursing home for years, and to Joel it seemed that a woman of her talents could have taken her pick of places to work, places considerably more glamourous than Hilltop. He grumbled at the football as he ate.

"Can't decide if it's bad management, or crappy players, but one way or another, we're one god-awful team, eh, Miller?"

Miller was silent. He never said a word at suppertime.

"Honestly, someone's going to start getting worried about your mental health if you keep talking to Mr. Miller, Joel."

Liam had come through the door with the medication. Again. He would insist on staying while Joel took it. Again. Joel suddenly found this infuriating.

"Just leave it on the stand please, Liam," Joel told him brusquely.

"That's not how it works and you know it, Mr. Monroe."

Mr. Monroe. It was always Mr. Monroe when he was being told what to do. Oh, it was fine to be all "Joel this" and "Joel that" when Nurse Liam was trying to be all chummy, but as soon as he got to giving orders and dishing out demands, it was suddenly Mr. Monroe. Joel hated the duplicity of it all.

"On the stand please," he said more firmly.

"Absolutely," Liam replied, changing tack. He put the medication on the stand by the bed and then folded his arms and stood there.

"Help you with something?" Joel asked.

"Nope. Got nowhere to go, and nothing to do."

"Your shift ends in an hour. I can wait that long."

"I'll make overtime out of you yet, Mr. Monroe. I ain't going anywhere until you've taken the pills."

The fact that Joel needed the pills was absolutely irrelevant. That he'd once had a stroke, a tiny one by all accounts but a stroke nonetheless, and the medication was likely the only thing keeping him from having a much more serious event, was secondary to the fact that Joel Monroe mightily hated being told what to do. Regardless of whether or not it may save his life.

They stared at each other. The nurse was implacable with

his steady hands and his blue-eyed stare. The argument was pointless. He was going to lose. He knew it. There was little value to be had in engaging in the row in the first place, but a sour energy had taken a hold of Joel and made him pugnacious.

He backed down eventually, but refused to break eye contact, even as he reached out for his pills and the glass of water. He didn't blink as he washed them down, but grimaced at the slight nod of satisfaction from Nurse Liam. He turned back to his television in disgust.

"Is there something bothering you, Joel?" Liam asked.

Joel again. After he did what he was told like a good little boy, he went back to being Joel.

"Don't know what you're talking about," Joel replied, but in his gut, he knew. He'd been desperately avoiding asking himself that question all day long.

"You're not yourself. I mean, you're cranky and everything, nothing new there, but there seems to be something else."

"There's nothing the matter with me that won't be fixed by a little peace and quiet, boy," Joel said, returning fire.

"Are you sure? It's just that Una mentioned…"

Before he could finish, Joel exploded for the second time that day.

"Well, maybe she and you ought to mind your own business," he shouted. "Maybe my problem is that it's not enough for all of you to run my life. Eat this, eat that, take these, drink this, drink that… You also all seem to think that you have a right to know what's in my head. Maybe my problem is that there's no such thing as privacy around here and I'm not allowed to have a thought without everyone around here poking at me."

Liam looked shocked, but he was a career nurse, with a long track record working in Hilltop. He'd seen worse, encountered worse. He got past it quickly. His kindly face seeming to absorb the shock.

"I think we both know there's plenty of evidence that there's something going on with you, Joel," he said softly, empathetically. "If you want to talk about it, I'll be here in the morning. In the meantime, do you want a cup of tea?"

He was smooth. Capable of adjusting. If he had taken offense at the outburst, he gave no sign of it. This was enough to infuriate Joel. Did Liam think so little of him that he couldn't even be bothered to be offended when he was being insulted?

"I don't want any damn tea," he lied.

Liam nodded and withdrew. Joel tried to watch the football again. The game was still going on, the players moving here and there, but Joel didn't see any of it. He was trying to answer the question Liam had asked him. What was bothering him?